Please turn
for an inter

D0173406

"POWERFUL EMOTIONAL INTENSITY . . . THE BOOK HITS YOU WHERE YOU LIVE."
—*The Washington Post Book World*

"Icy suspense . . . you won't put it down."
—*The Toronto Globe & Mail*

"Spring keeps us guessing to the end."
—*San Francisco Chronicle*

"Michelle Spring, born in Canada but long settled in England, retains the best of the English tradition."
—AMANDA CROSS

"*Standing in the Shadows* gives readers a female private eye comparable to V. I. Warshawski and a twisty psychological plot worthy of Elizabeth George."
—*Alfred Hitchcock Mystery Magazine*

"Laura is a fascinating woman of the Nineties, confident in her ability to perform her job even though it can turn dangerous without a warning."
—*The Midwest Book Review*

Please turn the page
for more reviews. . . .

"A COMPULSIVE READ . . .

One of the most quietly impassioned thrillers of the year."

—FRANCES FYFIELD
The Mail on Sunday (London)

"[An] excellent series . . . Spring's books, featuring complex plots, just keep getting better."
—*The Toronto Star*

"The books move between Cambridge and London, using the contrasting locations to good effect. Laura is cool and practical, tenacious and capable of great empathy with the people caught up in her investigations, which usually engage with contemporary social issues. . . . With each book, Spring is maturing as a writer, discovering how far she can push her talent and exploring the darker recesses of the human psyche."
—*The Times* (London)

"A FASCINATING MYSTERY."
—*The Snooper*

"Spring delivers an engaging cast of characters, builds a well-calibrated puzzle plot, and asks troubling questions of why children kill."
—*Ellery Queen's Mystery Magazine*

"[A] thought-provoking yet compelling page-turner that stays in the mind long after the covers are closed. With *Standing in the Shadows*, Michelle springs into the front rank."
—VAL McDERMID
Manchester Evening News

"[An] entertaining, well-constructed plot."
—*The Baltimore Sun*

STANDING IN THE SHADOWS

Michelle Spring

BALLANTINE BOOKS • NEW YORK

*To David
for the past and the future*

A Ballantine Book
Published by The Ballantine Publishing Group
Copyright © 1998 by Michelle Spring

All rights reserved under International and Pan-American Copyright Conventions. Published in the United States by The Ballantine Publishing Group, a division of Random House, Inc., New York, and simultaneously in Canada by Random House of Canada Limited, Toronto.

Ballantine and colophon are registered trademarks of Random House, Inc.

www.randomhouse.com/BB/

Library of Congress Catalog Card Number: 98-93419

ISBN 0-345-42492-1

Manufactured in the United States of America

First Hardcover Edition: May 1998
First Mass Market Edition: April 1999

10   9   8   7   6   5   4   3   2   1

Oh, you are a mucky kid
dirty as a dustbin lid
when he hears the things you did
You'll get a belt from your Da.

—STAN KELLY
"Liverpool Lullaby"

Author's Note

The city of Cambridge is much as described in this book. I didn't invent Newnham or Midsummer Common or the University Library, nor the traffic jams that take hold of parts of Cambridge on a Saturday afternoon. However, the characters in the novel began their lives in my imagination, and the events described in these pages are fictitious. Astute readers will notice that I have also taken certain liberties with the area of Chesterton where Geraldine King met her death.

Chapter 1

HOWARD FLATT'S DESCRIPTION of the murder was flecked with hesitation: just the facts. Geraldine King had died, he told me, on the fourteenth of October.

He left out all the important things. He didn't tell me that Geraldine had dressed with care, as always, on that day—that she'd chosen a blouse in a tone that lifted her sixty-something complexion, and a cardigan, in a blue of the palest shade, that found an echo in her eyes. He didn't tell me that her hair was white and fluffy, nor that her panties, ripped from crotch to hip, turned up at an arm's throw from the body.

Howard said that Geraldine had been found on the ground under a walnut tree. I only learned later—from Becca Hunter—that blood from the head wounds and runoff from the evening rain had puddled around the body as it had impressed slowly into the soft earth. That by the time Geraldine was found, her pastel cardigan was as wet as sea moss, her skirt so drenched that the pattern of tiny tea roses showed scarcely at all. It was Becca who reported that, when she touched Geraldine, the plushy arms were surfaced with the chill of death.

"And next to her body, just a few feet away," Howard explained, as if he had omitted nothing, "was the tree. And partway up the tree, at the head of a ladder, was a platform.

1

And that was where—" He came to a halt, a frown on the scale of the Cheddar Gorge splitting his bony brows.

"It's all right," I said quietly. "I remember."

We were nursing drinks at a small round table in Parker's Bar. I work in Cambridge whenever I can, but I haven't gotten around to opening an office there. It's a question of economics. Why pay rent on another suite of rooms when Sonny and I have a well-established and even (though it's taken time) a comfortably furnished office in Camden Town? It's there, in north London, that information is recorded, correspondence entered into, and junk mail junked.

For a working base in Cambridge, my house on Clare Street does just fine. A filing cabinet, a fax machine, a computer that gives instant connection to Camden, and there you have it—all the convenience of an office, with few of the drawbacks. No commuting into work, and the chance to shift between desk and bed as inspiration strikes.

However, there is one distinct disadvantage. Old clients, or new clients who are friends of friends, are welcome to ring my doorbell. But I don't fancy letting every Tom, Dick, and Harry know where I live—especially not those Toms (or Dicks or Harrys) whom I might have photographed necking with a partner's wife, or slipping their employers' secrets to the competition. For clients I don't know or don't trust, I need to have alternative places to meet— places that can deliver on my three criteria for a successful professional encounter. Top of the list, discretion; it is interesting how many clients don't want the world to know they've consulted an inquiry agent. Number two, privacy; it's no good passing on the secrets of your soul if you are overheard by a goodly portion of the local population. And, finally—for me, rather than for the client—hospitality. It's easier to endure the sometimes sordid confessions that come the way of a private eye if you have a comforting cappuccino at hand.

That's the problem in a nutshell. The solution—honed through years of trial and error—is to circulate among local bars and cafés, anywhere you can nurse a drink for an hour or two without being ushered to the door. Some of the most common Cambridge haunts rule themselves out—Browns and Clowns are too noisy for serious conversation; the tables are too close together in Auntie's Tea Room; and some of my favorite pubs are so underpopulated during the day that even whispered conversations wing across the room. But—lunchtimes excepted—I can usually find a suitable spot in Eaden Lilley's restaurant, or in Hobbs Pavilion, or as now, in the bar that overlooks Parker's Piece in the University Arms Hotel.

Howard Flatt had rung me at home—number supplied by the Camden office—at 8:30 A.M. on the dot. "Miss Principal?" he asked.

"Laura Principal," I confirmed. "Can I help you?"

Indeed I could. Howard Flatt wanted to hire a private investigator to follow up a murder that had taken place two years before—the killing of Geraldine King.

"Your connection to this crime?" I asked. But even as I asked, the answer came to me. The name of the child—only eleven years old at the time—who had been convicted of the murder, was Daryll Flatt.

What must it feel like, I wondered, to have a killer for a baby brother?

IN PARKER'S BAR, while he described the murder, Howard had his back to the room and his front to me. He was a big man, large and square and slow-moving. His shirt was navy-blue, patterned with white squiggles that from my side of the table looked like pasta bows, and the edges of the fabric were hard-pressed to meet across his chest. His neck was nearly as wide as his head. I'm not crazy about big men, especially the kind who expend more energy on their muscles than on their minds; but there was something about Howard's bulk that I found oddly reassuring.

He cleared his throat and spoke again, measuring out each syllable. "You remember?" he asked, baffled. Howard was an avionics technician—a helicopter mechanic—trained by the British Army, now working for a commercial company in Australia. His talents lay more with the monkey wrench than with words.

Did I remember? Well, yes and no. Howard had sketched in events surrounding the murder for me, and they were matched by a series of internal images—of a Viyella skirt, of a fluffy cardigan—as vivid as memory. But in fact I had never seen the body of Geraldine King. Not in the flesh; not even in a photo. At the time of the murder, several newspapers had carried a picture of the place where she was found, but none showed—none was permitted to show—the body itself. Had my brain locked onto a reporter's mention of the details of the outfit she wore when she died? Or had I simply clothed Mrs. King from the wardrobes of my own imagination?

"The murder of Geraldine King was a cause célèbre. A famous case," I explained. One of the less amiable hangovers from my academic past is an inability to resist translating any phrase even mildly obscure. "Taken up by the national papers. You wouldn't know that, since you were out of the country at the time. But it was certainly the most sensational crime to hit this city since the 1970s."

"Since the Cambridge Rapist," Howard concluded. Slow, but far from stupid. I regretted my translation.

"Yes," I agreed. I didn't want to be callous, but there was no point whatsoever in having this conversation if we had to pussyfoot around the facts. "It isn't every day," I said, watching his face, "that a little boy murders his foster mum. A crime like that is bound to be noticed. It feeds into people's worst fears."

If Howard heard me, he didn't respond. He made no attempt at denial. No Daryll-didn't-do-it. Instead he placed his hands on his brawny knees and pushed himself up to a standing position. "Excuse me," he said, "while I get another drink." As he lumbered to the bar, he seemed indifferent to the glances that followed his progress. Members of the Cambridge Chamber of Commerce, fellow patrons of Parker's, were clearly brought to attention by the size of those shoulders. Clearly to me, that is; like I say, Howard had other things on his mind.

While he waited to be served, I opened my mental files on Geraldine King and considered what to censor. I was astonished at how much detail leapt to mind.

Chesterton is a quiet residential area in the northeast corner of the city of Cambridge, alongside the river Cam. In theory, if you ignored the lock at Jesus Green, it would be only a two-mile boat ride from King's College Chapel. Two years ago, almost to the day, a local widow—an elderly widow if you call sixty-three elderly, as most of the papers did—was murdered there. An acquaintance found her body lying facedown in her garden near the base of a sturdy tree. She had been, the *Cambridge Evening News* proclaimed, "stoned to death." This, like many other stories, was not strictly true, but it did succeed in sending shivers down local spines and wooing readers away from the *Exchange and Mart*. "Stoning"—with its connotations of execution, of martyrdom, of public dispatch for private sin—remained on the tips of tongues in connection with the King case long after the police had revealed the more likely instrument of Geraldine's death: not a stone, but a concrete block, hauled up perhaps by means of a pulley system and hurled with devastating effect from a fort high up in the tree.

The fort acquired its own celebrity. The Fort of Death *(Hideaway of Horror; Treehouse of Terror)* was frequented by a boy who had been in temporary foster care with Geraldine King. Daryll was by some accounts a rambunctious lad of eleven—a tearaway, a troublemaker, a wilding. In other versions he was the epitome of an unhappy child, whose catalogue of misfortune—the unmanaging mother, the deserting father, the brutal stepdad—might look excessive even on a soap opera. Geraldine King's brief had been to offset the instability in the little boy's life, to provide the support of a motherly—or perhaps a grandmotherly—presence.

When Geraldine's body was discovered, Daryll was nowhere to be found. No suspicion fell upon him. There were, instead, fears for his safety. Had he too fallen victim to the *Fiend of the Fort*?

Alongside the Cam a towpath edges past the front of Geraldine King's bungalow, all the way from Chesterton to Bait's Bite Lock. Farther along, the landward side of the path is fringed with crack willows. A boy was found, after a prolonged search, huddled in the vast open base of such a tree, some quarter of a mile from where Geraldine's body was being loaded into a mortuary wagon. "Daryll?" the police officer asked cautiously, edging his flashlight toward the tousled head. "Is it Daryll Flatt?"

To the constable's relief, there was movement, a ponderous unfolding, and two luminous eyes with pupils the size of five-pence pieces opened, staring wildly at the night sky. After a moment's silence the little boy uttered an agonized cry, the substance of which was taken up the next day by all the media. They described it—rightly—as a slap in the face for the stubborn British belief in childhood innocence.

"I did it. I did it! I killed her!" Daryll shrieked as the other searchers thundered down the towpath toward him.

HOWARD RETURNED FROM the bar carrying a cup of black coffee, with a miniature jug of cream and two cubes of brown sugar perched on the side of the saucer. He put it in front of me but was immediately overtaken by anxiety. "I'm sorry, I should have asked," he berated himself. "Maybe you'd rather have a soft drink? Or tea?"

I thanked him for the coffee—"It's okay, really it is"—and set it to one side. Another dose of caffeine this morning and my fingers would do a river dance on the tabletop. I could see from the expression on his flat-nosed face that Howard had used the time at the bar to steel himself. "I'm ready now," he said.

And so was I. By the time Howard lowered himself back into his chair, my mind was made up. I didn't want to make money out of this man's mistaken expectations.

Don't get me wrong. On some issues I can be—as my partner Sonny labels me when I race for the moral high ground—Ms. Principle. But when it comes to business, I am as hardheaded as the next skull. If people feel the need to pay for something to be done, if they are not deterred by my warnings that the police have greater resources, that this is a long shot, that the chances of success are slim—if, in short, their need for closure is greater than their financial prudence—then who am I to refuse to follow their particular wild goose?

But this case—or rather this client—was different. The phrase *what you see is what you get* might have been coined with Howard in mind; he was as transparent as springwater. Deceiving him would be like offering poisoned candy to a baby. Howard would take my agreement as encouragement; he would count on me to solve the case, to put the world to rights, to prove the unprovable—that Daryll Flatt didn't murder Geraldine King after all.

No way.

"Howard," I said, planting my elbows firmly on the table, "it's no go. Your brother confessed to the murder. His guilt was confirmed in court. He's got to serve the sentence. You can't do anything now except make sure he knows you love him. And I— Well, I can't do anything at all."

This was lecturelike, not really my style. But blunt was the only way I knew how to do it. My mother always says that you don't do people any favors by hiding the truth. This seemed to me a perfect instance of mother-knows-best.

I thought then that Howard would give up. That he would surrender to my straight talk and trundle off. But I didn't at that point know Howard, not as I came to know him later.

He responded to my attempt at a brush-off with a smile of boyish confidence. Then he reached into the shirt pocket that bulged over his left pec and pulled out a snapshot.

"I'll pay for your time," he insisted. "I want you to know about Daryll."

Anyone's curiosity might be engaged by the chance of an insight into the mind of a child who had killed before reaching his teens. I know mine was. But it was the photograph that kept me in my seat.

It was a glossy snapshot with a white border, showing a boy of perhaps eight or nine. He was perched on the back of a sagging sofa, his arm upraised, poised to hurl a cushion at the camera. His triangular face was impish, with a smile that spelled mischief and teeth too big for the slender jaw. The eyes were sad, closed down somehow; they didn't match the smile. Some of my child-free friends would insist that boys of this age all look alike, but I know better, and I was shocked to find that I recognized the gleeful expression, and found that dusting of freckles across the nose familiar.

I quickly asked a question to cover my confusion, and that's how we came to pass another parcel of time in Parker's Bar. I let Howard spin it out in his own slow-talking way, let him sketch in for me the type of boy Daryll was, before the current crisis. How chatty the boy was, how irrepressible, sidling up to adults at the slightest encouragement and releasing great currents of conversation. About football, about his toy figures, about Australia. "We always had a thing about Australia, Daryll and I," Howard said. "The outback, that's where we planned to go someday. But now . . ."

I drew him back to the description of Daryll's character. "He was a confident kid?" I asked, missing the boat entirely.

Howard shook his head. "Not at all. Well, maybe when he was tiny—when Dad was still around. He was a happy baby, a chuckler. He'd race along the hallway in his walker, checking the world out. I wish you had seen him then. But by the time he went to school, he talked all the time. Like he was anxious, that's what I think—that Daryll was afraid of the silence."

Daryll's anxiety had a deep root. The kid brother hadn't had it easy, Howard said, and that struck me as a straight-up case of understatement. Not that things had always been bad; the Flatts were a happy family in Daryll's earliest years. Janet and Peter Flatt had married young, but they married for love, and they carried the responsibilities of three children—Howard the eldest, Mark much later, Daryll the baby—firmly on their shoulders. Until, that is, there was a downswing in the building trade and Peter was laid off from his job as a bricklayer. He didn't handle unemployment well; and Janet couldn't deal with his descent into depression. At the end of two years much of their mutual commitment had leached away, leaving anger and disappointment in its wake. When Peter was arrested for handling stolen goods, his removal to prison shattered the family forever. Peter never returned home. Janet, who had been an enthusiastic if unsystematic mother, took to drink. In the face of her husband's desertion, Janet's maternal resolution dwindled away.

"So your father left, and to all intents and purposes your mother collapsed. But Daryll still had you?"

The response was fractionally slower in coming even than usual, enough to tell its own tale. For a time Daryll had Howard. Howard tried to be like a parent to him, taking him to school in the mornings, preparing his meals, listening endlessly to his chatter. But important as Howard's presence was, it didn't quite make up for the loss of his father. "He usually refused to talk about it," Howard said, "but I could tell. A month or so before his birthday, Daryll would start going downhill. He would become sullen, he'd get in trouble at school; he even ran away a couple of times. He was hoping against hope that Peter would remember his birthday—send a card, perhaps. Better still, return."

"And when he didn't?"

"Well—you know—he'd be upset. I found him crying in the shed once. Things like that."

"And aggressive? In his distress, did Daryll become violent?"

Howard looked uncomfortable. "All boys get aggressive sometimes," he said. "He might, you know, hurt himself a bit. Bang his head against the wall. Or lash out at Mark."

The middle brother. "But Mark must have been a lot bigger than Daryll."

"It was a bad idea," Howard concurred. "Because our Mark"—he gave an ironic twist to the *our*—"loved to have an excuse to lay into Daryll."

Howard's dislike of Mark was intense, and I had to pull him up short before his indignation at some of the things Mark had done carried him too far away from the story of Daryll.

"And what happened when you left?"

Again that longer pause. Howard brought his two hands together, the right one cupping the fist of the left, and pressed until the knuckles on the left hand cracked. "I *had* to go," he said, defensively. Janet Flatt apparently found a new boyfriend, named Ian Miller. He clouted Howard and undermined him, until the teenager just couldn't take it anymore.

"Did your mother ever stand up to him?" Trying to get a picture of the family dynamics.

Howard shook his head. No. "She—She never said a word to him. Just looked scared, begged me to hold my tongue. So I left. And it was three years before I could bring myself to get in touch again. I was that angry, especially with her." He sighed. "I left, and little Dary—that's what I used to call him—he just had to manage on his own." He laid a gentle finger on the photograph. "That picture was taken just before I went, on Dary's eighth birthday."

We had been talking for a long while now, and I noticed a couple of customers standing by the door of the bar, looking around for an empty table. I reckoned, in the interest of good business relations, that it was better not to

overstay my welcome. But there were two more things I
wanted to know. First, I wondered, what kind of state was
Daryll in now? Howard had visited him in the secure unit
where he'd been held since his arrest.

"It's not so bad there," Howard said, in an effort to be
reasonable. "Not as bad as I expected. Oh, it's shabby, and
the boys are watched like hawks. But the teachers and
youth workers seem okay. His social worker from before
the murder still visits every week, without fail. Daryll gets
a lot of support from Mr. McLeod." Howard paused again
for a few seconds, looking down at his chunky hands. He
seemed too nice a guy to be anything other than pleased
that his little brother had someone to depend on, but that
didn't spare him the pain of the contrast. He cleared his
throat. "Daryll tells me that they got along really well right
from the beginning. McLeod had lost someone in his
family, I think maybe it was his wife, and so he understood
how Dary felt when our granny passed away."

I'd listened now, as Howard had asked me to. I knew
more about the Flatt family than I would have chosen to
know in a perfect world. But there was one issue that
Howard had skated over.

"Howard . . ." I waited until he looked up. "When your
brother talks about the murder, what exactly does he say?"

"What does Daryll say?" Howard thought for a moment,
the crease opening up again between his brows. "Mostly,
he cries. He is thirteen now, you know. He's been locked
up in that place, with murderers and rapists, for two years
now, but still he cries like a baby. Like he's going to choke.
Like he'll never stop. 'Do we have to talk about that,
Howard?' That's what Dary says." Howard looked around
the room, and, for the first time during our meeting, appeared to be aware of the other people in the bar. He lowered his voice to a baritone whisper. "He was mad at her.

That's what Dary says. He didn't mean to kill her, he just had to make her stay away from him. Had to make her shut up."

"What had Geraldine King done to anger him?" What did she say that he didn't want to hear?

Howard shrugged. "Daryll says a lot of the stuff just before the murder is a blur. He's got a therapist who is helping him to remember, but they haven't got very far."

"Do you have any doubts about Daryll's guilt? That it was Daryll who killed Geraldine King?"

"Sure he killed her," he said in a stolid voice, shaking his head. There was something—maybe his dignified acceptance of the inevitable—that put me in mind of a wounded elephant. "Sure he killed her. He dropped stuff on her head, and when she was lying there dead on the ground, he freaked out and ran away. He killed her, but . . ."

I was vastly relieved that he wasn't insisting on going against the investigating officers, against the prosecution, against the well-considered opinions of judge and jury. Against Daryll's own confession.

"But . . . ?"

"But I'm also partly to blame. If I had been here, Daryll wouldn't have got in such a state. Social Services would never have got involved. I could've taken care of him, he could've lived with me. He might never have met this Mrs. King, and he certainly wouldn't have killed her. . . . That's the long and short of it, Laura. Daryll killed Mrs. King. But I'm the one to blame."

I wished I had something to offer, something that would ease his sense of guilt, but my repertoire of services doesn't extend into the territory of the conscience. It was crunch time.

"So what is it that you think I can do?"

Howard's mood lifted the minute I asked. "There's one

thing I want from you," he said. "W-H-Y. That's what I want to know: why. Was it because Daryll was unhappy and all alone? Because his family wasn't—because I wasn't—there? Or did something else happen 'round about that time, before the murder, something that set him off?"

Howard looked down again, shifted his body, plucked at his trouser legs as if to prevent them from bagging at the knees. Why do people do that? I wondered. But wondering was just a way of putting off the hardest question of all.

"Howard, I'll have to think it over. Give me a few hours. But in the meantime, I need you to think about something, too. What if I take the case? And what if after investigation, it seems to me that Daryll did murder Geraldine out of sheer unhappiness—that your presence would have made all the difference. What then?"

Howard looked at his huge hands as if seeing them for the first time. He studied his knuckles for a full thirty seconds before he replied. "I went to see my mother again yesterday, Miss Principal. I begged her to tell me if she had any idea why Daryll did what he did. And do you know what she said?"

He looked at me, daring me to guess. I nodded, not to suggest I knew Janet Flatt's view on the issue, but to encourage Howard to tell me.

"My mother—our mother—said we were just like our father. Dary and me both. We're bad seed, that's what she said. I don't believe in bad seed," Howard said doubtfully. "Do you?"

"Not for a minute," I replied. But I imagined that if my brother was a murderer, an anxiety about genetic determination might find a place to root.

"I have to know the truth," Howard concluded. "I have to be able to say to myself, that is the reason—that's why Dary did it. I have to understand." He paused, his right hand once again compressing the knuckles on his left. "Otherwise," he said, "sometimes I think I won't be able to bear it."

Even the thickest body armor is feeble proof against that kind of pain.

THE SUN WAS low, hiding in the topmost branches of the trees, by the time I arrived at the river. My only company on the bank where I did my stretches was an ardent couple snuggled on the damp grass, who appeared to judge their embraces well worth the risk of pneumonia. Thank heavens for love—and for antibiotics.

But once settled into my sculler on the river itself, I was plunged into perfect solitude. I had to struggle through the first few strokes, my body still closed in on itself, still resisting. I concentrated on the rhythm—forward and back, forward and back, forward and back—controlling it with my mind and will, until quite suddenly I began to breathe more fully, more deeply, more pleasurably, the cool moist air. My body was in gear. The chant of forward and back receded; the cadence became a rhythm of wood and wind and water. I became a mere element rather than the conductor, and at last I could hear the sounds of the river itself. The sweep of breeze in the willows; a hiss as my paddle crossed the path of a swan; the steady resonant slap of water on the bank.

As soon as I came alongside the start of the towpath, I stopped rowing and trailed a paddle. The boat glided gently to the left. Past one home with a brace of gnomes standing sentry over an otherwise empty stretch of lawn; past another with elaborate borders and a fastidiously clipped hedge; losing momentum, finally, opposite a bungalow that had to be observed through gaps in tangles of shrubbery.

I grabbed a handful of grass, pulling the boat to rest against the bank, and stared curiously at the house. It was large, and given the generously sized plot, probably pricey, but it was not particularly beautiful.

The house must have been built in the 1930s, with a regular pattern incised in the brick. The front door was set inside a porch with a rounded arch. To the left of the porch a large picture window dominated; to the right, a line of smaller windows set high in the wall indicated the position of the bedrooms. The sitting room had an excellent outlook on the river—potentially, anyway, though in practice the view would be striped by branches of buddleia and jasmine. The bedrooms, with their stingy windows, had been designed with privacy, rather than aesthetic considerations, in mind. There was something prissy about the house. Only the garden, with its wide frontage and dense planting, showed any sign of passion.

Here, in this bungalow, Geraldine King had lived and died. Here Daryll Flatt had made his home for the best part of a year before he killed her. I let go of one clump of grass and reached for another, pulling the sculler a few feet farther along the bank. But though I craned my neck, I couldn't catch a glimpse of the tree house beneath which Geraldine's body had been found. It was farther back, I guessed, outside my range of vision.

There was not a single light on in the house. For a moment I was tempted to leap up onto the bank and search for the tree fort. But there was no way to secure the boat, and I would be dead conspicuous creeping through the garden in my rowing gear. Even if the current owners were away— even if the house were unoccupied—the neighbors with the daintily trimmed hedge were surely the types to be involved in Neighborhood Watch. In fact, I thought I had seen a flick of a curtain as I drifted past their plot, and an assault from the river would hardly go unnoticed.

I pushed off again into midstream. I had lost the rhythm, the physical flow, and I was too deep in thought now, too absorbed in the past, to recapture it. So I drifted, at a cruising-down-the-river sort of pace. It wouldn't count as serious exercise, but to be on the river was, nevertheless, pure pleasure; if you achieve pleasure while managing a bit of a workout, you are still, in my book, ahead of the game.

This meandering brought me and my sculler soon enough to the railway bridge. It's a neat construction of metal fretwork that spans the Cam at an oblique angle and disappears into the woods on either side. There was a time, some years ago—while Geraldine King was still alive—when this bridge was the only thing that shadowed my enjoyment of rowing. The problem began one bright winter morning. I can recall now in my muscles as well as my memory how it felt as I sped along, head bent into the task of rowing, looking over my shoulder from time to time to navigate. The gloom of the bridge passed over me in two strokes. But as I flashed out into the sunshine again, there had been a rush of air past my ear, and a resolute splash. Something had hit the water beside me, leaving a chaos of ripples in its wake. I brought the sculler to a halt and looked up at the bridge, shielding my eyes against the glare of the sun.

For a second, nothing. Then three small heads rose up and peered hungrily through the ironwork. "Hey, you!" I roared, putting my shock and anger into the shout. My indignant adult voice froze them in alarm. They stared at me for a moment, while I made furiously for the bank. But just as I landed, I heard the clank of the sleepers under their pounding feet, and they shot off into the woods on the opposite side.

There were other occasions. They became more daring,

relishing the chase, waiting for me to commit myself to left or right before they dashed in the other direction. I never caught them. I'm lucky that their missiles never caught me.

Boys' faces. I stared at the bridge again now, resting on my oars. Reached for my backpack, wiped my hands on a tissue, slid out of its envelope the photo that Howard had given me. At the time of the trial, Daryll Flatt's snapshot had appeared in grainy black-and-white in many of the papers. But I could never be certain it was him. The silhouette was too dark, the features too obscure, and, above all, the expression—the downward tug of the mouth—didn't match. But now I saw him as Howard must have seen him: an imp of a boy, narrow jaw, brown hair springing up off his high broad forehead, looking sideways to share a laugh, and I knew I was right. It was him. The brat on the bridge, the tearaway who had made me a target for attack—that child had been Daryll.

Chapter 2

IF SONNY MENDLOWITZ showed up at an audition for the part of private detective, he'd be shuffled to the back of the casting line. My partner simply doesn't look the part. There's a grace about him that doesn't mesh with the Sam Spade image. People don't see private investigator in the warmth of his glance; they can't read inquiry agent in the cut of his clothes.

But maybe those people have been watching too much television. Maybe they've been deluded into thinking that private eyes are of necessity cynical men, weighed down by contempt for humanity. Maybe they've swallowed the myth that any detective worth his salt will have a face and a physique that have been ruined by recklessness and whiskey.

If Sonny matched that popular image, I'd probably never have been drawn into this business myself. And I'm certain our personal relationship wouldn't have gotten off the ground. He's a formidable investigator, in spite of being lean and rather beautiful. He has the temperament: he is practical and patient, quick-witted and cool in a crisis. He has the social skills: Sonny's childhood, where fitting in depended on winning over the bullies, taught him a trick or two, and Sonny can turn a situation around with bonhomie where others might have to fall back on the uncertain authority of muscle. And, like all outstanding investigators, Sonny is seldom wracked by regrets. How can an investigator do what an investigator's gotta do—quickly—if he's busy agonizing over what he did last?

That was one of the toughest things for me about starting out in the business. When I first met Sonny, I was an historian; the habit of swift decisive action had been swept aside by the discipline of scholarship.

Not that I didn't have qualifications. I wasn't put out by the physical demands of the job—you don't row for your college without a good pair of shoulders and stacks of stamina. But I'd become a woman of words, not of action—someone who ensured that every sentence was polished, every interpretation solid, every fact well-founded, before exposing them to the public gaze. A person more certain about events in the nineteenth century than about those in the present. The habit of action had to be dredged up, worked on, cultivated. Had to be hammered into shape. And my biggest sticking point—the only aspect of the job that made me hesitate before leaping from an academic life to this one—was the little matter of physical danger.

Dealing with danger is not, as people often think, about mastering karate or shaping up on the shooting range. I learned the hard way that it is about mental readiness, rather than muscle. There was an occasion when we were following a gang of men. Men who came home from the office, changed out of their suits, and stalked the neighboring borough of London, looking for someone—someone smaller, younger, alone; above all, someone nonwhite—on whom to release the rage that they kept locked in during the day.

Sonny and I were seeking proof for the parents of a boy in long-term hospital care that these were the men who put him there. When they turned off the high street into a warren of alleys, we followed at what we thought was a safe distance. And miscalculated. We rounded a corner into a cul-de-sac, and there they were, waiting for us. They spotted us. Their shouts of challenge ricocheted off the high surrounding walls. They swaggered toward us with the confidence of numbers, all boots and bomber jackets and concentrated hatred. Sonny signaled to me and turned to run. I froze. I couldn't scan for an escape route: my vision could take in only the onward march of ten booted feet and the metal bar that the leader held crosswise in his hands. Sonny did a double take, saw me crouched against the wall, and lunged at them, charging straight for the center of the pack. The bellow that issued from his throat would have stopped an elephant in its tracks. They hesitated. Only for a second, but it was enough. Sonny grabbed my hand and got me out of there.

Never again, I vowed. Never again would I need to be rescued from my own inaction.

Since then I have taught myself a range of techniques to enable me to act decisively, even when alarm is battering at my brain. I've learned, when in danger, not to contemplate the possibility of failure—to forbid every corner of my mind to images of injury and death. I've trained myself by trial and error to channel adrenaline into unreflective response, so that when I get the feelings of fear (wobbly stomach, hard to breathe, something coming at me), I don't stop to analyze. I act.

And if it happens this way often enough, let's say from time to time, the sequence becomes second nature. I'm that much readier for the next occasion. Ready to move from the stirrings of fear to doings that disable a bad guy without even having to think.

As I came off the river Cam that October evening, after my encounter with the Daryll of my memory below the railway bridge, I had reason to draw on those techniques. In the dregs of daylight I made my way easily up the concrete apron to the entrance of the boathouse, then hesitated on the threshold. The interior was as dark as sin. I groped around the door frame for the switch. The overhead fixture flickered on. Its cold light extended only to the central corridor of the boathouse, making no inroads into the gloom that furnished the outer walls.

Like the resonant hush when someone holds their breath, something in the silence made me uneasy. I'd sooner have showered in the Bates Motel than in the boathouse that evening. Working swiftly, I secured my belongings, pulled a sweatshirt on against the chill of the evening, and prepared to leave. But as I hoisted my backpack, I picked up a flick of movement in the far corner of the building.

My muscles screamed *Run*—out and onto the path, among the passersby, away from this island of darkness. I wavered for only a second, afraid to look foolish: what if it was another rower, moving casually about the building, eyes adjusted to the gloom? The flash of my fleeing backside would provide the substance for a tale that I'd be long in living down.

Then an eerie sound—my name, *Laura*—echoed out of the darkness, slicing clean and sharp through my hesitation. I propelled myself toward the stairs, still plunged in blackness; and I was almost on him before I made out his features.

His familiar features. The casual pose, one knee bent, boot resting on the wall. And even in the gloom, that knock-you-out smile.

"Sonny!" I exclaimed, and action turned to anger. "What the hell are you doing, lurking there in the dark?"

"Getting in touch with my past," he teased. "Reminds

me of school. The creak of floorboards in the gym, the smell of sweaty socks—"

"The schoolboy pranks," I interrupted, trying to sound lighthearted. Not succeeding.

Sonny didn't answer. He put his hands on my shoulders and maneuvered me so my face was touched by a trickle of light from the entrance. He leaned forward and peered into my eyes. "You're really upset," he murmured. "I frightened you."

"Don't be ridiculous."

But of course he was right. After all my efforts, Sonny had trifled with my hard-won courage. Slithered under my defenses. He had all but disarmed me.

Twisting away from him, I walked my wounded dignity back to the locker. Closed the door, spun the lock, snapped it shut. I heard Sonny's footsteps, placating footsteps, close behind me. He touched me lightly on the shoulder, then withdrew his hand.

I turned around slowly, chin in the air, refusing to meet his eyes. I didn't want to make up with him just like that.

"Sorry, Laura," he said in a voice soft with apology. "I didn't mean to scare you. I was only joking." And he leaned forward with the offering of a kiss.

"Behind every joke . . ." I reminded him.

"There's a germ of truth. A grain of aggression. Yes, I know."

I've always been a sucker for "Sorry." I considered his behavior. Rare for Sonny, that mixture—the attempt to terrify and the tenderness. And then I knew.

"You've been to see your father," I said.

He nodded. Pushed the flop of fair hair off his forehead in a get-thee-behind-me gesture. And as we walked slowly back along Chesterton Lane and up Alpha Road, hand in hand, he told me about his visit to Alex.

It was always the same. Sonny maneuvered time from his current case because Alex was feeling unwell. Arrived at his father's flat to find Alex full of complaint: about the G.P., who was incompetent; about boredom; about inefficiencies at the local library; and, of course, about Sonny. *Who never came to see him.*

Sonny propelled an abandoned Tango tin off the pavement with a sudden kick. The ferociousness of the gesture made a passerby turn and stare. Sonny didn't notice.

"He always says that, 'You never come to see me,' though I'm standing right there in front of him. It makes me feel as if my presence in the room counts for nothing. As if for my father, I don't really exist."

What could I say? It wasn't the first time, but it always seemed to hurt him like the first. Alex makes a demand—usually at short notice, always non-negotiable. Sonny complies, tries to give him what he asks for. But what Alex asks for—help with the taxes, painting the balcony, trimming the hedge—isn't really what Alex wants. Poor Alex. He wants, too late, to be loved. He who never managed to show Sonny any convincing signs of affection is now demanding in his querulous way—*Why don't you ever come to see me?*—a share of love.

And since Sonny cares about his father but isn't sure whether or not he loves him, he's silenced by the complaint. Finds it impossible to reply. Feels trapped. Feels resentful.

The grains of my earlier annoyance dissolved. The skin on Sonny's palm was roughened; his boots smelled vaguely of diesel oil, some memento of his current case; but I knew his stride as well as my own, and there is no one I'd sooner walk home with. Even at moments like this.

"I love you, Sonny." It didn't make up for his father, but I said it anyway. He put his arm around my shoulder and relaxed just a little.

By the time we reached my house, his anger had subsided. We were hungry. Sonny laid the fire and put a match
to crumpled balls of newspaper, while I prepared coffee
and sandwiches. "There's not much in the cupboard," I
called from the kitchen. "You want mayonnaise with your
ham, or mustard?"

"Mustard, Mother Hubbard," Sonny called back. He's
never gotten used to the meagerness of my food stocks.

We draped ourselves over giant cushions on my sitting
room floor, side by side, where we could talk while we ate.
The glow from the fire ruddied Sonny's face. I told him
everything I could remember about Howard Flatt and
Daryll Flatt and the murder of Geraldine King.

"So Daryll Flatt was one of those children who pelted
you with bricks?" Sonny asked, astonished. He remembered the weeks when I'd been locked into battle with
those lads. If Sonny had had his way, we would have put
the police on to them, made them confront the full majesty
of the law. "Maybe if you'd let me catch them then, we
would have—"

"Saved a life?" I interrupted. "Prevented the murder of
Geraldine King? Finish your coffee, Sonny, and give us a
break." I reminded him that one of my favorite childhood
pastimes had involved standing on the Clifton suspension
bridge and spitting on the boats below. "Lots of children
do that sort of thing," I pointed out. "It ain't necessarily
criminal."

"Not at all," Sonny agreed. "But then spit's not in the
same league as a boulder."

"It was a concrete block that killed Geraldine King," I
rejoined.

"Same difference. With a concrete block you can build
walls—or you can crush skulls. With spit, the most you're
likely to do is to ruin a hairdo. If they had been my kids out

there"—Sonny made this pronouncement with the authority vested in a father of two sons—"if they were my boys, I'd soon have brought those games to an end."

"One of the things I'll have to consider is whether that's precisely the problem." Consternation crossed Sonny's face. "No no, I don't mean you, Sonny, I mean the absence of a father. From what Howard says, Daryll was a much happier child before his father went to prison. He felt the sting of rejection afresh, poor lad, each time his birthday rolled around. Maybe that had something to do with Geraldine's death."

"You mean maybe he blamed his mother—or women in general—for the father leaving? And finally flipped, and let his anger loose on Geraldine?" Sonny half smiled at the lurid picture he'd created, to show he only half meant it.

"I wasn't thinking of anything quite so twisted," I replied, resting my chin on my hands. "Something more mundane. Lots of boys have a wild period. A phase where they flirt with trouble. And most of them pull back before it gets too serious. Maybe without a father, it's just that much harder to get back on track."

"Especially," Sonny added, "if your mother deals with problems by trying to pickle them in alcohol."

It sounded trite and unconvincing. Lots of children lose touch with their fathers; more than we know of have neglectful mothers. But, in Britain at least, where the guns that can cushion a killer from the immediacy of death are rare, very few of those youngsters move on to murder.

Even so, I couldn't pooh-pooh it completely. After all, Howard Flatt wanted an explanation, and beggars have to take the theories that they're offered.

"You're going to take the case?" Sonny asked.

I thought of Sonny's children from his marriage to Morag. Daniel, the youngest boy—open and volatile, easily hurt but easily won over, too, sensitive to the feelings of others. For whom I had a soft spot (though I tried not to make it obvious) because he had always shown an interest in me. Not so Dominic, who often seemed to feel that friendship with me would mean disloyalty to his mum. Brighter, perhaps, and more brittle. Practical, energetic, self-contained. The elder of the two, but still a child.

They've never been in trouble, those boys, not real trouble. How far was that a matter of character, of upbringing? How far a matter of circumstance: no need to steal, to cheat, to lie, when your parents are able and willing to provide for all of your needs and many of your desires? How far a matter of luck: didn't I read somewhere that children who kill a mother or father generally have no history of delinquency? Generally are "good" children, have never been in trouble, not real trouble—until they take an axe and give a parent forty whacks. Until they kill.

"I tried to resist, Sonny. Chances of a decisive answer to Howard's question are small—I told him that. But something about the issue of violent children fascinates me all the same. I'll start with Nicole tomorrow."

"Detective Inspector Pelletier?" Sonny and Nicole had never really hit it off.

"She's agreed to talk me through the files. Nicole was on the murder team, you know—it was an astonishing case. I remember some of the things she said at the time."

I stood and did a cat stretch to loosen my spine. "I'm for the shower," I said, pulling off my hooded top. "Can you nip to the off-license for a bottle of wine? Helen's expecting us at seven."

Sonny followed me into the bedroom while I undressed. He hovered behind me as I pinned up my hair. "What's up?" I asked. It didn't take a detective to tell he had something on his mind.

"I thought maybe I could use a shower, too."

I spun around to check him out. Under my gaze he swept his blond hair off his forehead and looked at me again with that half smile.

"You look clean enough to me," I countered. Smiling back.

"On the surface, maybe. But deep down," Sonny said, with the waggle of an eyebrow, "I'm feeling kind of dirty."

Whether it was the secret housewife in me coming to the surface, I wouldn't like to say, but I couldn't resist the challenge of a man who needed a thorough cleaning. I set myself to do my best in the short time available. I scrubbed Sonny—and Sonny scrubbed me. We polished till we shone. When the warm water ran out, and we emerged finally from the shower, the soles of our feet were as wrinkled as prunes. We didn't mind a bit.

Sonny outlined his new case while we dressed. Divorce, he explained—marital property dispute—but with a special twist. Belinda Bennett was a good-natured soul who had devoted twenty years of her life to the family charter boat business. She had nurtured its growth from a single houseboat to a considerable player on the Norfolk leisure scene. All informal family labor. But the brothers Bennett denied that she'd been involved. She did nothing at all, they declared; not a penny shall she have. And they proceeded then to sit on the company records. Enter Sonny, with instructions from Mrs. Bennett's solicitor to find the evidence to prove that the good lady hadn't idled the last two decades away.

He finished his sketch of the story just as I was getting ready to dry my hair. I held off so I could hear the finale. "So," he concluded, "that's why I can't make it tonight."

"You what?"

"I'm off to Norfolk to interview the bookkeeper who filled the office chair after Mrs. Bennett got the boot."

"But what about Helen? She's cooked up one of her feasts, especially with you in mind."

"I rang Helen earlier today," Sonny explained. "How did you think I knew you'd be out on the river? I apologized and Helen accepted. We're all square. But I got the impression that she was anxious to talk. Has she been worried about something lately? As far as you know?"

I shrugged. Helen Cochrane, like lots of single mums, with children to nurture and careers to keep on course and houses to maintain, always had a lot on her mind. But if there was something special—a cause for anxiety—I'd winkle it out soon enough.

"I'll look into it," I said, using a blast of air from the hair dryer to blow him on his way. "And you come back soon, hear?"

Chapter 3

Helen Cochrane is, apart from Sonny, my closest friend. Our paths have run parallel over the years. As undergraduates at Newnham College, we firmed up our friendship by exploring the deep problems of human existence and the shallower ones of taste, in talks that lasted late into the night. We moved in tandem: through graduation and postgraduate study (gang labor in East Anglian agriculture for my history thesis, library management at Loughborough for Helen); in and out of failed marriages (only one each; in each case, one was enough); into home ownership (Helen's Victorian terraced house in Newnham is only a mile or so away from mine); and, not least, through the age barriers that mark the stealthy passage from being young to what is, to the young, unthinkable.

There are differences, of course, the most obvious being that Helen's daily schedule revolves around a near-teen's needs and mine doesn't. But in one way or another, Ginny Cochrane has been part of my life, too. That's another thing Helen and I have in common.

If Helen was disappointed that Sonny had backed out of our dinner in Newnham that evening, she gave no sign. When I pushed open the front door, she was pinned to the rug in the tiny Victorian sitting room, with tears of laughter in her eyes. There, between the chaise longue and the aspidistra, Ginny and her best friend, Karen, were subjecting Helen to a tickle terror.

"Promise. Promise. Promise," they chanted. Almost-twelve is a ruthless age.

"Can this be the head of library services for Eastern University?" I asked, staring in mock horror at Helen's disarrayed form. "Which way to the stacks?"

Ginny and Karen turned to me with mischief in their eyes, but being forewarned, I managed to fend them off. Helen plumped herself with relief onto the rocking chair. The girls retreated upstairs, most likely to regroup and strike again.

"What was that all about?"

"What?" Helen asked, looking around as if nothing had happened.

"That stuff about promises. Are they angling for designer jeans, or what?"

Helen rose to get me a drink. "I haven't started yet," she said, returning with two antique glasses and an impressive bottle of Côtes du Rhône. "I was waiting for you." She poured the wine, and passed the fuller of the two glasses to me. "Cheers!" she said, taking a nourishing sip. "What."

"What?" I asked. This was getting to be a habit.

"It's not jeans—well, not at the moment. They want me to promise not to go to the police."

"You're thinking of turning them in for tickling? Bit harsh, Helen, wouldn't you say?"

Helen stood up abruptly. "It's not funny, Laura," she said, with an absence of humor so unusual for her that I knew she meant it. "Maybe food will sober you up," she suggested, consulting her watch. "And the green mullet is, by my reckoning, more or less ready. So help me serve the meal, and as soon as we're seated, I'll tell you the whole sordid story."

Nestling on an old platter painted with whimsical crocuses, the fish looked almost too good to eat. Almost. I bit back my questions until our plates were full—until the parsnips and broccoli had been passed, and replaced under cover; until the sauce had been sprinkled over the fish; until the candles were burning steadily, and the only sound apart from our munching was a trickle of music from Ginny's room upstairs. Then I beckoned Helen to begin.

"It's about Ginny," she said. "I don't know what to do." Helen paused to organize her thoughts.

"Is it school?"

"Indirectly," Helen replied, and she was off. Ginny, she reminded me, had started bicycling to school at the beginning of the term. It wasn't a short ride to Chesterton Community College, but by going along Grange Road—or the Backs—and then up Mount Pleasant, it was possible to avoid confrontation with heavy traffic for much of the way. And she had company there and back, in the form of Rachel and Karen, two school chums who lived nearby.

"It started last week," Helen said. "I mean, that's when I first learned about it. I was sitting at the desk in my bedroom, drafting a report, when the girls pulled up in front of the house. I stood up to wave to them from the window, but they didn't notice me. Then Rachel took her helmet off and I could see she had been crying. I didn't want to interfere, to embarrass her unnecessarily"—that's Helen all over—"so I waited a minute before going down."

"And what did Rachel say when you saw her?"

"Nothing," Helen replied with a shrug. "They all tried to act—shielding Rachel, talking brightly to distract me— as if nothing had happened. So I left it, for a couple of days. Until it happened again."

I felt worried now, too. Ginny has secrets with her friends, like all kids her age—but she has always been open with

Helen about things that matter. I polished off my fish and pushed the plate to one side.

Helen suddenly recalled herself to her hosting responsibilities. "Salad, Laura? More vegetables?"

Not now, thanks, I signaled. This was shaping up as the kind of story where my concentration ought not to compete with my jaw. "*What* happened again? Was Rachel in tears?"

"Red noses, blotchy faces—all of them showed signs of being really upset. All on edge. So I gave them a drink and some comfort food, and didn't say anything until the other girls had left. Then I cornered Ginny and made her tell me. She was reluctant at first—they had some kind of pact. But I think when she started to talk, she was actually sort of relieved."

"So what's wrong? What was it? What *is* it?" I urged.

"Promise me you won't laugh, Laura. It's a man in a gorilla mask. A stupid rubber mask, the kind kids wear at Halloween. He was waiting the first time, this man, near the end of Grange Road, just where they slow down to check the traffic before turning into Madingley Road. He stepped out in front of them, with his arms outstretched. Made them stop. His fly was open—and well, you know."

It didn't take heaps of imagination. "How did the girls react to that?"

"That first time, they giggled. From nervousness as much as anything. But since then, Ginny says, his manner has become a lot more menacing. They think it might be their fault for having laughed at him."

"Does he say anything?"

"Yes. This makes it worse, Laura—the guy thinks he is a joker. Standing there, with his ape face, he says"—Ginny imitated his tone, it was mocking and sly—" 'Hey, girls, you want to see my banana?' "

You wanna see my banana? I almost giggled at . . . what? At the music hall swagger of it. At the adolescent obviousness, the sheer preposterousness of the remark.

But then the nastiness that was also part and parcel of the incident slithered in and overwhelmed me. That this man displayed his swollen genitals but kept his face hidden. That he got his kicks from shocking, from causing anxiety and fear in, children. That he took a part of the male anatomy about which Ginny and her girlfriends were mildly, cordially curious, and tried to turn it into an instrument of fear and domination. His arousal; their distress.

But he hadn't said: wanna see my gun? He'd referred to a banana. And the meaning of this hit me, late, like a ton of bricks. What do children do with bananas? This was no comical comparison; it was an insidious warning.

Silence. I reached for the salad, took Helen's plate, solicitously, and served her first. Comfort food for grownups now. And bit my tongue against the outburst. No point exploding in Helen's face, like a faulty grenade. No point in letting rip with the outrage that I felt, with the what-sort-of-a-person and the how-can-he-do-this-to-children that leap so easily to my tongue, to anyone's tongue—to Helen's tongue, I'm sure—in cases like this. These sentiments establish the speaker as having her elbows on the right side of the moral fence. But they don't do anything to change things. In fact, if they use energy that might better be used in devising proper systems of protection and restraint, they probably get in the way.

"How many times?" I asked.

"Three so far. Once at the corner of Grange Road. Once, near this end of Grange Road, by the university football ground."

"Both busy areas," I commented. That made me more uneasy. Not a behind-the-bushes sort of flasher, this one.

Not timid. He was audacious. Confident. "And the third time?"

"That was the worst. He cycled up along side them on Gilbert Road, shortly after they left the school. His physical style was hampered by the bike, of course. But he used the same catch phrase. 'You wanna see my banana, girls?' And by now they were so sensitized that all he had to do was stare at them through the mask—with terrible, glittering eyes, they said—to reduce them to tears. And you know what the most alarming thing is?"

"Yes," I answered, with a sick feeling in the pit of my stomach that had nothing to do with the fish. "It looks as if he knows their route. As if he might be stalking them now." I took Helen's hand. "And even if he isn't, even if he's going for schoolgirls in general, even if it's sheer coincidence that Ginny and her friends have been intercepted three times, the effect is the same."

"He makes them feel hunted," Helen burst out. "He's got them looking over their shoulders, dead nervous, suspicious of any male, pedestrian or cyclist, on their route. And I don't know which frightens me more, Laura. That he might try to abduct one of them. Or that they might be too preoccupied with watching out for him, maybe, to keep a proper eye on the traffic."

"What have you done so far?"

"What can I do? I've told them I'll be late for work for the time being. I'm driving Ginny to school—and Rachel and Karen, when they want to come."

"What about Rachel and Karen's parents? What do they say?"

"Well, that's another problem. They've begged me not to tell their parents. But I feel terrible about it. Here's a threat to their daughters, and I'm keeping it from them. What shall I do?"

"Will they ride with you to school?"

"They're too scared to cycle at the moment."

"So, for the time being, they're safe. Give it a week. Maybe by then this guy will have given up, or at least shifted to another area of town." I didn't really believe it could be that easy, but there's no harm in hoping. "In the meantime, Helen, what about the police?"

"You saw the girls, didn't you, when you came in? They were laughing, but they meant it. Ginny is convinced—Rachel and Karen, too—that going to the police would be humiliating. That talking about this kind of thing with a policeman—even a policewoman—would be too embarrassing for words. Yes, Laura," Helen added, heading me off, "I've told them that they have a right to be angry, that indecent exposure is a crime, that it's Apeman who should be embarrassed, not them, but . . ." Helen shrugged again, and picked at a stalk of watercress.

"They still say they don't want anyone to know. Okay, Helen, I understand. You can't drag them down to the police station kicking and screaming; and to expose them to an interview that they might find humiliating wouldn't be a step forward. After an experience like this, they need their confidence to be built up, not further undermined. I can see all that. But . . ." I paused, thinking it through.

"But . . . ?"

"But they didn't make *me* promise," I concluded. "So why don't I talk to the police on your behalf?"

Helen looked as if this possibility had never occurred to her. I took this as a sign of just how disconcerted she'd been by the whole experience. "Is Nicole back in Cambridge yet?" she asked.

"Yes, Nicole is back." Not only back, but I had a meeting with her the next day to get the lowdown on the Daryll Flatt case, and there was no reason why we couldn't stretch to a conversation about a flasher. "What's the use of having an ex-student in a secure position on the force if you can't tap her brains occasionally for a problem like this?"

"Off the record?" Helen asked hopefully. I nodded. "But," she asked, assailed again by doubt, "what good could that possibly do?"

"Maybe nothing. Maybe lots. For example, maybe the police know about this flasher already. Maybe they even have an idea who he is. Maybe they can talk to him. And maybe Nicole can persuade a few of the patrols to check the route between here and Chesterton School a little more often. Okay?"

Helen smiled and raised her glass to me.

But we both knew that *maybe* was a long way from good enough.

Chapter 4

IF YOU HAD asked me a few years ago, while I was still teaching history at Eastern University, to designate one of my undergraduate students for a career in the Criminal Investigation Department, I wouldn't for a moment have selected Nicole Pelletier. She didn't fit the bill. At least, she didn't fit the bill as I knew it at the time, from television programs. She wasn't a hard-as-nails cynic—like Taggart, to put it in today's idiom. She didn't have the rough appeal of a New York cop like Sipowicz or the polished pushiness of Frank Pendleton; she wasn't blessed with the melancholic courtesy of Inspector Morse, or with Jane Tennison's dry wit and magnificent bone structure. Nicole Pelletier looked, I would have said, very much like what she was— a sturdy, athletic girl of marked intelligence and little scholarly bent, a girl whose talents were best engaged on the netball court.

Just as well I never opted for a career in personnel. Here is Nicole Pelletier today, a detective inspector, and doing very nicely, thank you. The qualities—swift judgment, teamwork, strategic flair—that made her a damn good netball player in those days make her exceptional at policing now.

"Sorry," said a civilian clerk, popping his head around the door of the interview room. "Inspector Pelletier sends apologies—she's had to take a statement. Won't be free for a few minutes more."

With Nicole, I never know quite what to expect. There was a time when she could hardly speak to me without resentment threading her words. It started in her final year at university, when Nicole suddenly resolved—in spite of her neglect, up till that time, of all things academic—that she would be satisfied with nothing less than a very good degree. Every fiber of her tenacious spirit went into the project. It was an impressive effort; I began to think she'd pull it off. But shortly before exams, something happened to blow her concentration, and Nicole's final results were less than she had wished. Less than she deserved.

"You did well," I had comforted her. "In the circumstances." If she'd merely passed so soon after her mother's death, it would have been pretty damned impressive.

But Nicole rejected all attempts at consolation. She was convinced she'd let me down. She found intolerable the thought that I or anyone else might feel sorry for her. Her mediocre degree was a weakness, an embarrassment, never to be forgotten, and despite—no, probably because of—my support, I became identified with her humiliation.

But Nicole's disappointment didn't last forever. It was smoothed away by her success in the police service—and, in an odd way, by my change of career. When I took up my first case in Cambridge as a private investigator, I came to Nicole, cap in hand, for information. "So," she said, "you need help," and she couldn't disguise the exhilaration in her eyes. Couldn't resist the satisfaction of turning the tables on her former tutor—of becoming my ally, the experienced one, the one with the knowledge, the skills, the contacts. Lucky me.

But from time to time Nicole's disappointment washes

over her again and she lashes out. Sometimes, like now, she keeps me waiting.

I drew the clerk back for a second. "Excuse me. Any chance of a coffee? And"—I took encouragement from his weak smile of acquiescence—"I don't suppose there's anyone here who remembers the case of that local lad, the one who killed his foster mother a couple of years back?"

The clerk eyed me reprovingly. A you-should-know-better look. "Ask the inspector," he instructed. "She'll know. I'll send someone with coffee. White no sugar?"

"How did you know that?"

"Be forty-five pence," he replied, and disappeared.

"Why should I?" I muttered. I emptied the contents of my shoulder bag onto my lap to search for the coins, and then the door reopened and Detective Inspector Pelletier stepped in. Following on her heels was a young constable, with unbecoming bags under his eyes and a stack of box files balanced in his arms.

"Laura," she saluted me. She extended her hand and flashed me a smile of genuine welcome. She glanced at my lap, took in what looked like a miniature train derailment, and in a tactful gesture—since I was temporarily immobilized—withdrew the offer of a handshake.

I breathed a silent sigh of relief. This was the Nicole I had become used to, and definitely the Nicole I preferred. "Nice to have you back on the old home patch, Nicole." The last time we'd worked together—when I had reported the absence of a person in Kensington who turned out to be more dead than missing—the D.I. had been on temporary contract with the Metropolitan Police. "Did you find you couldn't flourish without the morning mist on the fens?"

The smile grew mischievous. "In the end, Laura, it was the loss of you that proved too much for me. The streets of

London seemed bare without your lovely face; the days were empty without those little chores you set me . . ." She became aware at the same moment as I that the constable's cheeks below his baggy eyes were reddening. Any woman who has done as well as Nicole in the police service knows better than to let rumors of this kind circulate.

"Constable," she said sternly, getting his full attention, "it's a joke."

"Ma'am." He smiled, nervously, and tried for a look of nonchalance.

"I've brought the files," Nicole told me. She pointed at the table. The constable set the boxes down, arranged them in a straight line, waited for a nod from Nicole, and then scooted away. "They were in the section of records known colloquially as H-W-S-B-O-T." Nicole paused, raised an eyebrow at me.

"Here's where sergeant buried our things?" I ventured. Not bad for ten A.M.

"Even less accessible than that. H-W-S-B-O-T. Hope-we've-seen-the-back-of-them. Took the best part of an hour to resurrect these, but they look to be intact. I went over them first thing this morning with D.C. Chalmers. So ask away."

"I don't suppose I could—"

"Not a chance," she said.

So I asked.

About, first, the events leading up to the murder of Geraldine King. I needed a fuller picture of what had happened. "What day of the week was it?"

"It was a Wednesday," Nicole recounted, glancing at her notes. "A pretty unexceptional day, by all accounts. Daryll Flatt went off to school in the morning, as usual. Geraldine King had one or two routine callers, but nothing out of the ordinary. She must have tidied the house—it was more or less immaculate. In the early afternoon, two things happened. Geraldine left the house and went out. She was gone for over an hour and a half. A neighbor saw her leave, on foot—which suggests she couldn't have gone too far, because apparently she was none too steady on her pins. We never discovered where she went. None of the taxis, none of the bus companies, could recall seeing her, she didn't visit any of the local shops, and—in spite of our appeals—no one came forward to say that they had met her or been visited by her at that time. Her destination remains a mystery."

"And the second?"

"Mrs. King made a phone call to Dean and Frammell, her solicitors. Told the secretary that it was absolutely imperative that she see Mr. Begbie that very afternoon. They found her a cancellation at 4:45—but of course by then she was dead."

"Was this after her outing?"

"Yes. The secretary recorded the time of the call as half-past two. Geraldine gave no hint, apparently, of what the appointment was about."

"So, on the day she was killed, Geraldine King went on a mystery outing, the destination of which remains unknown. And when she returned, she desired urgently to consult a lawyer, for reasons also unknown."

"Right," Nicole agreed. She showed all the signs of absorption. When the wind is behind Nicole on a case, she can really fly. "Then Daryll returned from school. The old lady gave him a sandwich—cheese with lettuce, if you want to know—and some homemade cookies, and a glass of milk—"

"Wholesome," we agreed in unison, and laughed.

"—and then she tried to persuade him to come to the

lawyer. She had ordered a cab for half-past four, insisted he should accompany her. Daryll refused."

"He told you this?"

"He told us lots of details about the last hour they spent together," Nicole said with a shrug. "How Mrs. King was very worked up, very emotional. How she took a piece of paper out of her handbag and cried over it. And then she ripped it up, very aggressively, into little pieces. How she kept shouting at him to hurry, to tidy up, to put his best jacket on because they were going into town."

"But he refused? Why?"

"He usually saw his social worker after school on Wednesday. Apparently, that day, Kelsey McLeod—that's the social worker's name—couldn't make it. His wife was poorly and he had to rush home from the office to see to her. She's got some kind of chronic illness, you know. But Daryll is very stubborn, and he kept insisting that he had to wait, that McLeod would turn up."

"And then?"

"Then Daryll retreated to his fort in the tree, Geraldine tried to follow him, and bingo—another job for the CID." There was a brief rap at the door. "Enter," Nicole called.

My civilian clerk came in. He was carrying a coffee in one hand and a poster announcing a lunchtime match of five-a-side soccer in the other. He began to retreat when he saw Nicole. "Sorry, Inspector," he said, "but I thought you were—"

"Well, I'm not. Thanks for the coffee. Perhaps you could get another one for Dr. Principal?"

The clerk looked as if he were relieved not to be ticked off. All other considerations and commitments, including his promise to provide me with caffeine, went by the board. "Here," I said, forcing him to look in my direction, "forty-five p." He avoided my eyes, took the coins, and left.

I watched Nicole as she sipped my coffee. "Who found Geraldine's body?" I asked.

"A woman who had been counseling Geraldine in connection with her husband's death. No," she said emphatically, in response to my upraised eyebrow, "nothing suspicious there. Stanley King simply ate too much, drank too much, took too little exercise. Died of a coronary thrombosis in his early sixties, leaving Geraldine a reluctant widow. Eventually, she joined a national support group for the bereaved. CRUSE, it's called. Was assigned a helper, a mentor, a counselor—I can't remember what they call her—someone to share experiences with. Anyway, this woman, name of Becca Hunter, always visited Geraldine on Wednesday evening. That's why there were freshly baked cookies in the house. When no one answered the front door, Mrs. Hunter made her way around to the back, and that's how she stumbled across the body lying in a puddle. She called for an ambulance, but it was too late. Geraldine was dead."

"And the pathology report?"

"I have it here. You want to take a look?"

You bet.

Nicole didn't bother to wait for my nod. She checked her watch. "I've got to make a call," she announced. "I can give you ten minutes." And she left me alone with the files on the King case.

I scanned the labels on the spines of the boxes, alert for anything that might refer to the interviews with Daryll Flatt. And sure enough, inside one of the box files I found a stack of papers, some of them handwritten notes, others typed transcripts of recorded interviews. Different people were present on different occasions, but the formula remained the same: a D.I. and sometimes a DCI; a social worker; and the boy himself. Not his mother. No one from the family.

I had time to skim only one of the transcripts. The interview began with a gentle introduction, a few questions from the inspector: *You feeling any better, Daryll? How's that cold today?* and then shifted to the terrain that had gradually been mapped out in earlier interviews. *So you hadn't been able to find your alien doll, Daryll. What made you think Mrs. King had taken it?* This line of questioning went on for two or three pages, going over and over the same ground, with dots to indicate silences on Daryll's part, and little advance on his initial response. *She didn't like it. She thought it was ugly. She only liked those stupid shepherdesses. She got rid of it somewhere, I know she did.* And then, after *menacingly, angrily,* penciled in the margins: *She shouldn't have done that.*

Ten minutes isn't long in anyone's book. I had just returned the interview notes to their box and located the pathology report when Nicole strode back in. She used the occasion to demonstrate the power of her memory, and so saved me a lot of trouble.

"So, now you know," Nicole announced. "Injuries to the shoulders, arms, and back from blows with heavy objects before death. No lacerations in the genital region, no sexual interference, no semen, though Geraldine's underpants had been ripped off and tossed behind the tree. And the head—"

"Wait a minute," I interrupted her. "Her knickers had been removed? But she hadn't been sexually assaulted? Isn't that odd?"

"Not particularly," Nicole replied. "He felt the urge but was too scared to try anything. It's what you might expect from a murderer so young."

She may have had in mind that little Jamie Bulger,

who was murdered in Liverpool in 1993, had also had his underclothing removed. In the interview, the rumor goes, that was the one thing his young killers shied away from talking about. It's a strange world where the facts of desire are more taboo than those of killing.

"You started to say about the head, Nicole," I prompted her, and was disappointed with myself for referring to *the* head as if it weren't part and parcel of the woman.

Nicole's voice was low and quiet. She found the subject sobering. "Geraldine's head may have been hit a dozen times by rocks, for all we know. Most indications of head injuries were obliterated by the lump of cement that tore the top off her skull and destroyed a portion of her brain."

"Not likely, then, that she suffered a lingering demise," I concluded.

"Nope," Nicole agreed. "This was a Chicken Little kind of death. The sky fell in." She swept her fingers through her blue-black hair, forcing it flat for a few seconds. On release, it sprang back into its usual exuberant shape. "Anything else you need to know?"

Just one thing more. "Do you know why? Tell me, Nicole: why did he do it?"

It was not the sort of question that the inspector prefers. Hows and wheres and whens are more her cup of tea. *Why* is too slippery. It's too open to interpretation and argumentation and disputation, more the province of barristers, Nicole reckons, and less the kind of territory she likes to tread. But she had a go. And how.

"Why?" she asked, and her eyes narrowed. "Well, I could say it was because of that bloody doll. Daryll Flatt owned some kind of cuddly toy—or not so cuddly, depending on taste. Made of brown leather. An extra-terrestrial figure, like E.T. He took it everywhere with him. Even took it to school, until the other children made fun of him. Anyway, it went missing. He says"—and she spat out the *he* as if she had the taste of sickness in her esophagus—"that Geraldine had something against this doll. Claims that she had destroyed it. Certainly, it seemed to have disappeared."

"That's all?" I asked.

"Also, Daryll says, on the day it happened, he wanted to wait for his social worker, but Geraldine said, in effect, to hell with McLeod. Both these things made Daryll furious."

I could hardly go back to Howard with this. "You're telling me that an eleven-year-old boy was pissed off about a doll? Upset because he might miss an appointment with a social worker? You're telling me that this is why he smashed the top of a woman's skull, as if her head was a soft-boiled egg?"

I had misunderstood. "No," Nicole declared with force. "I'm not telling you that's why he killed her. I'm telling you that's what he said. But if you want to know *why*, I'll give you a different answer. One you might not like to hear."

Nicole suddenly stopped. She shook herself, a small solid tremor, and began again. Her voice was no less emphatic, but lower in volume now, barely above a whisper. I had to lean forward to catch the words.

"Look," she said, and took a deep breath, "during this investigation, I had it up to here"—she chopped at her hairline with the side of her hand—"with sympathy for Daryll Flatt. *He was only a kid,* people said. *He couldn't have meant to kill her.* Over and over, like a ritual response, from folks who had never even seen him. But if you'd seen that body, Laura, like I saw that body—if you had seen the effort it took the crime-scene team to scrape up the scattered pieces of her brain, and if you had seen what Mrs. King had done for that boy, how she'd given

him as nice a home as a child could want—and then you
had seen how coldly he spoke of her, how little he cared
for her . . . you wouldn't waste your time asking why.
You'd just be glad he's off the streets."

I could see her point. But it didn't really answer my
question. And I felt a stab of conviction that the answer
wouldn't be found here, at least not now, with Nicole reliving the anguish of that investigation.

I made a lame attempt to divert her onto a different
track, to interest her in the issue of Ginny's flasher. "Before I go, Nicole, do you mind if I ask one more thing?"

"No, Laura Principal, you just listen. Maybe Daryll
Flatt had a hard life. Maybe he was just a child. But the
why of it is this: Daryll Flatt killed Geraldine King because there was no love in his heart, no compassion. Some
people say that he's an animal." She tapped her forefinger
on the table to emphasize her words. "In my book, he's
worse than an animal. No animal I've ever seen would do
that sort of thing to one of its own kind."

Inspector Pelletier more or less turfed me out then,
without coffee, and I didn't have the heart to argue. My
forty-five p probably went straight into the Police Benevo-
lent Fund.

It might just be that they deserved it.

Chapter 5

A COUPLE OF years ago I traveled to Tel Aviv to deliver a six-year-old girl to her father. Her Norland nanny looked perfectly capable of negotiating the airport and settling them both into their first-class seats. But when your father's capital adds up to something like one percent of Israel's privately owned wealth, some fellow travelers are likely to regard you not as a child, but as a ticket to a fortune. My job was to thwart attempts to cash that ticket in.

We flew into Ben Gurion Airport in the early evening. I hefted our suitcases, one by one, onto a counter for the standard security check. Mine came last. It wasn't a flight bag, as you might expect for such a job, but a soft-sided airline case, big enough to hold (on the off chance) an orange silk cocktail dress and high-heeled sandals, as well as a swimsuit, snorkel, straw hat, and suntan lotion. I wasn't flying this far without traveling on to test the temperature of the Red Sea.

My bag lay innocently on the counter, but the reaction to it was more telling. I watched as a security officer focused shortsightedly on my luggage, adjusted her glasses and peered again. She strolled in the direction of a supervisor with an unconvincing show of nonchalance. I put my hand on little Celina's shoulder and pulled her nearer to me. We both watched as the supervisor caressed a walkie-talkie with his lips, as doors slid back on either side of the room, as two soldiers entered from one door and two from the other. Within seconds there was one Uzi pointed at the spine of my suitcase, one at the Norland nanny, and two at me.

I stood stock-still. "It's all right," I told Celina. "Nothing to worry about." If only.

They beckoned me around, pointed with their guns at an offending object protruding from the bottom of my baggage.

"What is that?" the supervisor asked in a tone cold enough and hard enough to sink the *Titanic*.

From the spine of my suitcase hung a string of diminutive droplets of chrome, like miniaturized pop beads. What is it? I remembered just such a chain, purchased at Woolies by my brother Hugh and me for a Mother's Day long ago, with an enameled disk on the end that said MUM. I recalled playing hopscotch on the pavement, blowing into the palm of my hand to infuse my little chain with luck. It landed on square five, its clasp coiled just inside the chalk line that marked the boundary. I recalled spinning such a chain around my forefinger, children in the playground urging me on, one-two-three-four, and not quite overtaking the record of twenty-two cycles established a week earlier by Yolanda Longstaff from Year Five.

What is it? Words failed me.

"A key chain?" I suggested, my friendly wouldn't-hurt-a-fly tones a feeble bulwark against their suspicion that the suitcase harbored a bomb. "I've no idea what it's doing there."

We went through all the usual questions, again and again. While Mr. Haruvi waited in the VIP lounge for his daughter, and while the chocolate in my duty-free carrier softened and spread, I insisted that I had packed my own bag, that no one had added anything, that I had never been to Israel before—nor, for that matter, to Syria or Lebanon or Iran. And once they had made their security checks and found me not to exist in their files of female terrorists, I stood in the now nearly emptied security hall, with semi-automatics pointed toward me, and unlatched the case.

By then, I have to admit, I was nervous. Given the right context, even a whatchamacallit begins to look sinister. The lid went up slowly; I groped beneath my goggles, beneath my orange silk chemise, and my fingers came to rest upon the name tag that had been issued with my luggage. Its tiny chain had, presumably, been caught between the edges of the case when I snapped it shut. It pulled free with a grating sound. The episode was over.

If the security staff felt a little foolish, they gave no sign of it. Just doing their jobs, I guess. I, however, do think of this episode at Ben Gurion whenever I feel myself in danger of overreacting to a loose end. Though it is comforting to tie things up neatly—to tick one item off an agenda before moving on to number two—there are times when it's wise to let a loose end dangle for a while and go on about your business.

Like today. There were several more questions about the King case that I had failed to put to Nicole: about the nature of Daryll's confession; about the evidence against him; about other members of the family. Most of all, I needed to discuss Ginny's flasher with Nicole. But when Inspector Pelletier had turfed me out of the police station, she clearly hadn't been in the mood for further inquiries. So for the moment I had little choice but to leave my questions dangling.

It was a day for walking. For Cambridge walking, with collar pulled up, and the wind off the Urals raking its

fingers through my hair. I reached Burleigh Street from
the police station in no time flat. Nipped into Nadia's
Patisserie, laid out good money for a piece of white chocolate fudge, and settled into the curves of a metal bench
where I could watch the weekday shoppers and enjoy
every pleasure-laden, high-fat bite. Between swallows I
went over the information that I needed from social services. By the time I wiped my fingers on a tissue and
climbed the stairs to the Cambridge City office of Social
Services, I was primed with calories and questions.

The woman at the desk had auburn hair and some of the
same vices as me. I could see the patisserie bag perched in
her in-tray, and this gave me a warm, sisterly feeling.
Maybe she picked up the vibes; when I stated my business, she seemed genuinely keen to help.

My first choice was Kelsey McLeod, the man who had
apparently stood by Daryll Flatt, through thin and thin. No
luck there. But I learned that the social worker who had li-
aised with Mrs. King would be in shortly.

Shortly, as it turned out, overstated the time I'd have to
wait. I hadn't even checked out the spring fashions from
the office copy of *Prima* when a man pattered into the
room. The receptionist whispered a few words to him and
gestured in my direction. His pace had suggested someone
with a pressing schedule, but he looked me over with
friendly interest.

"Laura Principal," I said, extending my hand. He pumped
it swiftly up and down.

"Murray Eagleton," he announced. "I worked with
Geraldine on her Homefinders application. Pop along with
me to my office, and you can tell me why you want to talk
about poor Mrs. King."

Murray Eagleton was younger-looking than a senior social worker has a right to be. Everything about him was small and neat and speedy.

We sat in armchairs with drooping seats. I explained about Howard Flatt's need to know. This hit the right note. "An important part of healing," Eagleton agreed. "I'll tell you what I can, off the top of my head, but if anything needs checking from the files," he warned, "it will have to wait until later in the week. Fire away."

I began with a general shot in the direction of the victim. "Since you were Mrs. King's social worker, you must have known her reasonably well. What kind of woman was she?"

"Friendly," came the unequivocal answer. "Vivacious. Rather charming, I think you could say. She was a widow—that was why she came to Homefinders in the first place, looking for an outlet for all that care that became surplus after her husband died. But if widowhood got her down, she kept it to herself. When we talked, she was always smiling. Do you know," Eagleton said, and his perky voice slid down a register into solemnity, "I was one of the last people to see Geraldine King alive. Well, apart from . . ." For the first time, he faltered.

I helped him out. "Apart from Daryll Flatt."

"I was just going to say that." Eagleton gave me that smile again, short and swift. "I called 'round there on the morning she died. Just after ten. Mrs. King was baking cookies. She asked me to stay until they were ready. They smelled delicious, but I had another appointment. Had to leave. Do you know," the social worker said, meeting my eyes abruptly, "that even now, the aroma of baking makes me apprehensive. When I go into the patisserie across the street, I get a queasy feeling in the pit of my stomach."

"I'm sorry," I said, and meant it. "What was Geraldine's

mood like when you called 'round? Did she seem worried at all?"

"Of course, I've asked myself that lots of times. But do you know, she seemed right as rain to me. Very lively. She had purchased a new porcelain figurine and she was keen to show it off. And then she filled me in on Daryll, and we talked about the Homefinders social coming up, and about one or two other things, and then I had to go. She was a bit quiet when we talked about the social, but I think that's because the idea of going to a party reminded her about being on her own. She belonged to that generation of women, you know, who never had any experience of socializing without a male escort."

"What do you mean when you say that Geraldine filled you in on Daryll? Was there something wrong?"

"Routine stuff." Eagleton shrugged. "Or that's how it seemed at the time. Daryll was a 'bit wound up'—that was exactly how Geraldine put it. He had lost a doll he was fond of, a battered old thing. He was apparently quite agitated."

"So Geraldine reported to you on the morning of her death that Daryll was in a state?" I didn't realize how like a cross-examination this must have sounded until the words were out of my mouth. It was a mistake.

Eagleton's chirpy approach yielded to a detached, professional air. He drew himself up as best he could in the sagging chair. "Of course," he said emphatically, "if Geraldine had given any indication that this was more than Daryll's usual moodiness, I would have intervened. But she seemed only mildly concerned. That's how I summed it up in court: mildly concerned. Not distressed, not panicked, and certainly not frightened. Mildly concerned."

"And you knew," I added, "that McLeod was coming 'round that afternoon? Daryll's behavior was really, I imagine, his concern."

"That's so," Eagleton agreed, looking more at ease. "I advised Geraldine to speak to McLeod. To get Kelsey to check it out."

"Did Daryll and his social worker have a good relationship?"

"Did," Murray replied, "and do. From the time Daryll first came to the attention of Social Services, he and Kelsey hit it off like a house on fire. Kelsey's a good social worker, and he put everything he had into working with that boy—into providing Daryll with somebody to rely on. The boy had had more than his share of disappointments, and Kelsey believed that he was at a turning point. Either he could get back on the straight and narrow soon, or he would be a lost child."

"A lost child?"

"Someone who's gone too far. A boy for whom you can never make it all right." Eagleton sighed. "Like Daryll now," he said.

"And this McLeod was very involved with him?"

"How can I explain?" Murray asked, then launched off again immediately. "As a social worker, you meet all sorts. You know that saying—to know all is to forgive all? There's something to it. Say someone shambles into the office; they look hopeless, feckless, careless—unlikable. You talk to them; you learn about the odds they've had to struggle against in their lives, about their courage, about the sacrifices they've made, and bingo . . . the wall of dislike fades." He looked up at me again with confidence. Dashed me a smile. "They become human again. How could you do this job, what kind of a social worker would you be, if that didn't happen?"

"So Daryll became human for McLeod?"

"Exactly. Strictly off the record—I wouldn't like this to get around—it seemed to me that Kelsey identified with the boy. That Daryll became, in a sense, the son that Kelsey never had. There was a kind of attachment there, and heaven knows he put in more hours on that lad than the time sheet showed. I wondered at times whether I should warn him about getting too involved." He sighed, his liveliness at an ebb. "Hindsight." He shrugged. "Easy with hindsight. Are you planning to interview Kelsey?"

"If he'll see me."

"Go easy," Murray Eagleton urged. "He was deeply shaken by the murder. We all were, I suppose. But McLeod—well, he blamed himself. Took the responsibility on his own shoulders. Felt if only he had seen the signs, if only he had noticed Daryll's deterioration . . . Well, you can imagine."

"I can imagine," I agreed. "The old lady is dead and Daryll is in lockup. McLeod feels that it's all his fault."

"Something like that." Eagleton nodded. "I suggested that he might see one of the counselors for advice—informally, of course—but he refused. So I'd appreciate it . . ." He cocked an inquiring eye in my direction.

"Kelsey McLeod is safe with me. I'm not as dangerous as I look," I said, and was rewarded with a chuckle. I drew the conversation back to the real victim, Geraldine. "One thing I don't understand. How did a woman in her sixties come to be a foster mother?"

"Foster care provider," Eagleton corrected. "At Homefinders, we look for suitable local people to provide temporary care for children who must be away from their families for a time. Age doesn't have anything to do with it. What matters are personal qualities—are they stable and reliable? Have they something to offer a child? Character," he concluded.

Eagleton's voice had taken on a recitative quality, as if he were reading a prepared speech. I guess responding to police inquiries and internal investigations had fixed events in his mind. "The thing that precipitated Daryll Flatt being offered time-limited foster care," he explained, "was the death of his granny. She was an important person in his life. You know, of course, about the shock he had?"

Eagleton told me the story, in rapid, deadpan tones. How Daryll's maternal grandmother, Harriet Johnson, died quietly of heart failure. Daryll, aged ten, had been staying with her; he had fallen asleep on the sofa watching television. He awoke in the dim dawn to find his grandmother slouched beside him. When Daryll tried to rouse her, her body tumbled to the floor. Daryll took himself off to school. He mentioned it to no one. Didn't cry or complain. At the end of the day, his teacher found him huddled in a corner. He didn't say a word about his granny, not then. But he did mention, in response to direct questions, that his stepfather beat him, and this information was passed, as it must be, to Social Services.

"So that's how Daryll ended up in foster care?"

"That's it." Eagleton shook his head. "Daryll's mother, Janet Flatt, didn't take it well. Saw the involvement of Social Services as a slur on her mothering. But she clearly couldn't cope. There was lots of conflict in the home and she'd relied heavily on the granny to provide support for Daryll. So . . . Well, we placed him with Geraldine King in the hope that she would be a grandmotherly figure, a soothing presence. That's what we hoped. . . ." His voice trailed off.

And was she? I almost asked. But it would have been too flippant and too unkind.

Chapter 6

Wʜᴇɴ I ᴇᴍᴇʀɢᴇᴅ from Social Services and checked my watch, it was already twelve o'clock. Later than I had expected. Lunch would have to wait.

I walked to the corner of Burleigh Street and then, as the pedestrian lights turned green, crossed to the other side of East Road and broke into a run. Slowed my pace alongside the Zion Baptist Church, where a knot of men in front of the night shelter impeded my passage. Hit a gap in the traffic, carried straight on across Mill Road, ate up the pavement on Gonville Place and kept my pace, more or less, up the stairs leading into the sports hall.

It was worth the effort. The game had only just begun. Five a side—nine men and one intrepid woman. They looked to be in their twenties and thirties, neatly turned out, reasonably fit. They played with moderate skill and much good humor—apart, that is, from the woman, who played as if her life depended on it. She set up a sharp shot in the final few minutes, helping to propel her team into the lead, and followed through shortly after with a decisive goal that came out of nowhere to clinch the win. Atta girl.

I was waiting by the drinks machine when she finished her shower. She hadn't bothered to do more by way of prettification than run a brush through her blue-black hair.

It stood out from her head in triumph. "Nicole," I called out. "You were great out there."

She didn't argue. She was gloating still about the victory, and scarcely noticed when I steered her past the police station and on to the Free Press for some homemade chili: even in the face of mad cow disease, Nicole's a carnivore.

But she couldn't fail to notice when I asked her what the evidence was that had confirmed Daryll Flatt's guilt.

"Give me a break, Laura," she sighed. "I was only one member of the murder team. Why don't you go and speak to Daryll Flatt himself?"

"Simple," I said. "I don't want to meet Daryll until I have a clearer sense of the people and events involved. The kind of thing you're so good at." This was flattery, but it wasn't empty flattery. Nicole's judgment can be razor sharp, and I preferred to face an interview with Daryll armed with the weapon of her insight.

"Anyway," I continued, "I don't want to meet Daryll until I know exactly what I think about the case. About his motives for killing. I'm not a psychologist. Not a Cracker, with instant access to motives that no one else can penetrate. I've got no illusions: my mere presence in the secure unit won't induce Daryll to offer me the first-ever satisfactory explanation for his crime. The best I can hope for is this: maybe, if I dig around enough before we meet, I'll figure out what questions to ask." I had a swig of Abbott's ale, more to keep Nicole company than because I am a lunchtime drinker. "It's like that old Gertrude Stein anecdote."

Nicole didn't need telling. She must have heard it before: how, on her deathbed, Gertrude Stein had thrown out a challenge. "What," she had asked her companion, "is the answer?" When there was no suitable reply, Stein raised her head from the pillow, fixed Alice B. Toklas with a beady eye, and added, "Tell me, in that case: what is the question?"

Nicole relented. "Hush, Laura, while I do some recalling," she ordered.

So I dug into my peppery spinach soup and watched the wheels turning in her brain. When Nicole wiped her mouth with a napkin and leaned back in the chair, I knew she was ready.

"I'll give you evidence," she said, rising to the challenge. "First, there's Daryll's confession. Constable Dagherty found him curled up in a crack willow tree, hours after the discovery of Geraldine's body. The kid confessed straightaway. We didn't even have to break the news of Mrs. King's death. 'I did it,' he said, plain as night. 'I killed her.' He admitted that he'd stockpiled rocks and lumps of concrete— the kind that sit at the base of the railway bridge—in his tree fort, hauling them up with the pulley. Defenses, he said, for his castle. And when Mrs. King had tried to mount the ladder, he used her as a target. He claimed he didn't intend to kill her, and who knows?" Nicole shrugged. "Maybe it's true. But he's a bright enough lad, and any eleven-year-old who's not completely off his trolley knows that dropping a lump of concrete the size of a small suitcase on a human head will get rid of more than just the dandruff."

"And this confession," I pressed, "was there corroborating evidence?"

"We found Daryll's fingerprints on some of the rocks that surrounded the body. The surface of the concrete was too slick with brain and body fluid to hold an image." Nicole said this in a detached way, but I've seen her in the presence of a body; I know full well that detachment is for Nicole a matter of style rather than a state of mind. "His shoe prints were all over the ground. And in a Lion King lunch box inside the tree house, we found three thousand pounds of Geraldine's money."

It was the first I'd heard. "What money would that be?"

"Didn't I tell you? Stanley King, Geraldine's late husband, was careful with his money. A miser, some would say, but that's not the issue here. He laid a nest egg and nested it in the old-fashioned way, in a building society deposit account. Geraldine transferred this money to Lloyds Bank. Then—a few weeks before she died—she waltzed into the Gonville Place branch and withdrew forty thousand pounds in cash. The assistant manager had a word with her, advised her to take the money in check form, for security reasons, but Geraldine was adamant that only cash would do. And off she went."

Nicole's shake of the head reminded me of the way Dixon of Dock Green used to tut-tut over the carelessness of honest citizens who plant themselves in the path of crime. But I had to agree; if there is any proper use of the term *asking for it*, it has to apply to a little lady with a carrier bag full of cash.

"We found no expenditure to match that money," Nicole continued. "No lavish living, no new pension, no Mediterranean cruise. And, when she died, not a trace of the dosh. Except for three thousand pounds in large bills, hidden away among Daryll Flatt's things."

"So, the confession, the forensic evidence, the missing money—this is what went against Daryll Flatt in court?"

Nicole sighed, a long sigh as if she were humoring the village idiot. "Put it like this," she said patiently. "Daryll's confession; Daryll's prints on the murder weapon; money stolen from the victim hidden among his things—none of these went in Daryll's favor. But there was other stuff. Like his statements over and over again during interviews that Geraldine King didn't like him—this in the face of overwhelming evidence that Mrs. King was a dedicated foster mum. Plus, his over-the-top anger about his doll—"

"Yes. I know about that."

"Well, these things created a clear picture of a child who wouldn't—maybe couldn't—be loved. What they used to call a sociopath. Not crazy, but cold. Unable to respond, to feel concern for anyone else. The more Mrs. King did for him, it seemed, the more he hated her. Did you hear about the letter she wrote to him shortly before her death?"

Uh-uh. I shook my head. There was a lot that Howard Flatt hadn't gotten around to telling me.

"Well, you should read this letter before you take yourself off to see Daryll Flatt. It was found among Daryll's things, though he claims he can't remember it. I can tell you the substance. All she wanted, Geraldine wrote, was for him to be happy. To live with her forever and be *her* little boy. To erase the memory of that horrid woman forever."

"Meaning?"

"Janet Flatt, Daryll's mother," Nicole explained. "Horrid may be a bit strong," she allowed, thinking it over. "Some maternal jealousy there, perhaps. But Janet's not the angel in the house, I can tell you, even when she's sober."

I was beginning to see how the court case went. Like a television courtroom drama, with clear stereotypes and a neat boundary between good and evil. "The victim was a sweet little old lady, right? Pretty, white-haired, a respectable widow. And in court, when the letter was produced—evidence that Geraldine showered commitment and love on this unlovable child—her saintlike image was confirmed. Not a dry eye in the house, I assume?"

"More tears than Bambi," Nicole agreed. She had to smile. "Of course, Daryll's defense team tried to use it in his favor—why, they asked, would a lonely boy, a boy so clearly in need of affection, kill the one person who cared?

But on the whole, the letter weighed heavily against Daryll; the jury were, I think, shocked that a boy could return such commitment with violence."

"Ungrateful?" I asked. Is that how they thought of him?

"Cold," she countered. "Incapable of affection. Look at the history. During the time he lived with Geraldine King, it was one thing after another. Temper tantrums—one of the neighbors heard Daryll shouting that he wished Geraldine would die. Being sent home from school for walloping a smaller child. I don't suppose you heard about the episode with the pigeon?"

"Nope. Not a peep. Enlighten me."

"Well, this came from Daryll's social worker. Throughout our investigation, McLeod always tried to put the best gloss on the boy's behavior. You know the sort of thing. We'd say volatile, he'd say confused. Wild? we'd ask. No: scared, he'd say. We'd mention Daryll's temper, he'd plump for anxiety. And so on."

"That's his job," I suggested mildly.

Nicole shrugged. "Sure. But if you ask me, he pushed it a bit far. It wasn't until he was on the witness stand, under oath, that he disclosed that Geraldine had a specific worry about Daryll. Little Daryll, it seems, had captured an injured pigeon and had proceeded to make its injuries a great deal worse. Specifically, he had nailed the pigeon's wing to the fence, had strangled it with a string and had then tried to set fire to it, to cover up what he'd done. And the tormenting of small animals is—well, even you must know . . ."

"One of the signs of a child who's on his way to some bigger form of violence." They try it out first, have a rehearsal, see what it feels like. And then if they like it . . .

"You reckon the social worker was covering up earlier on?"

"Yep. And that's *not* his job. Kelsey McLeod wanted

that kid to be innocent. You could see it in the set of his jaw. It was only when the lawyers pressed him that he reluctantly admitted he knew about Daryll torturing the pigeon."

"Anything else?"

"Isn't that enough, Laura? It was enough for the jury. Enough for the judge. Daryll Flatt is a dangerous boy. He is a murderer. He's banged up where he belongs."

"That's not what I meant. Anything else to explain why Daryll did it? Why he killed this woman who was—as you yourself pointed out—determined to mother him."

"As I told you before—"

"Right," I interrupted quickly. "I remember. Daryll's a nasty piece of work." So I bought her another beer—a half this time—waited while she downed it, and then walked with her the short distance back to the station, doing my level best to avoid any further sources of irritation. I was nice as nice could be. Inquired after her father's health, asked about her dog, recalled the glories of that final, triumphant goal.

But she's no fool. "Right, Laura," Nicole said as we turned into Warkworth Terrace. "Why do I get the feeling that you want to ask me for a favor? Again," she added, with a wary glance.

"Nothing too demanding," I said. "I need some advice. Have you ever come across a local pervert, a flasher, who wears a gorilla mask and exposes himself to schoolgirls?"

"Not only schoolgirls," Nicole replied, without breaking stride. "Apeman's an equal opportunities flasher. Girls or boys—it's all the same to him. As long as they're prepubescent."

"So he's not a newcomer?"

"*Au contraire,*" she said, with the accent of someone who has used her school French only on shopping trips to

Boulogne. "He's been around for years. We've gone after him a few times, but he's smarter than he looks. He only works a particular area for a few days, then digs himself in for a while. Later, like a groundhog, he pops up somewhere else."

"You've no idea who he is, then. Is he dangerous?"

We reached the parking lot of the police station. Nicole stopped abruptly, gave it two seconds' thought. "Dunno," she said. "Probably not. These guys who expose themselves to kids—these inadequate little pervs—they're more pathetic than dangerous. Most cops will tell you—if they could do anything with it, they wouldn't be waving it around."

"How do they know?" I asked.

"Meaning?" Nicole was less friendly now.

"Meaning, simply, that if guys like him don't get caught, then you don't really get to know anything about them. And you won't know—for example—if today's rapist was yesterday's flasher."

"Oh, come on, Laura," Nicole said scornfully. "Let's not be melodramatic. This isn't *NYPD Blue*, you know. This is real life."

And then, before Nicole could demand to know why I was so interested, I told her. "It's Ginny," I explained, "Helen Cochrane's daughter. Apeman has approached her and her friends—they're eleven going on twelve—three times now on their way to and from school."

"How are they taking it?" Nicole asked.

I shrugged. "They're rattled, but far too embarrassed to bring this to the police. I was hoping that you might be able to do something, informally."

So I told her what it was and where it happened, and Nicole, ever diligent, wrote it all down. But I could tell that this was not what she would call high priority. With a spate of burglaries in the Latham Road area and the usual chaos

on Saturday nights and the unsolved shooting of a man in
Fulbourn, the antics of an ill-mannered ape would hardly
be at the top of her agenda. Especially if you believed—as
Nicole clearly did—that as long as he kept waving his banana, he wasn't likely to wield it as a weapon.

And then I remembered May Pearl. That's the name I
knew her by, a little person from Hong Kong who used to
feed the ducks early every morning on Jesus Green. I often
saw her near the pelican crossing on my way to the boathouse, and after a few days we began to exchange the odd
word. She used to chat to the joggers as well, and to a few
of the college staff and the council workers who were up
and about at that time of day. It was May Pearl's little community. It was somewhere to go, somewhere she was welcome, recognized, secure.

Until one day, a man—no, it was a boy really, in his late
teens—stood behind her and masturbated. Used her presence as part of his fantasy. She knew someone was there
for minutes before she turned and discovered what he was
up to. She dropped her bag of bread crumbs and fled over
the footbridge. Her little community was shattered. She
never reappeared.

And in place of Nicole's bland reassurances, I thought
of a man who was for years the chief forensic scientist.
Nobody begins with rape, Professor Blugrass said. A
rapist doesn't emerge out of nowhere. He works up to it,
with minor offenses. And if he likes the reaction he gets—
the drama, the tears, the fact that he's looked at—he esca-
lates the level. Until someone gets hurt.

Every violent rapist, every serious sexual offender, started
out with something smaller, Professor Blugrass said.

Maybe, I wondered, with a banana in his hand?

Chapter 7

THE WOMAN WHO opened the door of the neat little terraced house didn't look like Daryll's mother. You might think, with her Lycra miniskirt and her dry platinum hair, that she didn't look very much like anyone's mother, but that would be jumping to conclusions. At least she had the kind of legs miniskirts were made for.

"Janet Flatt?"

"Yeah?" she asked. The voice belonged to a woman who knew from experience that any stranger must be the bearer of bad news. "What do you want?"

"I'd like to speak to you about your son, Daryll. Just for a few minutes," I coaxed. I showed her my ID. She fished a pair of reading glasses from a pocket and settled them on her nose.

"Investigator, huh?" she said, with a glimmer of interest. "I didn't know they let women do that kind of thing." She lost the glimmer, and returned my card. "Anyway, you're too late."

"Too late? What do you mean?"

"Just what I said," she snapped. "It's already gone. Daryll's story. I've sold it—to a man who's going to make it into a book."

I was gob-struck. So, it was gone. Daryll's life. Sold, for a lump sum, to a man who would make it into a book.

I looked at Janet Flatt's lovely legs, at her ravaged face. A woman of contradictions, I decided. "A deal is a deal," I agreed. "But I'm not a writer. What you say to me won't end up in print. So there's really no harm in explaining one or two things to me, is there? Like for instance"—I searched for a question that might do the trick—"how did your son get along with Geraldine King?"

"That cow," she exploded, whipping her glasses off her nose. "My Daryll had problems enough, God knows, before she got her claws into him. But living with that prissy missy, with her peep-toe sandals and her airs, that really pushed him over the edge."

"What did she do to him?"

Janet responded angrily, rising to an unspoken challenge. "I was always a good mother. After his dad left, I worked my fingers to the bone to see that he and his brothers had food in their stomachs and clothes on their backs. Daryll never went to school with holes in his trousers, like some. And then they took him away." Her eyes glazed with tears. "You don't know how hard it's been for me."

"Geraldine King," I prompted gently. "Did you see her and Daryll together?"

"She never cared about him. All this stuff about how fond she was of him, that was total crap. If you ask me, she was just out to impress the social worker." Janet Flatt gave me a quizzical look, as if to check whether I had yet understood the awfulness of Geraldine. She appeared to conclude that I hadn't. "Do you know what sort of woman she was?" Janet asked. "The sort who never once in her life had to worry about where the electricity payment was coming from, or whether there'd be enough for bus fares. Probably never had to clean her own floors. And yet she thought she had the right to sneer at women who do all that and more."

"And Daryll? You said he went downhill when he lived with Mrs. King. What sort of boy was he before that?"

The answer came out as smooth as clockwork, well rehearsed. Like the story line for a book.

"He was the sweetest baby you ever saw," Janet Flatt said. Her tone dripped coochy-coo. "Was always laughing and rushing about. 'Slow that boy down,' we used to say. But I can see now," she continued, and it was gravity rather than sentiment that drove her mood, "that he was more like his father than I realized at the time. And after his father left, he got much worse."

"How worse?"

"You never knew what Daryll was thinking. He'd talk and talk and talk, until sometimes you wanted to shake him, but he never told you nothing. If you know what I mean."

"And Kelsey McLeod, Daryll's social worker. How did they get along?"

"That man's a saint," Janet declared. "I never thought I'd say it—that I approve of a social worker. But before McLeod came along, Daryll was always in trouble. Always fighting with his stepdad." Some memory made her flinch, and she looked up at me anxiously. "It wasn't good for me, all that stress. But Kelsey McLeod knew how to handle Daryll, sort of instinctively."

Instinctively, maybe. But if a murder is anything to go by, not all that well.

Behind us, on the street, a car pulled up to the curb. The engine rattled and died, the music—Whitesnake or some other heavy metal group; they all sound alike to me—crashed for a few seconds against the silence and then faded away. There was a ratcheting sound as the hand brake engaged. The car door slammed and heavy footsteps clumped in our direction. All these noises seemed in high relief, like sound effects in a poorly produced radio play.

". . . wouldn't do as he was told," Janet was saying. "Even at that age. Ian—his stepdad—couldn't stand it. All that sulking and hiding in corners. It used to drive Ian wild. He couldn't help himself." She stopped. Looked up at the man who had generated the footsteps and who was now, I could tell by her eyes, hulking behind me.

I didn't turn around. My hunch said that the minute I acknowledged the presence behind me, the interview would come to an end. "Couldn't help himself what?" I asked.

Janet focused her eyes on me again. She looked at me, but I was certain she answered for the newcomer. "Just a slap from time to time," she said nervously. "Nothing serious. And," she added, eyes flicking over my shoulder, "Daryll was never one to make a fuss. He didn't mind, not really."

I turned, expecting to find myself face-to-face with Ian Miller. With Janet's second husband, the man who had rescued her, probably, from alcoholism, and then had driven away her eldest son.

The man who couldn't help himself.

But instead there stood someone much younger. My client, Howard Flatt, was massive; this man was fat. His stomach was slung over his jeans, his jeans hung low on his hips, and even his fingers were pudgy. But he was unmistakably Howard's brother. "Mark Flatt?" I asked.

"Miller," he growled. "Mark Miller." He had, apparently, taken his stepfather's name, widening the wedge between him and Howard. "And who the hell are you?"

I explained who the hell I was. And why the hell I'd come. And that my client was Howard Flatt.

Mark Flatt Miller turned on his mother, with a ferocious

air. "You know what that writer said. We shouldn't speak to anybody else about Daryll."

"But Mark, she's not writing a book," Janet pleaded. "And anyway, I didn't say anything important."

What would count as important? I wondered.

But Mark Flatt Miller had something else on his mind. The thought of brother Howard brought out the surly in him. "Who the fuck does he think he is, asking for information about Daryll? He deserted the family. What Daryll did is as much down to Howard as anyone."

"I told him that, Mark," Janet placated. "I did."

"What did Howard have to do with the murder?" I asked.

"Howard ruined that kid," Mark snarled. A neighbor came to the front of her house, peered out, and retreated, slamming the door behind her. "Pampered him. Tried to turn him into some kind of sissy. Called him Dary!" Mark sneered. "What kind of name is that for a boy?"

Janet's jaded appearance was gone, replaced by an air of anxiety that blanketed her face, her eyes, her posture. She touched my sleeve. "It's hard," she pleaded, on Mark's behalf. "It's hard to be the middle child."

"Shut up," Mark growled at her. She did. "It was always like that," he snapped. "Daryll was always a cunning little shit, playing the goody to her face"—he jerked his thumb in Janet's direction, a gesture heavy with contempt—"but underneath a manipulating little rat. I took the blame for everything," he shouted, the anger as raw now as it might have been when he was a little lad.

No, I thought. Not everything. Nobody claims that you were the one who murdered Mrs. King.

I'M A SLEEPER.

When I'm with Sonny, I wrap myself around him, pull the quilt up as far as my ears, and slip contentedly away.

It's marginally more difficult when I'm alone. Sometimes I read, propped up in bed, the CD playing quietly on the other side of the room and a glass of wine by my hand. I always reach the end of the wine, but rarely the end of the story.

I'm a person, in other words, who knows when it's time to nod off. But I don't always manage to remain asleep at the morning end of the night, particularly if something's preying on my mind.

Like the morning after my discussion with Janet Flatt and Mark Flatt Miller. I awoke at six A.M., went to the bathroom, and on the journey back to bed found myself framing lists of things undone. Tried to soothe myself back into a thought-free state, so that sleep could reclaim me. But by then my conscious brain had taken over. It was posing questions far too challenging for a woman without caffeine in her bloodstream.

Like: what does it mean to get to know someone? What does it mean especially when your knowledge comes from other people, and those other people don't agree? Howard Flatt suggests Daryll was an uneasy boy, his spirit crushed by his father's desertion, his fears disguised under gushes of conversation. Janet Flatt distinguishes between the adorable baby and the uncontrollable child—more like his father every day. Detective Inspector Pelletier appears to be in agreement with, of all people, Mark Miller. One introduces Daryll to me as a nasty piece of work, the other calls him a cunning little shit. Mark Miller may be the pot who called the kettle black—but you wouldn't make the same claim for Nicole.

Is one view of Daryll right and the others wrong? Or could Daryll be a bit of all these things—a person of paradox, like his mother Janet, with her photo-session legs and her morning-after face? Perhaps there is no single

Daryll, not even a contradictory one. Maybe Daryll is a different person with Howard than he is with Mark. Maybe all these witnesses are right, but only in terms of their own relationship with Daryll. Maybe these terms are the only terms there are.

And Geraldine King—who was she? The pampered, intolerant middle-class woman that Janet Flatt saw? Someone quick to scorn other women because their struggle to maintain their families left its mark on their manner and their appearance? Or was she the sweet lady whom Eagleton approved for fostering, the grandmotherly figure for whom widowhood left an emptiness that only a foster child could fill?

One question prowled through my restless brain more than any other. Daryll was a killer, but no one suggested he was mad; how to make sense of his belief that Geraldine didn't care for him? What happened inside that bungalow to make Daryll deny the appearance of love?

The urge to look was irresistible. I dressed warmly against the morning chill. Rummaged about in the understairs cupboard until I located a couple of tent pegs and a hammer and a length of twine. Loped off down the hill toward the river, the key to the boathouse dangling from my backpack.

It's surprising how many people you encounter alongside the Cam in the early morning: postal workers cycling to the sorting office, students emerging after a night's hard play, isolates who prefer their landscape untainted by human presence. We all—last category excepted—smile at each other, we sometimes nod, we never speak. We're co-conspirators sharing the secret of our dusky world, and to speak might break the spell.

I took extra time over the stretching exercises, chasing the sleep out of my bones. I was loose and alert by the time my boat came parallel with the section of the towpath that fronted Geraldine King's bungalow.

I drifted to the bank and grasped a clump of grass, pulled myself alongside. The ground was soft from rain. Two quick blows with the hammer and the tent pegs held firm. I threaded the twine through, attached it to the rope at the front of the boat, and leaped up onto the path. Without pausing—it's the person who takes their time who looks suspicious, not the apparently purposeful one—I entered the property and made straight for the back garden.

The garden was arboreal, framed in the retreating shadows of early morning. At the base of the trees the darkness was impermeable; at their tips, where a raucous chorus of birds gathered to greet the dawn, leaves were silhouetted against a silvering sky. The chitterchat of birds, that insistent assertion of territory, grew more intense as I padded up the walk. But the moment I drew level with the house, passing an invisible line that divided the front garden from the back, the din fell away, leaving in its wake a profound silence. It was impossible not to imagine scores of little bodies that shook with outrage at my intrusion, hearts thrumming in feathered chests, tiny eyes trained balefully upon me. I could almost hear their resentment humming in the air. The sense of being under surveillance stopped me for an instant in my tracks.

I took stock. Checked first that the bungalow was still plunged in darkness. Then turned my attention to the garden.

The back garden was wide and surprisingly deep, far from the usual mean plot allotted to an urban bungalow. It was bounded along the sides by wooden fencing some three feet high, its disrepair largely hidden by overgrown shrubs. A more formidable wall of local brick ran along the back boundary. It was shadowed by well-spaced trees.

But the largest tree sat to the side and slightly to the rear of the house. It was a remarkable specimen, an ash or more likely a walnut, surrounded by a bold circumference of naked lawn. Its two lowest branches formed a V, and this supported a sturdy wooden platform upon which a fort had been built. It had been designed with care. There was a door in the front wall, and in the side an unglazed window that faced vaguely in the direction of the bungalow. The roof disappeared among a higher layer of branches. The weathered board from which the fort had been constructed had the same gray look as the bark of the walnut, so that from the ground, under cover of full summer growth, the tree house would be scarcely visible.

A crude ladder made of slats of wood nailed to two stout poles gave access. I mounted slowly, testing each rung before entrusting it with my weight. I was painfully aware of the possibility of the vertigo that occasionally grips me, stripping the muscles from my legs, and of the fact that the ladder had been built to accommodate someone lighter and smaller-limbed than I. The birds had started up their chorus again, more tentatively than before: *be careful, be careful, be careful,* I imagined them singing. My movement up the ladder was inelegant and halting; the fleeting sense of being watched remained with me. When I managed to swing myself onto the platform at last, it was with racing heart and slippery palms.

I edged around to the front of the fort, hunched through the door, and sat with relief on the floor, leaning back against the warm planks that made up the wall, taking comfort from the solidity of my position. *What goes up must come down.* Don't remind me. I looked around.

The ceiling of the tree house was perhaps five feet high, the dimensions four by four, making it a tight squeeze for someone like me. Like Big Alice, I was constructed on the wrong scale. But I could see that for a child it would be perfect. The sun filtering through the leaves would dapple the walls and floor with light, the wind would whisper through the window; the house might easily seem to be far and away at sea, removed from the mundane world below.

The furnishings were sparse. A child's deck chair, with dirt-encrusted stripes. An orange crate perched on end as a cupboard, another arranged as a table. Was that where the lunch box had sat with its curious cache of money? There may once have been candy wrappers, or a flask with cocoa, or scrap paper with cryptic notes, or even a dart board, but not now. Someone—probably the forensic team—had gathered such items away. Two years on since Daryll last climbed that ladder, the interior of the tree house had fewer marks of individuality than a public toilet.

Except, that is, for the walls. The two unbroken walls were ringed with pictures. Faded cutouts from magazines, attached with thumbtacks and carpet nails to the soft planking. None of the pictures corresponded to what one might most expect to find from an eleven-year-old boy. No pop stars or football heroes or characters from soaps, no moments of sporting triumph. Not even the more forbidden images, Pamela Anderson or a tabloid stunner. But the pictures did have a consistent theme.

They were outdoor scenes, all of them, landscapes, showing a vast countryside that was definitely not British. An image of plains, or of a veldt, with depressions in the landscape filled by tall grasses and eucalyptus trees. Of crops—sugarcane—lush and green and taller than a man, stopping abruptly at a highway where oil tankers rushed past. Of relentless surf, rolling onto an unnetted beach where no surfer in her right mind would risk an encounter with a great white. And, most telling of all, an image of the desert, out of which rose an astonishing russet mountain.

Australia. The place where Howard Flatt had gone, and Daryll Flatt had not. Here, in the tree house, Daryll had kept his dream alive.

But investigators are ill-advised to daydream. I should have attended to that sensation of being watched. Instead I let the posters summon up the exotic sounds of kookaburras and didgeridoos. I sat on the floor of the fort, hearing my imagination play, and failed to register that there was silence once again in the garden below.

Then in the bushes along the boundary the rustling began. A snap crackle at first, like the crack of a whip, that just maybe could be written off as the march of a wren among dry leaves. Then a brushing noise, as if someone pushed along the fence, using the shrubs as cover. I was once convinced that a hedgehog in the ivy at the back of my house was an intruder, and so I know from experience how the dry foliage of autumn can magnify sound. But something about the scale of this sound suggested a body many times the size of a hedgehog. Given the scarcity of large mammals in Cambridge, I was inclined to say *human*. And probably, if I'd been a betting person, *man*.

I edged to a crouching position next to the window and peered out. The window faced in the wrong direction. The upper reaches of the ladder were empty, I could see that—but little else.

I stretched out full length, my legs inside the tree house and my head peeping over the front of the platform. The wheel of the pulley was just above me. A good view from here: straight down between the arms of the V, I could see a wide sweep of lawn, all the way to the towpath. Empty. I could see a considerable stretch of the boundary fence with its shrubbery. Still and quiet.

I didn't move. The birds seemed to be holding their breath, and so did I. For several minutes I lay, watching and waiting, as the pale morning light crept across the grass. Saw, from my vantage point, a pair of swans nudge into the bank on the opposite side of the river. Heard a train in the distance as it raced toward the railway bridge where Daryll and his pals had pelted me with stones. Noticed a long depression in the earth, below me and slightly to my right, where Geraldine might have lain with her angora cardigan and her peep-toe shoes, while the rain washed her blood and brain matter into the soil.

It hit me suddenly, like a minor earthquake, from behind. Not crackling branches this time, but footsteps thudding swiftly across the lawn. Toward me. I froze, unable to rush the descent, but dreading the thought of being trapped in the tree. *Was that how Daryll had felt? Beleaguered? With only a few rocks between him and danger?* Armed with a stash of stones, I would be impregnable, but . . . My knees had melted; I couldn't rise from the platform. Directly below me, out of my range of vision, someone shifted the ladder and scraped it into position. The platform trembled. Heavy footsteps sounded on the lower rung.

Finally, I managed to move, to coil myself back into the hut. I fell against the wall with a thump, and saw through the window a hand reach up and grasp the edge of the platform. Just at that moment, somewhere nearby, a dog began a hysterical bark. The hand was snatched away. The thud of footsteps resumed, but it dawned on me that they were moving away now, toward the back of the garden. My courage returned.

I descended as quickly as I could, toes clenching the rungs, refusing to look at the lawn below—*don't think about falling*—and drawing on adrenaline to suppress my fear of heights. I jumped the last three feet and hit the ground running.

The garden behind the walnut tree appeared to be empty. Morning light had penetrated between the trees that clustered along the back wall, and an intruder couldn't go unnoticed for long. I stalked the length of the wall, feeling as a child does when a game of hide-and-seek lasts too long, wanting the others to come out so I could go home. No one did. The trespasser—the other trespasser—must have escaped during the far-too-long that it had taken me to shake myself into action.

I looked over the wall, supporting myself on my elbows, and surveyed the chain of narrow gardens behind. A woman came out of one of the back doors with a bowl in her hand. "Caesar! Caesar!" she called in an urgent voice still full of sleep. Caesar stopped his barking at last and trotted toward her.

I watched for moments more until my shoulders ached. There were no other signs of life—no trail of the intruder who had happened on the tree house at the same time as me. Just *happened*? Was it coincidence—or had he known I was there? Had he watched me row up to the riverbank, seen me hammer my tent pegs into the ground, watched me swing myself up onto the towpath? When I approached the ladder, had he been standing in the shadows? Had he stalked me? Had he noted the wobble in my knees, savored the vicious knowledge that once I was on that platform I would be too shaky to defend myself?

And if he had, then what did this mean for my investigation?

The moments I had spent in the tree house had animated my understanding of Daryll. I had looked where he looked and seen what he saw, from the dreams of Australia to the river in the distance. I had made that much of his vantage point my own.

But that was Daryll Flatt, the child. My sense of Daryll

the murderer was no more concrete than before. For a few
seconds I had grasped the echoes of the panic that might
have engulfed him as he cowered in the tree—I had known
something of his vulnerability. But I hadn't seen the murdered woman through his eyes. Seen what it was about
Geraldine that might have triggered in him the urge to kill.

Howard had said *Daryll killed her* with a certainty that
was as sturdy as it was painful. Howard was convinced
that the question of culpability had been laid to rest. That
we no longer needed to ask who or how. That the only
question remaining to be answered was why.

My search for the *why* was far from over.

I checked my watch. Still no spark of life from the bungalow, but time for me to make tracks. My eyes scanned
the bushes, senses alert for movement or shadow. And I
asked myself, as I padded back to the boat, that if Howard
were right—if Daryll's conviction had settled the who and
how of Geraldine's death—then how could I make sense
of this past half hour? Who else but her murderer would
have an interest in an abandoned tree house? Who else
would take the trouble to scale a rickety ladder, and then
retreat at the sound of a high-pitched bark? Who—besides
me—would be out and about in the early morning, sneaking through the garden where a woman had been killed?

Whatever Howard thought about it—or Nicole, for that
matter—there were fresh questions that couldn't be set
aside. To consider: might the person who snap-crackled
through the bushes, who watched in silence as the shadows retreated, who thudded across the lawn—might that
man (was it a man?) have been involved in the murder of
Geraldine King? And if involved, how? As the murderer,
drawn again to the scene of the crime, two years down the
line? Or could involvement mean something else—some

other relationship to the killer, to the dead woman—that I hadn't yet even begun to imagine?

With a final glance over my shoulder at the now-distant crown of the walnut tree, I pressed with the end of my oar into the bank and slid away into the current.

Chapter 8

I DIDN'T EXPECT to learn a great deal about Daryll Flatt from Mrs. Joiner. She had been his class teacher at Grove Junior School before he was taken into custody. Teachers do their best with their little charges, but there's not a great depth of understanding of one little lad that can be educed when they're dealing with a class of thirty-four. The best I could hope for was an angle of vision, a scene or two that would help to fix the child in the context of his peers.

But I struck lucky.

Mrs. Joiner, as it turned out, looked rather like a bird—an oyster catcher, to be precise. She had a long thin nose, small bright eyes set close together, and a habit of tilting her head to one side.

I stood waiting at the door of her classroom, while a woman with twins in a double stroller went over the arrangements for an outing for her daughter in Class Four.

"On Friday, wearing rainwear and wellies," Mrs. Joiner repeated, her eyes glazing by the time she'd said it twice. No more than one pound spending money. Back in time for normal pickup. You may come, too, if you like.

That did it. The mother maneuvered with difficulty out the door, one twin sleeping over a bag of crisps, the other clutching a felt-tip pen taken from the teacher's desk. Mrs. Joiner raised a weary eyebrow in my direction.

No point beating around the bush. "You used to teach Daryll Flatt," I said. "The year he got into trouble."

Mrs. Joiner's wooden chair had a cushion on it with a blue and red patchwork cover. She sat down on it with a whoosh. "Who are you?"

It was not said in a curious voice, nor an aggressive one. It was the voice of someone who knows correct procedure, and adheres to it.

"Laura Principal," I replied, offering my card. "I've been asked by Howard Flatt, Daryll's brother, to look into some details surrounding the case. There were one or two things that I hoped you might help with. The kinds of things that only a teacher would notice."

Mrs. Joiner returned to my opening statement. "Think again," she said. "He was in trouble *every* year. The worst time was when he struck a younger child in the playground. I'm not certain that Daryll intended to harm him, but he was—I beg your pardon, *is*—quite a big lad, and that sort of thing cannot be allowed."

"You remember him clearly, then."

"He's not the sort of child you forget. Understand me," she instructed. The bright little eyes were fierce. "He didn't seem a bad boy. But then, none of them do. Not in primary. Between you and me, Daryll was what I would call borderline disturbed. He was always mildly disruptive. Lacking in self-control. He would get incredibly wound up, impatient, about little things."

"Such as?"

Mrs. Joiner tilted her head to one side and considered. "The class planted some sunflower seeds, and Daryll couldn't bear the waiting. He raced into the classroom—often late, not stopping to put on his indoor shoes—and demanded my attention. Every single morning. 'Please, Mrs. Joiner, are they grown yet?' "

"Surely he wouldn't get into trouble for that?"

"You've obviously never tried to keep order in a class of thirty-four juniors, Ms. Principal. Daryll was difficult, believe me. And changeable, too. One minute, upset that he might have done something wrong. Then he'd catch the eye of his mates, and fill with defiance. I never knew what to expect from him."

"How would you rate his academic skills?"

"Oh, Daryll wasn't stupid," she said quickly. "He had a good sense of number, and he was quick to learn. But his English suffered from lack of concentration. Reading, writing, comprehension—all below par."

"Mrs. Joiner, I understand that the school contacted Social Services after Daryll's grandmother died. Was it you who called them?"

"No. That happened the year before. Hilary Simpson's class. She's moved now, somewhere in London. You may be able to get her new address from the office."

She stood up and brushed down her skirt with brisk strokes.

I rose, too. "One more thing," I said, "before I go. In the weeks leading up to Geraldine King's killing, did Daryll seem any different from usual? Was his behavior any worse?"

"No," she said. "In the weeks preceding the murder, as far as I can recall, Daryll was his usual, hyper self. I told the police that." Mrs. Joiner's head had been tilted at a thirty-degree angle during most of this conversation. Suddenly she righted it and looked directly at me. "But," she added, as if she had suddenly made up her mind, "there's something I didn't tell them. The day before, on the Tuesday, Daryll was exceptionally excitable." She stopped, as if waiting for permission to continue.

"The day before the murder?" I felt a rush of excitement. "In what way?"

"Agitated. Couldn't settle to his work at all. Kept rocking in his chair, back and forth, back and forth. It made an awful racket and distressed the other children. Several times I asked him to stop. Finally, I went over to him and put my arm around his shoulders. 'Daryll,' I said, 'is something wrong?' "

From the playground, I heard the staccato shouts of children at play, but inside Mrs. Joiner's late afternoon classroom, it was quiet and still. I could imagine an earlier afternoon, the rhythmic movement of the boy's chair, the teacher's whisper, the other children curious, straining to hear.

She continued. "Finally, he lifted his head from his arms and looked up at me. 'It's a secret,' he whispered. 'And I'm the only one who knows.' From his face, the secret couldn't have been a happy one. I asked him if he wanted to share it with me, but he said there was someone else he had to tell first. And no," she said crisply, heading me off, "I have no idea whatsoever."

"You didn't mention this to the police? Why was that?"

"I would have," she said, with a hint of challenge in the tilt of her chin, "if they had asked. But I'm a teacher. It's not up to me to do the police's job for them."

Although it was like looking a gift horse in the mouth, I had to ask the obvious question. "So why are you telling me?"

Her eyes closed for a few seconds, as if she were scanning for an answer, and then popped open. "Simple," Mrs. Joiner declared. "You work for Howard Flatt. I don't want to be harsh, Ms. Principal, but really, that brother was the only good thing about the whole Flatt

family. If you had seen Howard delivering Daryll to
school when he was little, helping him with his gloves
in winter, touching cheeks with him for a moment before letting him go—if you remembered that, you would
want to do anything you could to give that young man
peace of mind."

I left via the playground, and on my way out I came
across two lads doing wheelies with their bikes in the street
outside. I stopped to admire the show. They elaborated
their performance, and soon they were monitoring my reaction from the corners of their eyes. I was impressed—
didn't have to fake it.

Eventually we fell into conversation. It flowed smoothly
over the merits of their respective makes of bike, but
foundered slightly when I inquired after a man in a mask.

"You mean . . ." said one, and paused.

"The pervert?" his pal put in knowingly. He had a partially shaved head.

"What do you mean by pervert?" I asked.

"A guy who goes around with his dong hanging out," he
declared, with a you-asked-for-it look. Priding himself on
his boldness.

"That's the one. Have you seen him around lately?"

"Sure," they insisted. But they had difficulty pinning a
sighting down, and I concluded that the Apeman hadn't
been in evidence for a while. I believed them, though,
when they described him as a regular—someone who
showed up at periodic intervals along the route to and
from school. "Just over there." They pointed to the playing fields near Arbury Road. "And down on Stourbridge
Common, near the river. Everyone knows him," they
chorused.

"He's been around for years," added the boy with the

shaved head. "My dad says if he ever catches him near me, he'll cut it off."

Nice to know the problem was in hand.

THE FOLLOWING MORNING, I rang Social Services on the off chance that Kelsey McLeod, Daryll's social worker, had returned from leave. I was in luck. "But you won't find him here," the receptionist warned. "He had to rush off first thing this morning to deal with some emergency at the residential home on Mill Road. Ditchburn Place. I can make you an appointment, but you'll have to be prepared for a wait."

Just to show I was willing, I made an appointment. But I wasn't prepared to tolerate a wait. So a few minutes later—after a short drive and a long search for a parking space—I strolled into the lobby of Ditchburn Place. Once a workhouse, then a maternity hospital, now a residence for what North Americans call senior citizens. So much more dignified than *old-age pensioners*. Primary identification as citizens, rather than as dependents of the state; on what they share in common with the rest of the adult population, rather than on how they differ.

The matron didn't seem at all surprised when I expressed an interest in Kelsey McLeod. "Morning tea is on its way, and Mr. McLeod won't be far behind," she volunteered. "Why don't you wait in the lounge?"

She showed me into a large square room with armchairs lining the walls and senior citizens—mainly women—lining the chairs. I lined a chair myself and became an immediate focus of interest. "Are you Lilian's girl?" the plump woman on my right inquired. I told her truthfully that I was not, and, as if that was the signal she needed, Mrs. Partridge launched off on the subject of figure skating, which she had adored as an activity in girlhood and taken up again as spectacle when she matured. While she filled me in on the forthcoming world championships, I kept my eyes on the door through which, the matron had assured me, Kelsey McLeod would soon emerge.

Matron was right. He entered with a quiet flourish, gallantly holding the door for a beak-nosed woman using a walker. At the same moment, a helper lumbered in from the other passage pushing a tea trolley, and heads—including Mrs. Partridge's—swiveled in the direction of refreshments. Mine swiveled toward McLeod, whose attention remained fixed on the face of his elderly companion. In spite of the obvious effort required for her to get about, she was talking a mile a minute, immersed in a story intended for his ears alone. He listened with wholehearted concentration, as if they were bosom friends on a quiet stroll instead of social worker and client in a crowded lounge. When they arrived at a suitable place to sit, he offered his arm in an intimate gesture and gracefully conveyed her to her chair.

Matron herself brought me tea. "Yes," she said, following the direction of my gaze, "he has a knack with the old folks, doesn't he? His visits are a real highlight. They adore him."

"Some more than others," Mrs. Partridge broke in. There was a spiteful edge to her voice. I had a feeling she was miffed at being included among the old folks. "That Winnie Pollitt. Quite gooey-eyed around him, she was."

Matron looked mildly shocked. "Now, Ellen," she reproved. "Anyway, Winnie has moved to Huntingdon. To be nearer her only child. What was her daughter's name? No, I can't recall. A saint, you know."

"Winnie's daughter?" I asked. Only ten minutes, and already confusion was setting in. Can a person become institutionalized in such a short period of time?

"She means Kelsey McLeod," Mrs. Partridge said with a knowing wink.

"His wife is very ill, you know," Matron explained. "Heart disease—cardiac dysrhythmia. She's really very unwell, especially for someone so young. He's sacrificed everything to look after her, and you never hear him complain, poor love. A regular saint."

"But I thought—"

"Cheryl," Mrs. Partridge said triumphantly.

"His wife? But I had heard—"

"Winnie's daughter. Cheryl. Never did know her last name."

I took a custard cream with my tea. Two custard creams. To hell with it, three. Chatted with my neighbor about the prospects of the British entrants. Kept my eyes on McLeod, whose simple acts, like arranging a tea table for one old lady or fetching a magazine for another, were overlaid with courtesy. But he didn't accept refreshments himself, even when they pressed. Too much work, apparently. No time to indulge. I stood up as he made his way toward the door. Matron intercepted him and steered him to me.

"You don't know me," I broke in before he had a chance to ask. "But I urgently need to speak with you. In private."

Kelsey McLeod gave me a long wary look. He didn't want to stop, didn't want to talk with me, but for some reason, he acquiesced. "What's this about?" he asked. The warmth, the attentiveness, that had characterized his interactions with the residents in the lounge had drained away. Either the elderly brought out the best side of Kelsey McLeod, or I, for some reason, brought out the worst.

I told him about my commission. How I had spoken to Daryll's brother and mother and some of his teachers, but how I was still a long way from finding a reason for Daryll to murder Geraldine King. "Do you know?" I asked, going straight to the heart of the matter. "Do you know why he killed her?"

McLeod asked the matron if he could use her office for a few moments. She smiled, nodded, eager to please. "Of course, Mr. McLeod, of course." I'm sure if he'd asked, she would have allowed him to use her lingerie.

McLeod sat down behind the matron's desk, and I occupied the chair that was intended for visitors. Up close, his face was still attractive, but thin and lined, as if it had been gouged by grief. In some odd way, his mustache with its crimson flecks accentuated the impression of sadness.

There was a pause, the longish kind that raises questions about whether one party to the conversation has fallen asleep. When Kelsey spoke, he seemed genuinely distressed.

"He's only a child," he pleaded. "How could there be a reason? Fears, maybe, or urges that he doesn't understand. But reasons? It's impossible." He stopped again, and I waited again. I was sure that his train of thought hadn't yet reached the end of the line.

"When I first saw Daryll," he continued, slowly, "he was only ten years old. A strong-looking boy. Big for his age. But still . . . still, he only came up to here on me." McLeod pointed to his chest. "And Daryll's strength was all in the body. His soul had been trampled on by life."

"I wouldn't have thought *soul* was a category much used by social workers," I objected. A bad habit, pondering aloud.

McLeod was not amused. "Don't patronize me, Miss Principal. I'm answering the question. You asked why. I'm telling you."

"I'm sorry," I said quickly. "I didn't mean to offend. You're saying that Daryll's soul—"

"His life force, his human sense of self," the social worker interjected.

"—had been trampled on by a father who deserted him?"

"For starters. But, as I say, misfortune rarely travels alone. Add in one brother who bullied him. Another brother who claimed to love him and then left. And the death of a grandmother. It was too many losses for one little lad to bear. Do you wonder he was violent sometimes?"

I remained silent.

"Do you wonder he got into trouble at school?" Kelsey continued. "That his mother couldn't cope?"

"What about his mother?" I asked. "Where does she fit in?"

"Janet Flatt," he said, and his lip all but curled with disgust. "I've seen one too many like her. One too many. Prostitutes, drug addicts, all sorts. Put their babies into care at the first hint of trouble, and then months later wail that they are devoted mums, they have to have them back."

McLeod made no attempt to hide the contempt in his tone. I couldn't be certain how much of this attached to women in general and how much specifically to Janet. "You're not saying that Daryll's mother is—was—on the game? Or an addict?"

"Nothing of the kind. What I'm saying is that Janet Flatt is the type of woman who should never have gone in for motherhood. She was hostile toward Mrs. King from the word go, would you believe? I explained to her that a good relationship with the foster carer was necessary for Daryll, but she couldn't take it in. Insisted that Mrs. King had usurped her position."

"And how about you? Did you have any doubts about placing Daryll with Geraldine King?"

McLeod looked away from me, out the window. Maybe to conceal the flicker of pain that pinched his features. He picked at a hangnail. "Like I say," he said (although he hadn't), "I honestly thought it was for the best. Geraldine King was a simple soul. I thought she could help Daryll begin the healing process. Help him confront some of the losses in his life."

"Did you have any advance warning that it wasn't working out?" I asked.

"Warning?" His fingers were working still. A sliver of skin ripped away along the side of his thumb. He looked at it blankly.

"Signs of Daryll's distress. Like his reaction to the missing doll," I suggested. "Or the way he tortured a pigeon." McLeod looked at me askance. "I've heard about your testimony in court," I explained.

"Yeah, okay." He shrugged. "Like I say, Daryll blamed Mrs. King for the loss of his doll. He had this fantasy that she had destroyed it." He appeared not to notice as a tiny droplet of blood from his thumb deposited itself on the matron's desk blotter. "And, yes, he did behave cruelly on at least one occasion."

"Why didn't you tell the police about this, when they first interviewed you? Why hold back until you got to court?"

"I explained in my testimony," McLeod insisted, "that the pigeon, and his attitude toward the doll—these meant that Daryll was angry. He was projecting his hurt and disappointment, which is not a bad thing. It's better than keeping it bottled up." He stopped again, and glanced at me, then shrugged. "Anyway, I was upset. I forgot about it."

"You forgot? Months passed between the murder and the trial. For all that time, you forgot?"

Another extended pause. Then he started in again, looking defeated. "Okay, I'll tell you the truth. Off the record. I hoped when it came to sentencing, that the judge would be lenient. Daryll did a terrible thing, but he isn't a monster. I knew that stuff about the pigeon would look bad. It's a funny thing in this country, you know. When someone kills—well, sometimes the court can see that they were pushed to it, they didn't mean to do it, it was out of character and so forth. But if an animal has also been harmed, then the whole picture changes. That puts him beyond the pale. Makes him into a sadistic killer."

"And you didn't want to do that to Daryll."

"I'd spent a year acting on behalf of that child—trying to do my best by him. I couldn't just throw him to the wolves." McLeod turned on me, for the first time during our interview, the sort of attentive gaze that he had lavished on the beak-nosed woman with the walker. I saw that he had an exceptionally sweet smile. A confiding smile. "Can't you understand that?" he implored.

I resisted the urge to say, *It's all right, I understand.* Random reassurance isn't on my fee schedule. Instead, I pressed my point. "But didn't the incident with the bird . . . Didn't it suggest to you that perhaps Daryll needed psychiatric help? That maybe foster care wasn't the answer?"

"I was shocked, of course, about the pigeon. But I thought I could turn him around. He'd come on so well since I'd been working with him. And really, Miss Principal, what good does it do anyway to put a little lad like that into a residential home?"

"Now he's in prison," I pointed out.

"Not prison," he shot back. He seemed almost angry. "Children don't go to prison in this country. He's in a secure unit for young offenders. Nothing like a prison."

"Locked up," I said. Scarcely ever able to go outside—

well, maybe the occasional view from the back of a van on the way to court, or a few rounds of basketball on a dirty square of concrete with wire walls fifteen feet high. Escorted to and from the classroom. Under constant surveillance. Surrounded for the foreseeable future by murderers and rapists and mini-mobsters—surrounded, that is to say, by his peers.

Locked up. He didn't argue with that. But he did let me know that our interview had come to an end. He checked his watch, made dismissive noises, and showed me out of the matron's office. He headed toward the back of Ditchburn Place, presumably to a car park, leaving me to dawdle my way to the front.

So I did. Dawdle, that is. I hung around the front of Ditchburn Place, where the driveway intersected with Mill Road. And sure enough, a couple of minutes later the social worker pulled up in a VW Beetle and stopped at the intersection. The window on the driver's side was rolled down so he could check the traffic. I squatted so my eyes were level with his.

"Hi!" I said. Friendly-like.

"Excuse me, Miss Principal," he said, craning to look past me at the traffic on Mill Road. "I'm in a hurry." A tissue was wrapped tightly around the pad of his thumb.

"Sure. Just one more little thing. The day before Mrs. King was killed, Daryll was hanging on for dear life to a secret. He wouldn't share it with his teacher. He was saving it for one special person. Would that be you?"

McLeod didn't even glance in my direction.

I tried once more. "Do you know what Daryll's secret was?"

Without a further look left or right, McLeod slammed his foot down on the accelerator and screeched out into the

traffic, causing agitation among the cars that were bar-
reling down on him from farther up Mill Road.

Well, I wondered, would that count as a yes?

Chapter 9

In the last week of October, autumn was using golden
foliage to distract from the coming of winter. I had a treat
in store: I scuffed through the leaves along the Backs to
West Road, and enclosed myself for most of a blustery
afternoon in the University Library. The U.L. has a tower
like a Mormon temple and a facade more suited to a power
station, but for me it carries an emotional kick. Although I
was a willing refugee from academic life, the prospect of
pacing the corridors of the west wing has the potential to
stir me still.

But excitement doesn't guarantee success. The material
on children who murder is thin. There are few such cases,
and even fewer authors who have chosen to make them
their theme. I found pockets of analysis in textbooks on
forensic psychiatry and on the legal position of children;
and I turned up one or two rather lurid volumes of true
crime that had crept somehow past the librarian. None of
this took me as far as I had hoped toward understanding
the brief violent career of Daryll Flatt. I made dutiful entries in a hardcover notebook and abandoned the library,
feeling virtuous but little wiser.

I traced a long route back, crossing the river at Garret
Hostel Lane and picking up appealing bits of food in the
marketplace, at Marks & Spencer, and at the deli on Bridge

Street as I strolled past. I even allowed myself an ice cream at Quayside before I hefted my shopping bag for the final push home.

On the corner of Chesterton Lane two grubby-looking boys stood sentinel over an even grubbier-looking guy. I made a show of inspecting the dummy. It lolled on a wooden wagon. The head—newspapers stuffed inside orange-toned tights—didn't claim to be authentic, but the clothes looked and smelled as if they might have been worn by Guy Fawkes himself.

I smiled encouragement. They pounced.

"Penny for the guy, miss."

It was a few days early for Bonfire Night, but then who am I to stand in the way of youthful initiative? I set my shopping bag down on the pavement and scoured my purse, and then my pockets. A twenty pound note was out of the question, even if that whiff of urine on the trousers showed real ingenuity. That left only some very small change. I shrugged, raised my hands in apology—it is many a year since "penny for the guy" was taken literally—and placed my scant offering in his outstretched hand.

He could tell by the weight of the coins that something was amiss. He inspected his palm and unloosed his anger. "You fucking bitch," he jeered in my direction, bursting with outrage. He displayed the coins to his friend, who echoed his disgust.

Bitch is a word to which I particularly object, but I decided against a reprimand.

The issues were too complicated. Sure, he shouldn't speak like that to a fellow human being. Sure, he should learn a little restraint, a little understanding, a little respect for women—not as women, but as people. Maybe he should even learn that humor at today's bad fortune can be the basis of tomorrow's good; it had crossed my mind to return later with a more substantial offering, but at the sound of *bitch*, I ditched that plan.

I also thought of teaching him a lesson in manners. Lads like that don't expect a woman to stick up for herself. I could bend over, grab the little smartmouth and lift him up by his T-shirt, at the same time twisting it around his neck. I know how to do that. I could wring a highly satisfying apology out of his skinny little neck. I could bend over close and warn him off in my nastiest bad-guy manner. Given that I was almost twice his height, he'd certainly be intimidated. If I really wanted to ram the lesson home, I could deliver him one hard slap across the face before releasing him. Or propel him to the public toilet near Jesus Lock and wash his foul mouth out with soap. Or frog-march him down to the Cam and simply toss him in.

But I didn't.

"YOU WANT TO tell me why not?" Stevie asked. I'd been hoping Sonny would make it to Cambridge for dinner that evening, would abandon the Bennetts on the Norfolk Broads and spend some time with me. But when I struggled up the hill with my groceries, it was Stevie—our right-hand woman in Aardvark Investigations—who was waiting outside my house. I recognized the leg—the narrow jeans, the cowboy boots—protruding from the half-open door of her car. The rest of Stevie was in the driver's seat, more or less asleep. One of the qualities of an effective inquiry agent is the ability to catch up on your sleep anywhere, anyhow, anytime you get a chance. And Stevie is good at her job.

I set my parcels down again, approached the car, and placed my lips inches from Stevie's ear: "You'll never catch the Bennetts this way." For the past two or three days, Stevie had been pairing with Sonny on surveillance duty in Norfolk.

She didn't jump. Didn't even open her eyes. "I'm off duty" was all she said. "And I'm hungry."

So we carried our stuff into the house and unpacked the shopping. Stevie's overnight bag told me she was planning to stay, and over a cup of tea I told her about my run-in with the two lads on the corner.

"You're not cut out to be a philanthropist," Stevie remarked dryly. "Why didn't you thrash them? Teach them a lesson?"

"Oh, I don't know," I said. "I can't explain."

And then, suddenly, I could.

How for one thing, it's hard to see the glory in intimidating someone half your size.

How that phrase, *teach him a lesson,* with its hypocritical educational overtones, has always rubbed me the wrong way. When adults set out to teach a child a lesson, you can bet that their curriculum puts power and revenge ahead of the three R's.

How when you get right down to it, you'll not curb aggressive behavior by demonstrating that what counts is the willingness to hurt and humiliate. "That kind of kid," I finished off, "has had that lesson rammed down his throat many times before."

"Okay." Stevie took it in, neither agreeing nor disagreeing. I knew that she would offer her opinion, her view, sometime later, and that when I heard it, it would almost certainly be worth listening to. "Was that one of the things that was wrong with your client?" she asked.

"Daryll Flatt? He's not the client," I reminded her. "I'm working for his brother, Howard. And I'm not sure what you mean."

"Should have thought it was obvious," Stevie said. "Shall

I wash those salad leaves?" She swung over to the sink and went to work on the salad. Stevie knows my kitchen, and she's a much keener cook than me. "I asked you why you didn't thrash those little hooligans. You said, in slightly different words, that aggression breeds aggression."

"And so it does," I interrupted, helping myself to another cup of tea. "Stands to reason. Kids whose childhoods are punctuated by violence come to see violence as the solution to problems. Don't learn other ways of dealing with frustration. So?"

"So, I'm asking, simply: was that what turned Daryll Flatt into a killer? Did he have to endure too much discipline—too much violence disguised as care? Did his father take the belt to him, his mother lock him in the cupboard? Did he have"—and she smiled as she shook the water off the leaves, a smile intended to show me that her tabloid style was deliberate and ironic—"a surfeit of discipline and a shortage of love?"

"That's just like you, Stevie," I said, rummaging through the refrigerator. "The rest of the world is clamoring about the failure to discipline—about kids running wild, about the need for curfews. While you're worrying about the consequences of its overzealous application."

"Well, and why not?" Stevie asked. "Violent parents don't say, 'I beat my child because I'm a sick bastard—because I like hurting kids.' Most of the time when they beat a child, it's for the kiddie's sake."

They teach him a lesson.

"Well?" she asked.

"Don't rush me," I fired back. The whole question of why—the crucial question, as far as my client was concerned—made me edgy. "Sure, Daryll Flatt was on the receiving end of violence. He was an unhappy little boy, and his unhappiness enraged his stepfather. The stepfather couldn't help himself, Janet Flatt says. Just a slap from time to time."

"Like answers to a smoker's survey?" Stevie suggested.

"You got it. For five or six fags, read a pack a day. And after the stepfather, there was the next brother up. Mark Flatt Miller."

Stevie raised an eyebrow at the surname Miller.

"Identified with the bully," I explained. "You can see it in his scowl, in the way he carries himself, in his meat cleaver hands." Mark had the body language of a man who wants to intimidate. "Mark Flatt Miller has a grievance against Daryll that goes back a long way—real sibling rivalry stuff—and I'm sure he used to lay into his baby brother whenever he could. Even his mother is scared of Mark."

"So the answer to my question is yes?" Stevie asked. She whisked the salad dressing, set the jug on the table, and waited for my reply.

"That Daryll Flatt became a killer because he had experienced so much violence himself? Didn't know any other way of getting along?" I shook my head. Negative. "If I had to guess now—on the basis of what I've learned so far—I'd say that Daryll Flatt was moved by loss more than anger. All the people he had most cared for left, suddenly. His father, his brother Howard, and finally, his granny."

"And Daryll's mother?"

"Janet Flatt has a big line in self-delusion. 'Daryll never minded,' she said. I suppose she was trying to convince herself."

"Unable to face the fact that her son was hurt? That the man in her life was harming her baby?"

"Something like that. Janet Flatt loved Daryll. But the notion that love is all you need didn't last out the Seventies, and with good reason." I finally thought of a way to answer Stevie's question. "Look at it like this, Stevie. I spent the afternoon in the University Library, learning what I could from books about children who kill. And sure enough, juvenile killers have often witnessed violence or been subject to it themselves. Sometimes they're trying to defend themselves from abuse."

"On the other hand?" Stevie asked. She wrapped foil around a smart-looking fish—fresh from the coast, she said—and popped it in the oven.

I took the cue she offered me. "On the other hand, some children who murder are brought up in mundane circumstances. You can't use the idea of exposure to violence to account for the fact that they kill."

"And of course," Stevie added, poking through the cupboards, "there are other children who survive horrific abuse and grow up to be considerate, if wary, citizens." She was searching out ingredients with the energy of a wild boar nosing for truffles in the forest. My stomach did handsprings at the thought of homemade pudding, but my sense of duty couldn't let her carry on without help any longer, and I wasn't in the mood to assist. So I did the decent thing. I opened a bottle of fizzy white wine and enticed Stevie to abandon the pudding in favor of a drink and some marinated olives. We moved to the sitting room, where it was cooler.

"You're equivocating," she announced as she plonked herself down. She wasn't prepared to drop the subject of Daryll. "All this yes, no, maybe so, is more suited to an academic than a private investigator. Let's get down to brass tacks: have you found a history of violent behavior?"

"What do you count as history?" Is there any little child who hasn't hit or pinched or bitten a playmate? Who hasn't screamed with rage when she's dragged away from the fun fair? Who hasn't used his fists to defend a favorite toy? "No one—that is, no one who knew Daryll before Geraldine was killed—characterizes him as a violent boy. His teacher, Mrs. Joiner, recalled an incident involving a younger child in the playground, but she doubts that Daryll intended to do harm. She seems to place him as sad, rather than bad."

"Not mad?" Stevie asked.

"Apparently not. Except . . ." The pigeon was a bad sign. That was one of the few conclusions I carried away from my cull through the library that morning. Both textbooks on forensic psychiatry had agreed: the torturing of animals is a pretty chilling portent of violence to come.

I provided Stevie with the gory details.

"Nasty," she agreed. "No wonder McLeod tried to hold this information about his precious Daryll back from the police. But aren't you avoiding something?" Stevie reached over and turned on the table lamp. I hadn't realized how gloomy the room had become. "I heard about the boys who threw rocks at you from the bridge. Among them, Daryll Flatt. He could have killed you, Sonny said."

"I wouldn't have nominated him as a Child of Courage," I admitted. "But even if he had intended to harm me—and I'm not at all sure about that—there's still a crucial difference. When Daryll killed Geraldine King, he was alone. When he threw those stones at me, he was surrounded by pals. A lot of youngsters can be persuaded to do dangerous things in a gang that they wouldn't dream of doing alone."

"Right down to murder?" Stevie asked.

" 'Fraid so. It's not as unusual for children to kill as it's sometimes made out to be. From Mary Bell and Norma Bell, to gang killings in big cities, murderous children do crop up from time to time. What's really unusual," I said, "is for a preteen to kill. For him to kill an adult. And for him to kill alone."

Stevie looked none too contented.

There was a knock on the door. "What's the matter?" I asked her as I moved to check it out.

"Nothing that dinner won't cure," she replied, and returned to the kitchen.

Sonny stood on the doorstep, overnight bag in hand, looking like something the cat dragged in. I kissed him, but got more than I bargained for.

"You're soaking wet," I exclaimed, pulling back.

"Got caught in a shower," he explained. "Frank Bennett wandered into a field outside Hoveton. I had just positioned myself behind a hedge to watch, when the heavens opened up. Like Zeus drained his bathtub over me."

"Speaking of baths, why don't you go get your clothes off and have a hot one," I suggested. "Stevie's here. She's doing wonderful things to a fish."

"The tub sounds good." Sonny shoved the hair off his forehead in a distinctly weary gesture. "I'll think about the fish later."

He lumbered upstairs, footsteps heavy on the treads like those of a man who has spent too many hours of the past forty-eight slouching in his car.

Minutes later—after refilling Stevie's glass and setting the table for three—I climbed the stairs myself and found Sonny stretched out, still a little stiff, in my big cast-iron bathtub, his long arms clutching the sides as if he thought that without holding on he might slip forever beneath the waves.

"Tired, huh?" I said fondly, handing him a glass of wine. I fetched a folded towel from the closet and eased it behind his shoulders. He leaned back and stopped clinging to the side of the tub, a happier man. Or at least a more comfortable one.

My bathroom isn't the size that allows for a chair. "Any luck with the Bennetts?" I asked, perching on the edge of the toilet.

He shook his head, but gently, so as not to dislodge the towel. "I've secured affidavits from three former customers who are happy to say that the person who arranged boat charter for them was Belinda Bennett. As far as I'm concerned, that's three out of three. But the barrister acting for the brothers will point out that I managed to turn up only three customers who knew Mrs. Bennett, out of the thousands who dealt with the business over the years. And the judge will be less than impressed."

"So you still need documentary evidence."

"Precisely," Sonny sighed. "I need accounts, pay slips, bills going back years with Belinda's signature on them. I need diaries and appointment books in her own handwriting. I need instructions from the brothers to her, or from her to the brothers, that will confirm she was actively involved. Active being the operative word."

"Inland Revenue?"

"I've tried. They won't release the file. Not even to her."

"What about your bookkeeper? The one you were having drinks with the other night?"

"She was nice," he said. The shine in his eyes suggested that sometimes in-the-line-of-duty can be fun.

"If you're feeling that much perkier," I said, "you can put on some clothes and come downstairs for dinner."

For much of the meal, Stevie and Sonny chortled their way through reminiscences of the last few days in Norfolk. Their adventures were testimony to the difficulty of doing investigative work in rural areas, where any newcomer stands out. Testimony, too, to the loutishness of the brothers Bennett. Sonny couldn't decide which was worse: following Bryan Bennett as he wove homeward from the pub, avoiding by a hairbreadth a collision with an oncoming lorry; or the moment when—posing as an inspector from the National Rivers Authority—he came face-to-face with the real thing.

But eventually, after we'd had our fill of rural humor, we returned to Daryll and the Geraldine King murder case. Stevie gave a clipped and efficient account of our conversation so far. With her usual fair-mindedness, she recalled how she'd fished for the source of Daryll's action in a brutal childhood, and how I had tossed objections in and thereby muddied the waters.

Sonny refused to be drawn into this debate. "What's odd about your conversation," he said, "is the starting point."

I hadn't the faintest idea what he meant. Neither, from the look on her face, did Stevie.

Sonny helped himself to another forkful of fish. "Let me give you an example," he said. "In Hartlepool, some years ago, there was a little boy who killed his baby sister. Strangled her with a skipping rope."

"Yuk!"

"Hang on, Stevie, there is a point to this story. Seems this wasn't the first injury he had done to a baby. He had previously dropped the same little sister down the stairs."

"We've been through that," I said impatiently. "With Daryll Flatt, there is no sustained history of violent behavior. No record of attacks."

"Why wasn't he stopped?" Stevie asked. She saw the point where I hadn't.

"Precisely," Sonny said. "Why wasn't this little Hartlepool murderer-in-the-making unmasked before he managed to kill? Why—when he had squeezed his baby cousin so hard that a rib cracked—didn't someone refer him for treatment? Answer: because he was a child. Because children are not—that's how we tend to see it—capable of studied, calculated violence. Do you know what the parents said when they were questioned about the broken ribs? 'He was hugging the baby,' they said. 'He doesn't know his own strength. He loves the baby sooo much.' "

Sonny stopped to finish off his food, and I did my best to follow up. "So, we assume kids are innocent, and because of this, killers occasionally go unnoticed. But it can also mean that people ask the wrong questions about children, even when they know they're guilty. Yes?"

"Yes," Sonny said, beaming at me. "If the convicted killer that you two had been talking about was an adult, you would have looked for the reason for this death at this particular point in time. In short, for the motive."

"But because we were dealing with a child, we set motive to one side, and rushed to examine causes instead. We didn't ask why did he do it, with what motive, what intention, as we would with an adult. We asked what is the cause—the family trauma, the abuse, the exposure to videos—that gave him no choice."

"I'm sorry to throw a spoke in the works," Stevie said, "but when I covered that case for the NSPCC a couple of years back—you remember . . . ?"

We remembered. And nodded to show we did.

"I spent some time in the waiting room below the courtroom with a forensic psychiatrist. We got to talking about the boot on the other foot—kids who commit murder. When children kill, she told me, they often do so for reasons that don't make a whole lot of sense to adults. For things that seem trivial. Like a broken promise, she said. Or because somebody owes them baby-sitting money. Or—"

"Or in revenge, maybe, for destroying a doll? That's the suggestion in Daryll's case."

"Precisely. It has to be faced, Laura. Your dogged pursuit of a motive for Daryll—a motive that makes sense in adult terms—may turn out in the long run to be so much wasted effort."

"I won't accept that," I said. "It's too depressing, the idea that a woman could be murdered merely because of a missing doll. There's got to be more to it than that."

"You're just feeling discouraged because of those boys this afternoon," Stevie suggested. She filled Sonny in on my street-corner adventures.

Sonny was so tired, he had to prop his chin up with his hand. He managed one last question. "So how did you leave it with them?"

I chuckled. "Simple. I smiled at them. Warm, calm—beneficent even. There they were, pretending to be hard, and that smile made them feel about three years old. They hated it. Then I directed myself to the one who had sworn at me. 'It's a pretty interesting guy,' I told him, 'but if you mean to collect real money, you've got a lot to learn.' I promised to pass that way again before Bonfire Night. Suggested they might want to think about volunteering an apology."

"Are you really going back?" Stevie asked, skeptical. "They'll never apologize."

"Ten pounds says they will," I insisted.

What's Bonfire Night without a few fireworks?

WE NEVER GOT on to motive that evening. Sonny excused himself early. His moment of lucidity following the meal was quickly clouded by exhaustion, and he trundled off to sleep. Stevie made up the sofa bed soon after. I did the dishes, had a shower, and curled up around Sonny, savoring the smell of sandalwood on his skin. But while those two enjoyed the dreams that they had earned the hard way—tramping around Norfolk—I spent the night flicking in and out of sleep, trying to imagine what might, through eleven-year-old eyes, look like a motive for murder.

Chapter 10

IT'S NOT ONLY villains who return to the scene of the crime. I had several hours of contract work—the kind of thing that rolls around every month—under my belt already that day when I parked my car in one of the spaces that looked out on the river, just next to the Pike and Eel. The car was conspicuously alone. It was too late, I suppose, for mothers and children on the way home from school, and too early for young lovers. It was the time of day when dinners are prepared and television sitcoms pursued and the domesticated lifestyle of the British is acted out over ovens and on sofas. Add to that the damp and gusty winds that put umbrellas out of the question and flecked the surface of the river, and my solitude was hardly surprising. Not the sort of circumstances to tempt people down to feed the ducks.

Geraldine's house lay a short walk along the towpath from this point. Once again I counted down the houses. First, the house with the pair of gnomes that stood sentry over an otherwise empty stretch of lawn. It would be easy to imagine that the gnomes sprang to life at night and busied themselves in the garden. Next, a bungalow—in shape and layout much like Geraldine's—with wide borders and a hedge whose carefully clipped planes said much for the steadiness of its owner.

I decided on impulse to visit this house. To introduce myself to the neighbors.

Call me a pessimist, but when I show up unannounced on someone's doorstep armed with intimate questions about dead neighbors, I expect to have to plead and cajole, to convince and persuade, before they open their hearts to me. I have amassed a repertoire of reassurances and white lies for such moments, and I know to brace myself for disappointment. Even I, with my silver tongue and charming looks, am as likely to be turned away with a flea in my ear as to be welcomed. But Emma Caudwell didn't so much as blink an eye at my approach. "Come right in," she said, as if providing information to a private investigator about a murdered neighbor was part of the housekeeping routine.

"I know everything about her," she said. "You only have to ask."

I wasn't complaining.

Not at that point.

The interior of Emma Caudwell's house, like her garden, was what my mother would describe as *tickety-boo*. For my mother, this is a term of approval. She admires people who can so arrange their lives as to keep their houses in a tickety-boo state—no sash unpainted, no opportunity for ornamentation missed—even though her own aspirations run in quite different directions.

Emma Caudwell was a robust-looking woman, with a rounded figure and a bob blackened by L'Oréal. She wore tailored slacks and enormous gilt earrings. "Poor Geraldine," she cooed, leading me into an immaculate living room, "I don't think I'll ever get over it!"

Nor, I imagined, would Geraldine.

Enthusiastic would be a restrained way to describe Emma Caudwell's conversational style. She spoke like a woman in a race to say as much as possible in the shortest conceivable time. Relevance didn't come into it. We're talking marathon efforts here.

I learned about property prices in the area, from the blip in the market after the murder to the impact of a new greenhouse built onto their home. How Patrick, Emma's husband, had taken a job involving shift work—he was an administrator at Addenbrooke's Hospital—in order to pay the costs of said greenhouse. How the title on Geraldine's house had passed on her death, jointly, to her sister and to her son; how it had been quickly sold, at a giveaway price, to a retired couple from Didcot. How the Didcotians had since returned to the home counties and the house had stood empty, without a flicker of interest, for months. The impact of this neglect on the garden, and indeed on Emma's own garden, was a source of considerable comment: the un-pruned shrubbery was not nearly as worrying as the glim-mer of Russian vine. *Didn't I think?*

And so on and so on and so on, ad tedium.

We were standing at Emma's sitting room window. You couldn't see Geraldine's bungalow from there. That didn't prevent Emma from pointing vigorously and making ges-tures that encompassed the whole of the neighboring prop-erty as she spoke.

"Sit down, sit down," she exclaimed, indicating that our property survey had come to an end. "What do you want to know? You've come to the right place, let me tell you. If anyone can tell you about that boy, it's me, living right next door to him. Don't you think that's terrifying? That I lived next door to a killer? I often say to Patrick, of an eve-ning, 'Are we lucky, Patrick, or are we lucky?' Living right next door to a killer, I mean, and still alive."

"Did you ever—"

"Mind you," she interrupted, "Daryll didn't look like a killer—and they're the worst kind, the ones with appealing little faces. But I should have known. Always up that tree—like those road protesters near Newbury, did you hear about them? Always hoisting rocks up. If poor Stanley had known when he made that tree fort. He made it for Edward, of course, the year Edward started school. Too young, if you ask me. He'll break his leg, Geraldine, I used to say—or maybe his neck—climbing like that. But she never listened. Never had a brain in her head, that woman."

"Edward is Geraldine's son?" I broke in.

"Well, of course he's her son," Emma said, rather testily. "He wouldn't be her husband, would he? Far too young for her. Her husband's name was Stanley."

"Could we talk about Daryll Flatt?" I tried again. "Did he ever say anything to you about Geraldine? Did he ever indicate to you that he was angry with her? That he wanted to hurt her?"

"Well—" Emma said, and came to an abrupt halt. She folded her hands neatly in her lap and was silent for all of three seconds. I held my breath. "Well." It was time out, a pit stop; then Emma was off again. "Daryll Flatt never talked too much about anything. He was always on the go. You'd see him scooting out of sight, out of the corner of your eye, you know? He'd be hiding in the bushes, or behind one of the willows along the towpath. They found him in a crack willow, you know; I can show you which one if you want? No? Well, later then. Never said a word about her. Not even to me. Not a word. Most he would say—when I asked him if he wanted to come in for cake or something—most he would say is 'I'll have to see if it's all right with Mrs. King.' I ask you! Really. As if I were dangerous. As if a piece of cake would hurt anyone. As if Geraldine King and I hadn't been neighbors for years. What do you think of that?"

I threw in a mild word about the importance of teaching children to take precautions, but Emma Caudwell cut me off again, and just as she did, a door shut quietly in the hallway. I heard gentle footsteps approaching the living room.

"Oh, I know," she continued airily, "tell them not to take candy from strangers and all that. I always warned my girls. Don't take candy—well, anything, really, brussels sprouts or vindaloo for that matter—from a stranger. But am I a stranger? Patrick, is that you?" she called loudly, without a break in monologic flow. "What do you say? Am I a stranger?"

A quiet-looking man in a neat suit came through the archway. He shuffled in sideways, as if putting as little of himself as possible into the room. He looked at me, smiled a nervous-looking smile.

"Patrick?" Emma insisted, demanding his attention. "Am I a stranger?"

Patrick was a man of practiced tact. "Not to me, Emma," he replied, and ducked back out of sight.

I have an image of myself as a person who is reasonably tenacious, willing to keep trying, able to endure. But Emma Caudwell wore me down. One more go, I promised myself. "Geraldine King," I interjected loudly. "Mrs. King. Did she have any other friends?"

Apparently, I had uttered the magic word. "Friends?" Emma repeated, as if this were an entirely unexpected question. "Friends? Well. It wasn't 'friends' she was after, was it? Stanley King was only dead a month or so, and she was over here, asking for Patrick, wanting help with her lawn mower. She didn't have me fooled, not for a minute.

I knew what *that* was about. Told her she could *pay* for a gardener if she wanted a man."

It was my turn to be surprised. "But I thought you two were friends?"

"Friends?" Emma snorted again. "Whatever gave you that idea? Geraldine King and I had nothing in common apart from a postal code."

MY STEALTH IN approaching Geraldine's bungalow on previous occasions had been, it turned out, quite beside the point. According to Emma Caudwell, the house stood empty. Had done so for some time. I didn't fancy another trip to the tree house, didn't want to make myself vulnerable to whoever it was that had spied on me before, but I could see that the bungalow windows were uncurtained. It wouldn't do to retreat without taking a quick peek inside.

Wind was gusting at the large front window as I pushed aside the buddleia and winter jasmine and peered into the sitting room. It looked long unoccupied. Where the carpet had been taken up, the floor was freckled with fragments of underlay. Above the fireplace a rectangle marked the place where a picture had hung long enough for the surrounding wallpaper to fade. On either side of the hearth, shelves—a pale pink, as far as I could tell—marched up the alcoves, untenanted except for a crumpled ball of paper and a grimy-looking mug. It wasn't an elegant room, but the proportions were pleasant, and the fireplace provided a focus. I could easily imagine it as an attractive room—if Geraldine King had chosen to make it so.

A rasping noise behind me brought me up short. I spun around. Found myself standing opposite a man—and though I had only glimpsed him for a few seconds, I had

no doubt that this was Patrick Caudwell. He had changed
into casual clothes and looked more at ease than before.

"Where did you come from?" I asked, astonished that I
hadn't heard him on the path.

He apologized profusely for startling me. He was just
coming to check that the house was all right—keeping a
promise to the most recent owners—and had been surprised to see me standing there.

"I've been trying to get a fix on Geraldine King," I said.
"The kind of person she was. You were neighbors for a
long time. Did you know her well?"

He shook his head. No. Explained—apologetic here,
too—that though there had always been civil relations between the two households, they were never close. Emma
and Geraldine had never really hit it off, he said. They
rubbed each other the wrong way. Anyway, he, Patrick,
thought it prudent not to get involved. "It seemed best," he
said, "in the circumstances, to keep a bit of a distance."

He looked rather shy, which is not a quality you generally expect in a man of his age. But also expectant and
anxious. As if he were waiting for me to do something or
to say something else. Finally he plucked up courage.

"I liked Daryll Flatt," he said, glancing nervously in the
direction of his own home. That was all.

"What did you like about him?" I didn't know what
to say.

"He was quiet. He got on with his games. Didn't bother
anyone," Patrick said. "He was just a nice kid, not like
some of them around here. You know, smart alecks."
Patrick Caudwell shoved his hands in his pockets as if
putting away an unpleasant memory. "I was sorry about
what happened," he said. "About Daryll being convicted.
About going to prison. You don't expect that kind of thing
to happen to a child."

"You don't expect a child to kill his foster mother," I returned.

"No?" he asked, and made his way back down the path.

BECCA HUNTER WAS the woman who had stumbled upon the rain-drenched body of Geraldine King. She recounted the experience in sober detail—how wet the body was, how chill. How her first reaction was wonderment that Geraldine would sleep outside on such a showery evening. How this thought vanished the instant she registered the little that was left of Geraldine's skull.

"It's odd, you know," Mrs. Hunter said reflectively. She had a gray bob with a thick fringe, and wore jeans. She looked much younger than her years. "Finding Geraldine like that. I hope this doesn't sound bizarre, but finding the body makes me feel more closely connected to her than I did when she was alive."

"You didn't like her?"

Becca Hunter glanced out her window, as if the answer to my question could be found in the houses on the other side of Pretoria Road. Then she stood up and crossed to a bureau, lifted a bottle of sherry and two glasses from a tray. I accepted her invitation to a drink, though sherry is not really my tipple, and arranged myself on a sofa covered in a fabric with a William Morris design.

"What do you think of the word *widow*?" Mrs. Hunter asked.

I confessed I had never thought of it at all. Then I mused my way through various meanings. Dismissed the idea of merry widow.

"A figure of fun," Becca agreed. "Someone to snigger at."

That left two serious meanings—one good, one bad. On the honorable side, I suggested, *widow* reminds us of

shared histories. Of plaited lives. Of commitment and relationship, of loyalty and love.

I was warming to the topic. On the other side, I noted,
there's a stigma attached. *Widow* refers to women rendered
useless, worthless, washed up, by the death of a partner.
Women who are forced by lack of alternatives to throw
themselves—figuratively speaking—on a husband's funeral pyre.

Which one was Geraldine?

"The second," Becca said emphatically. "She had completely submerged her identity in that of her husband.
When she lost Stanley, she seemed to lose herself. Do you
know, I noticed—a good two years after she became a
widow—that she still signed her letters 'Mrs. Stanley
King.' Not Mrs. Geraldine King, but Mrs. Stanley. I asked
her about it, gently. Thought it might do her good to talk."

"And Geraldine said?"

"Geraldine drew herself up, all straight-backed, and she
said—it was one of the few times I ever heard her express
a strong opinion—she said, stoutly, 'I'd rather be a widow,
Stanley's widow, than be a Ms.' "

So Geraldine King had not railed at the narrow compass
of the title widow. Whatever her weaknesses, Geraldine
knew precisely where she stood. She was a widow—
Stanley's widow. Not a Ms.

It occurred to me then that I had a firmer image of
Geraldine King's corpse than I had of her as a living,
breathing woman. How had she presented herself, this
militant widow, this dedicated wife? Had she resembled
the farmer's spouse in the painting *American Gothic*, all
gray and narrow and gritty? Or was she ample and rosy
and domestic—a woman busy in the kitchen, trying to fill
the passage from her man's stomach to his heart?

"Any chance you've got a picture of Geraldine?" I asked.

Becca opened a cupboard and brought out a yellow envelope. She extracted half a dozen photos and handed them to me.

"I'm not a great one for photographs," she said. "But birthdays are a bad day to be alone. So I organized a little tea party—cakes, the neighbors, a few family members—for Geraldine. And I finished off the film in the camera." She shivered slightly. "It was almost as if I knew that she would be gone soon."

I was studying one of the photos. "Yes," Mrs. Hunter said, leaning closer, "that's Geraldine."

Geraldine fitted into neither an American Gothic nor a British domestic mold. If I had to sum up her appearance, I would say that everything about her looked soft. Her skin was powdery and pink, as if she'd just tiptoed out of a sauna. Her lips were plump and coral-tinted. Her eyes were shy beneath eyebrows as feathery as duck down. Her hair was fluffy, dove-white, and dense. Even her ears looked soft, with tiny pearl studs dimpling the tender lobes. Geraldine had the usual complement of wrinkles, the pleated neck, the spotted hands that give away every man or woman of her age—even the astonishing Joan Collins—but the overwhelming physical impression was of softness. Geraldine King was like an elderly lamb.

"How old was she when this photo was taken?"

"Sixty-two," Becca replied.

Sixty-two and soft all over.

There were four other adults in the photos. I recognized Emma and Patrick Caudwell, she looking garrulous and sharp-eyed, he trying to dissolve into the background. The other couple, Becca told me, were the Holtbys, Faith and William, sister and brother-in-law to Geraldine King.

Faith had the same thick hair as Geraldine, but she was taller, leaner, more spare. Her shape was comprised of angles, whereas Geraldine appeared to have no edge at all. "You wouldn't take them for sisters," I said. "Did they get along?"

"Get along?" Becca considered. "I sometimes had the feeling that Faith resented Geraldine. Nothing more specific than that," she added, in response to my raised eyebrow. "But that didn't keep them from shopping together; they met, regular as clockwork, second Tuesday in the month."

"And Geraldine's son? His name is Edward, I believe? Was he invited?"

Geraldine rarely saw him, Becca explained. He lived in the nearby village of Papworth Everard, but Edward and his father had had some sort of falling out over money, and Geraldine felt, in deference to Stanley, that she had to keep him at a distance.

This clearly wasn't to Mrs. Hunter's taste. "Her own son!" she declared with disapproval.

And what about Daryll? I asked. He didn't appear in the birthday photos.

"He was around," Becca said, "but he didn't spend much time indoors. He never seemed to care much for adults, you know—except for that man with the mustache from Social Services. As I recall, Daryll scuttled in, at one point, and loaded up on cakes and cookies. Geraldine tried to get him to sit down, but he wasn't having any of it; he took his food and dashed out. Actually, it was rather embarrassing. None of us knew what to say. Except for Patrick Caudwell— he stood up for the boy. Said of course he'd want to be out of doors, it's just the age and all that."

I asked how Geraldine King came to be involved with Daryll in the first place.

"That's down to me," Becca Hunter admitted. "I thought it might help her to make a new life. It was like this: one day we happened to be in Geraldine's bedroom, and I noticed two mugs on the bedside table. 'Overnight visitor?' I teased. Geraldine went bright red. 'Oh, no,' she said solemnly, 'that's Stanley's cup.' She saw the astonishment on my face, and explained, 'If I didn't make myself fetch him a cup of tea every morning, I might not get up at all.' I realized for the first time how desperate she was."

"So you suggested Homefinders?"

Poor little mites in difficulty, Becca had said. Need a motherly type to help. Come along to the next meeting. It'll do you good. She wouldn't take no for an answer, and Geraldine was soon attending training sessions run by Social Services.

"And did it work?" I asked. "Did Geraldine and Daryll develop a good relationship?"

"It worked a treat for Geraldine. Her confidence improved dramatically. She perked up no end once Daryll Flatt came along."

As I stood up to go—drawn by the prospect of a pint at the Fort St. George on my way home—I returned to my earlier question.

"You never said, Mrs. Hunter. Did you like Geraldine King?"

Becca considered for a moment. "The single most important fact about Geraldine," she said, "was that she had made her man the center of her life. She adored him. And this adoration made it difficult for anyone else to be close to her."

"How do you mean?"

"Here's an example. I mentioned to her once, light-heartedly, that men of our husbands' generation—I lost

Charles, in a car accident—had never been willing to take responsibility in the kitchen. Geraldine pooh-poohed this idea. 'Not *my* Stanley,' she said indignantly. 'My Stanley was a fine man. He had his responsibilities, and I had mine. I wouldn't have dreamed of asking him to help.' " Becca Hunter sighed. "Do you see what I mean? Always my Stanley this, my Stanley that."

Holding him up, even in death, as a shield between her and the world.

Chapter 11

I SHOULDN'T HAVE let it get to me, but it did. For the best part of an hour I had sat in the library at Eastern University, poring over the past months' papers, reading reports of violent crimes. Crimes committed by children. I read headline after headline, and as I did, my image of the world lurched sickeningly to the bad.

Disabled woman tormented by gang of youths; man who goes to her rescue kicked to death. Young mother found unconscious next to her traumatized toddlers after attack by schoolboys in public park. Sixteen-year-old convicted of the rape and murder of a widow in her eighties. Head teacher stabbed to death by teenage gang. Schoolgirls take the life of a thirteen-year-old from a neighboring school. Gang of boys aged nine and ten accused of raping a classmate in the toilets at a primary school. Boys put petrol-soaked rag through letter box and set it alight; three members of the family die.

It's not good for the soul to dwell on these things. That's not a principle; it's a practical conclusion, drawn from considering my own reactions. Minute by minute, as I skimmed the columns, crime news became the only news. Civil war in Albania, the breaking of the cease-fire in Northern Ireland; at home, the axing of thousands of jobs in the steel industry and the vindictive campaigns of the national election;

flooding in America and economic failure in Russia; even—
on the good side—the glories of Hale-Bopp, its tail arcing
millions of miles across the night sky—all receded into the
distance. All became less real than the violence that lurked
around every corner, in every classroom, behind every neutral (child's) face.

From amidst the headlines, a hand landed on my shoulder. I shuddered. A bad sign, that, when friendly human
contact makes a person jump.

"Lunch by the river?" Helen asked. She bent over and
scanned my face more closely. "What's the matter, Laura?
My invitations don't usually bring on that glassy-eyed
look. Have you seen a ghost?"

"Ghost of horrors past." I worked on a smile. Helen
plumped down next to me, waiting for an explanation. She
wore no makeup. Her blonde hair was slicked back in a
mini-ponytail, a hairpin catching the stray curl near the
left ear. She looked pretty and crumpled and workaday.
She looked like the real world—like chores to be done;
like plans no more threatening than a policy meeting. The
real world. Not murder and mayhem.

"Thanks, Helen," I said. "I'll do a raid on the deli and
meet you at the top of Norfolk Street in, say, ten minutes?"

She checked her watch and nodded. "Egg mayonnaise
baguette," she said. "Thank you for what?"

But I was off.

I couldn't shake that gloomy feeling. Even after we had
threaded our way through Barnwell to the river, even after
we had reached Riverside. Even after we had settled ourselves down on a friendly patch of grass where the river
laps the edge of Stourbridge Common, in the swishing
shelter of a young willow tree, to eat lunch, I still felt as if
bad news hovered somewhere near. As if the scatterings of

yellow leaves on the rough surface of the river might tell a sordid story.

As if I should be vigilant.

"Relax, Laura," Helen urged. She dug into her food. I unpacked my Greek salad and checked the scene one more time. Stourbridge Common stretched away from the river, open, innocent, and mostly empty. Ten yards behind us, the playground with its rough-hewn equipment; then off to our right, the breadth of the common, only partially tamed by the efforts of the council, sweeping out toward its distant fringe of trees. And, farther along the river, the cast-iron footbridge that carries pedestrians and cyclists to Chesterton.

For a lunch hour it was quiet. In the whole panorama there weren't more than half a dozen people in view. On the riverbank opposite us, a man wearing deck shoes hosed down a trim little boat. Another cycled along a diagonal path that crisscrossed the common, and veered off toward the woods, a carrier bag flapping stoutly from his handlebars. His fisherman's hat was firmly pulled down against the breeze. In the playground, an infant broke free of her stroller and made a dash for the fireman's pole; her plump young mother scrambled along behind. Two schoolchildren at the far end of the common tested the wind with a cheap plastic kite. It all looked normal; but an apprehension had been triggered in me, and I couldn't let it go.

"I saw you studying the newspapers, Laura—even, I noticed, the tabloids. What gives?"

"A long shot," I said. "Just trying to get a grip on issues of children and violence. What they do. Why they do it." I shrugged. "I looked through the scientific findings last week, but they didn't get me very far. Thought I'd just

skim the news, catch up with recent cases—see if they gave
me any ideas."

"And did they?"

"Too many. None of them pretty. I get cold in my bones
when I read these stories. Children kicking, beating, stab-
bing, shooting. For money. Or sex. Out of hatred, or boredom. Or just because they want to do what they want to
do—won't let anyone stand in their way. Gives me the
shivers," I admitted.

"But why?" Helen asked. That girl is so damn rational
sometimes. "Why so distressed? Is it really worse being
kicked to death if the attackers are celebrating their fif-
teenth birthday rather than their fiftieth? If you ask me,
dead is dead."

I laughed. "Can't argue with that." The historian in me
surfaced for a dangerous moment. "If you really want to
tease me, you could see me as a victim of twentieth century
ideas about childhood. Pure little children—unthinkable
that a child would murder."

"What's wrong with that?"

"Only that any decent inhabitant of sixteenth century England would have thought me mad. In those days, children
were expected to pull their weight when it came to work.
They weren't sheltered from sexuality; in fact, they were often
exposed to coarse jokes. But above all, they weren't considered innocent. The whole idea of childhood innocence—
babies born without stain and all that—developed later."

"So," Helen said, making the link I hadn't yet mentioned,
"you reckon that your average Tudor had a stronger sense
of children as people—the good, the bad, and the indifferent? And that a murder—let's say, for the sake of ar-
gument, of a woman by her foster son?"—she grinned
cheekily at me—"would anger people, but it wouldn't be

so unexpected? Wouldn't seem like the world turned up-
side down?"

"Could be." I grinned back.

"And today?" Helen asked. "Look, Laura, you've been
wallowing in tabloid tales of teens gone mad. But that's
only one side of the picture. What about all the accounts of
child abuse? Of pedophiles who prey on innocent kids?
Could be," she said, echoing my words, "that we're on a
point of decision today. Unable to make up our minds
whether children are victims or villains."

No wonder I felt confused.

It was dark for midday. I searched the sky for signs of
rain. The playground was deserted now. The man with the
deck shoes had stopped watering his boat and disappeared
indoors. Only the kiddies with the kite remained. The
breeze was catching their little red diamond, pushing it
puff by puff toward the most distant corner of the common.

Helen put historical speculation behind her. Sounded a
more commonsense note. "That's the trouble with reading
the crime news, Laura. You can easily get the wrong idea.
That when kids are not downing drugs or joyriding,
they're doing people in. But what proportion of kids get
involved in really nasty scenes? Laura, are you listening?"

"Sorry, Helen." I dragged my eyes away from the scene
on the common, away from the children's efforts to keep
their kite aloft. "You're right. Crime reports in the papers
are poor preparation for a peaceful lunch. But those children bother me."

Helen followed my gaze. Studied them for a moment—
the boy's shiny shell suit trousers, the girl's thin bare
legs—before reminding me that detective work doesn't
give me a license to spy on truants. "None of our business," she said.

To hell with truancy. It wasn't truancy that sent prickles

down my spine. What disturbed me was the man whose presence I could just make out in the shadow of the trees.

Helen continued, her unstoppable logic undercutting the insecurities peddled by the press. "Aren't most of the kids we know more interested in music and clothes and whether Liverpool will take the cup than they are in violence? When we talk violence, we're talking something rare, aren't we?"

"No!" I shouted, rising to my feet as a loud crack sounded in the distance. Abandoned by its owners, the red plastic kite had arrowed to the ground. It quivered, tip embedded in the earth, for half a second, and then toppled over.

"What now?" Helen asked, seeing the alarm on my face.

The girl and boy who minutes before had leaned backward, using the weight of their small bodies to counter the pull of the kite, were racing in our direction as fast as their legs could carry them. The girl gripped the boy's arm, urging him on. Helen swung in the direction of their footsteps.

I didn't dare stay to help them. Already my man had slithered out of the woods. Already he was cycling smoothly away, as if nothing had happened. Already he was halfway to the footbridge.

I pointed at the children. Now that they were closer, you could make out the panic on their faces. "Speak to them, Helen," I called over my shoulder. "Check that they're all right." And I set off at a run toward the footbridge.

It isn't easy to go from a position on the ground, knees drawn up, to a full-scale run, and it's sure as hell not recommended for those who want to carry their tendons and joints intact into middle age. But I had no choice. If this was the flasher who had been eluding the local police for four years now—the Apeman who had taken the shine off Ginny's first term at secondary school—then I had to catch the bastard. I'd let a hot bath, a masseuse, an osteo-path, deal with the consequences later.

His pace was leisurely, dignified, as close as a cyclist could come to ambling—the perfect cover for the prac-ticed pervert. People look askance at a man running away; they smile and tip their hats to the one with the relaxed, unhurried pace.

Maybe he would have pushed himself just a bit harder to escape if he'd realized that Helen and I had been damp-ening our bums on the grass behind the willow tree. It's all academic—he had spotted me now. Guessed—from what I was wearing, probably, or from my focused expression—that I wasn't just a casual jogger. Cottoned to my inten-tion. Realized his danger.

Suddenly he bent low over the handlebars and pedaled like a hot favorite in the homestretch of the Tour de France. *"Allez!"* I exclaimed to myself, and stepped up my pace.

We were equidistant now from the bank of the river, coming at the footbridge from opposing angles. The end of the bridge was only ten yards, nine yards, eight yards, away, and though he was ahead of me, I stood a good chance. At each end of the footbridge were metal obstacles, designed to force cyclists to dismount. He would have to slack his speed—to stop—to jump off his bike and ma-neuver it through the posts. I'd get him when he did.

Breathing like a walrus now, I gulped in air for one last push. He raced up to the bridge. The brakes on the old bike squealed as he swung his leg off, slipped through the posts, and snatched the bicycle through the now-open gate. Mounted again just as I reached the end of the ramp. I was on his tail across the bridge. My fingers grazed his rear mudguard and came away dirty.

But there was another gate at the Chesterton end. I

should have had him then, should have gained the two seconds I needed, should have cornered him as he climbed back onto his bike. Should have thrown him to the ground. Should have tugged off his slouchy fisherman's hat, exposed his face to the world. Should have opened his carrier bag, found inside it a cheap Halloween mask, his emblem of shame.

But I didn't. The gate at the far end was jammed open; it pointed uselessly, helplessly, toward the road.

The cyclist didn't need to dismount. Didn't need even to slow up. With a steadiness that infuriated me, he swung through the narrow opening on his battered black bike, veered to the left, and just as I hit the end of the bridge, he streaked out of sight along Ferry Path.

I GLANCED LONGINGLY in the direction that he'd gone. I had a little wind left in me and a lot of motivation, but I knew in my heart of hearts that I hadn't a hope in hell of overtaking Apeman now.

My hot pursuit cooled when I heard someone calling.

"Laura Pritchard! Over here!" Not my name, exactly, but near enough to capture my attention.

Immediately opposite the footbridge on Water Street was the Green Dragon. Framed by its black timbers and pale salmon walls, Emma Caudwell (neighbor to Geraldine King—but not friend) waved to me from the open doorway of the pub.

"Just the person I wanted to see," she declared. "Why oh why, when you called 'round the other day, didn't you leave a business card? How can I help when I don't know where to get hold of you? I looked you up in the phone book, but there's no Laura under Pritchard."

"Principal," I said. Not that I thought she'd listen. "Did you see that man? That cyclist?"

"What cyclist?" she asked. "You'll never survive in business without proper advertising. Marketing is your key to success." Her finger waggled in mild reproof. "What are you doing here?" she asked.

"Out for a run." I didn't feel like going into details. "And you?"

"Oh!" Emma looked around, as if suddenly aware of her surroundings. She reddened. "Goodness, you'll think I'm a secret drinker!" she exclaimed. " 'Observed coming out of the Green Dragon at midday.' I expect that's what you'll put in your report."

"Rest easy, Mrs. Caudwell," I said. "I'm not doing a report on you."

"Nicotine," Emma said, naming her poison. "Every day after lunch I slip down to the Green Dragon for a cigarette. The bartender keeps a packet of Silk Cut behind the bar for me. I have just the one. With a double tomato juice. No Worcestershire sauce. And a slice of lemon."

"But why—" I began to ask, and then stopped. Why ask?

Emma had already begun to answer. "You don't imagine, do you, that I would have that terrible smell in my house? On my soft furnishings? I won't let Patrick smoke inside, and I won't do it, either. You wouldn't want your home smelling like an ashtray, Miss Pritchard, would you?"

In fact, though I don't smoke myself, I sometimes take great pleasure from the smell of a fresh cigarette. Sometimes it wafts back to me the happiness of the first few moments as a child when my father returned home from a long distance haul. When he would settle himself into his armchair; when I would bring him his ashtray, and snuggle myself on his knee. I buried my face in his shoulder, in his flannel shirt, and breathed in the smell of father, of man, of safety.

But I wasn't telling her that.

I made my exit line. "You wanted to speak to me, Mrs. Caudwell? I've got a friend waiting on the common. I'm afraid I have to hurry."

That's when she took me by surprise.

"You asked the other day about the relationship between Daryll Flatt and Geraldine King?"

"You've remembered something?"

Trust Emma to take the roundabout route to answer any question. She berated herself for not thinking of it at the time. She explained how it had struck her—*of course*—just before she went to bed that night. How she had been watching a video, something she'd recorded off the BBC the night before.

"I never rent videos, do you? Dirt on the heads. Just an extra thing to clean, I tell Patrick." She smiled at me. In spite of her quirks, it was a good-hearted smile. "And then I remembered," she said.

"Remembered?" I glanced back across the Cam, but could not see a trace of Helen and the children.

"The video film. Daryll and Geraldine."

That got my attention. "Together?" I asked. "In the same frame?"

"Together," Emma confirmed. "That's what I'm telling you. Pop along to my house and you can see for yourself."

My eyes swept the common again. "Give me five minutes," I begged. "You go on home. I'll be there soon."

On Stourbridge Common all that remained of Helen and the kite flyers was an abandoned paper napkin with a swipe of egg mayonnaise. I know how Helen operates; I'd wager the price of another baguette that she had escorted the children home. And from there, if she noticed the time, she would probably make her own way back to work. But in case she paused to seek me out, I scribbled a message as best I could alongside the smear of egg mayonnaise and secured the napkin under a rock beneath the willow tree.

Gone to the movies, it said.

Chapter 12

THE BACK OF Emma Caudwell's house was as tickety-boo as the parts I'd seen before: clematis under control, fish knocker gleaming, and door propped open against my arrival. Emma's voice trickled through from the sitting room, urging me to enter.

"I have it here!" She brandished a videotape, insisted I hold it, as if something was to be learned by inspecting its unremarkable surface. On the spine of the box was a Letraset number, a solitary 1. No other markings.

"It's the first film Patrick made," she said. The first? I hoped she didn't intend this screening to stretch to the entire oeuvre.

Emma occupied one end of a pale blue sofa and patted the seat beside her. "He brought the camera home one Saturday, and from then on there was no stopping him. Film, film, film. The girls. And anything else that moved. Even filmed fifteen minutes of me gardening," she said coquettishly. "But I won't force you to sit through that."

I felt a surge of genuine gratitude. Somebody up there likes me.

"Then he went next door and filmed the neighbors." Emma straightened her arm and aimed the remote control at the television as if it were an exploding device to be kept at the greatest distance possible from the chest. "Just you watch."

I watched, but that didn't mean I could see. In the background of the image was a window, blazing with light. The rest of the picture was uncomfortably dark, with the people in the foreground visible only in silhouette. Patrick Caudwell's development as a photographer had a long way to go. Then, with a swoop that disclosed a pair of leather loafers and took in a long stretch of empty wall, the camera altered its angle and the picture was clear.

There, on a patterned carpet, in the middle of a sitting room, was a square board. There were two stacks of cards in the center and a border of smaller rectangles imprinted around the outer edge. A boy lay to one side of the board, with several small piles of paper lined up neatly to his right. A man echoed his position on the opposite side. Daryll Flatt and Kelsey McLeod were playing Monopoly.

"They're playing Monopoly," Emma explained.

I moved closer to the screen, knelt on the carpet near the television monitor, so I could scan every gesture, every nuance. Daryll seemed oblivious to the camera. He picked up the dice from a corner of the board, blew on them as if for luck, and shook them strenuously. When he released them, it was with a dramatic gesture that sent the dice rolling toward Kelsey, stopping just short of the edge of the board. "Ten!" Daryll declared triumphantly. (On the video soundtrack it sounded like *Den!*) "Doubles!" Then, with a grin that made his freckles dance, he stretched across the board and counted out the move, slowly and deliberately (*one ... two ... three ...*) until his counter came to rest on Free Parking.

An excited muttering passed between boy and man— something about hotels on Park Lane and you're-done-for-now. McLeod clutched his head in a parody of despair:

Wall Street financiers in the crash of '29 must have looked a little like this. McLeod's long arm snaked across to snatch an unearned fistful of pound notes; Daryll intercepted him, easily, and the grin of delight on his face was an image of pure pleasure, the kind only children can achieve, and then only when they are lost in the moment.

From somewhere nearby the microphone picked up a rattle of china. The camera swerved. Patrick Caudwell had a steady hand, but his technique for moving the lens left a lot to be desired. Feet—the window—the corner of a chair— a tray with biscuits and cups of tea—galloped across the screen.

And at last the camera rested on a woman who proffered the contents of a tea tray in Daryll's direction. Showed her face in close-up. It was Geraldine King, sure enough— sixty-two and soft all over. And smiling. A vulnerable smile—a smile of longing—as if she were trying with her coral-tinted lips to bind Daryll to her. You could almost feel the tendrils of affection reaching out, twining gently around their target, cosseting, cushioning.

"Daryll?" she said. Little more than a whisper.

And still the camera remained fixed in close-up on her face. I could see her need—indeed, it was almost palpable— and I could see her eyes and her smile, but not what I wanted to see, which was Daryll's response.

But it was only a matter of seconds until I did. Caudwell, the amateur cameraman, focused once again on the players. On Daryll, to be precise, who had shifted his body so he faced away from her, away from the camera. He played as if there were no one but himself and McLeod in the room. He seemed completely indifferent to Geraldine's presence.

"Daryll!" A full-blooded whisper now, downy and clear.

McLeod's voice—accepting biscuits, issuing an apologetic thanks—ran as a backdrop to the solid image of Daryll's indifference. To his continued rejection of Geraldine's offerings—the biscuits, the tea, the affection. The boy's indifference bulged in each vertebra of his stiff, stiff back. Showed in the line of his profile, like a Florentine death mask, unresponsive, cold.

Then, under urging from McLeod, Daryll turned to face Geraldine and the camera. Retrieved a biscuit, and a drink from the tray. Said, with a disciplined voice, *Thank you, Mrs. King.* Did it all in a perfectly modulated way, correct and cool, his childish face showing no emotion that I could read.

Then McLeod shook the dice and moved his piece to Bond Street. He and Daryll laughed uproariously at the change in fortune.

What a game! exclaimed the voice of Patrick Caudwell.

A game, yes. But who was playing what?

I STOPPED BY Helen's house in the early evening. Before the door was fully open, we both launched into questions. A duet of *Did you?*s, uttered in unison, dissolved into laughter.

We agreed to drop the doorstep quiz. To sit down and share a bottle of beer.

"Did you catch him?" Helen began again, glass in hand.

I told her how what might have been an exhilarating chase—should have been, if only the gate hadn't jammed, if only I'd been a few seconds faster—turned out to be frustrating and fruitless.

Helen recounted her conversation with the kite flyers after they had fled from the Apeman. *Are you all right?* she had asked, in her most motherly tones. And was greeted with such snuffling and muffled distress that she'd insisted upon accompanying the children to their home.

"I knew you would," I said smugly.

"Anyone would," Helen retorted.

Not so.

The mother had responded to her children's story of a gorilla and his willy with equal measures of alarm, relief for their safety, and suspicion. The suspicion was directed at Helen, who made an excuse and left. The mother had no intention, Helen told me, of reporting the incident to the police: in her view, bygones were bygones and well enough was best left alone.

"And what about you?" Helen asked. "How did you know what that cyclist had been up to? You were off in hot pursuit before I'd even begun to suspect that the Apeman was in the area."

"Didn't know," I admitted. My reputation for infallibility, dashed in one go. "But I kept trying to think of reasons why a man would ride a bicycle into that clump of trees. Near those children. And I couldn't think of any good ones."

Speaking of good ones, I wondered where Ginny had gone to. Upstairs, Helen said. Tucked away in her room.

"Alone?" I asked. "Without her sidekick, Karen?"

Ginny had been alone a lot lately, Helen explained. She'd been quieter than usual. Even restrained. There had been less of the familiar clamor to be out and about. There'd been no quarrels with Helen about fanciful projects—no pleas to accompany friends on out-of-the-question camping trips, or to join midnight boating parties on the Cam. There had been none of the reckless enthusiasm that marked the preceding months, none of the groans about homework, none of the fits of giggles, none of the declarations of war that had become part of the complex pattern of Ginny's first year at secondary school.

"It's worrying," Helen said. "She's become a model

daughter. Comes in, goes straight to her room, does her homework, goes to sleep early. It's like something has shut down."

Like Ginny had decided already—at eleven going on twelve—that maybe the world out there was too scary for her to handle.

"Does it have to do with the flasher?"

Helen nodded. "What else? Have you spoken to Nicole?"

Days had gone by since Helen first told me about the flasher, since I had asked Nicole to look into it, and I'd been so focused on Daryll Flatt that I hadn't followed it up. Tomorrow, I promised Helen, with a stab of guilt.

But when I called the station later that evening and asked for the detective inspector, it became clear my promise wasn't worth a penny. Inspector Pelletier had gone to Birmingham to interview some suspects in a burglary case; my inquiry would just have to wait.

Missing the Apeman. Then missing Nicole. Two in one day.

Didn't make me feel good.

And Sonny was out in the wilds of Norfolk somewhere, hiding behind hedges, refusing to answer his mobile phone. Only one thing to do.

I ran the bath with water more hot than warm, to within three inches of the overflow. Added bath oil at an early point in the proceedings, and swished it about with a whisk. By the time the bath was fully run, it looked and smelled like a gigantic vanilla milk shake. Fetched the special bottle that Stevie had brought back for me from her last trip to the Highlands, poured myself a finger-width of single malt whiskey and set it beside the tub. Then I eased myself into the suds and lay back with my head resting on a soft towel and my eyes closed. For a full minute I heard nothing but the soft wet sound of tiny bubbles popping. Saw nothing but the shifting image of my own blood vessels on the inside of my eyelids. Felt nothing but the lapping of the bath waves as I breathed peacefully. In and out. In and out. In and out.

And then another, more poignant scene began to play behind my shuttered eyes. Of a board game, in a quiet suburban home. Of two people, a boy and a man, in happy competition. Playful, intense; loving not the winning but the skirmish. The boy's face in close-up—mischievous, thoroughly engaged. The man, hamming it up, pretending to mind when his young companion took Free Parking. Locked into the excitement of the game. They were a pair, those two—Daryll Flatt and Kelsey McLeod. And Daryll Flatt seemed to have so much eagerness in him, so much warmth and enthusiasm and capacity for joy—how could such a boy change into the cruel, murderous, hate-filled (surely hate-filled) person who had murdered Geraldine King?

And yet, she had been murdered. Her tremulous smile, her offerings of affection, had been met with a hail of stones. With a lump of concrete. With death.

Interrupted by an insistent pulse, I wiped my hand across a towel and snatched up the telephone. It was Sonny. I told him all about the Apeman and all about the video.

"It's as if I were looking at two different children, Sonny. The boy who played Monopoly with such gusto didn't seem like a boy who could kill anyone at all. It's almost impossible to imagine that that child could have murdered Mrs. King. Makes me want to shout, 'He couldn't have done it. There must be some mistake.' "

"And the other?"

"The other Daryll—the one who looked at Geraldine with that cold, flat stare. As if she wasn't his foster mum.

As if she were scarcely human. That boy—I wouldn't put anything past him."

Sonny refused to be drawn into this speculation. Good twin/bad twin is not a story line he likes. His reaction to the video was direct and constructive.

"You don't know her," he said.

"Come again?"

"Mrs. King. You don't know her. Oh, you know she's a widow and a long way from a feminist; you know she was determined to have Daryll for her own; but her background, her other relationships, how she got to where she is—"

"You mean dead?" I interrupted.

"That, too," he said. "Look, Laura. Whether you're searching for the why of Geraldine's death—assuming still that Daryll killed her—or whether you've begun to think that someone else might have had a hand in Geraldine's death, either way what you need is clear."

"So tell me!"

"You need more information about Geraldine: who she was, who she rubbed up the wrong way, and why. So," he prodded, "over to you, maestro. What are you going to do next?"

I had already worked it out. "Never let it be said," I said, loosening up at last, "that Laura Principal is afraid to turn her inquiring mind to royalty."

"Meaning?"

I drained the final amber drop of whiskey.

"Meaning, it's time to tackle the Kings."

Chapter 13

KING, IN SPITE of its regal provenance, is a far from exclusive name. In the Cambridge area telephone directory there are no fewer than twenty-three entries with the surname King and the initial E. Still, it wasn't difficult to find my man; Edward, son of Geraldine and Stanley, was the only candidate in Papworth Everard.

He spoke with a faint lisp, which weighed in his favor, and an abrupt manner, which didn't. Yes, (*yeth*), I was disturbing him; what did I want? No, he hadn't time to talk. No, he didn't wish to answer questions about his mother.

About, as he called her, The Deceased.

"I'm a bithy man," Edward concluded grumpily.

Now, I'm not someone who believes that every time I dial a telephone number, the person on the other end of the line is obliged to respond. I'm not moved to indignation when my calls are met by an answering machine. I don't expect my friends to account—even less, to apologize—for occasions when a call to them couldn't get through.

But telephone tolerance has its limits. The phrase *I'm a busy man* makes me bristle. We're all busy: to fend off a caller by declaring yourself so is irrelevant, and arrogant to boot. I'm far more impressed by the simple rebuff: "I don't want to talk to you."

"I don't want to talk to you," Edward King added. He was trickier than I'd expected.

Outright rejection can be difficult to circumvent even for private investigators, who are—by occupational definition as well as training—thick-skinned. But Edward King couldn't resist doing verbal battle with me, and that was his downfall. Our skirmish ended with an agreement from him to entertain my questions the following morning, at his market stall, in Cambridge.

Cambridge Market is in many ways the center of the city, its hundred or so stalls towered over by Great St. Mary's Church on one side and the blanked-out windows of Marks & Spencer on the other. King's Hardbacks occupies a double stall near the telephone kiosks. I had spent many a happy moment there in the past, leaning against a piece of scaffolding to scan the opening paragraphs of a trumpeter's memoirs or a volume on the design of Venetian bridges. Though shopping is not my thing, I make exceptions. Delicatessens escape the general prohibition, as do shops selling quality chocolates; and any time spent browsing for books I place under the heading of research.

So it turned out that I had seen Edward King in the past. I recalled him now as a man who looked cold in face and body, as if the waxed green jacket failed to protect his gaunt frame from the Cambridge winds. When he spoke, it was with a sour restraint; if King possessed any warmth, he kept it to himself.

As I approached the market, pacing down the central aisle from the direction of the Guildhall, I spotted Edward King sorting through a box of books. He set them to rest deliberately on their opening edges, so that—like a row of runners bending over the starting block—their spines were exposed to public gaze. His face and lips had the bleached hue of someone who reads too late and laughs too little. But as he leaned forward, a shaft of morning sunlight touched his head, and his chestnut hair gleamed red. That was the only vivid thing about him, his red hair, as if it had soaked up all the brightness of his person.

I introduced myself. King glanced at me sideways, then returned his gaze to the books he was aligning. "Don't expect me to go all soft on you," he muttered, "just because she's dead. I don't believe in rewriting history the minute someone pops it." His tone was less abrupt than on the telephone, and more sardonic. Face-to-face, the lisp was barely audible.

"You and your mother had had a serious disagreement, I gather?"

"You could say that," Edward said slyly. While we spoke, he kept his eye on two students who were laughing over a volume of cartoons from *Private Eye*. I thought that the matron who was flicking through the vegetarian cookery books looked dodgier, but refrained from telling him his business.

"What was the quarrel about?"

"I don't mind who knows," Edward replied. "It started with my father, Stanley King. A man of strong opinions. One such opinion concerned my future as an accountant. When I had to give up my training after two years . . ." He dragged his eyes away from the students and focused them on me. "Have you ever studied accountancy, Miss Principal? Or bookkeeping?"

"Checking till receipts is the closest I've come."

"When I couldn't stick it out, Father more or less disowned me. I asked him to lend me the capital to start a bookshop. He had that much in the building society easily, but he refused. Didn't care to know whether it would be a good investment, let alone whether it might be what I wanted." Edward hefted another carton of books, slammed it down on the planks. "And I wanted it, Miss Principal, make no mistake. To run a bookshop is the only thing I've ever felt passionate about. But my father rejected the idea out of hand. He ordered me out of the house until I came to my senses."

"Your father sounds an uncompromising man," I said. And I felt a stab of sadness for Edward King, who had nothing other than a shop to feel passionate about.

He shot me a glance tinged with suspicion. But when he had satisfied himself that I wasn't making fun, he relented. "Father said bookselling was a hobby, not a business, and none of his hard-earned savings was going into it. And, to make certain he had his way, I was disinherited. He wrote me out of his will. Everything to Mother, not a penny to me."

"And how many pennies were there?"

"More than you'd think. The old man was mean. Didn't take vacations, hardly ever went out. Salted away a small fortune. Two hundred thousand pounds, if you count the house."

Not in George Soros's league. But it would make a difference to someone with debts piling up. Or, for that matter, someone who wanted to open a bookstore.

"And your mother? She didn't side with you?"

"My mother never took my side," he spat out. "Never once. If Father said, 'Send the boy to his room,' she did. If he slapped me, she told me not to whimper. And when he disinherited me, all she could say was 'Why didn't you do what he asked you, Eddie?' She was his puppet," he concluded. "No mind of her own."

The matron had departed, with a swish of her shopping bag, and the students had moved on to a hat stall down the way. There were no other customers at the moment. Just as well. With Edward King so absorbed in his family drama, I doubt whether he would have noticed them cart his volumes away by the truckload.

"I went to the funeral, you know," he said, out of the blue.

"Your mother's funeral?"

He shook his head. "I'm talking about Father's. I couldn't believe he was dead. He always seemed so—invulnerable. I went. To check, I suppose, that he really was gone."

"And? Did you speak to your mother there?"

"Oh, yes, I spoke to her. She started up again. Blamed me for upsetting Father. And when I tried to defend myself, she told me not to speak ill of the dead." He removed his gloves and looked at his long thin fingers. They were blanched with cold. Rubbed them ineffectually on his trousers, and put the gloves back on again. "Never went back to see her again."

"Mr. King, what happened to the family money after your mother died? Did you inherit then?"

A pale cold smile crossed his features. "I certainly did," he said with triumph. "I certainly did. Half to Aunt Faith. And the other half to me. I have a shop now in Biggleswade, as well as this stall. Doing very nicely, thank you."

"So your mother's death was convenient for you? Nothing more?"

"What do you expect me to say? That I miss her dreadfully, when I hadn't seen her for a year before her death? Or that I'm sorry I inherited her money? I may be many things, Miss Principal, but I'm not a hypocrite." He looked pleased with himself, in his own sour way. "Anything else? I've got a business to see to."

I asked him how I could contact his aunt Faith, and was rewarded with an address in Cromer, on the Norfolk coast. Then my curiosity got the better of me.

"One more thing," I said. "Have you still got a copy of *Cordon Vert*? Gourmet vegetarian menus?"

"Just over here," he said, and his obvious pleasure and pride at being able to answer in the affirmative underlined his point about passion; he did indeed care deeply about the book trade.

But hard as he looked among the vegetarian cookery books, he couldn't seem to find it.

"Never mind." I shrugged. "Easy come, easy go."

THE WIND WHIPPED up during the drive to Norfolk, sending great smoky clouds scudding across the sky. When I stepped out of the car in Cromer, I reached for my jacket. The temperature appeared to have plummeted in the past two hours.

The home belonging to Faith and William Holtby was nearly identical to others in the terrace, except for a poster in the front window that advertised a choral performance of Britten's *Peter Grimes*. Faith, her husband informed me, with considerable amusement and less discretion, was a member of the local operatic society—never missed a Thursday afternoon rehearsal.

Not their most tuneful singer, he chortled, but one of their keenest.

I added him to my private collection of people who are curiously willing to disclose things about others—and, in passing, about themselves—to strangers. It's a human quality that works consistently to the advantage of certain occupations—not only the obvious ones like market researchers, pollsters, and reporters, but also the less visible types such as palmists and society gossips, estate agents, auditors, or diplomats. And, yes, it has to be allowed, private investigators. Someday I would face up to the ethical implications of being included among that unsavory crew. But for now, I had William Holtby to attend to.

Holtby had a wide, amiable-looking mouth and pendulous earlobes. He'd been a P.E. teacher before retirement. His profession had been chosen, apparently, because it provided a way of pursuing an interest in games after the condition of his knees had restricted his performance as a player. Like his wife, perhaps—not talented but keen.

He seemed pleased to see me, but had little to say about Geraldine King. "That's Faith's department," he insisted, and wouldn't be budged. William stepped out onto the doorstep to point the route to the seafront where Faith was walking. "An hour every day," he said, shaking his head, as if walking was a mysterious female ritual.

Holtby's slippers testified to a man who had no intention of taking the salty Cromer air. He did invite me to come in and wait, but something in his expression told me I wouldn't be comfortable; the sound of the television issuing from the sitting room was, anyway, far less inviting than the cries of the seabirds that echoed from the direction Faith had taken.

"How will I recognize her?" I asked. Even on an overcast day, Faith wouldn't be the only person on the front.

"Just look for a woman who's plain as a stick and past her prime," he insisted, "with a copy of the *Daily Mail* under her arm." He chortled at his own joke. I didn't.

I tramped along the seafront, gloveless hands buried in my jacket pockets. Faith was the third person I encountered, and the first who was encumbered by a *Mail*. She stepped along vigorously, her white hair whipped by the wind. Faith's prime, I reckoned, must have been something to see.

She started at my approach, but after I had introduced myself and outlined my business, she allowed me to fall into step with her. When I explained how I'd located her, she asked, sharply, "And what did Bill have to say about my sister?"

"Nothing. He referred me to you. Said Geraldine was your department."

Faith seemed to find that satisfactory. "I have no objection to talking," she said. "Never a day goes by that I don't think about her, you know. The good and the bad. Talking helps to keep her alive in my memory."

"Did you and Geraldine grow up in this area?"

Faith painted a somber picture of childhood in rural Norfolk. Of a village where winters were dominated by mud and wind and isolation. Of fen women whose long shifts at the vegetable packing shed, sorting carrots in the bitter cold, were valued as much for the measure of companionship they provided as for the income. Of summers when children like Faith and Geraldine could roam free— a freedom tarnished by the fact that there was, in truth, nowhere to go and, when you got there, nothing to do. Of two sisters whose adolescence was dominated by the desire to escape. Who did move on to bigger towns—Faith to Cromer, where she worked in a hotel, and, much later, married Bill; and Geraldine to Cambridge, with Stanley.

"Geraldine often talked of moving back to Norfolk, you know. To Cromer, so we could be neighbors."

"She never tried to make the move?"

Faith smiled a rueful smile. William Holtby was quite wrong about his wife. Faith's style was not the compliantly feminine image that Geraldine had presented, but she was far from plain. Faith had the same alabaster skin as her sister, the same abundant hair; but she was more angular and more assertive in her physical stance. She seemed to me altogether a more confident, and maybe more abrasive, person. If Geraldine was the lamb, Faith might be the bright-eyed collie that returns the flock to the fold.

"Stanley wouldn't hear of it," she explained. "He was a difficult man. Never believed in compromise, always laid down the law. He was Cambridgeshire all the way. And when he was gone—well, Geraldine would never dare do such a thing on her own."

We had reached the point on the return journey where the road turned abruptly inland. "Do you feel up to a few more minutes by the sea?" I asked, in spite of the chill in my fingers. I wasn't content just yet to retreat to the house where William Holtby hunkered over Eurosport.

In reply, Faith scrambled down the embankment and set a course straight across the beach. She stopped just short of the water, where the sea's broad tongue licked the pebbles, and stood facing outward.

I spied a perfect pebble—a small brown triangle twice the size of a guitar pick and nearly as smooth. I clutched it firmly between my thumb and forefinger, positioned myself as I'd seen others do, and flicked it out to sea. My perfect pebble sliced the surface of the water and sank without a trace, its chance of glory lost forever.

"My sister was a foolish girl, you know," Faith said, not remarking any more directly than this on my failure. "And perhaps a foolish woman. But it wasn't entirely her fault. No one ever allowed her to be anything more." She looked at me, saw in the set of my jaw how very cold I was. Took off her own scarf and wrapped it around my neck.

"Where we lived as children," Faith continued, brushing aside my protest, "the sides of the lanes were choked in late summer by blackberries. And I would always wear an apron, and take as many bucketsful as possible home to mother. But Geraldine used to laugh and stuff great handfuls of berries into her mouth, like someone at an orgy, until the juice ran down the front of her dress. If it had been me, I would have got a hiding. But not Geraldine. 'Father,' she exclaimed, 'they were delicious!' And he just laughed, and swooped her up onto his knee, stains and all. That's how she was. She always knew how to please men."

"And you?"

Faith bent her knees, lowering herself to the beach, and swept her palm over the stones. She chose one and examined it. It looked rougher and less promising than mine had. She straightened up, fixed her eye on a point ten feet out to sea, and flicked her slim wrist. Plip, went the pebble. And plip, plip, plip. Three leaps, three landings, before it dived triumphantly under the gray surface of the water.

"Geraldine had the looks and the charm. I was the older sister. Expected to look after myself. And, much of the time, to care for her, too."

The one who was never allowed to be frivolous, never excused for her follies. "You must have resented that sometimes," I suggested, watching Faith's immaculate profile. She was still looking out to sea, watching, as if she could discern the dark places where the halibut slid along the bottom. But she answered with the poise of a politician. "Geraldine was silly as a child. As an adult, she could often be infuriating. But she was still my little sister. And," she avowed, with an authenticity of passion that politicians rarely muster, "I didn't want her dead."

Goes without saying. Or so I would have thought.

"I understand that you two sisters met regularly in Cambridge?"

"It was a kind of tradition. The second Tuesday of every month. Geraldine always met me in the Arts Theatre Restaurant—or, while the renovation work was on, in

Henry's—for lunch. We used to share a meal, get down to the serious business of shopping, and finally finish up with tea."

"So you had your usual expedition the day before Geraldine was killed?"

"Let's walk," Faith said abruptly, and set out at a swinging pace across the beach. When I caught up with her a couple of seconds later, she carried on speaking as if there had been no interruption. "Briefer than usual," she replied. "You see, we quarreled that day over lunch. We decided— on both sides—to cut our meeting short." Faith was smiling, but her eyes scanned my face for a reaction.

"Quarreled about what?"

"It's private," Faith said firmly. "I would rather not say."

I digested this information in silence for a moment, listening, instead of talking, to the scrunch of our shoes on the pebbles. Caught the glint of a piece of beach glass, apple-green with frosted surfaces, and put it in my pocket for Dominic, Sonny's oldest boy. He has a collection.

"All right," I said. "But you were one of the last people to see Geraldine"—to a relative, you need never add the word *alive*—"and there are some things about that meeting that you must have gone over in your mind since then."

"Can you be more specific?" Faith asked.

"I can. First, you must have learned—at the trial maybe or from the police—that Geraldine rang her lawyer on the day she was killed and demanded an urgent appointment. Do you have any idea why she wanted to make a sudden visit to a solicitor, so quickly after seeing you?" Faith looked blank. "Did she express any concern about money, or—perhaps—about a will?" Still vacant. Composed. "You were due to inherit from her estate, weren't you?"

Not merely defensive now. Downright cool. "Yes. According to Geraldine's will, my nephew—her son, Edward—

inherited half the value of her estate at the time of her death, and I inherited the rest. Before you ask, let me tell you— it's no secret—that my share, after death duties, came to over £100,000."

"Your share would have been even larger, wouldn't it, had not almost forty thousand pounds of Geraldine's money gone missing in the months prior to her death? Have you any idea what happened to that money? Did Geraldine ever mention anything about it?"

"Not a word," Faith said. "But there's little doubt where it went, is there? Daryll Flatt took it. Geraldine brought it home, perhaps tucked it away in a drawer somewhere—I told you she could be foolish—and he waited for his chance and took it. Perhaps he gave it to that awful family of his. Or buried it somewhere. Who knows?"

We had reached the Holtbys' front door. Faith rang the bell. William opened it, his amiable grin still in place, a bottle of pale ale in his hand. Faith's smile softened her whole demeanor. "Here's your paper, love," she said, leaning over him where he had reseated himself in front of the telly, landing a kiss on his forehead. He grunted a reply.

I walked to the mantelpiece and picked up a photograph of a young bride and groom. Her sister's wedding photo, Faith confirmed.

"She was exceptionally pretty," I remarked, noting the sweep of her hair.

"Pretty?" Faith pondered, as if it were a new idea to her. "Would you say Geraldine was pretty, Bill?"

Bill didn't take his eyes off the telly. "Suppose so. She wasn't what you'd call a deep thinker," he snorted, turning his head toward me, as if this was information that I required.

"We can't all be Einsteins," I replied.

Conversation fell off while Faith hung up her outdoor clothes and put the kettle on for tea. She shepherded me into the kitchen, where we didn't have to compete with the television.

"You didn't think much of Daryll Flatt, then, Mrs. Holtby?"

"You know what it is like up there, in that place where they sent him?" Faith asked, answering and not answering at the same time. "There are tennis courts and televisions. Visitors whenever they like. It's a holiday camp," she concluded, "for killers. I won't say he should hang; those days are over, and probably for the best. But my little sister's dead, my Geraldine, and I don't see why her killer should spend a few years in a place like that and then go free."

Chapter 14

I WORKED MY socks off on Friday morning. Beginning with the notes I'd made after my meeting with Nicole and working forward, I organized all the information on the case. I began with the obvious: converted the scruffiest scribblings into readable typescript, listed outstanding questions, outlined follow-up tasks.

The hardest part of the job—the part that had me reaching for the Tylenol—was rereading the notes I had taken from interviews. Don't be fooled: this isn't reading in the normal sense of the word. You can't whiz through the words on the page; you can't even get by with the diligence, the concentration, that works for, say, instruction manuals. Either of these approaches would miss the point, because the words that describe an interview are the least of an investigator's concerns.

The words are merely cues—important for the memories they trigger rather than the meanings they contain. A smattering of observations from a much richer and more densely packed field. Reading isn't enough: you have to live the encounter over again. To dive back under the surface of the conversation, grasp the nuances and the gestures and the pauses that litter the bottom, and pull them up—along with all their possible meanings—into the clear clean light of day.

The interview itself is peanuts by comparison. It can be done on automatic pilot—knock at the door, switch on all your senses, and target them on the interviewee. The real graft is the work of recovery.

And sometimes, like today, this hard work pays off.

I immersed myself in fragments of conversation. I hovered over my exchange with Janet Flatt, and relived my sense of exposure when Mark Flatt Miller hulked behind me on his mother's doorstep; I recalled Murray Eagleton's quick patter at Social Services and the arrival of the tea trolley at the old folks' home in Ditchburn Place.

And as I worked, one fragment of memory floated to the surface. And lodged itself there.

I locked it in place, where I could get at it again, and went on to complete my weekly report for Howard Flatt just in the nick of time.

AT TWELVE NOON I met Howard in the familiar surroundings of Parker's Bar. He was seated at a table near the windows when I arrived. Beside him, her hands cradling a tumbler of juice, was a woman with a plain round face. She looked mature and childlike at the same time, as if she might have leaped in age from fourteen to twenty, skipping some of the steps in between.

The instant Howard spotted me, he lumbered to his feet and clasped my hand in both of his. "I'd like you to meet Donna," he said proudly. "My fiancée."

The girl at the table turned on me a broad toothy smile that brought her pretty close to beautiful. "Thanks for helping Howard," she said. She had a voice like a Mediterranean breeze, all soft and warm.

Only an idiot could mistake the accent. "You're Australian. Are you planning to stay in England for a while?"

Donna glanced at Howard. "This started out as a holiday," she replied. "But not anymore. Now that we've been reunited with Daryll, I don't see how we can leave without him."

Donna set out shortly after to do some shopping. Howard walked her to the door. As soon as he returned, I handed him my report.

Page one was devoted to the itinerary—who I had seen, and when and where and why. To put it bluntly, where the money went. Two visits to Cambridgeshire Constabulary. Meetings with Social Services in the persons of Murray Eagleton and Kelsey McLeod. Interviews with people who knew Daryll: Janet Flatt and Mark Flatt Miller; Mrs. Joiner, who had taught him; and Emma Caudwell and her husband, who had lived next door. And finally, interviews with individuals who knew Geraldine King—with Becca Hunter, with her son Edward, with her sister, Faith Holtby. The itinerary also itemized six hours of library-based research and two visits to the murder site.

"The tree house is plastered with pictures of Australia," I said when he reached that point in his reading. "Daryll didn't forget your dream."

Howard looked glum.

After that came my summary of what had been learned so far. "The results aren't conclusive," I warned him. "But we're making progress."

Howard reached across the table and returned the report. "Can you tell me the main points?" he said. "I'd rather hear them from you."

And he sat with his large hands folded quietly in his lap while I told him what I'd learned about Daryll's life and character after Howard had left home. I spared him nothing, not even the callousness of his stepfather, with its echoes of the brutality that Howard himself had endured.

I described Daryll's impatience, the difficulties he had

with self-control. When I mentioned Daryll's reaction to the seeds that were grown at school, Howard gave a nod of recognition and a faint smile. No more nods, though, when I mentioned one of the things I had picked up in the library.

"You probably know," I said, "that—statistically speaking—children who suffer neglect or abuse, and children who for one reason or another don't master impulse control, are much more likely to commit violent crimes."

Howard's gaze shifted to the scene outside Parker's Bar. He focused for a moment on a toddler who was being tugged away from the ice cream vendor by her mother. Her green wellies were dug in tenaciously on the muddy side of the path.

"Is that so?" he said. In the mouths of some people, *Is that so?* would indicate distance, or skepticism, a deliberate nonendorsement, a polite way of registering doubt. From Howard, at that moment, the phrase rang with defeat.

Then I told him about the pigeon.

"Daryll?" he exclaimed. His massive head shook slowly in disbelief. "I wouldn't be surprised if you told me that Mark had tormented animals. But Daryll's a completely different sort of boy. You should have seen him—how he used to curl up on my lap in the evenings, like a baby, and stroke my arm. As long as Mark wasn't there to scoff." He gazed out the window for a moment, collecting his thoughts. "But that was five years ago," he admitted. "What could have happened to change him so much?"

I didn't refer to Howard's departure from the family home.

Nor did I refer to my growing uncertainty about Daryll's guilt. Had Daryll changed as much as his conviction—as his confession—seemed to suggest?

I pointed instead to the information that was incomplete, still, about the killing. Where Geraldine went when she left her house on the afternoon of the murder. Why she was distressed when she returned. Why she arranged to see her solicitor. Where the £37,000 had gone that she had withdrawn from the bank. And what, above all, was the secret that Daryll was keeping to himself?

"Didn't the police get anywhere with these questions?" Howard asked.

"They never succeeded in tracing Geraldine's movements on the day she was killed, nor in finding the money. And I only just learned this week, from his former teacher, about Daryll's secret. Speaking of money, by the way, is there anyone in your family who appears to have enjoyed a windfall while you were away?"

Startled, Howard moved into denial—but then stopped abruptly. He didn't speak.

I helped him out. "Yes, I saw Mark's car. He bought it new?"

"That's what took me aback. Mark never was one for saving, and with his record of debt, I'd be surprised if any finance company would touch him. But there's probably some simple explanation."

"Probably," I agreed. "Just like there's probably some simple explanation for the curious relationship between Daryll and his foster mother. Geraldine appeared to be devoted to your little brother. She was regarded as successful in her role. I'm told by the police that Geraldine even penned a letter proposing a more permanent arrangement."

"What, adoption?" Howard asked, clearly surprised. "Mother would never sign the papers. I know she has her faults," he said earnestly, "but whatever else, she loved us." He gave a decisive nod. "Dary was her baby. She'd never let him go."

"That's what Social Services said. But what really interests me is how did Daryll feel?"

"About Mrs. King?"

"Exactly. There's a mismatch there—Geraldine was devoted to Daryll, people tell me; but Daryll himself says that she never cared for him. According to people I've talked to who saw them together—and this is borne out by the video I watched—Daryll kept his distance from Geraldine. Gave no sign of attachment. And this from the boy that you knew to be so affectionate. It doesn't make sense."

"You think it's important?"

"More than important. I've got a feeling, Howard, that this relationship is at the heart of things. That when I understand how Geraldine and Daryll felt about each other, I'll have a grip on why she died."

"Then you're willing to go on?"

"If you want me to. I'd be happy to give it another week. For one thing, I think it might be sensible to have a word with Daryll's doctor. His old doctor, when he still lived at home. Can you remember the name?"

Indeed, he could. Dr. Pryce, from the surgery on Campkin Road. "But he was already an old fellow when I was a teenager," Howard warned. "I doubt if he's still in practice."

"I'll find him. Did he"—I tried to sound casual—"treat the whole family, do you know?"

"Sure," Howard said. "He was Granny Johnson's G.P., and my mum just sort of inherited him."

I had one more thing to settle before we went our separate ways.

"Something more important than Dr. Pryce," I said. "I've reached the point now where I have to speak to Daryll. He's the only one who can tell me the answers to some of these questions. Is it all right with you if I meet him face-to-face?"

"Sure. But it's not up to me," Howard replied. "It all goes through the Social Services. Through Kelsey McLeod. If Kelsey thinks you're an okay person to visit Daryll, your name goes on the list. Simple as that."

I like a man who looks on the bright side.

SPEAK OF THE devil.

I had looked for McLeod in the Social Services office without spotting so much as a hair of his mustache, but as I trotted back toward the Grafton Center after my meeting with Howard, I passed within ten feet of his stationary vehicle. Even for a one-car woman like me, McLeod's VW Beetle was unmistakable.

It was pulled up at an inconvenient angle in the parking lot on Adam and Eve Street. The windows were steamy, but I could just make him out, slouched in the driver's seat as if he were at the wheel of a getaway car. Without pausing to think, I rapped my knuckles on the car window.

I should have looked before I leaped. The head that swiveled toward me belonged to a woman.

She was pale—not the alluring pallor of a fairy-tale princess, but the paleness of neglect. She had lifeless hair that should have been washed yesterday but wasn't. Only her eyes—blue and slightly bulging—gave evidence of vitality.

She stared at me with a curiosity that was frank and unfriendly.

"Sorry," I mouthed through the glass. The window descended. "I thought it was someone else," I explained.

She spoke at last. The voice sounded like it belonged to someone who had been everywhere, done everything, seen it all—and didn't much like any of it. "You thought it was Kelsey, I suppose?"

"I recognized the car," I admitted, "and . . ." My voice trailed off. I had been on the brink of explaining that I knew Kelsey McLeod's wife was chronically ill. That I somehow hadn't expected to find her behind the wheel of a car.

"What do you want?" she asked. It was a hostile question, not an offer of help. Her manner belied the cultural image of the uncomplaining invalid.

I decided to come clean. The situation was awkward enough without additional lies. "I need your husband's permission," I said, with the faintest of question marks over *husband*, "so that I can visit a boy—one of his charges—who is in a secure unit."

She didn't demur over *husband*, but her eyes betrayed the unexpectedness of my remark. "Daryll Flatt?" she asked.

She was surprised, and so was I—but only for an instant. Well, of course Mrs. McLeod would know the names of some of her husband's clients. And the odds are pretty steep against a social worker having more than one juvenile client in a high security unit. I nodded.

Mrs. McLeod responded with relish, each word drawn out as if she were savoring some secret satisfaction. "Well, well, well." Her colorless face took on a calculating quality that made no sense to me. She inclined her head out of the car window and took a moment to inspect me from the toe of my suede boots to the crown of my head.

"Are you a relative?" she asked. "Of Mr. Flatt?" She used *Mister* precisely the way Spider Simpson, the most sadistic teacher at my old grammar school, had used the title *Miss*. No one would mistake it for a term of respect.

"I've been commissioned by Daryll's older brother to produce a report on the case." I kept my reply bland and neutral. This woman seemed like the kind who might enjoy ripping bandages off babies. I didn't want to give her access to Howard's particular pain.

"You're a private eye?"

"Laura Principal. My firm is based in London," I added. Since she made no reply, just stared up at me with that inexplicable touch of insolence, I decided to take a chance. "I don't suppose you've ever met Daryll, have you?"

"Have *you*?" she shot back. Like a game of I'll-answer-if-you-will.

"That's why I need your husband's approval. To get access to the unit where he's held. No, I haven't met him yet. You?"

"My husband has to do it. That's his job. But I'm not in the habit of hanging around with murderers. Even if they are underage."

"But Kelsey was Daryll's social worker even before Daryll was arrested. And from what I've heard, he was quite attached to the lad. Maybe still is."

"He always gives too much," she insisted angrily. As if it were my fault. "To all his clients. Men who choose to drink their lives away. Women who can't look after themselves, let alone their families. Children who don't know the difference between right and wrong. They only have to sneeze, and he's there, working overtime, taking care of them." There was a resentful emphasis to the word *them*— them and not me?

Mrs. McLeod reached around behind the seat, pulled up a nylon rucksack, and rummaged inside it for a cigarette. When she touched the lighter to the tip and drew in deeply, I could hear a rattle, like bronchitis, in her throat. I watched without speaking. And luckily, even the nicotine didn't dampen her wrath.

"Was Daryll special?" I asked at last, when I began to think she had forgotten my presence.

She turned slowly back toward me, blew a long column of smoke in my direction. "You should have seen them," she said. Bitterly, not meeting my eyes. "Sitting on the grass, down by the Pike and Eel. Talking. Hand in bloody hand. You'd think Daryll was *his* child, the way he carried on."

"I thought you'd never met Daryll Flatt, Mrs. McLeod?"

She looked at me blankly, as if she'd forgotten who I was, and then she answered. "Seeing isn't the same as meeting. I was parked nearby."

"You were so close that you could see them? And you didn't say hello?"

She shrugged. "That boy broke his heart," she said. "He was ambitious, my Kelsey, and full of confidence. And that boy took it all."

"What did Daryll do to your husband? I don't understand."

"Do you really want to know?" she asked, and fixed me with her fierce blue gaze. "I'll tell you. And you can tell all those bastards who criticized him for—" She stopped and pulled in a deep breath.

"Anyway," she said, "Kelsey spent more time with that boy than he had with any other client. Not just the usual stuff, half-hour interviews and trips to the dentist. No, anything that Daryll Flatt wanted, Daryll Flatt got. Weekend outings. Soccer practice. Kelsey even took him on a camping trip. It didn't matter that the hallway needed papering, or that I wasn't feeling well—that kid always came first. He wanted the best for him, he said. And when he found that woman—that Geraldine King—he thought he had come up with the perfect arrangement for Daryll.

She would make up for the loss of his grandmother, he said. The brat would flourish."

"And he didn't?"

"Didn't what?" Flashes of anger were breaking through again.

"Didn't flourish?"

"Daryll Flatt killed her. You call that flourishing?" she sneered. "He was trouble from the beginning. Almost cost Kelsey his job. He was blamed, you know. People pointed the finger at him, said that he should have seen it coming, should have arranged psychiatric treatment for the boy. What do they know?"

"And would you say your husband is still upset?"

"Every time he goes to see that kid, he comes back wound up like a watch spring. Tick tick tick. Can't sleep. Can't eat. It's been two years now, and he still can't seem to shake it off."

When she spoke of Kelsey's distress, her aura of grievance receded, replaced by tenderness. So I pushed my luck a little further. "You don't have children of your own, Mrs. McLeod?"

"It wasn't possible," she said quickly. Neutrally. The lack of emotion was more touching, somehow, than a direct appeal for sympathy would have been.

Still I pushed. "Mrs. McLeod, 'round about the time of the murder, Daryll Flatt said he had a secret. He was saving it for one special person. It seems likely that that would be your husband. Have you any idea what the secret might be?"

"Something about Daryll's granny," she said, shrugging. No longer interested.

"Daryll's granny? Do you mean Harriet Johnson—the one he sometimes stayed with? What about her?"

The snap came back into her unfriendly eyes. "Can't you figure it out?" she said. "You're the detective."

"Is it to do with her death?"

Mrs. McLeod considered. Pressed the switch suddenly, so the car window shot halfway up and I had to draw back. She twisted the handle of the key, spurred the car engine into action.

"That's for me to know," she said, returning to the game playing, "and for you to find out."

HOWARD HAD DESCRIBED Kenneth Pryce in the most comforting of phrases. *Granny Johnson's G.P.,* he'd said; Janet Flatt *just sort of inherited him.* It had an old-fashioned ring, recalling the days when you could count on seeing the same G.P. on every visit to the surgery, when he would know the names of all your children and details of their ailments—when, in short, the description *family doctor* really meant something. But comforting phrases don't make a person easy to locate.

Retired, and moved away, the receptionist at the Campkin Road surgery declared. She clung to the secret of his current whereabouts like a burr on a dog's back.

Someone at the Community Health Council was far more accommodating, tracking Dr. Pryce to an address on the outskirts of Great Yarmouth. An address that was, as it happened, conveniently near the place where Sonny and Stevie were stalking the Bennetts.

Sonny himself blew into town that evening sounding pleased as punch. "We've got them," he said. He flung his scarf on the back of the sofa and stretched himself out full-length. "The Bennetts. Well, almost. Turns out that they were required to keep records of all transactions for the company that insures their boats. I have a contact in the insurance office who has promised to make an additional copy for me."

"Man or woman?" I asked.

"You doing a survey?" Sonny shot back.

"Just for the record." I laughed and changed course. "Pretty good timing, eh, tying up the Bennett case just before half-term holidays? The boys will be pleased. Any idea yet what you're going to do?" Dominic and Daniel were coming to him as usual for half-term.

"I have one more trip to make to Norfolk. And then I thought," Sonny ventured, "that we might come up to Cambridge and spend a day or two of the half-term with you."

This was a departure. The boys were used to me hanging out at Sonny's flat in London, or even tagging along once in a while on weekend outings. In those situations, I am the interloper, and can't pose much of a threat. Coming into my space was something they hadn't tried before. "Why not?" I said. "I'd love to have you." I squeezed up next to Sonny on the sofa, twining my legs around his. Part of my brain was already constructing lists—of kiddie food, of activities, of ways to win Dominic over.

So it was settled.

"And if you're going back to Norfolk," I interjected before we moved on to other things, "I've got a little job for you."

"In Norfolk?" Sonny sounded suitably surprised.

"Yarmouth, to be precise. I want you to interview Kenneth Pryce for me. He was G.P. to the Flatt family. He is the most likely person to have issued the death certificate for Harriet Johnson—that's Daryll's granny. And he may remember something about her physical health before she finally died. If he had any qualms about the death, sensed anything odd—or for that matter, had any reservations about Daryll—I'd like to know."

"Laura, what in the world are you talking about?"

"About the possibility of another murder." I explained how Harriet Johnson had died suddenly, in the night, with Daryll by her side. How distressing this was for her grandson, apparently. But also how troubling for me.

"Meaning?" Sonny asked.

"To lose one granny figure is a misfortune," I misquoted. "To lose two might be considered carelessness. Or worse."

"You're suggesting he might have killed his own grandmother?" Sonny was unconvinced. There was not a trace of *There's an idea!* in his voice. Nothing but astonishment.

I backpedaled. "I have to tell you, Sonny, that after seeing Daryll on that video with Kelsey McLeod, I find it hard to believe he could murder even a doughnut. But you've got to understand: I'm doing my best to keep an open mind here."

"An open mind. Not an empty one."

"Precisely. Ruling nothing out. Look, we know that Daryll Flatt was alone with two elderly women at the times of their separate deaths. Don't you think, Sonny, that as coincidences go, this is fairly farfetched?"

"In statistical terms, it's highly unlikely. But what about the police? Wouldn't they have wondered whether Harriet Johnson suffered foul play? Wouldn't they have checked?" Sonny asked.

"When Harriet Johnson died, there was no reason to be suspicious. And by the time Daryll had confessed to Geraldine's murder, the other death was too far in the past. The police had enough on their plates. They never gave Harriet Johnson's death a second thought, as far as I know."

My speech was punctuated by a long low rumble. It

came from an area just below my belt. The last I'd eaten was a sandwich at noontime in Parker's Bar. But I couldn't eat until I'd gotten this matter settled.

"So will you, Sonny? Speak to Dr. Pryce?"

Sonny made a feeble protest—used phrases like *fool's errand*—but it was a case of scraping a toe on the ground rather than digging his heels in. He took the address from me, stuck it in his pocket. "I'll give it a shot," he said.

I took that to mean that if Dr. Pryce was at home when Sonny called, and willing to speak, I'd soon have answers to my questions. Sonny's amiable manner disguises a fellow who could winkle the life story out of Howard Hughes.

But give-it-a-shot is not Sonny's strongest expression of commitment. If Dr. Pryce was out walking the dog when Sonny called, or if he was reluctant to discuss a patient, or if he expressed a distaste for private investigators in general and Sonny in particular, then Sonny would wash his hands of the whole affair. He wouldn't push.

Fair enough, I said. As if I had a choice.

Then, to lighten the atmosphere, I told Sonny about my embarrassment at mistaking Ann McLeod for her husband Kelsey. Sonny proceeded, with more good humor than tact, to rub my nose in my mistake. He declared me the winner of the Faux Pas Medal of the Month. I conveyed my excuse—that I hadn't expected someone with dysrhythmia to be driving—but Sonny insisted that I accept the prize regardless.

"The prize being . . . ?" I asked.

"Come here," he said, "and I'll show you." And when I nuzzled up to him, he gave me the kind of kiss that could make a girl forget to eat.

Well, almost.

"I'm starving," I said. "Food first. Prize-giving cere-
mony later."

Then I wrapped his scarf around his neck and dragged
him off to dinner.

Chapter 15

THE TEAM AT Radio Q103 promised, as they did most mornings, to get me out of the sheets and into the streets, but their winning words came a little too late. Sonny was up and gone by the time the alarm went off.

There was a depression on the mattress where his body had been. I didn't make the bed. Not for any sentimental reasons, just out of the-hell-with-it Saturday morning sloth.

I had promised to treat myself to the new John Lee Hooker album, and decided over a croissant that no harm could come of a quick visit to Andy's Records before the Saturday crowds converged on the city. I headed straight for the topmost floor of the car park, where the white honeycomb ceiling of the lower levels gave way to a big and damp East Anglian sky. There—apart from a Land Rover that pulled into the bay behind me—I was able to park my Saab in splendid isolation. I paid and displayed, and set out on foot for Fitzroy Street.

On my way, trotting through the central corridor of the shopping mall—past the escalators, past the cookie shop (where the aroma is alluring but the cookies taste like cardboard), past a scattering of teenagers slouched on benches, cigarettes in hand—I scanned the displays. This is the closest I come to shopping: in and out. I keep my eyes open as I pass by, and if I spot anything—fruit, a pair of sandals, an

171

armchair—that meets my needs and my budget, I grab it as I go. Helen despairs of me; such a haphazard approach, she insists, is downright decadent. But if you don't enjoy shopping—and I don't—then what's the point of hanging out in shops? Consumption heaven for me would be a mail-order firm that could meet all my commodity needs, from knickers to nachos, from the comfort of my fireside.

Nothing caught my eye today and I arrived at Andy's parcel-free.

On my way back from the record shop, it was a different story. I made a small detour and stocked up for the arrival of Sonny and the children. A video, recommended by a man who said he knew the kind of film that boys like. Bags of fruit—not only oranges and apples, but nectarines and melons as well. Cucumber and broccoli, the only greens that Dominic and Daniel will consume, and parsnips and spinach and salad for Sonny and me. A chicken. Cooking apples, in case I was ambitious when I planned dessert, and ice cream, in case I wasn't.

High above the throngs of shoppers, on the tenth level of the car park, the broad sweep of asphalt was almost as empty as before. There were only two cars besides my own. In the front seat of the Land Rover, two men slumped down, looking half asleep. I registered their existence in a back-of-the-mind sort of way. The other car, a Nissan, was empty. Sonny's not a person given to wild suspicions, but he had once informed me—as if it were a law of nature— that men who sit together in parked cars are invariably up to no good. I should have taken more notice.

Instead I unlocked the Saab and stacked the groceries in the small compartment behind the driver's seat. I arranged the bags so the chicken didn't bruise the nectarines, and the lettuce wasn't leaned on by the melon. My mind was on the food and my bum was in the air when the warning signals came.

The solid surface of a parking lot doesn't creak under pressure like old wooden floorboards. Asphalt doesn't squeak like linoleum, doesn't click like marble. So I sensed someone behind me before I heard him. I backed swiftly out of the car and banged straight up against another body. A body far too close for comfort. Too close for good intentions. At the last minute I brought my elbow up aggressively, but it was too little and too late. The intended blow veered off without any real force.

This only took a matter of seconds. In less than the time it takes to slice open a chicken, or to smash a melon, a forearm clamped around my throat. It was broad and muscled and smelled sickeningly of diesel fuel. The man was a good two inches shorter than me, but strong, and he clamped me close as if I were the designated loser in a wrestling match. We were locked, his sternum to my spinal column, in a pose of awkward intimacy. It took my breath away.

The invasion of personal space was nothing less than shocking. There wasn't room for a flea to crawl between us. I could feel his collarbones against my shoulder blades. His beefy stomach slammed into the small of my back, his thighs crushed mine. The sharp tendon in his lower arm put pressure on my windpipe. My nostrils were stung by the acrid smells of fuel and sweat and onions. My ears were filled with shallow breathing, the creak of denims, the alien rhythm of someone else's pulse.

He held me there for one second, two seconds, three, four. My head swam. I gagged. I thought I might black out from the unrelenting weight on my windpipe. I made a wild effort to lift my knee, thinking maybe I could slam my heel down on the base of his toes—but his arm jerked my jaw up, my head back, and I was thrown off balance.

"Get into the car," he said. Accent is in the ear of the listener. He had a round Norfolk accent that didn't sound warm and unpretentious, as it does when worn by friends, but cruel and rough and base.

He loosened his grip on my neck. I had a few inches of clearance. I hoovered in great gasps of air, and choked, and my mind began a scramble for possibilities. Where there's air there's hope.

Not far away was the mauve-doored emergency exit. Its alarm might summon the security guards. If he intended me to drive, I thought, he would have to move around to the passenger side. I could break for the exit at that moment, if I had the strength. If I made a dash—not a mad dash, but a sane one—I might beat him to the stairs by a good few feet.

I coughed and spluttered, drawing it out, stalling for time. Time to visualize the route to freedom, time to will my legs to speed. Now or never, I told myself.

But just as my head started to clear, just as my breathing returned to normal, a shadow darkened the asphalt beside me. There were two of them. My crazy plan collapsed.

"I said, get in." Oblivious to security cameras, he delivered a bruising blow to my back. I slammed against the car. Well, at least one thing was clear: there was no point in my playing the little lady card with these guys. Whatever they were up to, they had no qualms whatsoever about hitting a woman.

I turned slowly and for the first time faced my assailant. He was in his mid-fifties, with the kind of tan that comes not from lying about on the Costa Brava, but from working out of doors. His nose was large and fleshy, his eyes prominent with drooping lids. An unforgettable face, with an arrogance about it that repelled me.

I put a steadying hand on the door frame of the Saab, bent

my knees, and swung into the driver's seat. The oddest things come to you in a crisis. I recalled reading in a woman's magazine that the correct (read: feminine) way to get into a sports car is to swing both legs in at the same time, knees and ankles neatly together. No unflattering leg positions that way; no—heaven forbid—glimpses of panty.

I pivoted exactly so. My two heels left the asphalt simultaneously and landed together on the floor beneath the steering wheel. It was surprisingly easy. I smiled slightly, not because I have any commitment to being ladylike, but for the recovery of my dignity. When you are helpless and humiliated, when someone is coercing your movements, physical dignity is one of the few grips you have on your self-esteem. For some of the same reasons that black teenagers in Dalston may swagger when they're stopped, yet again, by the police, I got into my car as demurely as Jackie Onassis.

Resistance was useless, for the time being. Ladylike was all I had left.

The second man seemed less threatening than the first. He looked like someone who was auditioning for the part of a hard man but wasn't going to get it. From a standing position, I could have overcome him. But not now. Locked behind the steering wheel of the Saab, legs neatly parallel, I was anyone's. As they say.

And before I could come up with another plan, the first assailant had settled himself into the passenger seat. He twisted toward me and showed me what he held in his hand. It was a working knife, broad and short and sturdy. Like him. He didn't say a word. He let the weapon speak for itself. He stared at me with an intensity that made the hairs on the back of my neck stand to attention. I broke into a sweat. He wasn't touching me, yet, but I felt a sweep of claustrophobia, overcome by his malevolence—by the smell of him and the size of him and his insinuating look—in the cramped interior of my car.

I stared straight ahead, through the windshield, at the splashes of cloud that hung over the car park, at the turret that topped the Habitat store. I took deep breaths, trying not to betray by the sound of my breathing how close I was to panic.

In situations like this, time becomes distorted. The three minutes that a mugging takes often seem to its victims to be thirty, every second stretched out, lived at roller-coaster intensity. He stared at me for a lifetime.

Then he leaned toward me. He lifted the knife and placed its tip, slowly and deliberately, in the tender hollow on the left side of my throat. Just next to the jugular vein.

"Start the engine," he ordered. His partner, standing outside, took the keys from the door, where I'd left them, leaned into the car and inserted them in the ignition. He guided my hand to the keys—I couldn't look down because of the knife—and then slammed the door shut. Given the circumstances, there seemed no point in buckling up.

The engine began with an experienced purr. This car was already secondhand when I bought it some years back, but it would still take me anywhere I wanted to go. And in this case, where I didn't want to go.

"Where are we heading?" I asked. "And why?"

He answered the first part of my question and ignored the second. "A drive in the country?" he suggested, as if he had just thought of it, and instructed me to go in the direction of the A10.

I spiraled slowly down the curving exit ramp from the car park, the steering wheel locked on right, hampered by the knife. I toyed with the possibility that someone might notice that I had a hijack on my hands. No one did. From outside the car, I suspect, my passenger looked like an attentive boyfriend, turned toward me, arm resting fondly on my shoulder. Our passage went unnoticed.

Grafton Center is an unwieldy collection of chain stores, with less personality than the streets of terraced housing that were pulled down to make room for it. But on a Saturday it attracts enough shoppers to give birth to an all-day traffic snail on the main access route. I edged left into the traffic, circled the roundabout, and doubled back along East Road, struggling to give as much attention to my driving as I did to my passenger. He held the knife firmly against my throat—so firmly that, near the intersection with Norfolk Street, when the traffic slid to a sudden halt, a droplet of blood trickled down my neck. It formed a pool above my collarbone. The stain on my crocheted top was the last thing on my mind.

"Hey," I said, as if we were on the same side, "be careful."

My passenger had up until then maintained an uncompanionable silence. He stared at me, his hooded eyes clouded, his hands firmly on the knife. It was only after my outburst that he began to speak.

"Tell me," he said. An order, not an invitation. "What's your boyfriend up to these days?"

"Boyfriend? Which one?"

He made a noise in the back of his throat that signified disgust. "I'll tell him you said that. *He* seems to think you're something special. Went on and on about you, apparently, to my bookkeeper. I thought I'd better have a look for myself at such a paragon of female virtue."

Virtue, from the way he spat it out, wasn't one of his favorite qualities.

"You're Bryan Bennett?"

"You don't need a name. Just say that I'm a real Englishman. Someone whose home is his castle. My missus, she thinks she can pull the wool over my eyes, but no woman leaves me and takes my money. D'you hear?"

I nodded, groped for the button, and lowered my window halfway down. The traffic was bumper-to-bumper all the way to Lensfield Road. "I can get us through this," I said, indicating the jam.

Bennett glanced around and seemed to become aware of his surroundings for the first time. He was a man of considerable concentration, and up until now all of it had been focused on his grievance with Mrs. Bennett and on me. He kept the tip of the knife at my throat, but not quite so firmly, and sized up the line of cars in the distance. Then he swiveled his head nervously. He took in the sidewalks along East Road, and the upcoming forecourt of Eastern University, busy with students and skateboarders and passersby. He registered his own vulnerability. Here he sat, in the center of town, in a traffic jam, with the good citizenry of Cambridge on every side, holding a knife to the throat of an unwilling driver.

"How?" he growled.

"Down there." My eyes flicked to the right, along Dover Street.

"Do it."

I disguised my relief, didn't let it affect my facial muscles or shine the surface of my eyes. Bryan Bennett obviously didn't know Cambridge. "Move that knife away. I have to ease out into the middle of the road, so I can check for oncoming cars."

He thought it over for a couple of seconds. Then his wrist slid along my shoulder, and suddenly I could shift my head without feeling the prick of cold steel. "Careful," he growled. Like the sadistic warning of a torturer before he grinds out his cigarette on your cheek.

I pulled out into the traffic, waited for a gap, and then

twisted to the right onto Dover Street. Took a quick left onto Adam and Eve. Snaked into Warkworth Street. And all the while, Bennett continued as if there'd been no break in the flow of his complaint.

"Your boyfriend comes to Norfolk nosing around in my business, trying to help her cheat me. He's got no right."

And finally, left into Warkworth Terrace. He was watching my face again with a kind of intensity that made my blood rush with hope.

"So my brother and I thought it might be good if we showed him what it's like to have someone interfere with your woman." He leaned toward me, propelling the aroma of onion in my direction, and moved the knife closer to my jugular again. "Tell your boyfriend—" he snarled.

I pulled sharply left, slammed my boot down on the accelerator, and swung with a screech of tires into the parking lot of the police station. All I saw was a knot of police officers, a blur of white shirts, before I opened the door and flung myself onto the pavement.

He recovered quickly, I'll give him that. He was out of his seat and running like an Olympic sprinter before any of the astonished constabulary could shift into action.

I stood up and brushed the dust off my jacket while I watched his progress down the street.

"Tell him yourself!" I shouted as a police car backed out of the driveway and two constables took up the chase. I can't be certain he heard.

Chapter 16

THERE WAS NOTHING to be ashamed of, I told myself, in the way I'd handled Bryan Bennett.

Nothing, that is, if you discount the failure of my internal alarm system. Even when the Bennetts appeared to have bedded down in the Land Rover opposite me, I was more mindful of my melon than I was of their ugly mugs. That may testify to my good taste, but certainly not to my good sense.

But in any broken cookie, there's at least one crumb of comfort. I flattered myself that once they got the jump on me, my reactions left little to regret. When Bennett locked his arm around my throat, I felt shocked, yes, but not panicked. I managed later, in spite of the prick of the knife, to keep a semblance of calm.

Even after my leap from the car at the police station, I had dusted myself off and given a plausible impression of a person of composure. I answered questions smartly from the officers in the car park and fended off their jokes. I plied the police with information, and stoutly resisted a visit from a doctor. It was only after a pair of constables had returned with Bryan Bennett in tow, after they had sallied forth and fetched his brother Frank, that I reviewed my situation. I began then to quiver from the inside to the out.

The sergeant took my statement and pronounced me free to go. I couldn't bear to be alone. So I drove to Helen's house in Newnham and hunkered down in her pretty little sitting room. There I sat while the encounter with the Bennetts scrolled through my memory again and again.

After the third or fourth time, I rose from the rocking chair and confronted my face in the mirror above the fireplace. The image was skewed, somehow. My jacket was crumpled and contorted, as if the stiffness of my body during that drive had left it permanently distorted. My hair, though washed only that morning, had an abandoned look. My smile came out as a grimace.

And my neck . . . I turned to the side, raised my chin and looked closely in the mirror. Where Bennett's arm had gone around my throat, where the rough fabric of his sleeve had crushed, there was a dusting of dots, a stain dark red against my pale skin. Like a hickey, but delivered in hatred.

"I noticed that bruise." Helen was standing in the doorway watching me. "It must have really hurt."

I wanted to explain that though I'd been dead scared—though it did really hurt, for a time—this wasn't what mattered. I intended to tell Helen that my sense of being off center had to do not with specific damage but with the way my assailant had broken through my boundaries, invaded my space.

Instead I began to sob. My face twisted as I tried to suppress the tears, and then at last I gave in. Helen set the tea tray down and came to me. She hugged me and made a sound like pigeons cooing. And finally, when the tears slowed to a trickle, before I had time to retreat in embarrassment, she smoothed my hair with a gentle hand, gave the hem of my jacket a tug, and handed me a wide-toothed comb. The weeping left me with red eyes and the kind of complexion that would win a shudder from Estée Lauder, but you don't get something for nothing. And the truth was, I felt a whole lot better.

"When you came in," Helen reminded me, "you rocked in that chair for ages."

"Back and forth, compulsively" was Ginny's contribution. She had arrived in time to see the tears. "Like a hamster on a wheel."

I had to laugh. "No more rodent compliments, please."

My spirits were lifted enough that I could take solace in a wedge of blackberry and apple pie—and that of course raised spirits further still. Helen entertained me with stories of a construction project at the library where she was in charge. Renovations from hell, she called it. I managed a sour chuckle at the thought of the chaos caused by disconnection of the cataloguing computers at the point of peak demand.

But Ginny refrained from laughter, and it wasn't out of kindness. She had other things on her mind. "Are you working on the Daryll Flatt case?" she asked.

I smiled at her description—like something straight out of an old Perry Mason novel. All it lacked was alliteration: The Dilemma of Daryll Flatt. The Killing of Geraldine King.

"His brother has hired me to find out a thing or two," I agreed. "Why do you ask?"

"Well," Ginny said, kneeling down next to the rocking chair, "we think we know where the murder took place."

Helen's face was somber, a nonverbal signal that I should think before I spoke.

"We?" I asked, stalling for time.

"Karen and I," Ginny explained with a flush of impatience. "Someone at school, Tommy in my art class, told us. His father works with— Oh, never mind. I'll show you."

I put out a hand to prevent her from leaving, but Ginny was faster than me. She flew up the stairs to her bedroom, hands brushing the wallpaper, and clattered down again. She swung 'round the newel post at the bottom and landed breathless at my feet.

"Here!" she said.

The circular called attention to a house for sale in the "popular Chesterton area of the city." No mention of a murder. It sanitized the site of Geraldine's death by assimilating it to the lowest common denominator of real estate speak: 3 beds., low level w.c., large walled gdn. The photo in the right-hand corner, taken before the garden had gotten out of control, showed a bungalow with an uncurtained picture window. Unmistakably empty.

"It's true," I said. "That's where Geraldine King lived."

"And Daryll Flatt killed her in that very house? Have you been there?" Ginny asked, eyes wide.

I took my instructions from Helen's face. The truth, but measured, her expression called for.

"Outside it, yes," I said, in answer to Ginny's first question. "And no. I've never been in the house. I've looked through the window and I've walked around the garden. It's a perfectly commonplace property, but being there left me with a bad feeling."

"Is there a ghost?" Ginny interrupted. "When people are murdered, their souls often hang around, looking for revenge."

"No." I shook my head. "No ghost."

I censored any mention of the footsteps that had pounded across the ground beneath the tree house. "You don't need a ghost, Ginny. Sometimes just knowing that someone died violently is enough to take the hominess out of a house." I looked at her expectant face, knew exactly what she was thinking. "You keep away from there," I warned.

"I want to see it," Ginny insisted. "Karen does, too."

My counterarguments got me nowhere. *Ghoulish* didn't cut any ice; at her age, I suspect, it's a kind of compliment. *Nothing to see* was brushed aside; it's okay for you, you've seen it. When I pointed out that it is never wise to hang around empty houses at her age—*never know what you'll find*—Ginny silenced me with a simple retort. "That's why we're asking you," she said.

And then she trumped me, by "offering" to go alone.

I submitted. We would meet after French club on Monday afternoon, near the Pike and Eel pub. I would act as escort.

Together, we would make an excursion to the bungalow that would be dignified. And brief.

Ginny raced upstairs to convey the news to Karen.

"It doesn't feel right," Helen said. "Visiting murder sites is ghastly and gruesome and grisly. But it seems the safest thing in the circumstances."

As long as we didn't meet a ghost.

ON HER RETURN from Birmingham shortly after, Nicole called around and found me at Helen's. "Frank and Bryan Bennett," she exclaimed. "This is one of those times of year—maybe it's the cordite in the air—when trouble-makers seem to be stirred into action."

I walked to the station to see her, keen to be outdoors, needing the swish of the trees on Jesus Green to ground me again. On Midsummer Common, where council work-men were beginning the preparations for Bonfire Night, I paused. A large circle had been chalked on the grass about two hundred paces away from a riverside pub, the Fort St. George. There was a central pole from which the guy would be hung. Pieces of wood leaned like the supports of a giant tepee around it. Next week, I supposed, the gaps would be filled with old pallets and waste timber, creating a structure that would loom impressively against the night sky and then swiftly burn itself out.

A bonfire, a shower of fireworks—such a simple machinery of pleasure to inject magic into the everyday. To provide, for the children of Cambridge, an hour of enchantment.

Well, for most of the children.

Maybe not for Ginny, whose appetite for enchantment had recently been dimmed.

"Don't remind me about troublemakers," I said, returning to the Bennetts. But I described the hijacking incident to her anyway. Couldn't stop myself. And Nicole listened like a friend, as if she hadn't already heard the details from the officer in charge of the case. "You're intending to throw the book at them?" I asked.

"Willis had in mind something on the order of the *Encyclopaedia Britannica*. How will that suit you?"

I laughed. "Dropped on their heads, for preference, from an enormous height. Sonny's been keeping an eye on them, you know." She didn't know the details, so I told her about Sonny's surveillance in Norfolk. "He may have something useful to say about the extracurricular involvements of the Bennetts. But leave it until tomorrow evening, will you, Nicole?"

Nicole raised an eyebrow. I headed off her query with a shrug. "I'm just not ready to tell him yet. Not over the phone. Better to break it to him face-to-face, when he arrives with the boys."

At Nicole's nod, I made an effort to change the subject. "Any news about that flasher?"

Nicole had forgotten. She was betrayed by the blank look in her eyes. I felt a flash of annoyance, but threw a fire

blanket over it. Before the Apeman appeared on Stourbridge Common, after all, I hadn't clocked in at Olympic
speed.

Nicole dredged my request out of her memory. "The
man with the mask?" she said at last. "Turns out my colleague, Detective Constable Andrews, has a file on him as
long as a Roman candle. Let me give Andrews a shout."
Nicole let herself out, left me sitting at a scratched table in
an interview room on the first floor of the station. I occupied myself by trying to link infamous names to the ini-
tials carved in the wood. JR/HS/MH . . . Jack the Ripper?
Hillside Strangler? Myra Hindley? Not many children's
names to draw on here. Maybe MB for Mary Bell, or LB
for Lizzie Borden—but in general, juveniles are relegated
to a little league when it comes to murder. Children are
more done-to than doing.

Nicole returned with plastic cups of tea and a man in his
late twenties. The hopeful expression on D.C. Andrews's
florid face seemed more fitting for a clothing salesman
(*Perhaps sir would like to try the jacket?*) than for the
CID. He gave me an eager-to-please handshake and a
summary of the police file on the flasher.

Apeman had first emerged on the Cambridge scene four
years ago, apparently. He had popped up in the area between Arbury Road and Kings Hedges, where there were
several schools close together. He would be reported near
one school one afternoon, and another the next.

Since then Apeman had extended his territory over the
whole north side of the city, from Newnham to the Science
Park on Milton Road. There was a pattern to his sightings:
three or four appearances around adjacent schools in the
space of a week, and then nothing for a month or more.
"He seems to go underground," D.C. Andrews said. "Be-

fore we can arrange surveillance in a particular area, he's disappeared."

"And Stourbridge Common? Is that one of his haunts?"

"A favorite spot," Andrews replied. "You know something?"

We chewed over his appearance and my unsuccessful pursuit. The kite flyers' mother, true to her word, hadn't rung it in.

"Don't be cross with yourself," Andrews said. "You got closer than us."

"And his description?" I asked. "With all these sightings, it must be pretty detailed by now. Must be narrowing things down."

"In your dreams," Andrews said. "We get the description you just gave me time and again: medium height—maybe five-foot-nine; medium build; medium brown hair. Rides a battered black bicycle—indistinguishable from thousands of others in Cambridge. Tends to dress in corduroy trousers, a dark wool jacket, a fisherman's hat."

That's my boy. "Detailed," I concluded. "But not exactly helpful. You could fit this description to thousands of men in the Cambridge area."

"To thousands of men," Andrews agreed, "and, as it turns out, to none of the known perverts. But there's something else." D.C. Andrews was warming to his topic. "In the past few months, the pattern appears to be changing."

"How so?"

"Well, in July, Apeman showed up near Mayfield School. Shocked two little girls on their way home. But—here's the thing—the next day, instead of moving over to St. Luke's School, or Chesterton or the Grove, as we had come to expect, he turned up again in the same area. To be precise, 'round the corner from the home of the previous day's victims."

"Stalking them?"

"In effect."

"So what happened?"

"The father got wind of it and mounted shotgun for his children. Apeman went to ground. Until September, that is, when he fixed his sights on some first-formers from the Manor School."

"And did he stick with the same children over a period of days?"

" 'Fraid so." Andrews paused and then gave voice to the clear implication. "He's getting bolder, Miss Principal. Targeting specific children. I don't know what it means yet, but it doesn't make me sleep easy."

The stuff of nightmares, to be precise. "So the fact that Ginny has seen him several times confirms the flasher's new way of working."

"Confirms one thing, anyway: the sooner we lay hands on him, the safer."

"What do you plan to do?" I didn't underestimate the difficulties. Plainclothes surveillance—saturation surveillance— is the obvious course of action. But with so many schools involved, it would take half the police forces of Britain to provide the manpower. Besides, our man was an expert at avoiding adult witnesses. Any grown-up lurking near his target child, and he would shed the mask and ride away. Just another Cambridge cyclist.

"I'm hoping that we can use his change of pattern against him," Andrews replied. "Next time he singles out a group of children for his attention—assuming they report it straight away—we'll set up covert surveillance around those particular kids. We'll trace their route to and from school and make sure that behind every hedge, inside every van, there's an officer ready to pounce."

"Sounds like—"

"A long shot?" he interrupted.

"A risk. Wouldn't you be using the children as bait?"

"Well," he said, looking only mildly uncomfortable, "of course we wouldn't act without the full permission of their parents. And we would have to guarantee absolutely that once Apeman showed himself, he didn't get away."

Hmmm. *Absolutely guarantee?*

Nicole had been uncharacteristically quiet during this exchange. The expression on her face was unmistakable: *better him than me.*

Chapter 17

THE MINUTE ANDREWS walked out the door, Nicole put the flasher behind her, so to speak, and swung into action.

She shoved her chair a few inches back from the table. Off came the shoes. She tweaked her tights, making room for her feet to flex. And she lifted her right leg, and then her left, onto the table, so that one ankle elegantly cradled the other. Finally, she tugged down the hem of her short black skirt and settled down to listen.

Her demand was couched in simple terms, but that didn't make it simple to comply. "Right," she said, "I want to know everything you've learned about Daryll Flatt."

Everything?

About how Daryll had suffered at home after Howard left? How his stepdad roughed him up? How his older brother harassed him? How his mother—his poor, unmanaging mother—tried to ease her guilt by persuading herself that Daryll didn't really mind?

Did Nicole want to hear all of that?

Did she want to hear how, after moving in with Geraldine, the "fiend of the fort" had used the tree house to escape from a world that frightened him? How Daryll must have lain on the platform for hours on end, gazing out toward the river? How the walls of the fort were ablaze with images of Australia—where his brother Howard had promised they would go?

Should I explain to Nicole the kind of problem Daryll created for his teacher? How Mrs. Joiner characterized him as a handful, but not—with perhaps one exception—a violent or a dangerous lad? About his inability to tolerate frustration? How the time that elapsed between the planting and sprouting of seeds seemed to represent to the boy an eternity—perhaps because in his short life nothing had happened to convince him that waiting would bring a desired result?

Should I describe how Daryll Flatt, for all his irritating qualities, could inspire loyalty and love? Should I explain how McLeod's deep attachment had made an impression on Murray Eagleton and on his own wife? How even after the conviction, the social worker continued to make Daryll a priority?

In the end, I told Nicole everything—well, almost everything. I even revealed the most startling piece of information I'd turned up: that deep in the recesses of his mind, alongside the traces of his many sorrows, Daryll had stored away a secret. A secret intended for one person alone. Nicole had gone out of her way to help me on this case, and it would have been churlish not to share some of what I knew.

When she heard this information, Nicole's toes described small circles of excitement in the air. "So who told you about this secret?" she asked.

"Someone who spoke to Daryll the day before the murder." No point in bringing the police down on Mrs. Joiner at this point.

"So," she mused—so being D.I. Pelletier's favorite word—"it's one of the neighbors, those Caudwells; or it's the teacher; or McLeod himself." She looked sharply at me.

I drained the last few drops of tea from my cup, took careful aim, and propelled it toward the wastebasket in the corner of the room. It made a gentle arc and fell to the floor to the left of its intended target. I decided that the stuff about Daryll's granny could wait for another day.

"Besides that secret, Nicole, there are other things that make me uneasy."

Nicole picked up her cup. Didn't even look inside to guarantee it was empty. Just increased the slope of her chair, pulled her arm back as if she were in a darts championship, and let fly. The cup landed in the bottom of the basket with a satisfying clunk.

"Such as?" she asked. She was smiling.

"You haven't lost your touch." I stepped across the room, transferred my cup from the floor to the wastebasket, and sat down again.

Then I addressed her *such as*.

"First off, there are all the unanswered questions about the day of the murder. Where did Geraldine go on Wednesday afternoon? Why was she so distressed when she returned? Why the urgent appointment with her solicitor?"

Nicole made a gesture of impatience, but I raced on.

"Then there are unanswered questions about the money: to wit, where the hell did it go? And why in the first place did Geraldine—the wife, after all, of a parsimonious supermarket manager, a woman unused to frivolous living— remove forty thousand pounds from her bank?"

"Ancient history, Laura," Nicole grumbled. She didn't like this line of conversation. Police officers, like private investigators, are trained to go for cast-iron conclusions— for full stops, not commas. Nothing makes them more nervous than a collection of loose ends. "Ask me something I can answer," she challenged.

"Maybe you can answer this. Remember Daryll told you that when Geraldine returned from her outing on the day of the murder, she found a piece of paper—"

"She took it out of her handbag," Nicole interrupted.

"Right. And ripped it up, as if she were angry. Well, just for the record, what did he mean by 'sheet of paper'? Was it a letter? A newspaper clipping?"

"Your guess is as good as mine," Nicole replied. "Geraldine tore up the paper in the sitting room, according to Daryll. Left the bits lying on the floor. But we found only one fragment of paper. *Not* the remains of a sheet."

"So where did it go?" *So* was starting to crop up in my conversation, too. Maybe, like measles, it was catching.

"Go?" Nicole asked. "We only have Daryll's word that there was a piece of paper. The whole thing could have been part of his warped fantasy."

"Did you send it to the lab? That fragment?"

"For Christ's sake, Laura . . ." Nicole sat up and forced her hair back from her face in a characteristic gesture of frustration. "Why so excited about a scrap of paper?"

"Because it's the only link we have to Mrs. King's state of mind. To why she might have wanted to see her solicitor."

"The files are still in my office from last week," Nicole said with a conspicuous sigh. "I'll have a look later on, see whether there's a lab report buried away in a file."

"When do you get off duty?" I asked, anxious to keep the conversation going. "We could stroll over to Footlights. I'm willing to treat you to an enchilada."

"I don't suppose we'd carry on talking about the case, would we?" Nicole grinned. Was I that transparent?

"Well, we might just chat about whether the police had

other suspects at the time. Other than Daryll, that is. Whether anyone else looked dodgy."

"To a detective on a murder case, Laura, everyone looks dodgy. You know that."

"Like members of Daryll's family?" Nicole hadn't agreed to eat with me, but that was no reason to curtail the conversation.

She knew right away who I meant. "Wouldn't want that Mark character to marry your sister, would you?" she snorted.

"Haven't got a sister," I teased.

She didn't so much as chuckle. Policing hasn't done a lot for Nicole's sense of humor. "Mark Miller has 'nasty piece of work' written all over him." I could tell from the look in her eye that she was entering into the spirit of the exercise. Her formidable memory—the memory that had almost compensated at examination time for lack of work— was coming into play. "And in the case of Mark Miller, looks don't deceive. A conviction for grievous bodily harm, another for common assault. He's one book you *can* tell by its cover."

I nodded. "A thuggish sort."

"But if we're running through suspects," Nicole cautioned, "a criminal record isn't enough. Miller works— worked at the time of the murder—on a crew installing storm windows. They were somewhere in deepest Suffolk when Geraldine was killed. In short, he's fully alibied. 'He was here all week, never left the site,' they said. Of course," she added, with a philosophical air, "that kind of alibi isn't worth the paper it's printed on. They all lie, all cover for one another. But you'll never prove it. Anyway, he hasn't got a motive. Oh, by the way, have I ever mentioned to you that Mark visited Daryll at Mrs. King's before her death?"

"How much before?"

"Couple of weeks, something like that. Mark said he wanted Howard Flatt's address. But I think it was just a chance to snoop."

"There's your motive," I suggested. "Oldest in the book. Mark Flatt Miller spotted the money hidden in the house—forty thousand pounds, remember, we're not talking tens and twenties here—and came back later to grab it. Mrs. King tried to stop him. Murdered in the course of a theft."

"It's an idea," Nicole said dryly. There were echoes of the tone Helen uses when Ginny lobbies for trips to Euro-Disney. But I didn't mind. Nicole can patronize me until the cows come home—as long as she doesn't clam up.

"What about the mother?" I prompted. "Was Janet Flatt ever a suspect? She certainly resented Mrs. King. 'That prissy missy,' is how she referred to her, 'with her peep-toe sandals and her airs.' Janet probably felt humiliated about Daryll's placement in foster care. She had been, by all accounts, a successful mother until her husband left. What came after—her inability to protect her sons against their stepfather, for instance—seems like the actions of a weak woman, or a frightened one, rather than a mother who would happily sign her son over to someone else."

"You're suggesting she might have bumped off Geraldine? That it was a clumsy bid to get her son back?"

" 'Course not. But if you start with Janet's contempt for Geraldine, stir in some anguish over Daryll's care order, and then you add a final ingredient—the letter Geraldine wrote urging Daryll to make a permanent home with her—well . . . couldn't Janet Flatt have seriously lost her cool?"

"You think the letter might have been the trigger?" Nicole weighed it up, one stockinged foot rat-tatting against the other. "Well, the letter—you haven't seen it, have you? I'll look for it when I check about the lab report—the letter did refer to Janet Flatt as 'that horrid woman.' Not calculated to soothe the angry beast. On the other hand, we don't know for sure that Janet Flatt ever saw the letter. Or even knew of its existence. She certainly didn't let on, if she did."

"It's not the letter that's important," I countered. "It's what it implies: that Geraldine King wanted the child for herself. What if—no, it's too crazy." The only way to make Nicole even consider this possibility would be to make her drag it out of me.

"What's too crazy?" Nicole asked, right on schedule.

"No, nothing. Any chance of a cup of coffee?"

"Later," Nicole said. "When we're through, I might even take you up on that enchilada. Now out with it."

"What if Geraldine went to see Janet when she left the house? To put the possibility of adoption to her? What if they quarreled—as they almost certainly would—and what if Geraldine declared she would see her solicitor about adoption?"

"Hence the appointment?"

I nodded. "That would give Janet Flatt a motive for getting rid of Geraldine, and for doing it quickly."

"But a solicitor would hardly be in a position to take action on the spot."

"Janet wouldn't know that," I argued.

"I like it," Nicole said. She was smiling broadly. Though she wouldn't welcome anything that undermined her resolution of the case, Nicole enjoyed an intellectual challenge. "Too bad the whole scenario's off the wall. Janet and her family were relocated to Peterborough after the trial. But at the time of the murder, they lived at the far end of King's Hedges Road."

"Too far for Geraldine to walk," I acknowledged. "Not there and back in ninety minutes. Wasn't that the time the witness gave for the outing?"

Nicole nodded. "And we never found the driver of a taxi or a bus who would admit to giving her a lift. So . . . any other bright ideas?" Her smile was buoyant. Nicole likes nothing better than to better me. To take my ideas, kick them around for a while, and then boot them off the field. I might have minded this—except that she's often right. And playing ball with the inspector has always proved a fast way to improve my game.

"One or two," I said. "I've been thinking about the victim's family. Edward King, for starters."

Edward doesn't make such a powerful impression as young Mark Flatt Miller. It took Nicole longer to place him. "So," she said after a couple of seconds, "the bookseller. Dry-eyed on his mother's death."

"The same. Mr. Bitter: angry that his father had disinherited him. Furious that his mother had failed to intervene. Makes no bones about his hostility."

"The bonds of love wouldn't have prevented Edward from killing. I suppose you've worked out a motive for him, too?"

"It doesn't take a genius. There are two possibilities, and both of them have to do with the inheritance. Edward King wanted to open a bookstore—'the only thing I've ever felt passionate about.' Father refused to subsidize a son who wouldn't follow the route of accountancy into a secure middle-class future. Mother concurred. Edward might have done Geraldine in revenge. Or he might have lost his temper after begging Geraldine to provide him with capital—with money that was 'rightly' his on his father's death—and being refused."

"Can you work in the visit to the solicitor here?" Nicole asked. She didn't look impressed.

"No problem," I said promptly. "She wouldn't advance the money. They quarreled. Geraldine said she would write him out of her will, too, just as his father had. To forestall her meeting with the solicitor, Edward sneaked in and killed her."

"I like that last one," Nicole said. She was still grinning. "It has a certain clichéd flair. Too bad about the alibi."

"Oh. Edward was otherwise engaged when his mother died?"

"Decisively. As far as I can recall"—when Nicole uses that tentative phrase, I always know her memory is crystal clear—"at the time his mother died, Edward was halfway between York and Leeds on a book-buying tour."

"There's always the A1," I said, unwilling to part just yet with the son as suspect.

"Indeed," Nicole said, and raised a dampening eyebrow. I could feel my attachment to Edward draining away.

"Any final bids?" she asked. "Before hunger overtakes me?"

"It wouldn't be fair to neglect the other members of the family," I suggested. "How about the sister and brother-in-law—Faith and Bill Holtby?"

For the first time that morning, Nicole looked surprised. "Why them?" she asked.

"Faith intrigues me," I admitted. "There's something curious in her relationship to Geraldine. Fondness, yes. But sibling rivalry."

"Over what?"

"Well, Geraldine was prettier. Or at least, most people thought so. Geraldine got the attention, especially from men. Faith lived in her shadow. And then—or this is how I see it—Geraldine also married a more successful man.

Coming on top of a long-standing competitiveness, Geraldine's attitude to her husband when he was alive—my Stanley this, and my Stanley that—might have seemed like needling to our Faith."

Nicole laughed. "You're scraping the bottom of the barrel, Laura. That's a normal sibling relationship. You don't still buy the idea of supportive sisterhood, do you? Only someone who never had a real-life sister could swallow that line."

"Okay, sibling rivalry is pushing it," I conceded. "No need to get personal. But there's something there, all the same. They quarreled, you know, the day before Geraldine's death. By the sound of it, it was something deeply felt."

"You want to bring money in here, too?"

"It's not inconceivable. The Holtbys live modestly. Half of Geraldine's estate must have made a big difference to their retirement. After their quarrel, Geraldine might have threatened to disinherit Faith."

"So. The solicitor again."

You can only call on a solicitor so many times in the course of a discussion before the appeal of the law begins to ring hollow.

"And William Holtby? Do you reckon he had a part in this?"

I took the question seriously, more seriously than it was meant. I thought back to Holtby—to his carpet slippers and his bad knees, his telly, his surreptitious glances. Something about the man . . .

"I doubt he had a part in the murder," I replied. "At a gut level, it doesn't feel right. He doesn't have the passion, you see. You can't commit a murder without some kind of passion, even if it is a passion for cash."

I looked Nicole straight in the eye. "That's one of the unacceptable things about Daryll's conviction," I said.

There it was, out in the open at last. I was no longer convinced that Daryll Flatt was the person who had murdered Geraldine King.

Nicole removed first one stockinged foot from the table and then the other. She inserted her feet into her shoes, cleanly, decisively, without even looking. Such a competent girl. And then she faced me, leaning forward, elbows on the table, displeasure undisguised. Games were one thing; but Daryll had been convicted—after an investigation in which she played a part—and questioning that conviction was not her idea of fun.

"You think Daryll Flatt was lacking in passion?" she said. Colder than steel.

"Sure do. In spite of Geraldine's desire to make a life with Daryll, in spite of how she perked up in the foster care role, there's nothing to suggest that Daryll regarded Mrs. King as other than a landlady. Think back to that landlady you lodged with one summer, Nicole. What was her name?"

"Mrs. Fabish."

"Mrs. Fabish. A tyrant, wasn't she? Remember how she monitored the consumption of toilet paper? How she stood sentinel over the telephone? How she wouldn't allow men on the premises? A real tyrant. But—and here's the crucial thing—it never crossed your mind to kill her, did it?"

"No, not really," Nicole admitted, after a telling hesitation. "I enjoyed spinning stories about her in the pub. But all in all, Mrs. Fabish wasn't that important to me."

"My point exactly. I have the impression that Geraldine wasn't all that important to Daryll, one way or the other. She didn't stir enough emotion in him to make him swear at her—let alone drop a block of concrete on her head."

"But he admits he did it," Nicole protested. "We have a confession."

"Strange, isn't it?"

Chapter 18

NICOLE AND I never did manage an enchilada that day. She located the lab report we'd talked about earlier, and the note from Geraldine to Daryll, and allowed me a glimpse. You owe me, she pointed out as I departed.

Debt like this I'm happy to carry.

When I emerged from the police station, the autumn gusts had given way to rain, drops falling flatly on my hair, my trousers, my shoes. As I raced for the nearest call box, I came up against a witch with pointed hat and bloodstained claws, a skeleton with tiny trainers on its feet, and a full-fanged vampire—and not one of them over three feet tall. Party time for the preschool crowd. *Wooooooooo* . . . said the witch to me in a voice with less volume than a cheap personal stereo. An image of Apeman leaped to mind. I responded to the witch with mock alarm and hoped that this Halloween she'd be spared the sight of a real monster.

My first phone call was to Trendex, the local office supply firm. I gave them the technical specifications of the fragment of paper found in Geraldine's sitting room, and in just over a minute I came away with a list of standard uses for paper of that weight and finish. Formal correspondence was deemed unlikely, as were invitations, airmail letters, newspapers, magazines, computer printouts, and invoices; among the probable uses were price lists, advertisement circulars for upmarket firms, information sheets, or casual correspondence. It was a start.

Then I rang Social Services. Over the past few days, I had come to the conclusion that McLeod was reluctant to speak to me again. Three times now the receptionist had taken my name and offered to put me through to Mr. McLeod; on each occasion she'd come back within seconds with the claim that Mr. McLeod was in a meeting. He'd ring me later, she said. He never did.

This time, as soon as McLeod's presence in the office was confirmed, I hung up the phone and dashed for Burleigh Street.

"Take a seat," the receptionist said. "I'll find Mr. McLeod." She might be forced to fib to telephone callers, but she didn't look like the sort of woman who would lie to your face.

Sure enough, before I could flip through the magazine stand, the tall thin figure of McLeod appeared. He came toward me smoothly, arm extended for a welcoming handshake. "So glad you're here," he said, smiling. "I've been anxious to speak to you." At the warmth of his greeting, the temperature in the office went up a notch.

Perhaps I'd been mistaken about McLeod's reluctance to talk to me. Maybe it was a paranoid fantasy on my part. My line of business breeds paranoia, but I had thought up until now that Sonny and I were the exceptions that prove the rule.

I followed McLeod down the corridor to a quieter room. He didn't ask why I'd come. He encouraged me to be as comfortable as I could on a sagging chair, and then he took me by surprise.

"I believe I owe you an apology," he said. "An explanation, for my abruptness at our last meeting. You might have gathered"—he leaned toward me and lowered his

voice a notch—"that Daryll is more to me than just another client."

I put on my best don't-stop-now facial expression.

McLeod continued, in a reflective mood. "It's not easy
to explain to someone outside social work. My colleagues
understand," he said. "Look, I've been a social worker for
twenty years. The early cases, you're learning all the time.
Playing it by ear. Checking back with others more experienced, subjecting everything you do to scrutiny. Sometimes you mess up—but usually the consequences aren't
serious because someone else will put it to rights." He
smiled at me. "Like taking lessons from a driving school.
You might slip on the foot pedals, but the instructor also
has a set of controls, so no one gets hurt."

"And then you get your license," I said.

"Yes." McLeod nodded. "That's one way to put it. You
gain enough experience to trust your own judgment, most
of the time. From then on, there's a new set of worries.
You stop fretting that you'll mess up someone's life with
the wrong decision, or that your recommendation will be
overturned in court."

"What do you worry about instead?"

"Well, when you get to the point where you can put your
finger on what's needed, keep within the law—almost
without thinking—then . . ." McLeod tossed me a rueful
glance. "Can't you guess?"

"Then you worry that you no longer care."

"Right," he said. "You worry that the fire that made you
take up this job in the first place is gone. That you know
your clients inside out, and you are only a hairbreadth
away from despising them. That you act defensively. That—
although you never take a wrong step—you never really
help."

I could see what McLeod meant. And I could guess where he was heading.

"Daryll Flatt made a difference?"

"He made me care again," McLeod said. "I first saw that boy just after his grandmother died. He was crouched in a corner of his classroom. His arms were folded around his knees. For a long time I couldn't get a reaction, and when he finally lifted up his chin and his eyes met mine— it was like I'd known him all my life. I haven't got a child of my own," McLeod added. He met my eyes for a moment, and lowered them again. "Ann was never well enough; we had to do without. But Daryll—well, he's like a son to me. I only wanted the best for him." He shook his head and then fell silent.

"You mentioned the death of Daryll's grandmother, Harriet Johnson. I should tell you, Mr. McLeod, that I came across your wife the other day. She told me that Daryll had a secret connected with his granny. Since your wife never met Daryll, she must have heard this from you."

He remained quiet for a long time, thinking, chewing the edge of his mahogany mustache. Then he began, in a voice so subdued I had to strain to make out the words.

"It was after Daryll was found in the crack willow tree," he said. "After his initial confession. In the police station, Daryll didn't want to talk about Mrs. King much. He seemed to have forgotten great chunks of the preceding hours. He remembered throwing the rocks at Geraldine. Didn't remember much else. But he kept going on and on about his granny, saying he was the only one who knew what happened to her."

"Did you mention this to the police?"

McLeod looked at me with astonishment. "Of course not! The police weren't interested in Daryll's granny. That was years ago. And anyway—"

He stopped, before he dug himself in any deeper. I helped him out. "Anyway, Daryll was in enough trouble for killing Mrs. King. Why draw attention to an earlier death? Is that what you thought?"

McLeod seemed to shrink down in his chair. "All right, it was wrong of me to keep quiet. But maybe I handled Daryll all wrong from the beginning. Ann never tires of telling me so." He gave a wan smile, and swept his hand across his face, as if to brush the judgment away.

Finally, he drew his lanky self upright. "Tea?" he asked.

The kettle must have already boiled, because McLeod was back with mugs of a weak milky mixture—ostensibly tea—in two minutes flat. Just enough time for me to recall my other reasons for seeking him out.

As soon as he pushed through the door, I pounced, asking him to arrange for me to visit Daryll Flatt. Wouldn't be difficult, McLeod assured me. "Do you know the procedure?"

I shook my head. "Never had cause to visit a secure unit for children before."

"It will take a little time to set it up," McLeod said. "But I'll get you there as quickly as I can."

"Thanks," I said. "One final thing. Do you remember a letter that Mrs. King wrote to Daryll? It went something like this . . ." I handed him a rough version transcribed in my own fair hand.

Dearest boy, All I want is for you to be happy. You shall stay here with me and be mine. I will be good to you, and then you can forget about that horrid woman forever. G.

"Did you know that Geraldine wanted to adopt Daryll?"

McLeod looked at the letter and nodded sadly. "She would have liked the security, you see. The loss of her husband hit her hard. She worried that another loss would be too much to bear."

"But was adoption a real possibility in a case like this?"

"Without Janet Flatt's cooperation, or without monumental evidence of abuse, the courts would never have agreed to rescind Janet's parental rights. But that didn't stop Geraldine from hoping. It was a fantasy, if you like. But important to her nonetheless."

"She was fond of him, then?"

"Of course," he said emphatically.

As if there was never any doubt.

Chapter 19

THE GUSTY HOURS before a thunderstorm always bring out the tom in my neighbor's ginger cat. I spotted him the next morning, looking for trouble. I had just tapped on the window to discourage him from leaving his calling card in my border when Sonny's Cavalier slid into a parking spot opposite the house.

Sonny unfolded himself from the car and met me on the doorstep with a hug like that of a shipwrecked sailor embracing the solid shore.

The reasons for Sonny's relief soon slouched out of the car. Dominic and Daniel, that particular morning, were droopy and argumentative. What a journey it must have been. They didn't want anything: no to soft drinks, specially laid in for their arrival; no to a ham sandwich, or cheese sandwich, or egg mayonnaise; *yeah, all right* (grudgingly) to the video that I had selected after long deliberation.

Not wanting anything didn't mean, however, that Dominic and Daniel were happy. Not at all. They flopped onto the floor with exaggerated sighs; they plucked distractedly at Sonny's sleeve when he tried to talk; they bickered and scowled and kicked at the furniture. All in all, they presented an impressive but not pretty picture of discontent.

"What the hell's going on?" I whispered to Sonny in the

kitchen. We were assembling the makings of lunch on a tray. Just because the boys didn't want anything didn't mean they wouldn't eat.

"Gloomy day?" He shrugged, looking away. "Holiday blues? Colds coming on? Don't ask me. I'm only their father."

"Or," I suggested, turning him around so I could look in his eyes, "maybe they had destinations more child-friendly than Cambridge in their sights?"

"I'm sorry, Laura," he said, giving up on the pretense. He kissed the end of my nose.

I plopped ice cubes into tumblers of Sprite. Watched the bubbles whiz to the top. Resolved to make the best of it. "Leave it to me. Feed them first, and then I'll sort them out."

Sonny placed a tray on the floor within reach of them and retreated rapidly, like the keeper of dangerous mammals at a zoo. Then he pulled up a chair and joined me at the kitchen table. The boys had started to run a musketeer film. We listened for a moment to the lovely sounds of silence after the bickering died away.

"A Nobel peace prize for the inventor of the video?" Sonny asked.

I considered. Shook my head. "Tempting. But I suspect there are bigger issues on the world's stage than harmony in the Mendlowitz household."

"You might not say that if you spent more time with us," Sonny shot back.

I'd walked right into that.

"What happened to you yesterday, Laura?" Sonny asked, trying to strike a lighter note. "When you rang me about the arrangements, you were so evasive. I knew it must be something big. Did you win the pools? Lose a client? Get selected to row for England? Or what?"

I couldn't put off any longer telling Sonny about the Bennetts. It didn't take a psychic to predict that his engaging grin would disappear when he learned what his adversaries had been up to. When he learned what they had done—or tried to do—to his "woman."

He'd be upset. And angry. And when men like Sonny—well, in fact, most men I've known—get angry, there's always this imperative to action. They immediately want to *do* something—to fight someone, to take the thing that's wrong and put the world to rights.

But sometimes what's needed is just a chance to come to terms with the thing—to sort out feelings, to think it through. And when you're coming to terms, a man who's fidgety for action gets in the way.

"More like what," I replied. "Sonny." He looked up, guarded now. "Promise me you won't get angry."

"Me? Mr. Mild?" Sonny joked. I could already see the glitter of let-me-at-him in his eyes.

Sonny's arms were resting on the table. I placed my hands on top of his and touched the soft pale hairs on his fingers. "You know this divorce case you've been working on? Bryan Bennett took me for a ride yesterday. I had to hand him over to the police."

I guess, coming out of the blue, this wasn't easy to absorb. "You've been to Norfolk?" Sonny asked, groping in the dark.

"No, here in Cambridge. He and his brother grabbed me and forced me into the car. Ordered me to drive him in the direction of the A10."

"How did he force you?" Sonny looked dumbfounded. I felt his hand struggling to get free, an automatic gesture. I held on tight.

"Armlock around my neck," I said curtly. I didn't like going over this. Not in this way, with Sonny building up a head of steam across from me. "Two of them, only one of me. Knife to the throat. That sort of thing." I sat back and waited for the explosion.

"The bastards!" Sonny exclaimed. He jerked his right hand free, fisted it and slammed it down on the table with such force that Daniel leaped off the sofa and came racing toward us. He stopped a few feet away from his dad, suddenly nervous. I could understand why. In his current state, Sonny looked—well, not quite like Sonny. All the generosity, the humor, the affection, was submerged in a glinting anger that cut him off equally from Daniel and me. Like he had no feeling for us anymore. Like he was a prisoner of his rage.

"Sonny," I said quietly, warningly.

"Just when I've got them. They can't stand it, those Bennetts, not getting their own way. The fucking bastards . . . What did they do to you?"

The question came, it seemed to me, as an afterthought.

"Sonny . . ." I had to speak with great emphasis to get through to him. "Look at Daniel. You're scaring him." I extended my arm in Daniel's direction, and Dan, after a second's hesitation, used it as a shelter to move closer to his father. I curved my hand around his shoulder and gave him a pat. "No one's cross with you, Daniel. Your daddy has been investigating some men in Norfolk, and yesterday they had a go at me. One of them forced me into my car, made me drive him a ways."

"You mean the Bennetts?" Daniel asked, relieved to understand a little.

"Hey, you're not supposed to know their names," I teased him. "That's confidential information."

"Did they hurt you?" Daniel asked. Not in anger, but in concern. And he looked at me straight-on and friendly for the first time that day.

I gave his shoulder a squeeze. "Only a little." I rolled down my polo neck and showed him the discoloration between collarbone and chin. "No serious injuries. My limbs, my head, my heart are all intact. But they upset me. I need some fun today, to rinse the memory away. Want to help?"

"Sure, Laura." Daniel grinned. "But do you mind if I finish the video first? You want to watch, too?"

I stood up and reached for a large cookie with sprinkles on the top. And found its twin for Dominic. "Maybe later," I said, and just missed kissing the top of his head as he raced back toward the television.

"Freshly baked?" Sonny asked, in a making-conversation kind of voice.

"By someone." I shrugged. "Not by me."

He swept his hair off his forehead in an impatient gesture. "For Christ's sake, Laura, those Bennetts tried to kidnap you. Who wouldn't get angry?"

I didn't say anything. I walked to the doorway and checked to make sure Daniel had settled in.

"Well?" he asked.

"I'll tell you who wouldn't get angry, Sonny. Someone whose first concern was how I felt, and whether I was un-hurt. Someone who thought of my safety before he thought about his own fight with the Bennetts."

"You're saying this is a male thing?"

"What do you think?"

Sonny was silent. He looked at his hands, at the scat-tering of hairs that reached toward the knuckles, at the scar that trickled out from beneath his watch strap. He turned them over and examined the palms. Traced the happiness line, described by a palmist who operated out of a hut in a car park in Wells-next-the-Sea as the mark of a love that would last. He shook his hair off his forehead and smiled at me, tentatively.

"How is Daniel?" he asked. "Should I go and talk to him now?"

I stood in the doorway for a few seconds, taking in the sights. Dominic was perched on the back of the sofa, flailing the fire tongs in the air. Daniel's foot, shorn of its shoe, wiggled in time to the parries and thrusts on the television screen. Both boys had their eyes fixed on the action.

"They're enjoying it," I said. "It doesn't make sense to pull them away now."

"Did they eat?" Sonny was feeling solicitous.

"Nothing left but nectarine pits," I replied, and watched him relax.

I WANTED DOMINIC and Daniel to enjoy themselves. You think Cambridge is boring? I challenged them. Well, think again . . . and I rattled off a list of amusements from the armor collection at the museum to the indoor tennis courts at Long Road Sixth Form College.

In my desire to please, I made the kind of mistake that people who live with children soon learn to avoid.

"Anywhere," I said. "You choose."

So we ended up at Laserquest, and I had only myself to blame.

I knew little about Laserquest, and less that I liked. As far as I was aware, it was a kind of play area, with indoor mazes giving the illusion of an alien territory on which battles are waged. A militarized world—everyone shoulders a laser gun and there's a war of all against all.

I'm a woman of my word, so I took them there. But I didn't agree to play.

The approach to Laserquest is via Bradwell's Court, through an uninviting door and, finally, up a stairwell as broad and bleak as the fens. It is empty of everything, even litter. The walls are icy blue, the metal handrail is red, the balusters are custard-colored, the linoleum a dirty gray. The colors could have been comforting, like an eight-year-old's bedroom, but the hangarlike proportions worked against it.

Two flights up, we were arrowed through to Operations. The noise and jostle of the inner lobby came as a jolt. The long narrow room snaked off to the left. It had no windows, not a hint of daylight. There was an industrial carpet with missing chunks and tinned music that put conversation out of the question. The administrative heart of the operations— a counter where you acquired the token that animated a laser pack—occupied one long wall of the lobby. On the opposite wall were video games. Daytona USA offered side-by-side car racing: beat your companion on the race track from the comfort of your own stool.

But fighting, rather than racing, was the general theme. A line of boys in their mid- to late teens had taken on the challenge of electronic battle, and it didn't make a pretty sight. Like automatons, they stood in front of Virtua Cop or Killer Instinct or Mortal Kombat 3, their eyes in ferocious focus, their arms in jerky motion on the joysticks. They might be ordinary lads, nice lads, the kind who make way on the sidewalk, but somehow they didn't look it at that moment.

Sonny and the boys seemed right at home. Disconcertingly so. A member of the "crew" with black hair curling to his collarbones asked them to feed their aliases into the electronic scoring system. They reeled off battle names as if DESTROYER, GLADIATOR, and DREDD were tattooed on their hearts.

The game was about to start. Sonny and Dominic and Daniel were directed to a door marked AIR LOCK. I watched as they shouldered their laser packs and hefted their guns. I waved my menfolk off to war.

I bought a soft drink and tried not to look too much out of place. As a fantasy world, Laserquest reminded me of the Ghost Train at the fair—its black-painted scenery had limited shock value; its illusions were unconvincing. Still, there was something in the atmosphere—the anonymous silhouettes of the players, the twinkling lights on their shoulders, the way the air lock slammed behind them— that made me just a tad uneasy. As if Laserquest, for all its shabby props, might shelter something far more sinister. I experienced one of those piercing thoughts, those *oh no not that* images that have troubled me since adolescence: Sonny and Dominic and Daniel would never be seen again, and when I pleaded for help in finding them, the boys working the video games would look at me with eyes devoid of human feeling and shrug.

I shook my head to chase away this nonsense and found that the man with curly hair was watching me. He nodded toward an internal window set low in the wall. A hand-lettered sign above it read BATTLE VIEW. "You can watch them," he said, as if he had picked up my anxiety. "Through there."

Looking through that window was initially like staring into the bottom of a coal scuttle. But as my eyes adjusted, the darkness began to soften. I was facing the left-hand section of the battle area, dark walls set at curious angles. The only illumination came from the alternating flash of red and green spotlights. The short stretches of corridor within my angle of vision were empty.

Suddenly, a black-clad figure darted past me, circling and scanning, his laser gun held before him like an advance guard. Lights twinkled on his shoulders. Another player swept past when his back was turned. I found myself gesticulating like a pantomime spectator—*he's right behind you*—but no one took any notice. Perhaps it was one-way glass. Seconds later both players had dashed away. I was left once again with the ghostly silhouette of the scenery.

I checked the time clock. Nineteen minutes down, one to go. When I returned to the window, a murky figure filled the opposite alcove. He stood stock-still, only a meter or two from where I watched. I had an impression of mass and power. Then the lights flicked on above his head, and in the lurid glow I saw his features clearly. He stood, all 250 pounds of him, with his back pressed against a wall. I could see the fat fingers on the trigger and the midriff flopping over his jeans. His laser gun was aimed along the route from which he'd come, and his head was cocked in that direction, too, watchful, menacing. Appropriately, the speakers in the lobby began at that moment blasting out heavy metal, and I recalled the snarl of Whitesnake the first time we had met. It was Daryll's middle brother, Mark.

Seconds later the airlock burst open. Dominic and Daniel surged out. "Can we have a drink? We're going again," they declared.

"You, too?" I asked as Sonny finally surfed out on a wave of other adults. I thought he looked kind of bushed. He had that glow that comes from exerting yourself in a closed space. There was no sign of Mark Flatt Miller.

"Only if you come, too," Sonny retorted.

But if Sonny was hoping that he could retire and blame it on me, he was out of luck. I couldn't resist the chance to watch Mark Flatt Miller again in action in the anonymity of a game. I flexed my bicep at Sonny, buttoned a black cardigan over my white shirt, and announced to the man at the desk that Medusa was ready for battle.

I tried to watch for Miller, but within seconds of passing through the air lock, I was locked instead into the spirit of the game. Doing my bit as a rebel leader: scanning the tunnel ahead of me from side to side, sneaking up on other players, taking defensive action when my gun was disabled by enemy fire. Swept up in the edgy rat-a-tat-tat of Star Wars fantasies.

When I finally came across him, Miller's size made him easy to recognize. He stood motionless in the center of a bridge, legs astride. His gun was held at hip level. He fired indiscriminately, nonstop, raking both approaches to the bridge. No one could pass. No running and diving for Mark Flatt Miller, no thrill of the chase. He was—like Everest—simply there. What could be the fun of playing in this way? I wondered. Did the sense of being immovable appeal to Miller? Was it the refusal of interaction that he liked? Or was it just the winning?

Only one player challenged him, and that was by mistake. A girl in her early teens. Something threw her into confusion. In a temporary panic, she misjudged and made for the bridge. She wasn't even firing. The barrel of her gun was lowered. Miller could have given way—could have edged himself back against the parapet and let her pass. But the second she slid past him, he rammed her, slamming her side against the wall. She was less than half his weight. It was strictly against the rules of the game. More to the point, it was brutal.

The girl stumbled out at the opposite end of the bridge. She assured me that she wasn't harmed. But the smart of tears showed that for her, the game had moved out of the realm of good clean fun. She'd had a glimpse of something that goes bump in the night, and the darkness didn't seem playful anymore.

I leaped onto the bridge, disregarding the flashes from

Miller's gun. My score was plummeting. I didn't give a shit. I strode toward him and wrapped my hand around the barrel of the gun, forcing it down.

He wrenched it away, furious. He backed away, trying to get enough distance to fire at me again.

I was surprised at the depth of my own anger. And at my lack of caution. "You ever try picking on someone your own size? Or do you only manage to be tough when you're dealing with children?"

Suddenly he focused. "Fucking hell," he said—that impressive vocabulary again—"you're the snooper who went to see my mother. The one who's digging for information about Daryll."

I waited. It was hot in there. I could feel a rivulet of sweat poise on my hairline and trickle down my forehead.

"Well, let me tell you something, snooper," Miller continued. "That old lady—the one Daryll killed? She talked about my family like we were dirt. But she was up to something. She had something to hide."

The penny dropped. "You visited her, didn't you? Not that long before she died. Did she tell you about the money?"

He tried to look knowledgeable, but only managed a kind of sullen bafflement. "What money?"

"The forty thousand pounds Geraldine King had hidden in her house. Someone took it. There's a reasonable chance it was you."

He pulled back, angry again, and looked as if he were about to run me down. With his size, he could. He could flatten me like a steamroller on hot summer tarmac. But he changed his mind, turned and lunged off in the other direction. The bridge trembled.

Sonny came up behind me and put my gun out of action again before I had fully recovered. "What's the matter,

Laura?" he asked, stroking my bottom as he squeezed past. "You didn't even try to defend yourself."

"Nothing, Sonny," I said. "Guess I just lost my taste for gunfire."

In the course of the game—in spite of Mark Flatt Miller—I relinquished some of my prejudices about Laserquest. I had assumed that games that focus on guns and use people as targets communicate the joy of killing. That under the surface, they encourage players to suppress their shared humanity, to look at other people as objects to be dominated and destroyed. That Laserquest would whip up hatred. Worse, that in the long run, killing in the real world could become, because of games like this, reduced to a game itself.

But my growing hostility to guns doesn't fit with my experience of Laserquest. Racing through the maze, ducking and weaving, I certainly did feel alert, on edge, eager—even aggressive. What I didn't feel was murderous. The laser gun was an instrument of competition, not of death. I felt about it much as I would about a tennis racket during an exciting match, or about a baseball bat when I had to bring home the person on third base, or about a pair of oars during the Cambridge Bumps. And that probably applies to the rest of the players, too. Apart from Miller, I've seen more ferociousness, more murderous intent, on a squash court than at Laserquest.

And yet—even without the prejudices—I wasn't sure it was for me.

In the lobby afterward we examined our scores. Dominic was near the top of the list. Sonny and Daniel were respectably in the middle. Medusa chalked up a pathetic rank near the bottom.

Dominic started to tease.

"She's good at basketball," Daniel retorted.

"And rowing," I added. "And Scrabble." I felt touched by his support, but also a little defensive.

As we exited down the echoing stairwell, I noticed for the first time a large hand-lettered sign on the wall of the landing: HASTA LA VISTA, BABY, it predicted. YOU'LL BE BACK.

Well, I thought, we'll see.

HELEN AND GINNY were already seated at a large marble-topped table when Sonny and I rolled into the Pizza Express at six o'clock that evening with the boys. The minors knew exactly what they wanted, from Margarita Pizzas to the chocolate bombe. They ordered by rote, and then pottered off to plague the piano player.

Helen was in an optimistic mood. The flasher, she reported, had not been seen for days now. Gone to ground, the police had said. She hoped that if—not when—he emerged again, he would turn his attentions somewhere else.

Sonny was concerned. He completely understood Helen's eagerness to see the back of the Apeman. But it worried him that if the flasher went to ground, just at the moment when the police were finally geared up to catch him, he would be in the clear. He would have generated fears for Ginny and her friends and other children that might haunt them all their lives—and got away scot-free. And he might feel even bolder about peddling his wares in the future.

Helen didn't budge. "Of course, I want the man arrested," she retorted. "And put away. But most of all, I want no further harm to Ginny. I don't want her to have to think about this bastard and his bananas anymore. I'd rather she didn't have to repeat the sordid details, over and over, to police officers and to the court. The best thing for Ginny would be for it all to end. Finito," she concluded, as the waitress swung over to our table and deposited the first three pizzas.

While we wolfed down our food, and while the kids created a lively traffic in olives around the table, I diverted Sonny to the topic of Dr. Pryce. "You spent much of the morning quizzing me about the Bennetts," I reminded him. "Now tell me what you found out in Yarmouth."

"Pryce is a daunting old bird." Sonny began like a man with a story to tell, slowly, eking it out. "In his late seventies, I should imagine. Stooped and none too fit. But the glint in his eye would fell a malingerer at forty paces."

"No soft bedside manner?" Helen asked.

"I bet his patients wouldn't have rung him up in the night, unless the grim reaper was in hot pursuit." Sonny paused. "Anyway . . ."

"Anyway?" I repeated, urging him on.

"When I mentioned the Flatts, Pryce knew who I meant right away. Provided an instant family history that summed up Janet and her kids to a T. 'Young couple, three children—all boys. Husband up and left. Youngest lad got into serious trouble,' the old man declared in crisp no-nonsense tones. 'What do you need to know?' "

Sonny stretched out his legs under the table and paused for dramatic effect. Helen and I sighed. He grinned and carried on. "Well, I knew that if I asked him about Harriet Johnson just like that, cold, he'd probably clam up. So we talked instead about doctoring for a while. The guy is sharp as a 2H pencil. Completely up to date. He regaled me with the latest from the *Lancet* about several diseases that I would rather not have gotten to know. And he was exactly right."

"How could you tell?" I asked dryly. Sonny's lack of interest in matters medical, his refusal to consult a G.P., his fatalistic attitude to illness, are common knowledge among his friends.

"Touché," he said. He didn't look bothered.

"And then you got around to Daryll's granny?"

"I did. What was the cause, I finally asked, of Harriet Johnson's death? Was he surprised at her sudden demise? Did he consider the possibility that Daryll might have contributed in some way? And then"—Sonny fixed me with a glance intended to make me squirm—"then I cursed you for dispatching me on this ludicrous mission."

The glance made me laugh rather than squirm. "So, Dr. Pryce didn't think much of your suggestion?"

"*Your* suggestion," Sonny corrected. "He made me feel about two years old. As if I were a baby pontificating on the meaning of the universe." He paused, signaled the waitress to run through the puddings for the youngsters. When they had ordered, he picked up where he'd left off. "You want to know what he said? His exact words?" He took a notebook out of his overcoat pocket, flipped it open to a page headed *Terence Pryce*, and read aloud: " 'Don't be daft. The boy was only eight. Besides, she had a heart attack.' " Sonny swiped his palms together vertically a couple of times to indicate how he'd been dismissed. "End of interview," he concluded.

End of this line of inquiry? I wondered. Whatever Daryll's secret, with such an emphatic dismissal from Dr. Pryce it seemed unlikely that it included another murder.

"I'm sorry, Sonny," I said, and meant it. "I shouldn't have sent you on such a fruitless and embarrassing errand."

Sonny's confidence seemed undimmed by his encounter with Dr. Pryce. "Embarrassing, yes," he acknowledged lightly. "But who said anything about fruitless?" And he poured more wine for Helen and me.

I wished the piano player would take a break. The Jesus

Lane dining room was all high ceilings and hard surfaces, and the noise level was getting on my nerves.

"Come on, then, clever clogs. Give."

"It's about Ann McLeod," he said. "You know, that social worker's wife?"

I explained to Helen who Kelsey McLeod was. I had a funny feeling that I knew what was coming. "What about Mrs. McLeod?"

"Well, remember you came across her in a car just off Adam and Eve Street? You were taken aback to find her in the driver's seat."

"I had assumed she wouldn't be able to drive. She's got a serious heart disorder," I said for Helen's benefit.

"There's the rub," Sonny continued. "Someone with cardiac dysrhythmia—wasn't that what you told me?—wouldn't be driving. She'd be subject to random blackouts and dizzy spells. Your impulse was right after all. So—"

"So," I interrupted, intrigued, "either Ann McLeod is a very odd specimen, taking foolhardy risks with her life and that of others, or the diagnosis is wrong. Dr. Pryce put you straight on this point, I presume?"

"He was emphatic," Sonny said. "What do you make of that?"

"I don't know what to make of it, Sonny," I said, feeling at sea for the first time in this case.

The notion that investigations involve sleuths in unearthing clues—clues that make it possible to find missing persons, to solve mysteries, to apportion guilt—is one of the silliest myths of modern times. When detectives tread from door to door, posing patient but unspectacular questions, the individual items of information they turn up are, on the whole, of little value. What matters is the relationship between them. What sets alarm bells ringing, what leads to solutions, are the inconsistencies—the occurrences, images, sets of events that don't fit together. Not, at least, within the picture that the main participants are trying to paint.

One inconsistency had been glaring from the beginning of this case. I'd known there was something wrong with Ann McLeod—and I don't mean heart disease—from the time I went over my interview notes. It had lodged in my brain then, like the buzz of a fly in the room where you're trying to sleep—the contradictory things that had been said in passing about the social worker's wife.

Like D.I. Pelletier's account of how, on the day of the murder, McLeod had been called away from the office because his wife was ill; *some kind of chronic illness,* Nicole explained. And later, in even stronger terms, that Ann McLeod was an invalid.

Like the matron in the old people's home, with her admiration for the sacrifices McLeod had made. *His wife is very ill, you know.* Cardiac dysrhythmia.

And most of all, Howard Flatt's observation that death was one of the things that had bonded Daryll to his social worker. Daryll had lost his grandmother, Howard reminded me; McLeod had lost his wife.

Now, I'm not the sort of person who demands that doctors be infallible. I don't believe that medicine is an exact science. It involves, in my view, a hell of a lot of guestimation, of let's-try-and-see-if-it-works. And I don't even consider this a criticism. Plumbing isn't an exact science, either, but when a pipe leaks in your loft, a plumber is still your best bet.

In short, when it comes to medical diagnoses, I'm quite ready to tolerate a degree of uncertainty. To accept a margin of error.

But in the case of Mrs. McLeod, it was getting ridiculous.

According to different witnesses, Ann McLeod could be hale and hearty. She could be seriously ill, a chronic invalid. Or the poor woman could be—on some accounts, was—already dead.

I had failed to confront the inconsistency. Had told myself I was saving Ann McLeod for a rainy day. But now Sonny, and the inestimable Dr. Pryce, were forcing me to look at her more closely.

Rainy or not, here I come.

Chapter 20

THERE ARE FEW places less fun to be than a parked car when the weather is wet. If you sit with the windows closed, the vehicle steams up and you lose sight of the outside world. If you opt for fresh air, the rain sheets in through the open window, putting damp patches on your clothes.

So it was as I sat waiting for Ginny and Karen, the interior of the Saab resembling a steam bath one minute and a clifftop in a thunderstorm the next. I had parked facing the river Cam. The scruffy grassland of Stourbridge Common occupied the farther bank, and it seemed to me that the common was quiet, even quieter than I would expect for an afternoon in November. I could see a couple of ponies huddled together at the eastern end of the common, but not a single dog walker braved the downpour, and no children raced their bikes across the pasture. In the distance, a few of the houses that fringed the common had lights in the windows. Maybe the weather had driven people back to the telly, back to an early tea.

No sign yet of Ginny. I drummed my fingers on the steering wheel, checked my watch, went through my calculations again. Ginny and Karen would be out of school at 3:35, then busy with French club until four-fifteen. They had promised to make their way straight here. Allowing them a few minutes to visit their lockers, I expected them to pedal down Water Street at about 4:25. I'd arrived early. Just in case.

Just in case had become the watchword for Ginny during the past few weeks. Until today, she'd been driven to school in the morning and picked up by Helen after classes—just in case. No hanging around with her friends after school. Just in case. No playing near the bushes on Lammas Land, no walks to Grantchester with friends, no shortcuts through Coe Fen or Grantchester Meadows, no feeding the ponies on the wild patch of ground between Trumpington Road and Chaucer Road. Just in case.

It upset me whenever I thought about it. Ginny's transition to secondary school had been as smooth as they go. She had been given a little rope, and used it constructively, proving herself to be responsible and reliable—ready, Helen said with wistfulness and pride, for greater freedom. Then Apeman had set things back. All it took was for Ginny to be a few minutes off schedule, and Helen was afraid she'd find her in tears, or worse. Ginny herself couldn't bear to be separated from friends, wouldn't go as far as the corner shop on her own. It wasn't so much the abnormality, the unusual high security, that made me feel distressed for her. It was that, where Ginny was concerned, a state of vigilance was beginning to seem normal.

In fact, that's one of the reasons I had consented to this bizarre outing. Part of me felt that Ginny should have had enough chills without seeking out a murder site. But I also understood that visiting a house that was haunted by its past—like reading horror stories, or watching scary videos—constitutes an important act of defiance. It is not like getting in a car with a stranger, say—putting yourself in the way of real danger. But it is a way of refusing to be paralyzed by fear. Refusing to bow down to a world that offers no better advice than self-restraint.

Watch what you wear, watch where you go; keep a curb on your friendliness and your curiosity and your sense of adventure.

Stay alive—but at what cost? Thanks, but no thanks.

We would stroll around the property, that was my plan, and peer through the windows, like people interested in a house purchase. If any of the neighbors should notice— the talkative Emma Caudwell, for instance—I would tell her the truth: that there had been a great deal of talk at Ginny's school about this house and its history, and I thought that bringing the girls to have a quick glance— confronting them with the ordinariness of the place—was the best way to defuse the situation. The image of the house, and especially of the tree beneath which Geraldine met her death, was, I admitted to myself, accompanied by a shiver. I couldn't think of it without hearing again a whip-crack in the bushes and the thud of footsteps across the lawn. It's only the cold, I told myself, rolling the window closed again.

It was 4:25. I rummaged in the backseat, found a scarf, and used it to lift my hair into a loose ponytail. If it had to be wet, I would rather it didn't flop around my face. Then I got out of the car and stretched. It's only rain, I told myself as the first chilly drops landed on my skin. I sauntered along Water Street in the direction of the school, trying to summon up a chorus of "Singing in the Rain," but lacking the Gene Kelly spirit. Besides, as I remember it, Kelly boasted an umbrella.

When I reached the T bend with still no bicycles in sight, I began to worry. Surely they hadn't chickened out? Didn't seem likely. Ginny's interest in this outing had been close to unshakable, and even if she had changed her mind, she would have come and reported that to me. Could the teacher have kept them overtime? No, French club was voluntary, and Helen and I had made Ginny keenly aware of the need to keep to our agreed schedule. There was only one possibility. Something unforeseen had happened to delay them. Something, probably, between here and the college.

Four-thirty. I could feel panic welling up. What should I do? Jump in the car and try to find them? But there were two possible routes, and I didn't know which they would have chosen. I couldn't risk them showing up while I was gone and then, full of bravado, wandering on their own into that garden with its echoes of death.

I slid into the car, out of the rain, and seized the mobile phone. I didn't really expect to get any information. In a school the size of Chesterton, the whereabouts of individual pupils is hardly a matter for the office. But what they told me made my heart thump with anxiety. Miss Binet was absent that day; French club had been cancelled. The girls would have left the school grounds over an hour ago.

They wouldn't, I thought to myself. They couldn't, surely, be so stupid, so foolhardy, so . . . adolescent!

But as I made my way toward the towpath, I knew they could. And sure enough, there, near the small shelter at the head of the path, at a crazy angle, padlocked against theft, were two bicycles. One sported on its handlebars the purple helmet that I knew belonged to Ginny.

I ran in spite of the rain, my boots throwing splashes of water from the puddles that narrowed the path. I ran with my head held high, scanning ahead for the girls, ignoring the raindrops that slapped against my cheeks. I turned into Geraldine's garden and came to a halt. There was no one in sight.

"Ginny! Karen!" I called. I peered around the garden, scouring the perimeter bushes with my eyes, penetrating the afternoon shadows.

And that's when I saw her.

Ginny was wearing a yellow macintosh and fisherman's sou'wester. The color made her easy to spot against the dull skin of the walnut tree. She was posed awkwardly on the narrow part of the platform that fronted the tree house—on the door stoop, so to speak. Her arms projected stiffly in front of her, her wrists were bent back. Her hands moved slowly, convulsively, as if to ward off some kind of horror.

She was looking down. But not at me.

There, on the lawn, inches from the place where Geraldine's body had been found, was a man in a dark wool jacket. He stood facing the tree. At the sound of my voice, he half turned toward me, his fingers fumbling with the fly of his trousers. I knew without looking that his face would be inhuman: could see, before I saw, the overhanging brow and broad flat jaw of an ape.

My eyes were on him. My heart swelled with something akin to hatred—with a disgust and a rage so powerful that it almost stopped me in my tracks. But it was to Ginny that I spoke.

"It's all right, Ginny. You'll be fine now. Go back inside the fort."

She teetered at the edge of my vision, fifteen feet off the ground, and didn't follow my advice. Her hands continued to flail in mute protest, and her body, sheathed in yellow, looked doll-like, insubstantial, unsteady.

I cleared the rage from my throat. "It's all right," I insisted again. "You'll be fine, Ginny. Grab hold of the door frame and stand very still."

Even as I spoke, the center of my vision was reserved for

him. He was silent, but his body language said it all. Though his facial expressions were concealed by the mask, I could read the degree of alarm in his movements—in the way he stood, shoulders hunched, head bowed, rigid. In the position of his feet, not yet readied to run.

He had not thought to be intercepted. Perhaps he had acted with impunity for so long that he'd begun to imagine he was beyond discovery. Maybe even beyond guilt.

I could see his surprise, in the defensive way his left hand was flung across his crotch. It's one thing for a man like him to display himself to children, to use impropriety and unexpectedness to capture their attention—and then to delight in the illusion that it is the quality of his penis that grips them so. It's quite another to be exposed to an adult.

A head emerged from the tree house and Karen edged out alongside Ginny, shook her arm, pulled her down to the safety of the platform. Ginny wouldn't fall. I gave Karen a discreet thumbs-up. And then I turned my full attention to the flasher.

"Look at me!" I ordered. It sounded like someone else's voice.

He tried to turn away. Tried to avoid my eyes—just as children had, no doubt, tried to block out the spectacle that he had forced on them.

"Look at *me*." I did my best to convert my rage to command. Into that egocentric instruction, that flasher's phrase—*Look at me!*—I put all the authority I could muster. And it worked. Slowly, reluctantly, as if pulled by a wire, the head turned. Before it slithered away again, I could discern the glint of the eye within its pocket of rubber. To me it looked like the glint of cruelty, of selfishness, of monstrosity.

"What is it," I asked—not loud, asking myself as much

as him—"what is it that makes a man want to terrorize children? That needs their nightmares to fuel his pleasure?"

I found myself creeping closer, and couldn't help but notice that he flinched at my approach. For some reason, that made me feel more powerful and even angrier.

"What is it," I growled in a voice that even to my own ears resonated with menace, "what is it that makes a man like you regard his body as a weapon?" I looked at him closely. "Do you despise yourself so much?"

Both his hands were in the pockets of his jacket now, and I could see the fist on one side twisting in anxiety, tugging the fabric. The pocket writhed as if some unspeakable creature was struggling to escape.

Other than that, he stood perfectly still.

Except that when I inched to within breathing distance of his face, when I could overcome my loathing sufficiently to draw near, I could make out a tremor in his shoulders. And when I snatched the rubber mask from his face, up and over his forehead, snapping the elastic with the force of the movement, the eyes were not quite what I'd expected. Behind the mask, they glowed dark and diabolical. With the disguise pulled away, the eyes were frightened and pallid, and the glint came not from a core of menace but from moisture. Silently and miserably, under the mask, the Apeman had wept. A tear glistened in the furrow that linked his nose to his chin.

"So it's you," I said, quietly now, ashamed of my outburst. Ashamed of my desire to humiliate and hurt. How little difference is there between the pleasure he took in terrifying children and the pleasure I had taken in bringing him to heel? Except that one is wickedness and the other is heroism—or so they say.

"Patrick?" I said, and he averted his face.

It was the next-door neighbor, Patrick Caudwell. Emma

Caudwell's husband, the administrator who worked shifts at Addenbrooke's Hospital. In order to pay for their greenhouse, Emma had said. I could easily imagine another explanation: *Oh, Grandma, what flexible hours you have. The better to meet you after school, my dear.*

I recalled Patrick's gentle response to Emma, when she waxed indignant about being treated as a stranger by Daryll. You're not a stranger to me, Emma, he had replied, and there was something touching about this reply. At the time, I had imagined Patrick Caudwell to be wearing an ironic smile. Now I wasn't sure.

Of anything.

I knew that Patrick Caudwell had been looking after the house for the current owners. Keeping an eye on the property, watching out for intruders, redirecting the mail.

And, presumably, weaving stealthily in and out from his garden to theirs. When he had intercepted me as I peered through the window of the bungalow, I hadn't heard him approach.

I knew only one other thing of any significance about this man. I knew—because he had told me so—that he liked Daryll Flatt. Daryll was a nice lad, Caudwell said. *Not,* he had declared with feeling, *like some of the others around here.*

Like some of the others . . . Ginny and her friends? The two little girls he had followed home from primary school? Were they the not-nice ones? And as I thought this, a surge of rage swept over me again, at what this fellow—this quiet, unassuming fellow—had done.

And with the rage came the certain knowledge of what would hurt him most. "So," I taunted him, speaking in slow sly syllables, "whatever will Emma say?" I can be as nasty as the next guy.

He swung his head toward me. There was fury and desperation in his face. At that moment, one of the girls shifted position on the platform overhead and a boot scraped across the boards. I glanced up. I never saw the hand shoot out of his pocket, forefinger poised. Never saw the pressurized container.

Caught only the blur of movement on my right-hand side.

Heard only the sinister hiss, like a serpent.

Felt only, instantly, overwhelmingly, the pain.

My aunt Marjorie was burned once, badly, on her legs, when she was a child in Bristol. She was coloring, stretched out in front of the fire, ready for bed, savoring a last few moments with the family before being scooted away to the chill of an unheated bedroom. She felt a cone of warmth on her calf, and heard a crackle. When she looked down, her nightie had burst into flames. Her mother rose like a wraith at the screams and engulfed her daughter in the robe she was wearing, using her own soft maternal body to stop the spread of the fire. Both were badly burned. And now, with instant recall, I was reminded of what everyone in the family declared was a miracle—that at first Marjorie felt nothing, in spite of the blackened skin. The nerve endings were so badly injured that they couldn't convey even pain.

Not so for me. When that hiss struck, every nerve in my eyes seemed to shriek with the impact. But more dreadful than the pain itself was the awareness that with every second the chemical, the acid—whatever it was—might be etching out my sight forever.

I heard myself scream and then someone took my hand. Grasped it hard and tugged me along, swiftly. I stumbled, but I was pulled to my feet again and almost dragged along. And then there was a mighty shove on my back and I careened headfirst into the river. I'd stopped screaming now, but my eyes were stapled shut with pain, and I twisted to the surface without the benefit of light or sight to guide me. That's when I heard the voices.

"Laura! Open your eyes!"

I knew it was right. Without a shiver of distaste for the muck of the Cam, I raised my arms above my head and allowed myself to sink, down toward the muddy bottom. I used my fingers to tear the lids open. I could see almost nothing—the murky water of the river was overlaid with shadows. When I looked upward, I saw only shades of khaki filtering down. The surface of my eyes burned.

Then slowly I stretched and touched one set of toes to the bottom, pushed off and up, floated upward like a bubble in a glass, and with a final heave from my arms broke the surface. I shall never forget how, through the pain, I forced my eyes open yet again and saw . . .

Everything.

Saw the dark shadows on the far bank. Saw a pair of swans, wings outraised in indignation, advancing on me. Saw the sleeves of my favorite jacket, rimed with weed.

Saw Ginny, crouched on the bank, with her hand extended toward me.

"Karen's gone for help," she said. And she struggled me to safety.

Chapter 21

THE WORST OF it was over when my visitors departed later that evening. Helen and Ginny, Sonny, Howard and Donna, Nicole Pelletier on her own time—and of course, the police—all kept me company for a while. In some ways, it was useful that my incapacity brought them together. From Howard and Donna, Ginny collected information for a project she was doing about Queensland; Nicole persuaded Sonny to abandon any idea of confronting the Bennett brothers for what they had done to me. But most of these exchanges passed over my head. I was too pain-distracted to take advantage of their presence, and part of me was contented when they left.

I had been meticulously examined by a doctor in the emergency room—after a wait long enough to enable me to rehearse every detail that had ever come my way about blindness. I combed my mind for memories of the partially sighted skier, of the show jumper whose vision was confined to one eye, of composers and cellists and carpenters who functioned competently without the aid of sight.

I couldn't recall a single real-life instance of a partially sighted P.I.

The doctor provided tablets to dull the pain, and they did. Further treatment would have to wait, he warned, until I'd been seen by the consultant. Then he instructed the nurse to bandage my eyes. Just a precaution, he said. The less light they had to contend with, the better.

So by nine o'clock, when I would normally hope to be digesting a decent dinner with a friend, I was propped in a bed in ward G6—mixed medical—at Addenbrooke's, while Sophie Gathercole described the onset of angina.

I had made a bond with Sophie—partly because she occupied the neighboring bed, but mainly because no one else seemed to be fully awake. Sophie spoke hesitantly, always ready to rein herself in, as if she didn't expect anyone to take an interest. I did my level best not to put additional dents in her battered self-esteem. I asked what I hoped were reasonable questions about her condition, and all the while made lists in my head about quite other topics.

Top of the list was Patrick Caudwell. Ginny and Karen, from halfway up the walnut tree, had observed my meeting with Caudwell. They had seen him unmasked. Had registered his distress. Had noticed how agitated he became when I mentioned his wife, and had shouted to warn me—but too late—when he pulled the canister of ammonia from his pocket. When I screamed and staggered away, he apparently ran for the towpath. Ginny and Karen had rushed to my aid.

He hadn't returned to Emma, or so it appeared. He certainly wasn't there when the police arrived. They checked the closets and the cellar and even the garden shed, but the Apeman had, to mix a metaphor, flown the coop. His bicycle—a battered old thing, his wife said with distaste—was missing. According to Nicole, who took the trouble to collect all the details before popping in to see me, Mrs. Caudwell was staggered to hear the news. Discovering that her husband was a notorious pervert couldn't have been good for Emma's self-assurance.

So the police—armed with a description from me, a photo from Emma, and a few pathetic jokes about jungles—had put out a notice to neighboring forces. The consensus was that Caudwell had probably caught the train and headed off to distant parts. Pembrokeshire seemed a good bet—he had a sister there. But Edinburgh or Leicester or Southampton were also in contention. Above all, nobody thought he would hang around Cambridge waiting to be caught, not after he'd added assault to the indecency charges that would confront him in court. If Patrick had an inkling of what happened in jail to "vulnerable prisoners," he would keep on the move as long as he could.

"And you know, Laura," Sophie whispered, "I thought at first it was just heartburn. You know, from too much Christmas pudding. Can you imagine? Or another time, I had this new peasant blouse. You know the kind I mean— gathered at the neckline, with embroidery all around? Oh, it was lovely," she reminisced. "Well, when the pain started, I thought maybe the elastic in the wrists was too tight. I made up my mind to put another inch in."

She delivered this information in a voice that was like eiderdown. I strained to hear. The bandages blocked my vision. It was harder to follow a conversation without the extra information that comes from lips and frowns and smiles.

"And did it make a difference?" I asked. "Lengthening the elastic?"

But I was thinking about Daryll Flatt again. How the fact that the flasher turned out to be Patrick Caudwell made a difference. How it brought me, maybe, one step closer to figuring out what lay behind the murder of Geraldine King.

"Laura? Laura?"

"Sorry, Sophie," I fibbed, "I must have drifted off." With

these bandages on, who would know whether I was awake or asleep?

"I'm going to sneak down to the shop for a Galaxy bar," she whispered. "If Sister asks, just say I've gone to the bathroom, okay? Can I get you anything?"

"Nothing, thanks, Sophie. Is it dark out yet?"

"It sure is," she whispered. "Pitch-black. All I can see through the window is the lights on that tower over there. Maybe that's Men's Medical?" she asked hopefully.

"Check it out," I suggested. I liked Sophie. Perhaps she needed a little encouragement.

She left, and suddenly the room felt eerily empty. I listened for a moment. I could hear several sets of breathing—not in sync—deep and slow, probably drugged.

So much for the nightlife.

I could also hear the television, some kind of game show—a host with a Midlands accent who exclaimed, "You never know!" in answer to questions.

No sound of movement in the ward. "Anyone awake out there?" I called softly. No one replied.

Just checking. With maybe a tinge of apprehension. I suppose, after my abduction from the car park and the attack by the Apeman—all in the space of three short days—I was entitled to a dash of insecurity.

I returned in my mind to Patrick Caudwell. The Apeman had been operating in the northern part of the city of Cambridge for a number of years. And all the while, the Caudwells had lived next door to the Kings. It stood to reason that at some point along this neighborly timeline, someone from the King household would have spotted Patrick on one of his little jaunts. Seen him putting on or taking off his mask; when a grown man returns home in ape costume, it's not the sort of thing you are likely to forget. Seen him in his navy wool jacket and fisherman's hat, on his battered black bike, and recognized the description of the flasher who terrorized local kids.

And who better than Daryll to notice Patrick Caudwell's curious excursions? Daryll spent much of his time in the branches of the walnut tree. Perhaps lying on the platform of the fort, gazing out toward the river. Where he could see all the way to the water. Where he was unlikely to be seen.

And if Daryll Flatt had witnessed the transformation—seen Patrick Caudwell turn into the Apeman—perhaps the secret that Daryll had hinted of to his teacher had nothing to do with his granny. An important secret, he had implied. The identity of a man whose obscene antics were the undercover talk of the playground would certainly qualify.

And what if the person to whom he had revealed it was Geraldine? Wouldn't a boy tell such a momentous secret first to his foster mum? There were so many conflicting facets to Geraldine's character that it wasn't easy to predict what she might have done with information as weighty as this. But it did strike me that subtlety wouldn't be her forte. I could most easily imagine outrage, and denunciation, or cries of *pervert* and *animal*. Geraldine wouldn't sit, I somehow felt, on the oh-you-poor-man side of the fence.

But if she threatened to denounce Caudwell—to reveal to Emma, to the police, that he was the notorious Apeman—would Caudwell just shrug and walk away? When I thought of the man who had moved so swiftly in my presence from abject misery to attack, retreat seemed unlikely. Would he have gone so far as to kill?

As *kill* crossed my mind, I heard something that drew me back to G6. Just the mildest, thinnest, snick of sole on the linoleum floor. Then nothing again but the game show.

Without my eyesight, I couldn't see my watch, and without my watch, I had no idea how long Sophie had been absent. How long I'd been, for all intents and purposes, alone.

"Who's there?" I asked, holding my breath, the better to catch any sound.

No one answered, but I heard the slide of a shoe again, nearer. Suddenly, a hand clutched my arm.

"Thank God you're all right," a woman exclaimed. "You were so still, I thought—I was afraid . . ."

"I'm fine," I said, gesturing to the bandages. "Just a precaution." I'd recognized Emma Caudwell's voice.

She pulled up a chair, moving it to the left side of my bed, and sat down slowly. The situation was delicate. I waited for her to begin.

"I've come," Mrs. Caudwell said, "because I wanted to say how sorry I am. That you've been hurt, I mean. And also . . ." She sat perfectly still for three or four seconds, collecting her thoughts, then began. "Patrick's not a bad man," she pleaded, in tones slower and more humble than any I had heard from her before. "I'm sure he didn't want to do it. Couldn't help it. I had thought it was all over," she explained.

Patrick had left Ireland as a runaway adolescent. His father was an alcoholic, his mother had died when he was little. Lonely years in orphanages had left him depressed and brittle. But in England he struck it lucky. He found people who befriended him. He was bright; he studied and earned a degree. He met Emma, who for reasons of her own needed someone to mother.

Patrick had confided to Emma the abuse he'd suffered as a child. How he'd been made to parade naked to the showers with a priest watching; how he'd been rewarded for doing so with visits to his sister. Told her that sometimes he had an urge to do something terrible—that was how he put it: to show himself to someone (he didn't say a child) when he was sexually aroused. Promise me you won't, Patrick, she had said, holding him close. Promise me you won't. Don't do this to me—to your daughters—to yourself. And she'd thought he kept his promise. Until today.

"If you knew," she said—and there was only sorrow in this voice, not bravado—"what a kind man he is, how he loves me and the children. If you knew—" She stopped. Uncharacteristically at a loss.

"I'm sure he is," I said. I didn't add that the damage had been done to Ginny and to other children whether Patrick was a kind man in his private life or not. "Hate the sin, but not the sinner," I muttered.

"The sin?" she asked, aghast. "But is what he did that bad? It's pathetic, isn't it, rather than dangerous?" Her hand had drifted off my bed at some time during our conversation, but now it clutched my arm again.

I didn't reply, except to pat her hand in sympathy.

She moved the chair back and rose to her feet. "I have to go now," she said. "I'm relieved to hear that your eyes will recover. I'll come see you again."

Yet another white lie.

I WONDER IF anyone—a health economist, maybe, or a time-and-motion expert—has ever calculated the total amount of time that hospital patients expend on waiting. Waiting for breakfast, for dinner, or for a glimpse of tomorrow's menus. Waiting to find out if their pain can be dealt with, their infection overcome, their disorder rectified. Waiting for morning through the long dark hours of sleeplessness. Waiting for the oblivion of night.

It's not one of my specialties. When I relax, I like to do it wholeheartedly. Free me from work obligations—present me with a peak to climb, a novel to read, a meal to savor or friends to enjoy—and I'm your girl. Give me something to do—something playful, or adventurous, or sensual—and I can rise to the challenge of relaxation every time. But the prospect of forty-eight hours perched on a precariously high bed, with nothing to do and little in the way of company, is my idea of purgatory.

So when the consultant—with what I suspected was a sadistic glimmer—declared that he would keep me in for another twenty-four hours, I offered resistance.

There was a bed shortage, I reminded him. He knew it, only too well.

I had an appointment at Social Services later that afternoon, I insisted. Cancel, he advised.

I was reduced to begging. "Let me out, please. I'll come back tomorrow to see you. Scout's honor."

To no avail.

You can keep the bandages off, he conceded, and left.

I trudged to the telephone in defeat and rang Social Services. "Have to cancel my appointment with Murray Eagleton," I told the receptionist. "I'm in hospital." I couldn't keep the grumpiness out of my voice.

I armored myself against acid thoughts by reliving my meeting with Emma Caudwell the evening before. Looked at from the vantage point of a hustle-bustle hospital morning, our encounter seemed distinctly eerie. Her unexpected arrival and the shock of her hand on my arm; the fact that everyone else in the ward was, or seemed to be, asleep; and, most of all, the poignant tale she had told about her husband's childhood—about the powerless little boy who suffered still inside the man.

My own powerless self had fixed on one aspect of her account, like a pit bull on a postman's leg. And wouldn't let go.

Until the police had set her straight, Emma Caudwell

appeared to have not an inkling of what Patrick Caudwell had been up to on his afternoons off. At some level, clearly, she hadn't wanted to suspect him. Hadn't wanted to wonder why he was setting out in mid-afternoon yet again on that battered bike. I kept asking myself: what if Emma Caudwell was not the only person in the case who had been blocking out unpleasant information?

AN HOUR LATER, as I sat on the bed, eyeing with my now fully restored vision a carton of lukewarm orange juice, and recycling the same old sets of ideas, I was brought up sharp by a visit from the White Rabbit. Since our first meeting, that's the name that had stuck in my head for Geraldine King's social worker—for the quick patter of Murray Eagleton's footsteps, for his perky appearance, for his busy-busy-busy air.

"What are you doing here?" I asked.

"What happened to 'Hello' and 'Nice to see you'?" He chuckled, and let off an enormous, friendly sort of sneeze. "Excuse me." His nose received two quick swipes of a clean handkerchief. "A young client has helped herself to an overdose, poor thing, and I decided to drop in to see you on my way to visit her. Unless I'm intruding?"

"Not at all." I steered him into the day room and onto the territory of our previous conversation. I reminded Eagleton of his suggestion that Daryll might have had a special importance for McLeod—maybe even filling in for a child that McLeod never had. He made a lively little nod that encouraged me to continue. "But you also hinted that McLeod might have been getting overly involved with Daryll. Would you mind telling me exactly what you meant by 'overly involved'?"

Eagleton made a tent of his fingers and bowed his head over them. "Yes, I can recall saying that," he replied after a moment, looking up. "I was referring to commitment. McLeod was very committed to Daryll. Still is. Over and above the call of duty."

"Over and above?" I pressed. "In what respect?"

"I could give you specifics," he said, watching me closely. "If you think it's important."

"Please."

"Well, what I recall is this. Eunice—that's my better half—and I often take the children for a walk on Sunday afternoons. One of our favorite walks is beside the river, opposite Stourbridge Common. Do you know it?"

"Very pleasant," I agreed, suppressing a hint of impatience. "And?"

"Well, several times I saw Kelsey's car parked near the Pike and Eel. Near Mrs. King's house. When he wasn't on duty—when I would expect him to be at home, with his wife."

I shrugged. This was hardly a heavy-duty revelation. "Maybe like you, he'd gone for a walk."

"No chance." Murray's denial was emphatic. "I checked. No, Kelsey's commitment extended to keeping the Flatt boy company, even on the weekends. That's what I meant by 'overly involved.' "

"Nothing more sinister?" I was mildly ashamed of myself for feeling a dash of disappointment. But I had to be sure. "You never suspected that McLeod had feelings of a sexual nature for the boy?"

"Good grief, no," the social worker replied. He looked genuinely upset.

But then, come to think of it, I had never heard Eagleton say a bad word about anyone. Geraldine, Daryll, Janet Flatt, Kelsey, even me—to a woman and a man, the picture he painted was positive.

"We in Social Services see abuse of trust too often," he said with feeling. "But not Kelsey. Oh, my, no."

I apologized for being the bearer of such an upsetting series of questions. Then, before Eagleton remembered that the real purpose of his visit to Addenbrooke's was currently in the emergency room, having her stomach pumped, I rushed on to my next topic. Geraldine's state of mind on the morning of her death.

"You were one of the last people to see Geraldine alive, right? Can you go over your conversation? What she said?"

"I'll try." He tented his fingers again and after a thoughtful thirty seconds to organize his reminiscences, began. His recollections were crisp and clear. The man might have been over-generous in his judgments of other people—and if you must err in your judgments, rather that way than the other—but he was no fool.

"We talked about baking first," he said. "How could we not, with that wonderful aroma filling her kitchen? Then I asked about Daryll; she told me of her concern. Daryll had misplaced a toy and he was taking its loss rather badly—blaming Mrs. King. I suggested that she talk to McLeod that very afternoon and let him sort it out."

Eagleton sneezed again—" 'Scuse me"—and then continued. "I tried to persuade her to attend the Homefinders social that was coming up on the weekend. Geraldine had been dithering. Her social life virtually collapsed, I believe, when her husband died. I did my best to be encouraging—assured her that most of the other care givers and social workers would be there. That I would be there with Eunice, and Kelsey, that perhaps even Ann McLeod would be well enough to come. I tried to convey how relaxed it would be, how undaunting, but it didn't work. The more I encouraged her, the more anxious she became. In the end I dropped it. That was all."

"Nothing else you can think of? She didn't mention any other concerns she might have had? Anything about needing legal advice?"

"She showed me a porcelain figure she had bought, to add to her Lladro collection. But that's all. No solicitor, I'm afraid. Got to go," he said, rising to his neat little feet. "Is there anything else?"

"I don't know whether it's fair to ask you this," I said, on the impulse of nothing ventured, nothing gained. "Kelsey McLeod offered to arrange for me to see Daryll."

"In the secure unit?"

"Exactly. But I've been waiting awhile now, and my time is running out. How long does it usually take?"

"Varies," he replied, and shot a friendly wink in my direction. "Why don't I see if I can speed things up."

It was easy to look grateful. But less easy to look surprised.

At the door, as Eagleton was leaving, he paused, rummaged in his jacket pocket, and came up with a Kit Kat bar. Good, old-fashioned comfort food. He tossed it to me.

"Thanks," I said. "You must be a good social worker."

"Oh," he replied, with a glimmer of amusement, "I bet you say that to all the boys."

EAGLETON, AS IT turned out, was good for more than a bar of chocolate. I had just arrived home—feeling fragile still, but released with a clean bill of health—when he rang to tell me he'd cleared the way for my visit to Stamford House in West London. Laura Principal now appeared on Daryll's approved list of visitors. The rest, apparently, was up to me.

"Can I get in within the week, do you think?" I asked, accustomed to cumbersome prison procedures.

"You can go today," Eagleton said. He waved aside my amazement. "It's not a prison," he reminded me. "It's a secure unit for children—*children* being the key. The duties of those who run the units are to keep the boys secure, yes—they mustn't be a danger to the public or to themselves. But their duties are also defined under the Children's Act."

"Meaning?"

"Meaning that residents can have as many visitors from the approved list as security can cope with—as long as it fits in with their schooling and the rest of the schedule. In short, you're in."

Chapter 22

Take it easy, the doctor had said, and so I did. Driving into London is a mug's game at the best of times—I took the train. I rang Sonny to suggest that he book a table for dinner that night, folded three extra sheets of paper into my briefcase, and parked my car at the station.

The Cambridge Cruiser is fast and noisy. *Daryll Flatt, Daryll Flatt, Daryll Flatt,* the train intoned as we streaked through the countryside toward King's Cross.

First stop, the West End. Hamleys. I went straight to soft toys on the ground floor and emerged after twenty minutes with a handsome white carrier bag.

Second stop, Goldhawk Road, West London. I ignored the push and pull around me on the tube, and pondered how to get the information I needed from Daryll Flatt.

Access was straightforward, Eagleton said; but Daryll's therapist and his social worker had between them specified serious restrictions on topics for discussion, and these restrictions would be taken seriously. Daryll was under psychiatric supervision—not because he was considered mentally ill, but as a way of helping him take responsibility for his actions.

"In confidence," Murray had said, "I can tell you that there is concern about a lack of remorse."

"He isn't sorry?" I asked. "But the description I heard of his arrest, and of his demeanor in court, suggested that he was devastated."

Murray sneezed again and shook his head. "You're missing the point. Remorse has a specific meaning."

"The money," I exclaimed. "Daryll won't tell anyone where he's hidden the money."

"Precisely," Murray confirmed.

"If he hid it," I countered.

Murray didn't tell me explicitly what he thought of that suggestion. But he blew his nose at last.

THE RESTRICTIONS COVERING my conversation with Daryll Flatt were restrictive indeed. I could speak to Daryll about anything in his current life—soccer, films, the routine in Stamford House. I could ask him about his family, or about daily life with Geraldine. But I couldn't ask about his feelings for Geraldine, or anything else—like the money—that might touch on the motivation for the murder. And I couldn't ask—not a single question—about Patrick Caudwell. Nor about the murder itself. These territories had been roped off. One foot over the boundary and I'd be turfed out.

And just to make sure that I kept to my side of the fence, one of the residential social workers—a woman with a thick plait and round brown cheeks—settled down in a corner of the visiting room with a notebook on her lap.

But I didn't look at her for long. My attention was captured by Daryll.

It was him and not him—an adolescent of thirteen rather than a boy of ten. He was taller, of course, and a little heavier. He had the same hair, but more severely cut. It bristled up from the same high forehead. The same eyes—wary, refusing a frank look. His jaw had broadened; the face had shifted subtly to a more rectangular shape. The freckles had faded. The biggest difference was the mouth. There was no hint any longer of an impish grin to balance the bleakness of his eyes.

The visiting room was small. At one end was a table, cluttered with old copies of *Micronet* and *Beano*. There were four chairs with metal frames and padded vinyl seats. The social worker and Daryll sat at diagonally opposing ends of the room. I took the empty chair that was nearest to Daryll; he was on my left, only three feet away; she was farther off, on my right.

I adjusted my chair so I could face Daryll, and pulled a tissue-wrapped package out of the Hamleys bag. Without a word, I unwrapped it and balanced it on my knee. Daryll was quiet for a long time, but his eyes were unwavering in their focus on the toy. He cleared his throat and spoke in a small voice.

"Used to have a doll like that," he said. There was no covetousness in his tone. Only regret and distance, as if he saw the doll from leagues away, through a haze of loss.

"What happened to it?" At my question—perfectly natural, I thought in the circumstances—the social worker directed her unemotional stare at me. I changed the subject.

"It's E.T., isn't it?" I asked. "From the film?"

He nodded.

"The alien who got left behind when his spaceship took off?"

"The one who was locked in the hospital," he replied, looking down at a Game Boy in his lap. "In isolation." He flicked the switch, and the *dee-dee-dee* of Tetris pierced the room. It sounded like a bumblebee at an audition for *Miss Saigon*.

"Abandoned," I added.

Dee-dee-dee from the Game Boy. Silence from Daryll.

"Do you want it?"

He looked up. Unwilling, but interested in spite of himself. "Why would you give me something? Don't even know you."

"I know you," I said. "Do you remember, three, four years ago, how you and some friends used to hang out on the railway bridge near Stourbridge Common?"

"In Cambridge?" he asked in wonderment, as if Cambridge were the other side of the world.

I nodded. "You took rocks from one end of the bridge and tossed them in the river. Sometimes they landed near the boats. And one of the rowers often chased you. A woman? Do you remember?"

A light came into his eyes when he smiled. His cheeks took on a blush and I could see the ghost of the freckles.

"That was me," I concluded.

"You never caught us!" he exclaimed, exhilarated by the memory of the chase.

"Didn't really try," I bluffed. He knew my show of indifference was a sham, and laughed. Then he suddenly sobered, as if a brutal hand had wiped the smile off his face.

"Are you angry?" he asked.

"I was, at the time. But it's all in the past. Do you want the doll?"

He reached out and took it, and, after only a second's hesitation, lodged it in the crook of his arm. It sat there staring impudently at me, its bright brown eyes unblinking.

"Your brother Howard asked me to come," I explained. It was sort of true. "I have a few questions that I would like to put to you."

He scuffed with the toes of his trainers, hard, on an imaginary spot on the floor. "Payment for the doll," he concluded, and looked away.

"No. In the interests of truth," I said. "The doll is yours to keep, whatever." Daryll didn't answer, just stopped his scuffing. So I began. "Let's start with the most unpleasant topic," I suggested. "Your brother Mark. Why did he used to get so angry with you?"

Daryll shifted and for the first time appeared to take notice of the residential worker, wedged down in her chair in the corner. She seemed to be doodling in her notebook. He turned back to face me again, and shifted the doll across his chest, like a kind of shield. "Dunno. Never did nothing to hurt him. Tried to keep out of his way, but he would just do things to me."

"Like what?"

"Once he stood on a chair and lifted me up and set me on top of the wardrobe. Couldn't move—was all twisted—because the ceiling was too low. Hardly room to breathe."

"You didn't try to jump down?"

"Couldn't. That wardrobe was dead wobbly. 'Keep still,' Mark said, 'or the wardrobe will topple over and you'll be killed.' Had to sit there for hours," Daryll continued, with astonishing calm—why wasn't this boy screaming?— "before Howard found me and helped me down."

"And Mark used to hit you?" Daryll nodded. "And your stepfather did, too?"

"He wasn't as bad as Mark," Daryll said. "Ian used to lay into me something awful when he got drunk, but he wasn't . . . What I mean is, he just did it and got it over with. With Mark, it was worse."

"And your mother?"

"What about her?" He glanced again at the residential worker, nervous now.

"Did your mother beat you, too?"

"Never," he said emphatically. "She was good as gold,

my mum. She would have done anything—anything—for her boys."

Anything but stop the beatings. But then, what did I know about Janet Flatt? I who had a job I liked and a decent income and a home of my own and enough self-confidence now (though it wasn't always so) to cover two. I who had only been struck in the line of business—never in love. I who could afford to despise the people who hit me. Who didn't have to butter anyone up to pay the bills.

Who had never been made to choose between my lover and my child.

The social worker was glaring at me again. She was right: although Daryll protested too much, it wasn't up to me to score the surface of his feelings for his mother.

"Mark came to visit you at Mrs. King's house, didn't he, Daryll? Do you remember what he wanted? What he did?"

Daryll shivered, and clutched the E.T. doll more tightly. "Dunno." He shrugged. "He came in and sort of poked around. Said he wanted to see how his little brother was getting on. Didn't believe him."

"Were you scared?"

" 'Course not," Daryll retorted, but he looked anxious. "Anyway, Kelsey came. And Mark told him some story about wanting Howard's address. And then he left. Mark doesn't bother me when Kelsey's around."

As he said this, the air was pierced with high-pitched screaming. There were repeated crashes of wood on metal. The sound had the urgency of sudden death—as if someone had caught their leg in a man trap and was in overwhelming pain. I tensed. Daryll didn't even flinch. The woman with the plait strode to the door. As she peered up and down the corridor, I seized my chance.

"Daryll," I whispered, "when you threw those rocks at Mrs. King—"

He interrupted. Not a whisper but a low controlled tone, clear, carefully enunciated. Unmistakable.

"Rock," he said.

The residential worker returned and leaned against the door frame. Punched numbers into a mobile phone. "It's Henry," she said. "Gone over the top again, down in Visitors." She rang off and sat down as if nothing had happened.

"Rock?" I asked. I couldn't keep the surprise out of my voice.

Daryll's eyes fixed on mine. Not bleak any longer. Something other than despair, something questing, hopeful—cunning?—leaped out. He made sure he had my full attention and then he nodded. *Yes.*

Rock. Not rocks. Not lump of concrete. If this was true, then Daryll Flatt didn't murder Geraldine King.

I cast about for other legitimate topics, tried to reclaim the conversational tone I'd started out with. I cleared my throat. The woman with the plait cast me a suspicious glance.

"Kelsey McLeod comes to see you here, doesn't he?"

"Every Sunday. Sometimes during the week as well. Kelsey is my best friend."

"That's a lot of visits. What do you do when he's here?"

"Oh, you know." He glanced at the residential worker again. She was looking the other way. "Sometimes we play table tennis. Sometimes we kick a ball around in the yard, if it's not raining. Mostly we just talk."

"He's easy to talk to?"

He nodded, but there was a guarded note to his movement. One finger ran in small defensive circles over the leather leg of the doll.

"You have a lot in common?"

Daryll nodded. Out-and-out suspicious now.

"What did you think of Mrs. McLeod?" I asked.

He shrugged, but the suspicion faded. Nothing dangerous about this ground, as far as Daryll was concerned. "Never met her."

"You spent all that time with Kelsey McLeod, and you never met his wife?"

He rose to the challenge. Put on a so-much-for-you kind of voice. "She's dead," he said.

"Dead?"

"Yes. Of menin— Can't remember what it's called. You get a terrible fever and your head hurts. It happened the year before my granny died."

"Meningitis?" I asked. "She died of meningitis?" He nodded. "That would explain why you never met," I said.

Not.

But at least it narrowed down the possibilities.

The social worker crossed her corduroyed legs and tapped the glass of her wristwatch with the pencil.

"One last question," I agreed. "You told the police, a long time ago, that Mrs. King extracted a sheet of paper from her handbag and tore it into pieces. What was that paper like? Can you remember anything about it? Anything at all?"

"About the paper?" If Daryll regarded this as an odd question, he didn't complain. I could see from his face that he was working to recall. But after so much time, it was difficult. Finally, he spoke, sounding half fearful, as if he felt he might be blamed for failing to remember much. "It was just a piece of paper. It had a picture, in the corner. And lots of writing."

"What was the picture of?"

Daryll shrugged. "Couldn't really see. Maybe woods or something like that. There was a tree for sure."

"The words. Were they typed? Or written by hand?"

"Typed. With lots of spaces in between."

I opened my briefcase and took out three sheets of white paper, an A3, an A4, and an A5. When I bent over, my body gave a blip. I determined to ignore it. "Which of these is closest in size?" I asked.

"It was folded in half," Daryll pointed out.

I made a horizontal fold in each of the three sheets and then held them up one at a time. Daryll watched me with anxious eyes.

"Like that," he said, identifying the A4 sheet. "Do you know what it is?"

"Not yet," I said. "All I know is that it matters. And that you've been a tremendous help."

His smile was like a burst of summer. "Will you come again?" he asked. "Do you play table tennis?"

He caught me off guard there. "Are women allowed inside?" I asked, thinking that the interior areas of the secure unit would be closed off.

"Of course," he said indignantly. "It's not a prison."

On our way out of the room, Daryll exited first and I took the opportunity to whisper a query to the woman with the plait. "Does he never refer to himself in the first person?" I asked.

There was a trace of scorn in her look. "The last time Daryll said 'I,' " she replied, "was when he said 'I did it.' "

BY THE TIME I crossed the parking lot outside Stamford House, my blip had blossomed into full-scale nausea. The tube was out of the question. A taxi set down its passengers on Goldhawk Road within spitting distance, and instead of spitting, I climbed carefully in.

Once the cabbie had assumed responsibility for getting me to Sonny's place, my stomach stabilized. He tried to engage me in a discussion of minicab drivers. Scum of the earth, apparently. Trade-stealing, know-nothing layabouts. I wasn't in a state to argue. I looked out of the window and let the epithets hang in the air like acid rain.

I maintained control all through the cabbie's harangue, through the start-stop of rush hour traffic. But once I'd paid the driver and stumbled frantically up Sonny's stone steps, once I had rung the bell in the hope of attracting help and then—abandoning hope—let myself in, my self-control cracked. Couldn't even make the bathroom. I dropped to my knees, tugged the hem of my raincoat aside and was sick all over the Victorian tiles.

What is it about being sick to your stomach that changes independence into isolation? There's the helplessness, to start with. Your knees buckle, your strength seeps away, your mind refuses to focus. There's the way you lose proportion: I didn't care any longer about the case, about Daryll Flatt or Geraldine King, about the whys and hows and wherefores of the murder. To hell with it all: just make this feeling go away.

There's only one thing that can make me yearn for my mother, and this is it.

But of course, when I'd done the revolting deed, I felt immediately lighter. I stood up and eyed the evidence with distaste. If the world were fair, I thought, someone would sweep into the room at that moment and carry me off to bed. Someone would ply me with warm drinks and cuddles. Someone would clean up for me.

But it's not. I was alone. I would have to take myself to bed. And though I tried, I couldn't bring myself to sneak off without relieving the floor of its burden.

Nicole's phone call caught me on my knees again in the hallway. I set the bottle of Dettol down and reached for the receiver.

"Caught you at last," she said. She sounded like she'd just won the national lottery.

I stretched the phone cord and plonked myself on the floor, with my back propped against the wall. "You've caught me, more or less, being sick," I said. "Don't know yet whether it's a stomach bug or a reaction to the drugs they gave me in hospital. But I feel—"

"Like death warmed over?" Nicole interrupted. "Well, funnily enough, that's the subject of my phone call."

"Don't be cryptic. Have you caught Caudwell?"

"Not yet; we have a couple of locations still to check out. But we have searched his house."

"How did his wife feel about that?"

"Emma tidied up compulsively behind us. Almost felt sorry for her. And we found—any guesses?"

"A gorilla mask?"

"You're behind the times, Laura. Caudwell's mask collection was stashed away in an orange box in the tree house. Didn't you hear?"

That confirmed it. It was Caudwell who had left me shaking in the tree house. He'd been standing sentinel over his hiding place.

Nicole took my grunt of recollection as a signal to continue. "What we found when we searched—in the bottom drawer of a rolltop desk—was a plastic folder chockablock with clippings. Not just any old clippings. Every single one had to do with the murder of Geraldine King. It was all there, his own private archive, from the finding of the body right through the trial. He'd gone to some trouble. They were from several different newspapers, all neatly trimmed, and ordered and dated. Now," she asked, "what do you make of that?"

"More to the point, Inspector," I countered—my stomach was feeling blissfully steady—"what do you make of it?"

"Seems like more than neighborly interest to me," Nicole shot back. "I've had a constable combing through the witness reports from the time, and what has she found? Two witnesses reported a flasher—*the* flasher, you could hardly mix him up with any other—hanging about on the day that Geraldine was murdered."

"The Apeman was never a suspect?"

Nicole might have shrugged. I thought I heard the whisper of fabric. "Flashers aren't violent. It's not in the profile," she said. "And anyway, he was after kids, not old ladies." She cleared her throat. "And anyway, we never found him."

"But of course now, as soon as you locate him, you'll want to interview him about the murder?"

"Goes without saying," she said.

SONNY FOUND ME snuggled under the quilt, a couple of hours after my inglorious entrance. Snoring, or at least that's what he claimed. He didn't know that I'd been sick until I told him the whole grisly tale.

Sonny rose to the occasion. He warmed me a bowl of soup and brought it to the bedroom, on a tray, with thin slices of toast and a pot of raspberry tea. He removed his boots, shuffled an armchair broadside to the bed, and sat with his long legs snuggled under the quilt and his toes grazing mine.

I loved the attention. I demanded and got sugar in my tea. I ate all of the soup and some of the toast. I began to tell him about my day.

Sonny pounced upon Daryll's views about his mother.

I repeated what I'd said. " 'Good as gold' was how Daryll described her. So what?"

"What does that suggest to you?" Sonny asked. "Janet was a far from perfect mother: she drank, she allowed her children to be beaten, and then she sent her son away to be fostered. Or that's how it might look to little Daryll. But 'good as gold' tells us that Daryll couldn't face up to her failings. That he tried to hold an image of her as perfectly pure and good. Good as gold."

Easy to understand. Daryll's father, his brother Howard, even in a sense his granny, had all—from a child's point of view—abandoned him. Maybe for his own sanity he had to believe that his mother, at least, was perfectly loving.

"Poor little lad," I said. Poor little tyke, slouching in the interview room, a leather doll clutched in the crook of his arm.

Poor little killer?

"At the same time," Sonny continued, "there was bound to be some anger with his mother. For failing to protect him. For letting him be taken into care. And that might provide a motive for Geraldine's murder."

I didn't understand. "Don't understand," I said.

"Daryll didn't seem to care one way or the other about Geraldine. Then why in heaven's name would he bump her off? That's what you've always said—no passion, no motive. Right?"

"Right. But now—"

Sonny wasn't about to be interrupted. "Now we have to consider that Daryll's attack might not have been aimed at Geraldine herself."

"Sonny, what are you talking about?" My head hadn't stopped hurting, and I had no inclination for beating around

the bush. "You aren't seriously suggesting that we're deal-
ing with a case of mistaken identity? Maybe you think that
Daryll was eager to see his social worker that afternoon
because he wanted to drop a lump of concrete on his head?
That he had trouble telling Geraldine King and Kelsey
McLeod apart?"

Lapsing into sarcasm when I feel unwell is one of my
less appealing habits.

"Give me a chance, Laura," Sonny said in quiet reproof.

I crawled down the bed and touched my cheek to his.
"Sorry, Sonny. Mea culpa." I felt genuinely contrite.

"Stuff the Latin," he said, still annoyed. "And get back
into bed. You're not well enough to be moving around."
He waited while I retreated back to my end. "All I'm saying is that maybe the murder wasn't sparked by Daryll's
relationship with Geraldine. Maybe Geraldine was merely
a cipher."

I looked blank.

"A stand-in," Sonny explained. "A substitute. A sym-
bol for someone whom he was angry with but didn't dare
attack."

At last I understood. "And who else would a foster
mother substitute for but the mother herself! So maybe all
those rocks reflected his anger, really, with Janet Flatt?" I
considered. And sighed, overwhelmed by the unfairness
of it.

Sonny doesn't like it when I go all negative. He removed the tray from my lap and helped himself to a slice
of cold toast. "A straightforward scenario at last, Laura.
What are you fretting about now?"

I confessed to a sudden sorrow about Geraldine King.
"She was such an inconsequential creature, Sonny. For
much of her life, she trundled along in Stanley's shadow.
And now you've suggested that even in the matter of her

death, Geraldine was still just standing in for somebody else."

Then I recalled the rest of my conversation with Daryll Flatt, and immediately brightened. "Only one problem with your intriguing theory, Sonny."

"And that is?" There was a hint of smugness around his jawline.

"Daryll didn't do it."

I told him what Daryll had told me, but Sonny took some persuading. "Daryll insists he threw only one rock?" he asked.

I nodded.

"Not a series of rocks? Not a lump of concrete?"

Nodded again.

"And this changes everything?"

"Of course it changes everything! I've seen the pathology report, Sonny. There's no way Geraldine was killed by rock in the singular. She was struck by a hail of rocks and then—most decisively—by concrete. Daryll was emphatic. He threw one rock. And that means he didn't kill her."

"If you don't mind me saying, Laura, a word and a nod is not a lot on which to base a conclusion."

I did mind. Thinking about it made my head hurt.

Sonny fetched me a couple of painkillers. "Okay," he said, with a slight smile, bowing to my determination. "I'll buy Daryll's innocence, for now. But do you buy Patrick Caudwell as the killer?"

I padded my answer with caution. "Wouldn't go that far," I demurred. "But some of the circumstances can be made to fit. Motive is straightforward. Geraldine finds out that Caudwell's the flasher. Caudwell tries to extract a promise of silence. She refuses. He kills her. Maybe, when

Geraldine left the house that afternoon, she confronted Caudwell. Maybe that encounter triggered her appointment with the solicitor."

"Whoa," Sonny said. "Hang on, Laura. Surely she'd go straight to the police."

"We're not talking here about an independent woman," I reminded him. "It would be just like Mrs. Stanley King to consult an expert before taking the matter any further."

"Opportunity?"

"Not a problem," I continued. "Caudwell lived next door. He was accustomed to moving stealthily between the two properties. In fact, he gave me quite a start once when I was peering into the window of the bungalow. I'd had no hint of his approach."

"And have you noticed," Sonny chimed in, "even the fact that the knickers were ripped off the body makes more sense if Caudwell rather than Daryll did the killing. A flasher, after all, is more into looking than he is into physical contact."

"Isn't that a voyeur?" I asked, sitting up higher so I could study his face.

"Maybe they're two sides of the same coin—the flasher who wants to be seen and the voyeur who gets a kick out of watching." Sonny was hot on the trail of Caudwell at the moment, and unwilling to be deflected. "And as for the missing money," he said, "it's bound to turn up now in Caudwell's bank account, or tucked away in his desk at Addenbrooke's."

We closed on that note of optimism. "How's the headache?" Sonny asked, looking me over from head to foot.

"Tylenol didn't work," I complained. "And speculation has made it a lot worse. But there's a chance it might respond to some tender loving care."

Sonny took his clothes off. Slid under the covers. And massaged my headache away.

Proving once again that, even in this age of advanced pharmaceuticals, the old-fashioned remedies are often the best.

Chapter 23

WHEN I AWOKE, I was alone. The light through the windows proclaimed the arrival of morning. The cool sheets on Sonny's side of the bed suggested he'd been up for a while. He had a security conference in Birmingham that day. I hoped he hadn't left without a word.

O me of little faith. The door opened and Sonny slipped in with a mug in each hand and the telephone gripped between shoulder and chin. "It's Stevie," he said, setting the coffee down. "She's off to Cromer to tie up loose ends with Mrs. Bennett's solicitor. She fancies following that with some free days in Norfolk. Any objections?"

"Let me have a word with her." I scrambled to a sitting position and shook the hair out of my eyes. He handed me the phone.

"Stevie?" I added a veneer of gruffness to my throaty just-woke-up voice. "What's all this about wanting time off?"

Stevie seemed to take my boss act seriously. She had put in a lot of night work on the Bennett case and was owed some time, she explained, so she thought she'd loosen up at Wildfell Cottage for a few days. "If it's all right with you?"

All right with me? Stevie and Helen and I share a vacation home in the village of Burnham St. Stephens, near the north Norfolk coast. At the mention of Wildfell Cottage, I conjured up a welcome image of the mist rising from the meadow, of the moonlight silvering the apple tree, of the whisper of the grasses by the side of the stream.

"One condition, Stevie," I replied. "That you pick me up on your way past—drop me at the nearest Marks & Sparks so I can acquire clean underwear—and then take me to Norfolk with you. A couple of days at the cottage is just what the doctor ordered."

"Why do I fall for it every time?" Stevie groaned. "Okay, boss, I accept your company with pleasure. But I'm not sure I can go along with the underwear. Can't a girl like you do any better than Marks & Spencer?"

"Meaning?"

"Meaning, let's get some class here. Haven't you heard of Victoria's Secret? La Senza? Let alone Janet Reager?"

"I'll stick with Marks & Sparks," I insisted. "If it's good enough for Margaret Thatcher, it's good enough for me."

"Mrs. T.?" Stevie said, laughing. "Am I hearing right?"

"She was an expert on uplift, didn't you know?"

"No no, not the Iron Lady joke," Stevie pleaded. But she swung past Sonny's place on her way out of London anyway, and I piled my bag into the back of her ancient Mercedes.

"How you feeling today?" she asked as she pulled out again into traffic.

"I tested the state of my stomach with a shower, then added scrambled eggs and coffee. And so far, so good. Must have just been a passing bug. A transient."

"Or that water you swallowed when you plunged into the Cam," Stevie suggested. "Give me plenty of warning if you feel queasy again. I've just cleaned the upholstery."

Florence Nightingale she ain't.

We were on our way. We passed the time in easy conversation. The only awkward moment came when Stevie quizzed me about how Ginny had come to be in the tree house when Caudwell appeared. I explained about the real estate flyer and how the girls were determined to visit the bungalow. How I had escorted them there to avoid the risk that they might visit on their own. Or that was the plan.

I shrugged. "We all make mistakes."

But something about this conversation bothered me. I could feel a tightening in my gut again, and this time I was sure it wasn't a passing bug.

We pulled into Cromer around noon. As soon as I opened the car door, I was struck by the scent of the sea. Stevie headed straight for the solicitor's office. "You won't see me for a while," she warned. "Can you occupy yourself?"

Can a crab walk sideways?

I set out, briefcase in hand, to confront the funny feeling that had assailed me in the car. At the post office, I compiled a list of local real estate agents. It was longer than anticipated. Property sales, it seemed, were part of the seaside ambience.

In the first office on my list, there was an enormous ash-veneered desk with that bland emptiness that says lack of work. The girl behind it looked as if she ought to be in school. "Have you worked here long?" I asked, as a precaution. For two years, she replied. So much for my assessments of age.

I was trying, I explained, to trace the movements of someone who had been involved in a crime. I didn't say what kind of crime. I didn't mention that Geraldine was dead.

The estate agent applied herself conscientiously. She removed the smile from her face, straightened her shoulders, and gave careful attention to the photograph that I had borrowed from Becca Hunter. I had been carrying a snapshot of Geraldine King in my briefcase all this time.

"It's not easy," she said apologetically. "We get a lot of elderly ladies in here. And—" She cut off the remark before it emerged. Very wise, in my view. *They all look alike* is hardly good for retirement sales.

I thanked her for her time, and headed down the street. The next office on my list emulated the kind of olde English shoppe that Disney has made famous—bow-fronted window, with small panes; snow, whether it snows or not, at Christmas. Harmless, I suppose, but not likely to impress buyers with the firm's aesthetic standards.

Still, when Mr. Armstrong—*Call me Andrew*—recognized Geraldine, I forgave him his bow window. "You know her?"

"Certainly," he said, with a reserved smile. "Such a charming lady. And so very pretty, if you don't mind me saying. I remember her well. I can tell you her name. Wait." He held up a manicured hand. "Give me a moment, please." It was his party piece. Other people of his seniority might ask to be let off the detail. But Andrew Armstrong could recall, he assured me, every single client of the past five years. "Mrs. King," he said, and looked understandably smug. "Mrs. Gemma— No, I take it back, Mrs. Geraldine King."

He checked the file. Mrs. King had come in two and a half years ago. She was in search of what three-quarters of their clients desired, but fewer could afford—a bungalow overlooking the North Sea. There had been a house with a south-facing sitting room that she had been particularly keen on. But then nothing had happened. "They must have gone off the idea," Andrew said.

Such a little word—an innocuous, commonplace word—

for such a big impact. I experienced a kind of shock, as if someone had buffeted me across the back of the head.

"They?" I asked.

Yes, Andrew explained, Geraldine had been very keen to purchase. Even though she held back, was dithering, Andrew recognized all the signs of enthusiasm. Even, he said coyly, of desire. One glance at the built-in display cabinets in the sitting room, he said, and she was hooked. That's part of what a good estate agent does, weighing up the client. It's psychology, he proclaimed with pride.

"They?" I urged, leaning forward in my seat.

"Yes," Andrew explained. "Mrs. King was quite dependent on her son. Asked his opinion constantly. And though he gave an appearance of interest, I suspected from the outset that he was humoring her." He shrugged. "Guess I was right."

"Her son Edward?"

"Yes, indeed." The agent nodded emphatically. "Mr. Edward King."

"You have an amazing memory for names and faces, Andrew. How about a description of this Edward?"

He looked doubtful. "I was rather concentrating on the lady," he admitted.

"Could you try? What was his build?"

"A very narrow man," Andrew said. "What you might call spare. Pale complexion, long upper lip—clean-shaven, of course."

I had no idea what "of course" meant, but I let it pass. "Hair color?"

Andrew deliberated. "Burnt umber," he said. He gave me an apologetic smile, as if his phrase required explanation. "My wife paints, you see. Oils. If I had only seen him indoors, I would have said dark brown. But out of doors, when we drove to inspect the property, there were crimson highlights."

"You couldn't have been more helpful, Andrew, thank you. Not many people could recall a tenth of the detail you have. Is there anything else before I go? About your dealings with Geraldine or Edward King? Anything at all?"

Flushed with pleasure—I don't imagine that his line of work provides many opportunities for praise—the estate agent insisted on consulting his files again. "One more thing," he concluded. "For months, I didn't see or hear anything of the Kings. And then I had a phone call. From the lady. She was extremely agitated. Was the house ready, she asked, to move into? I was taken aback, as you can imagine. I'm sorry, Mrs. King, I said, but the sale didn't go through. Surely you knew that your son didn't pursue it? But apparently she didn't." Andrew paused for a moment. He looked stricken at the memory.

"She was very distressed," he concluded. "I don't know what was going on between those two, but it didn't seem to me to be any way to treat a lady."

Let alone your mother.

I SHOULD HAVE hung around and waited for Stevie to emerge from the solicitors, but the new information that had been lobbed into my lap made me hungry for answers. Here I was in Cromer, where the Holtbys lived. It was Thursday afternoon: Faith would be at the operatic society, rehearsing *Peter Grimes*. I would just have time for a meeting alone with Geraldine's brother-in-law.

If I hurried, that is. I raced along Hamilton Road, only stopping once to ask directions. On and on, until I came to the Holtbys' terraced house.

He came to the door on the third ring, his slippers slopping on the runner. "Well, hello," he said, dragging the syllables out. If he had been a character in a cartoon, his eyes would have stood out on springs.

"Mr. Holtby? You do remember me? I'm a private investigator, Laura Principal. I spoke to you and your wife a while ago about her sister, Geraldine King."

"How could I forget you?" he asked. Easily, I would have thought, since he spent most of our previous encounter glued to the television. "Come in, come in. You want a beer?"

"Let's split one," I said. "Thanks."

He shuffled about, fetching a beer and a glass for me, and then installed himself on a chair facing the television and invited me to seat myself nearby. "What can I do for you?" he asked.

Well, the man didn't seem to be a watchword for subtlety, so I decided not to beat about the bush. "I need your help, Mr. Holtby." When he smiled, I was fascinated to see that his earlobes trembled.

"Hang on, Lauren," he interrupted. "Let's start as we should continue. Call me Bill."

"Bill," I acknowledged, and raised my glass to him in salute. "There's a question that matters a lot to me. It's a question that only you can answer."

He took two large gulps of his beer and set the glass down. "Fire away," he said.

"The day before your sister-in-law died, she and your wife had a quarrel. A falling out. The sort of thing that's bound to happen occasionally between sisters."

"Yes, they did," Holtby said. He nodded in agreement. And smiled. "What's your question, Laurel?"

"Did this quarrel have anything to do with you?" I took a deep breath. Had I been too direct, had I rushed him, had I been—in a word—too pushy? Would this interview screech to a halt?

Not a bit of it.

"Sure did," Holtby said. His grin widened with pride. "It's something, isn't it, when a man has women fighting over him at my age?"

He was so puffed up at the memory that I had to prompt him again. "Faith and Geraldine were fighting over you?" I kept the astonishment out of my voice.

"Sure," he confirmed. "It happened like this. Geraldine complained to Faith that she had been propositioned. I'd been in Cambridge a few days earlier, on some business. Popped in to see my sister-in-law. Made a pass at her, Geraldine claimed. An indecent proposal." He said this in a voice that was supposed, I imagine, to mimic the prim tones of Geraldine King.

"And how did your wife react when she heard that?"

"She was livid. If you've never seen Faith when she gets angry, you've really missed a sight. Whoo-ee, that woman can blow up. Goes all red, she does, up her face and her neck. She was furious with Geraldine. Called her a vicious liar." He chuckled. "Don't you sometimes wish you could be a fly on the wall?"

"The next day, Geraldine died," I said. Bill Holtby had a curious sense of humor. "Was there anything in her accusation? Had you made a pass at Mrs. King?"

Holtby polished off his beer and headed for the fridge to get another. "Of course," he said, returning from the kitchen. "And you can't tell me she wasn't asking for it. The way that woman dressed and the way she was always talking talking talking, standing so close. Anyone could tell she was on the lookout for a man. It was bad enough while Stanley was alive. But after she became a widow— well! Anyone could see that what she needed was—"

"Funny, that," I interrupted. "Because she rebuffed you. Am I right?"

For the first time, there was a hint of recognition of the outside world in Holtby's face. A sign that something had pierced his complacency. He became rigid. Even his ear-lobes were still.

"Well," I nudged him. "Did Geraldine rebuff you? What exactly did she say?"

He looked at me, and there was something cruel in his eyes. "You really want to know what she said? She got out of it by claiming she had a sweetheart. 'I'm already seeing someone, Bill,' she said in that ridiculous voice. 'Some-one special. A gentleman. Not like you.' "

"Did she say his name? Give any clue as to his identity?"

He shook his head. Picked up the remote control that rested on the arm of his chair and pressed the button. Flicked rapidly from cartoon network to German soft porn to a war film. Submarines and strong jaws.

"Mr. Holtby," I prompted. I couldn't call him Bill again. "Mr. Holtby, why didn't you tell the police?"

He looked at me for the last time. "That was Faith's doing. Geraldine was wrong to make such an accusation, Faith insisted. She made me promise. 'Swear to me, Bill,' she said, 'that you'll never repeat such a vicious lie.' And until now, I kept my promise. Anything," he said, with a cruel smile, "anything for domestic harmony."

BY THE TIME I returned to the car, Stevie had come and gone. I felt ridiculous leaning against the boot of her Mer-cedes, mobile phone in hand—like one of those boys you see from time to time in suspenders, pretending to be bro-kers. But none of the phone companies had seen fit to set up a call box within sight of the parking lot, so what choice did I have?

Little choice, less luck. I made a perfect score, of a kind—zero out of three. My failure applied as much to the calls I should have made yesterday—could have made, would have made, if nausea hadn't intervened—as to the newly urgent. Howard's line was persistently engaged, so I wasn't able to bring him up to date on my meeting with Daryll. Helen couldn't be reached, so I was unable to confirm that Ginny had bounced back from her encounter with the Apeman. At the Parkside police station, the desk sergeant couldn't contact Inspector Pelletier and he wasn't prepared to give me news himself about Patrick Caudwell.

Stevie strutted back to the car, newly exotic in a waistcoat embroidered in purples and mauves. I admired the purchase and then popped the question. "Stevie, how would you feel about the prospect of taking next week off?"

Not a flicker of hesitation. "Would give me a chance to dust off my walking boots and check out the Pennines before snowfall," Stevie said. "Why this sudden generosity?"

"I have to get back to Cambridge quickly."

Stevie selected a choice specimen from her famous collection of curses and flung it in my direction. Then her agreeable side took over. She settled herself into the driver's seat and leaned across to unlock my door. "I guess Wildfell will still be here in a fortnight's time," she said. "You can tell me on the way to Cambridge what's triggered this change of plan."

We hit the road.

My brain liked to think of myself as fully recovered from the shock of Caudwell's attack and from my bout of sickness, but I guess my body knew better. As soon as the heater boosted the temperature, exhaustion settled in again, clouding my mind and burdening my eyelids.

"Give me a few minutes to catch my breath," I said, resting my cheek on the window and closing my eyes, "and then all will be revealed."

But I slept for most of the journey. We were on the out-skirts of Cambridge by the time I returned to conscious-ness. The car was hot and noisy. An old Joe Cocker track was playing on the radio, and Stevie was singing in sup-port of his sentiments about friendship. It's a mystery how I managed to sleep.

Stevie saw me move and winked at me. "You could have said straight out that you'd rather not tell me what happened in Cromer, Laura. It's not like you to take refuge in sleep." She polished off the track with a drum roll that left the steering wheel unattended for longer than I liked.

"No, honestly, Stevie," I began. *Honestly* brought me to a halt. Maybe I was putting it off. Something about the revelations that had emerged today had leached into my soul. I waited until the crest of the wave of sadness had swept over me.

"Geraldine King had a lover," I said quietly.

"So?"

"So why didn't we—me, the police—guess that earlier? We knew most of what we needed to know. Knew that she had been a heartbreaker as a girl. Knew that she was *interested* in men."

"And just how did 'we' know that?" Stevie asked.

I shrugged. "It was everywhere. In the history of her life with Stanley. Remember? 'I'd rather be a widow,' she insisted, 'than be a Ms.' In the positive descriptions—charming, vivacious, pretty—she earned from Murray Eagleton, Kelsey McLeod, the estate agent in Cromer. She flattered men, made them feel good. But the women I spoke to—Becca Hunter, Emma Caudwell, Janet Flatt—found her harder to like. Apart from her sister, she had no female friends."

"So? She was a man's woman," Stevie said. "Surely not the first you've come across."

"More than that," I insisted. "Emma Caudwell almost gave the game away, but I refused to see. Emma complained about Geraldine. 'Stanley King was only dead a month or so, and Geraldine was over here, asking for Patrick, wanting help with her lawn mower. It wasn't "friends" she was after, was it?' At the time, I disregarded Emma's remark. Filed it away as a blatant example of fear-of-the-unattached-woman. But Emma Caudwell saw perfectly clearly what I didn't allow myself to understand: Geraldine King was on the lookout for love."

"You're being a little hard on yourself, Laura. You're not the first person to assume that elderly women are past it. It's part and parcel of society's attitudes toward aging. Sexuality—we're made to believe—is for the young."

"And the beautiful," I added. "And the able-bodied."

"Exactly. Women 'past their prime'—now there's a phrase!—become invisible. As if, when they collect the pension book, they just kind of shrivel up and die."

"Isn't that going a bit far?" I countered. "You make it sound as if nobody values elderly women." I thought of my mother, happily tucked away in Bristol, whom I hadn't called in a fortnight.

"There's value and there's value. Sure, you can decide to be a granny type who does more or less what's expected. All lavender scent and cookies. But what if that isn't you? Or what if it is, but you want more?"

I looked her up and down. "Can't see you as a sweet little old lady, Stevie."

"I'm not going to go quietly into old-ladydom," Stevie agreed. "I'll take up hang-gliding and have lovers by the score. I'll wear purple, like the poem says, and do lots of forbidden things."

"But you're wearing purple now, Stevie," I interrupted.

"Road-testing it." She laughed.

We drove for a moment in silence, weaving through the traffic around Mitcham's Corner. But the topic was still with us.

"Personally, Laura, it's not the stereotypes that bother me. I can handle those—sticks and stones and all that. What gets to me is the physical vulnerability. The frailties of old age. The fear. I don't want to be afraid," she said. It was the first time I'd ever heard a note of fear in Stevie's voice. She continued. "While you were sleeping, there was a news report. Another elderly woman murdered. Not so far from Cambridge this time. Somebody Pollitt, in Huntingdon."

It didn't help my mood. Too many deaths, I thought sadly. Too much violence. Too much fear.

We slid across Victoria Bridge. The frame for the city bonfire could barely be discerned looming out of the darkness on the common.

"Where to?" Stevie asked as she approached the roundabout.

"Anywhere you're sure I can speak to Detective Inspector Pelletier."

"Let's try the police station," Stevie said. My practical pal.

Chapter 24

Bᴜᴛ Nɪᴄᴏʟᴇ ᴡᴀs not to be found—not until the following morning. I passed the intervening hours somehow, with snatches of sleep. I returned to the station at half-past eight and almost missed her.

Inspector Pelletier was on the move. She jostled down the corridor, meanwhile throwing off instructions to the pair of officers who shadowed her.

I blurted out my news. It brought her to a halt.

"Are you serious?" she demanded.

There was a touch of end-of-the-tethers in her tone. She was heading to a burglary scene in Waterbeach. Missing computers. Again. The same premises had been cleaned out by the same burglars only ten days before. They had waited for the insurance company to settle and the new computers to be installed. Then they had sauntered back for the replacements.

That kind of thing tends to make a police officer touchy.

"You're telling me, Laura, that you know what happened to Mrs. King's missing money?"

For a few seconds I savored the feeling of being the girl in the know. So rare, so deeply satisfying. Like sticky toffee pudding.

I took a risk. "What did the lady gnu say to her husband,

Nicole, after giving birth to triplets?" A silence forced me to make my own reply. "Darling, have I got gnus for you!"

Nicole glowered at me. Not a groan escaped her lips. She instructed the constable who was waiting to go on ahead to Waterbeach and keep the lid on till she came. Then she led me to an interview room and designated a junior officer to take notes. "This better be better than your jokes," she said through gritted teeth.

So I put the gnus behind me and went straight into the story. Starting with Cromer, and how I had come to be at a real estate agent's, flashing Geraldine's photo.

The missing money had been eating away at me, I explained. What would a woman like Geraldine want with forty thousand pounds? One of the few things that would make sense was buying a house; and I'd been told that Geraldine would happily have moved to Norfolk, if her late husband hadn't vetoed it. But I only connected these things when I was telling Stevie how I had been cajoled into taking Ginny to the scene of the crime. Ginny had seen the real estate flyer about Geraldine's bungalow, I said. And I suddenly knew—*knew* was the only word for it—that the paper Geraldine had ripped up on the day of her death was a real estate circular. The specifications indicated in the lab report fit, and so did the description of the paper that I got from Daryll.

"But you're saying that Geraldine didn't actually buy the house in Cromer," Nicole protested. "So where did the money go?"

"I'm coming to that. The estate agent—here's Andrew Armstrong's business card, by the way—says that though Geraldine was eager to buy, the man with her was less so. The money never materialized."

Nicole pointed her finger at the junior officer. He leaned

over and took the card and set it squarely on the table in front of him. "Meaning?" she asked.

"Meaning that Geraldine—a woman who couldn't mow a lawn on her own, much less buy a house—handed over forty thousand pounds to someone else. On the understanding that he would arrange the purchase. And that gallant gentleman pocketed the money. When Geraldine finally rang the estate agent herself, she found out she'd been fleeced. That phone call could well have been made on the day of her death."

Nicole was twitching in her excitement. She has lots of fine qualities, but you would never call her serene. "So who was he?"

"By name and appearance," I replied, "it was Edward King."

Nicole joined me for the refrain. "Geraldine's son," we chorused together.

Nicole stood up and briskly brushed her skirt back into place. "Constable," she said, "reserve me a car for"—only the slightest hesitation before that phenomenal memory clocked in again—"Papworth Everard. Six o'clock this evening. I'll want a sergeant with me." She started toward the door.

"Oh, by the way, Laura," she said, stepping aside so the constable could open the door, "Caudwell's been found. At his sister's place in Pembrokeshire. It was a desperate dash, rather than a successful one."

"When do you expect to see him?"

"He'll arrive in Cambridge under escort later tonight. Depends when we can find the manpower. Can I leave you to break the news to Helen Cochrane?"

Knowing that Caudwell was in custody—that there was no chance he would suddenly turn up in Ginny's path—

would do more for Helen's spirits than a full body massage. Not to suggest that the two are incompatible.

"With pleasure. But, Nicole, before you go . . ."

"One more thing?" She grinned.

"Two things," I admitted.

Nicole left the constable holding the door and plumped herself down again, but this time she remained on the edge of her chair. "Make it quick," she said.

"Number one. Geraldine King had a lover." We talked that over for a few moments, weighing up implications, tossing possibilities around—including the possibility that Geraldine had lied.

"Number two?" Nicole asked.

"A question. Do you know anything about this murder in Huntingdon? An elderly woman? Stevie heard the news on the radio."

"I know the outlines. Winnifred Pollitt, aged seventy-eight, apparently smothered, apparently with a pillow, in her bedroom. Sad case. Why?"

"Can you find out whether her son had been in touch with her? Whether he'd visited recently?" Nicole was waiting for something more persuasive. "I can't tell you more, Nicole, but if you're looking for promotion between now and retirement, you'll get on the phone to Huntingdon pronto."

"You won't tell me why?" Nicole asked.

"Trust me," I pleaded. "Just this once."

For an instant Nicole glared at me as if I were a scorpion that had scuttled into her lingerie drawer. Then she relented. "You've done a pretty nice job on the King case," she admitted. "I'll ring Huntingdon right after I've dealt with this B and E in Waterbeach. If you want to know the outcome, you could meet me back here in, say, an hour?"

I nodded my thanks. Turned to leave. But Nicole put a

hand on my arm and held me there. "A warning, Laura," she said. She looked stern now, the curve of concern wiped off her handsome jaw. More than stern. Forbidding. "I've given you a lot of rope in the past couple of weeks. So take notice: if my phone call to Huntingdon turns out to be a wild-goose chase . . ." She paused for dramatic effect, looked up at the ceiling.

"Yes?" I prompted.

"The gnus on your future won't be so good."

Then she disappeared down the corridor, with her constable in tow, leaving behind her the faintest trace of a smile.

I CAUGHT UP with Nicole and hitched a lift as far as Milton Road. She sped off toward the burglary; I counted down the homes on Highworth until I came to McLeod's house.

It looked, at first sight, as if no one was there. The car was in the driveway, but full-length curtains were drawn across the bay window and there were no lights visible in other parts of the house. But as I mounted the steps, I heard the bass beat of pop music from inside. I recognized the jangly background of "Dancing in the Street."

There was no response to the doorbell. The music continued. After a decent interval, I tried again. This time, "Dancing" stopped in mid-phrase and the front door swung open. I saw a hallway of polished oak, a large ceramic plant stand, and a slight woman in a leotard.

"Mrs. McLeod," I said, after a second's hesitation. "Do you remember me?"

Her eyes still bulged in a fierce blue gaze, but the pale and sickly look was gone. In her cheeks, instead, there was the hectic blush of exercise. "What are you doing here?" she asked. Her hair, pinned up on the back of her head, was damp with sweat. Her breath came in deep steady gulps.

"I wouldn't disturb you, but it's important," I said. "I need to ask you one or two questions."

"You can see I'm exercising," she objected.

"Is that Cher's workout tape I heard? The one where she wears that little spiderweb outfit? I used to do that one," I said, shuffling my feet in imitation of the aerobic routine.

"All right," she relented. "If you're quick."

She led me into the sitting room, where Cher and five babes—a redhead, two blondes, two brunettes—posed awkwardly on their right legs. A horizontal band of snow across the middle of the frozen screen made it look as if they'd been hit by a blizzard.

The room had an IKEA kind of neatness. Low-slung sofa. Low wooden coffee table. Cupboards made of stacked wooden cubes, with a scattering of reference books, bric-a-brac, and mementos. There was a collection of photos on one shelf in wooden frames. Most were of Ann and Kelsey, in holiday mood. One showed them resting against a wall. Kelsey, looking rested and clean-shaven, had his arm around Ann, was leaning toward her and whispering in her ear. There was a river behind them and a buttressed cathedral rising up on the other side.

"Paris?"

Ann McLeod nodded happily. "Our anniversary," she said. "Two years ago."

"Your husband's at work right now?"

"As a matter of fact, he's at a conference this week, in Manchester. I'm what they call a grass widow." She seemed lighthearted, as if managing on her own posed not the slightest challenge.

I braced myself. "Mrs. McLeod, I need to ask a personal question. How is your health?"

"My health?" She frowned. "I don't know what you

mean. There's nothing to say about my health. I'm just fine."

"I'm sorry, but I heard differently. I heard you had suffered from a heart disorder."

"Well, you heard wrong," she snapped. "Look at me! Do I look ill?"

"You certainly don't. Look, Mrs. McLeod, I'm sorry if this is awkward, but are you—" I stopped and rephrased. "Is this Kelsey's second marriage? Has he ever been widowed?"

Ann McLeod was slender and not very tall, but the effect of my question was to make her puff up. As if anger acted on her as a growth hormone. "I've had just about enough," she said. "What do you mean, coming in here with these ridiculous questions. 'Am I sick?' you ask. And then, in effect, 'Am I dead?' Like that appalling King woman. Well, you can leave right now. But before you go, get one thing through your head. I am not one of those people who thinks marriage is just a phase—something you try out, just for the good times. Marriage is for life."

I waited until she stopped. Until the echoes of her angry outburst died away. "When did you meet Mrs. King?" I asked.

There was a click and a whirr from the television as the pause mode flipped to rewind. Cher and her co-dancers began flying backward. They looked like drunken Barbie dolls, their legs and arms flailing.

"Get out," she said. "Out of my house. Before I call the police."

I moved in the direction of the door. She followed me, close behind, her fists beating the air to punctuate her sentences.

"I am Kelsey's wife. His *only* wife," she shouted.

"Now and forever," I heard her declare as she slammed the door.

NICOLE DIDN'T EVEN gesture toward an apology when she and her entourage swept back into Parkside—three-quarters of an hour later than expected, I observed. In police work, she replied, that looks almost overeager.

She brushed aside my polite inquiry about the burglaries in Waterbeach with a least-said, best-forgotten, wave of her hand, then hunkered down to business.

First, on the phone to colleagues in Huntingdon.

Then on to me.

"Huntingdon confirms that Winnifred Pollitt was visited by her son. Or should we say 'her son'? I expect a full explanation now, Laura. You knew, I assume, that Winnifred Pollitt has only one child? And that the child is of the female persuasion?" She raised an eyebrow in my direction.

"Name of Cheryl," I agreed.

"Let's not fart around," Nicole said. Vulgar but to the point. "Who is this 'son'? Do you know?"

"*Know* would be stretching a point. I have an idea. Winnie Pollitt, like Geraldine King, had a secret love. She was infatuated with a social worker who used to visit her old residence—Ditchburn Place—before she moved to Huntingdon. Who happens also to be the social worker with responsibility for Daryll Flatt."

"And you know this—how?" Nicole asked. I could almost hear her impatience tick-tick-ticking away.

"I picked it up when I went to interview McLeod at Ditchburn Place," I explained. "Though I certainly didn't see the significance of it at the time."

I described the scene for Nicole. The large square room with chairs lining the walls. Mrs. Partridge, who knew everything there was to know about figure skating and struck up a conversation with me as soon as I sat down. McLeod's entrance into the room—his avid attention to the old woman he accompanied.

A knack with the old folks, the matron had said. *They adore him.*

But adore wasn't Mrs. Partridge's term. *Gooey-eyed,* she insisted. *Especially Winnie Pollitt.*

"Don't take my word for it, Nicole," I said—as if she would. "Check for yourself. Ask Mrs. Partridge. Don't bother asking the matron, by the way. She thinks the sun shines out of McLeod's backside so brightly you could use it as a torch." Matron, I suspected, was gooey-eyed herself.

"Laura, remind me what this McLeod looks like."

"He's about six feet tall, slim build. Mid-forties. A bristly mustache. Hair a kind of chocolatey brown. Small-featured—one of those anxious faces that are lined and boyish at the same time."

Nicole nodded vigorously, so that her black hair took on a life of its own. She consulted her notes. "He's a dead ringer for Winnie's 'son.' Well, almost. They didn't mention a mustache. But then," she added, and now it was my turn to nod, "mustaches come and go."

Nicole had gone from grudging to gung ho in such a short space of time, I wasn't a bit surprised when she called a time-out. "Be back in five minutes," she excused herself. "Call of nature."

In fact, she returned in four. What's more, she brought coffee from a pot brewed in a back office by one of the junior officers. Real coffee, in real china mugs, dark brown and delicious. I certainly didn't miss the polystyrene.

"Let's take it step by step. Let's say that this Kelsey McLeod paid visits—unofficial visits—to Winnie Pollitt.

That he presented himself to the neighbors as her son. That she was infatuated with him. All very . . . bizarre, Laura. But a long way from murder. Do you think McLeod killed Winnie, then? What motive would he have?"

"The same motive that led to the killing of Geraldine King."

Nicole set her mug down with such a whump that a wave of coffee splashed onto the table. "I'm not sure I can take this," she warned. The edge of her sleeve absorbed some of the spilled coffee as she leaned forward.

"Earlier today," she said through gritted teeth, "you spun me a tale about Geraldine King and her son looking to buy a house in Norfolk. You moved Edward King center stage for involvement in his mother's death. If, that is—which I'm not granting—Daryll didn't kill her. But now—now you want to squeeze McLeod into the frame as well?"

"Bear with me," I said, and she did. While I began at the beginning and explained.

How Kelsey McLeod had preyed on Geraldine King. How he'd met her when she made inquiries about fostering. Had seen her as an easy target, desperate for affection. Isolated. Naive. McLeod had given a glowing report to Social Services on the quality of her foster care. He'd glossed over her ambivalence about fostering in general and about Daryll in particular. Had, in effect, encouraged the connection because it provided a cover within which he could develop his own relationship with Geraldine.

"Didn't anyone notice?" Nicole asked.

I shrugged. "Yes and no. His colleague, Murray Eagleton, noticed that McLeod hung around Geraldine's place more than duty required. He fretted that McLeod might be emotionally involved with Daryll. Never made the link to Geraldine."

"Nobody else?"

"Well, other people were puzzled—as I was, later—by the lack of attachment between Geraldine and her foster son. But as long as Daryll's social worker said the relationship was going swimmingly, and Daryll himself never complained, who was going to pursue it?"

"Daryll's mum?" Nicole suggested.

I should have picked it up sooner. "Janet Flatt almost cottoned on, didn't she? Geraldine didn't care about Daryll, she complained, to anyone who would listen. Geraldine only wanted to impress McLeod, she said. But Janet Flatt is a difficult and largely unlikable character, with her own reasons for hostility to Geraldine, so none of us took her accusations to heart."

"So what was McLeod after, Laura?"

"You'll have to ask him. My guess, for what it's worth, is that the reasons for his involvement with Geraldine changed over the months. Initially, he probably enjoyed her company. Don't look so surprised, Inspector. Men found Mrs. King attractive. The fact that she was no spring chicken is neither here nor there. She flattered them, made them feel important. But anyway, whatever pleasures McLeod got out of spending time with Geraldine, he soon saw other, more material, possibilities in an unworldly woman who would do anything to please him."

"Like a carrier bag full of cash," Nicole concluded.

"Precisely. Here's how I see it. Geraldine fancied the idea of setting up house with McLeod in Norfolk. McLeod persuaded her to keep their relationship a secret. Intimated, perhaps, that it might be conflict of interest, since she was foster mother to his charge. That he might lose his job if word got out too soon. Then he took her to look at houses, helped her select one, and relieved her of the cash. Promised to secure the deal."

"Like taking candy from a baby. But hang on," Nicole

objected. "The estate agent told you that the man who accompanied Geraldine was Edward King. Her son."

I knew it wouldn't take Nicole long to catch up. I waited. Sure enough, she was there in a matter of seconds. "Geraldine's son—Winnie Pollitt's son!" she exclaimed. "Both the 'sons' were Kelsey McLeod. What better way to cover up a relationship between an elderly woman and a younger man!" Then she thought of another problem. "But the description? The real estate agent in Cromer gave you a perfect description of Edward King." Nicole scrunched up her eyes, recalling the details. "Tall, gaunt, reddish hair. And—above all—clean-shaven, like Edward King. Kelsey McLeod has a mustache."

"They are both tall and thin," I amended. "And McLeod's hair is a chocolate color, with a reddish tone. And as for the facial hair—well, in his sitting room there's a photograph of McLeod, taken in Paris in the year Geraldine was killed. He was clean-shaven. As you said, Nicole, mustaches come and go."

There was a long pause. "If McLeod has kept quiet all this time," Nicole said, looking glum, "he's never going to confess. We'll have to open up the toolbox all over again. And nail him."

I threw in one last suggestion. "Spend a little time with Ann McLeod," I said.

"His wife? The one who's chronically ill? How does she tie in?"

"It's a phantom illness," I said dryly. "A figment of McLeod's fertile imagination. A perfect way of gaining sympathy from ladies young and old—the devoted husband, caring for an invalid spouse. And when it suited him to appear unmarried, he had no qualms about bumping her off. She became the late Mrs. McLeod."

"Poor woman!" Nicole exclaimed. "Do you think she knew how expendable she was?"

"Expendable is hardly how Ann McLeod sees herself. As far as Ann is concerned, Kelsey McLeod has no future without her. And that's precisely where Geraldine King comes into the picture." I paused for a moment, collecting my thoughts. "There's always been a mystery about the day of Geraldine's death, yes?"

"The missing ninety minutes," Nicole confirmed.

"Here's how I see it. The day of her death, Geraldine was visited by Murray Eagleton."

"Her contact at Homefinders. Her social worker, in effect."

"That's the one. Nice fellow." How can you not like a person who keeps Kit Kats in his jacket pocket? "Well, Murray and Geraldine talked about many things, including a forthcoming Homefinders social. Geraldine became agitated at that point. What got her going, I suspect, was Murray's suggestion that Kelsey would be accompanied by his wife."

"Do you mean that Geraldine might have thought up until then that McLeod was a widower? That his wife was dead and buried?"

"Precisely. That was the first hint Geraldine had that McLeod was still married. You can guess as well as I what happened next. When Geraldine learned this alarming news, she looked up the address and marched over to his house, as fast as her peep-toe shoes would carry her. Confronted Ann, told her that she and McLeod were planning to live together. Perhaps even showed her the agent's description of the house in Cromer. And probably—quite probably—Mrs. McLeod mocked her. Told her she was an old fool. Laughed in her face."

"All speculation, of course," Nicole said, falling back

on her give-me-the-evidence training. "But the sooner I get Mrs. McLeod down to the station for a little chat, the better."

And she did. Two hours later Ann McLeod—looking prickly as a pineapple—stamped her way into an interview room at the Parkside police station and put a nail in the coffin of her husband's innocence. Of course, she had no inkling that McLeod was involved in murder. The thought never seemed to have crossed her one-track mind. However, she did know—because Geraldine herself had broken the news—about his relationship with the older woman. Being reminded of this enraged Ann. And rage made her helpfully indiscreet.

"Scheming old bat," Ann shrieked. *"I'm glad she died."*

And then she obligingly named two more elderly women who had, in her delicate way of putting it, tried to get their claws into Kelsey.

"We'll have no difficulty," Nicole reported to me, "proving that McLeod made rather a habit of winning the affections of widows."

She was once again her own brusque and businesslike self, focused on the law-and-order issue of rooting out a killer. Her earlier insistence on upholding Daryll's guilt—we've got him and we'll keep him—had given way in face of the evidence. If only all police officers held that kind of commitment to the truth.

"So what do you reckon happened, Laura, after Geraldine had this shaking up encounter with Ann McLeod? Given the timing, she must have returned home pretty sharpish—wait, there's a call box on that route, isn't there? Could she have rung the estate agent in Cromer on her way home? She certainly didn't ring from her home phone. We would have picked it up."

"And learned from Andrew Armstrong that the deal had never been clinched on the house of her dreams. That McLeod had pocketed her cash. That's when she resolved to see her solicitor. If she couldn't have the man, she determined at least to get the money back."

Nicole's expression at that moment was a mixture of triumph and rue. "If you're right," Nicole said, "and I have to say it feels like a perfect fit—then Geraldine was having a hell of a day."

The image of a rain-soaked body beneath a walnut tree came unbidden to my mind. "It started bad," I agreed.

"But it ended even worse."

IT WAS GOOD to crawl into bed. To slip off all my clothes and abandon them in a heap on the floor. To pull the quilt up to my shoulders and let the music of John Lee Hooker wash over me, let his stubborn optimism—his hanging in there—provide a focus for my swirling emotions.

But when the phone rang, too late really for a phone to ring, I downed the volume on the blues and snatched it up.

"D.C. Andrews and I have been interviewing Patrick Caudwell," Nicole announced. No preliminaries, but echoes of triumph in her tone.

I pushed myself upright and maneuvered a pillow behind my back. "Has he—"

Nicole interrupted. "Apeman is consumed with remorse. Not only about his urge for indecent exposure—for which unattractive habit he has, by the way, requested treatment—but also for his part in the conviction of Daryll Flatt."

So there it was. "Did he—"

"If you can tear yourself away from whatever you're doing and get down to the station right away, you can ask him yourself. He insists he needs to speak to you. And since he's been so cooperative the last few hours, I couldn't find it in my heart to refuse."

And, of course, neither could I.

IF YOU'D ASKED me that morning, I would have laughed and said that Apeman's attack on me—that piercing spray of hospital ammonia in my eyes—was well behind me. A thing of the past. A minor occupational hazard. A bygone. Let it be.

But when I walked in the door of the interview room and saw Caudwell sitting there, with his shirtsleeves rolled up, his elbows on the table, and his head resting in his hands, it came rushing back. The hiss that the canister made as I turned my head. The searing pain. The terror that I'd never see again.

He looked up, just then, and saw the wash of hostility on my face. He didn't flinch. In an odd way, he even looked peaceful, at ease. Perhaps the arrest had lifted the weight of pretense off his shoulders. Perhaps knowing that Emma knew was less painful than the effort of keeping it from her.

"I don't expect you to forgive me," he said.

Just as well. I wasn't in a forgiving mood.

"For what I did to you," he said. "For what I did to those children. Or, most of all, for what I did to Daryll."

Well, that was something, I thought. At least he didn't try to kid himself that the attack on me mattered more than the things he'd taken—the innocence, the reputation, the childhood—from Daryll Flatt.

"You witnessed the murder?" I asked.

"Almost," he replied. "On the day of Geraldine's death, I was out and about for much of the day. Sometimes near the bushes along the towpath."

"In and out of costume, I presume?"

He met my sneering remark with a steady gaze. "Yes,"

he said. "From one of my vantage points in the bushes, I noticed McLeod's arrival. Saw him go directly toward the tree house. He stayed there for four or five minutes. Then he disappeared inside the bungalow. A few minutes later, when I glanced back in that direction, I saw McLeod searching the garden, quietly calling Daryll's name. Daryll usually rushed to be with McLeod. I thought it was odd that McLeod was having to look for him."

"No more than *odd*?"

"At the time, I didn't know about the killing."

"So when you learned that Geraldine had died—and heard that Daryll had confessed to the killing—you put two and two together?"

"Just so. I confronted Kelsey McLeod. I asked him why he hadn't told the police that he'd been at the murder site near the time Geraldine was killed." Caudwell paused, some of his composure, his apparent peace of mind, slipping away.

"And?" I insisted.

"McLeod trumped me. You see, Ms. Principal, after the murder, McLeod spent time with Daryll at the police station. Daryll told him what I'd been doing."

Caudwell lowered his head, and a flush of shame passed over his face. Not, I reckoned, for the fact that he was the flasher as much as for the fact that it was this that allowed McLeod to go free. For the first time in this interview, I felt compassion for Caudwell.

"Daryll's teacher mentioned," I volunteered, "that Daryll was harboring a secret. He was saving it to tell one special person. I guess the special person was McLeod. And the secret was . . ." I waited.

Caudwell nodded. The softness of my tone had enabled him to regain some of his dignity. "Me," he said. "McLeod offered me a deal. Mutual silence. I was to keep quiet about his presence at Geraldine's on the day of the murder; he would refrain from telling Emma, my wife, what I did to children. I sent Daryll Flatt to prison so that I could go on living a lie."

Caudwell looked me straight in the eye. Unflinching. "And now I'll have to live forever with the knowledge that what I did to children—showing myself like that—was actually the least of my crimes."

Chapter 25

BONFIRE NIGHT WAS mild and dry. The high winds that threatened to disrupt the celebrations earlier that day—that buffeted an oil rig in the North Sea and brought a wall crashing down on a farm worker's head—subsided before festivities began. At precisely half past seven, to the delight of twenty thousand people on Midsummer Common, the first volley of fireworks shrieked into the heavens and the skies above Cambridge were streaked with light.

Still, Bonfire Night wasn't quite what I'd expected.

For a start, Dominic and Daniel didn't make it. They had to go to a friend's party in north London, Sonny explained. He put a brave face on his disappointment. The phrase "had to go" hung in the air like smoke.

For another thing, we had arranged to make up a party: there was Helen and Ginny and Ginny's best friend, there was Howard Flatt and his girlfriend Donna. And since home leave had been granted pending a review of the case, there was Daryll Flatt. Three youngsters, I thought, of similar ages: won't they have fun?

But Daryll and the girls might have been slicks of butter for all the bonding there was between them. I don't know whether their styles clashed, or whether Daryll's reputation got in the way, or whether, simply, the differences in their circumstances made a chasm that couldn't be bridged.

Whatever the reason, they looked blankly past each other, and Daryll stood alone.

Truth to tell, Daryll kept his distance from all of us. When I tried to engage with him, I got nowhere. Helen couldn't find a chink in the armor, either. "Dunno," he would shrug. His refusal to call himself *I* was as steadfast here as it had been in Stamford House.

With Howard and Donna, Daryll's isolation took a more subtle form. They placed him between them as they walked, making him the insider, but he held himself aloof. He narrowed his shoulders as if to guard against contact. He kept up a quickfire commentary on everything around, words spilling in a ceaseless monologue that underlined his separateness. For though Daryll tossed endless comments in their direction, he never once looked them in the eye.

Except when Howard's attention was elsewhere. Then Daryll's gaze would creep to Howard's face, would slide hungrily over his features, as if searching for a resemblance. For physical reassurance of a brotherly bond.

The most exhilarating part of the evening, even for Daryll, was the promenade to Midsummer Common from the restaurant where we had stoked up with pizzas. Near Parker's Piece, throngs of spectators converged from different routes, giving the impression that all humanity was headed for once in the same direction, and that all were up for fun. The crowd moved smoothly in step, heads bobbing, in warm clothes and high spirits. People exchanged banter in a display of civic warmth rarely seen in England, aside, perhaps, from football crowds.

The closer we came, the more spectators there were. Bicycles were tethered three deep to the iron railings on Clarendon Street. People filled the pavements. They spilled over into the street. Cars crawled along Parkside, on a hopeless quest for parking space, but on the side streets closer to the common the night belonged entirely to those on foot.

And still closer we moved and the more magical the atmosphere became, until the tendrils of the fair—tinny music, neon lights, the smell of frying onions—reached for us over the heads of the throng. It was like a medieval carnival—a matte-black sky, the lurid glow of the bonfire on the horizon, bursts of noise and flares of light, and a crowd whose mood was laced by merriment and maybe the faintest hint of menace. Solitary fireworks whizzed and sparked their way into oblivion over our heads. How would all this wild energy seem, I wondered, to Daryll, who had spent one-sixth of his life in the minimalist environment of a secure unit?

Around the bonfire a stockade had been constructed to keep the throng at bay. We edged toward it. Daryll pushed up against the fencing, angling for a better position. He fired questions at his brother. Howard cleared his throat and offered slow and thoughtful answers. At one point Howard stretched out a huge hand and placed it tentatively on Daryll's shoulder. Daryll's stream of comment didn't cease; but he trembled, the tiniest of shakes, and Howard pulled his hand away.

For the fireworks themselves, we fanned out. Daryll stayed near the stockade, and Howard and Donna with him, while the rest of us took up a position on the periphery where the crowd was less intense.

In the minutes while we waited for the first explosion, and while spectators drifted into our portion of the meadow, Sonny and Helen and I spoke in muted voices about the latest developments in the case. I began with Ann McLeod's forthright revelations, confirming Geraldine's visit to her on the day of her murder, and Geraldine's plans to set up house with Kelsey; confirming also McLeod's habit of involvement with elderly widows.

Sonny couldn't resist probing for details. "But hadn't Ann McLeod been covering for her husband up to that point? Didn't she provide an alibi for Kelsey at the time of the murder?"

"No need to," I said. "The police never interviewed her. Why should they? As far as they knew, McLeod had a purely professional connection with the case. He just happened to be Daryll Flatt's social worker. No one in the investigation knew that the acquaintance between him and Geraldine was anything other than professional. You would no more suspect McLeod than you would Daryll's teacher, Mrs. Joiner, or—" I shrugged, running out of examples.

"Or the family doctor," Sonny supplied. "Have they searched McLeod's house yet?"

The search of McLeod's home on Highworth Avenue had turned up, I explained, a treasure trove of evidence. There was the leather doll to which Daryll had been so attached. Which he thought—which McLeod encouraged him to think—had been destroyed by Mrs. King.

"Don't ask me why McLeod hung on to it," I said, and shrugged. "Perhaps he guessed that to reveal it after the trial would raise questions that were better left submerged. And perhaps—given Daryll's attachment to the toy—he couldn't quite bring himself to pulp it."

"And did they find the missing money?"

Near enough. At the bottom of a tool chest in McLeod's garage, the police found a passbook. Some entries in it were of immediate interest to detectives investigating Winnie Pollitt's murder in Huntingdon. But the entry that mattered closer to home was the deposit made on the same day that Geraldine withdrew the carrier bag of cash from her bank. The entire £37,000.

Sonny considered for a moment before drawing a conclusion. "I'd say," he said, "that the evidence against McLeod is ominous. But it's not decisive. Nothing that puts McLeod at the scene of the crime. No proof that he dispatched the old girl."

"As opposed to defrauding her of her savings?" I asked. "Would a witness do?"

Yes, their faces said, it would.

I thought of Patrick Caudwell in the interview room—of his oddly dignified demeanor, free of self-delusion for perhaps the first time in his adult life—and reported what he'd said. How he had known all along that McLeod was at the tree house when the killing occurred. How, once he'd told McLeod what he'd seen, McLeod's reaction—the insistence on silence—left no further doubt: McLeod was the killer, and Caudwell knew it.

"So," Helen summed up, "McLeod used Daryll's secret about the Apeman's identity to blackmail Caudwell into silence?"

The fireworks began.

Helen and Sonny moved closer, inclined their heads toward mine. We must have looked like Bonfire Night plotters. "Has McLeod been locked up yet?" Helen whispered.

I shook my head. "Won't be long," I said, hoping that was true. "They tried to pull him out of a conference in Manchester, but he'd already left. He'll be back in Cambridge soon. And when he arrives home, there's a party of police officers waiting to give him a good old Cambridge welcome."

WE WERE TEN minutes into the fireworks, our attention shifted from murder to the skies, when we saw the unmistakable outline of Howard Flatt, who was making his way toward us through the throng.

"We left Daryll back near the bonfire," he said, ushering Donna into view. "He was keen to hang out with some lads his own age. Anyway, we wanted to have a private word."

"How is Daryll taking all this?" I asked.

"The police have formally reopened the case," Howard said. "They think there's a good chance that he'll soon be on permanent release." Howard and Donna exchanged a look of concern.

"So what's the problem?"

"That police inspector, what is her name?"

"Nicole Pelletier."

"Inspector Pelletier. Soon be over, she says. As if you can wipe this kind of experience away. Leave a blank sheet."

"She's an optimist," I said. And like all optimists, sometimes a little cockeyed.

"It's just that Daryll's had so many disappointments," Howard said, struggling to put his anxieties into words. "So many downright shocks. And mainly, he has had to deal with them on his own. It's bound to have made him . . . I don't know what the word is."

"Untrusting," Donna offered. He squeezed her hand.

"And now, another disappointment to add to his collection," I mused. "Though he may have sensed it before, he now has to live with the absolute certainty that Mrs. King didn't care for him. That she used him to further her relationship with Kelsey."

Sonny edged in closer to the center of our huddle. "But what about the letter?" he blurted, then lowered his voice. The rockets were making such a racket, he needn't have bothered. "The note addressed to 'Dearest boy'? Why would Geraldine write such a note, why would she be so indignant about Janet Flatt—"

" 'That horrid woman'?" I interrupted. "We were all taken in by that. When Geraldine wrote 'Dearest boy,' when she insisted he should live with her, she didn't mean Daryll at all. She was writing to her lover. Her *dearest boy* was Kelsey McLeod. And even after she knew that McLeod had betrayed her—that he already had a wife; and that he'd stolen her money—she was still ready to set up house with him. All he had to do was reaffirm his love, and Geraldine promised to forgive and forget. So the horrid woman in the note wasn't Daryll's mother, it was—"

"Ann McLeod!" Helen exclaimed. "Kelsey's wife!"

Two or three people from the crowd turned around to scowl at us. We stared at the sky for a moment, following the trajectory of a pair of purple comets, looking for all the world as if we hadn't been talking at all.

It gave me a chance to think.

Even without a confession from Kelsey McLeod, I could now reconstruct the day of the murder. How Geraldine had learned—in a passing comment from Murray Eagleton—that McLeod was a married man. How she had snatched up the details of the house she thought she'd purchased and gone to have it out with Kelsey's wife. How Ann—who had no intention of surrendering her husband—had laughed at Geraldine, and then, in turn, had rung her husband at work. McLeod had given his perennial excuse for absence—yet another lie that his wife had taken ill—and trundled off home.

And the murder itself? I knew now, more or less, how it happened. McLeod realized that Geraldine was on to his theft—that he was about to be exposed as a con man. He arrived at Geraldine's place, bringing three thousand pounds in cash, in the hope he could use it to delay her from taking action. He entered the garden surreptitiously. Standing in the shadows, he saw Geraldine try to entice Daryll down from the tree. Heard her mention the solicitor's appointment.

He realized then that the time for persuasion had past.

McLeod saw Mrs. King approach the tree, heard Daryll shout at her to go away. Saw Geraldine, undeterred, begin to climb. Saw Daryll, panic-stricken, hurl a rock in her direction. Watched impassively as Geraldine lost her footing, tumbled off the makeshift ladder and landed on the lawn, stunning herself in the process. Saw Daryll peek over the platform and—when he caught sight of the old lady lying there, facedown on the wet grass—retreat in terror into his fort.

McLeod seized his opportunity. *Quick thinking,* you might say, or *fast on his feet*—if the object hadn't been murder. McLeod stepped out in the open and finished her off.

Then he went into the bungalow, bent on destroying anything that would signal his involvement with Geraldine. He collected the remains of the house details that she'd torn up. But he overlooked the Dearest Boy note. Later, when the police showed it to him, it must have been a shock. McLeod must have known instantly the true meaning of that note—that there in a few short words, his illicit relationship with the murdered woman was exposed for everyone to see.

But the police didn't read it like that. To McLeod's astonishment—and then to his relief—the police assumed (and who can blame them?) that the dearest boy in question was Daryll Flatt. McLeod may have had no intention, initially, of implicating Daryll. He may have ripped Geraldine's knickers off with the vague intent of suggesting a sexual motive for the killing. Stuffed the money into

Daryll's lunch box just to be rid of it. Might even have believed—at that stage—that no one would seriously suspect a child. But from the point where he heard the police interpretation of the note, McLeod began to play along with the possibility of Daryll's guilt.

Even to embellish it.

Who better than Daryll's social worker to blacken the boy's character? To exaggerate the degree of Daryll's anger with Mrs. King? To invent a story about the torture of a pigeon in order to enhance an image of the boy as violent and disturbed?

Reluctantly at first—a reluctance that the court took for an urge to protect—but later, more and more convinced that what he did was for the best, McLeod established Daryll Flatt as a killer.

There was one thing troubling still. Helen put it into words. "If Kelsey McLeod framed Daryll Flatt," she whispered, "if it was McLeod who had lifted a lump of concrete above his head and hurled it down on her skull—then why on earth did Daryll Flatt confess? Why, when they found him in the crack willow tree, all alone in the dark, why did he exclaim, without any prompting, 'I did it—I did it—I killed her!' "

"Simple," Sonny insisted. "Daryll said he did it because he honestly thought he had. He threw a rock at Geraldine. He saw her still form lying on the ground. He retreated into his tree house. He didn't hear McLeod arrive. He didn't see McLeod deliver the death blow. And he fled while McLeod was inside the bungalow, getting rid of evidence. You see? From his own point of view, Daryll looked to himself like a killer."

I saw.

But I didn't believe.

Even a child younger than Daryll knows the difference

between a glancing blow and a crippling one. A boy might feel bad about throwing a rock at Geraldine in the first place, but he would be more likely to protest "I didn't mean to hurt her! I didn't throw it hard" than to claim he'd killed her. Children of ten, eleven, twelve, from what I've seen, are zealous in defending themselves from the unjust accusations of the adult world.

So why would Daryll accept—rush to embrace—responsibility?

There was a lull in the fireworks. As the cracks and crashes subsided, all the sights and sounds of the fair—the sweet smell of cotton candy, the hum of the motors that kept the wheels rotating and the arms gyrating, the manic rhythms of "Dance City"—filtered through to our corner of the common.

And at that moment two boys shoved in front of us. Their mood didn't match the ooh-and-aah air of most of the spectators. They pushed past roughly, indifferent to other people. The wagon they were pulling grazed Helen's ankle. Sourly, thoughtfully, I watched them go.

"Laura?" Howard whispered. He bent his head so his words would be heard by me alone.

I nodded to show I was listening. My eyes followed the ragged progress of the wagon.

"Laura, I'm really concerned about how Daryll will cope—whether he'll cope—when he learns that Kelsey McLeod let him take the rap for murder. He is very fond of McLeod."

Kelsey is my best friend. "There's no getting around it, Howard," I said. "It'll be another blow to the boy's self-esteem."

And suddenly I realized what it was about those lads with the wagon that made me feel jittery. "I'll be back in a minute," I called over my shoulder to Howard as I set off.

Weaving and bobbing my way through the crowd, I heard Ginny shout after me, but I didn't stop even for her.

This was unfinished business. It had been nagging at me for the past week. I'd been up to my ear holes with the investigation, and I'd let it slide. But here they were—the two louts who had called me a bitch. Time to settle my bet with Stevie. Time to make them apologize.

I wove my way between groups of spectators—tossing out *excuse me*'s and fending off complaints. I skirted a ring of students who were waving sparklers, paused while a pair of toddlers ambled out of my path. And the chance was lost. The lads with their pathetic little wagon were nowhere in sight.

Just then came a resounding explosion and boisterous exclamations from the crowd. I looked up, at twists of white fairy lights that writhed through the sky. At the purple rain that dripped down, ending in great blue beads of fire over the tops of the trees.

The spectacular display lit up the margins of the meadow. Lit up the gray-green leaves of the willow trees.

Lit up, even, the pale freckled features of the thirteen-year-old boy who stood beneath a tree. His shoulders were narrowed, his face a twist of agony. A man hunched opposite him, fingers gripping the boy's arms, knee on the wet grass. He addressed the boy urgently, emphatically. From my position I could only pick up the ghost of his words.

I skirted the crowd, shifted around behind the tree and edged up beside a group of spectators, who were still staring at the night sky, oblivious to the drama being played out nearby. I got within three or four feet of McLeod, with my best ear toward him.

And I heard what he had to say.

"It's no good, Daryll. That won't make you feel any better. Remember what it was like? When you saw her lying there, all cold and dead? How you didn't save her? How you let her die?"

"But Kelsey," Daryll pleaded, eyes on the ground, "you've got to believe me. My therapist at the unit has helped me remember. Only threw one rock, Kelsey. Only one. And it didn't really hit her, not hard anyway. She just fell . . . and then . . . She wasn't moving, Kelsey. Thought she was dead. Just like—"

"Just like your granny. That's right, Daryll." The voice was gentle, soft, insinuating. The voice of love gone mad. "Your granny died when you were with her, didn't she? Of course, you didn't mean to kill her, but you must be responsible in some way, mustn't you? That's what you've always told me. And with Mrs. King, it was the same, wasn't it? If you hadn't been so stubborn, Daryll—if you had come when she called, if you hadn't hidden in the tree house, hadn't disobeyed her, Mrs. King wouldn't have tried to climb, would she? And if she didn't try to climb—well, there's no getting around it, Daryll. Except for you, Mrs. King would still be alive."

I'd been listening so intently to their voices that I didn't notice the footsteps coming up behind me. Fingers scraped my arm. "What in the world are you—" Ginny whispered. Then I clamped my hand over her mouth.

"Fast as you can." I hissed in her ear, blocking debate through the urgency of my tone. "Bring Howard and the others. Now!" Ginny changed course as smoothly as a whippet, and sped off.

Daryll was speaking again, more quickly this time, desperation raising the pitch of his voice, blurring the edges of his words. "Not sure, Kelsey. Please forgive me. Not sure anymore that it was my fault. Sorry. So sorry. Just not sure."

McLeod released his grip on Daryll's forearms. His

voice took on a tortured quality that sent a shiver down my spine. "Daryll . . . Daryll, think of the consequences. Someone saw me near Mrs. King's house on the day she died—looking for you. If you say you didn't kill her, they're bound to decide that it was me. They'll put me away for the rest of my life. Do you want me to go to prison, Daryll? Like your father? Never see me again?"

"No." The child began to weep, oblivious to the knots of people around, the nervous glances in his direction. "No, Kelsey, don't say that."

But Kelsey did.

And more.

"Whereas if you stay in the unit, Daryll, it will only be for a little while. Only a few more years. And you're happy enough there, aren't you? You've got everything you need. I've seen to that, haven't I? I've always wanted the best for you, Daryll. I'll visit you every week, as I've been doing, and look after you. Please, Daryll. Do this for me. For both of us?"

There was a pause, while McLeod fixed his powerful gaze on Daryll, waited until Daryll met his eyes. I took a deep breath to steady myself.

"Daryll, don't you love me?" McLeod asked. And waited.

I stepped out into the open, positioning myself equidistant from McLeod and the boy. McLeod looked at me. There was a sheen of shock on his face.

"Daryll," I said firmly, and waited until Daryll's head swiveled in my direction. "Daryll, you do care for him, don't you? I know you do. But you don't have to lie for him. Not anymore. That's not part of love."

There was no movement from Daryll. He stood, hands pressed deep into the pockets of his jacket, stiff as a post.

"If he loves you, he'll let you go. Let you have a life. You're only thirteen. You have a right to be free."

When McLeod rose to his full height, he towered over Daryll. "Daryll needs me," he insisted, with his eyes on the boy. "He needs me to look after him. If I went to prison, it would be Daryll who would suffer. He'd be all alone again."

Daryll Flatt had begun to shake. He looked thinner now and more brittle and his body trembled as delicately as a bowstring. His cheeks were wet with tears.

And at that moment, while we waited for Daryll to speak—to make a decision too vast in its implications, too cruel, too inhumane—Howard came lumbering up and stopped, a few feet from his brother. "Daryll!" he called. There was sorrow in his voice, and anxiety, and unmistakably, there was love.

Daryll looked from one to another, from McLeod to Howard, with misery in his eyes. His throat worked convulsively. What emerged was a cross between a cry and a stutter.

"I . . . I . . . I . . ."

And then he stepped forward blindly, awkwardly, as if his skin held him back, and collapsed against Howard. Howard scooped him up and embraced him as if he were an infant again. Daryll almost disappeared in the massiveness of Howard's body.

That's when McLeod made a run for it. He spun on his heel, slipped a little on the slick grass, and raced off down the path that runs beside the river. He moved quickly, with a grace that surprised me, shifting in and out of the clusters of people strolling away from the fireworks.

I was close behind, but he was fast. I swerved in the crowd to avoid a low-slung cigarette, and lost sight of him for a second. But his height worked in my favor. There he was—heading northwest, toward the footbridge.

I put on a spurt, breathing deeply, forcing more push into my legs and my lungs. Arrived at the base of the footbridge three long strides behind him, the space between us crammed with people on their way home from the display. I thought I'd lose him in the crowd. Then my shout and the sound of our headlong rush caused a few people to fall back against the side of the bridge. Just for a second, there was an open space between McLeod and me.

I tightened my muscles and flung myself at him, launched myself out in a rugby tackle, sailed through the air and landed on the stony surface of the bridge with a shout. My arms were locked around his legs.

McLeod crashed facedown a half second after me. I heard a crack—one of his teeth broke. He crawled forward along the bridge, dragging me. I was the plough behind the horse. I clung to his legs as if my life depended on it. His kicks bruised my chest but he didn't wrench free. I was only dimly aware of the daze of activity around us— of people approaching the bridge and falling back aghast, unable to make sense of what they were seeing. Uncertain whether to intervene.

I knew I couldn't hold on much longer. In a desperate move, I tried to climb toward his head, arm over arm, without slackening my grip. McLeod wrenched to the side and delivered two ferocious kicks that loosened my grasp on his legs. His right foot shunted into my shoulder. I wrapped my arms around my head and struggled to stand, but he delivered a vicious kick to my thigh and my legs gave way.

At that very second, I heard an authoritative voice clearing the crowd, demanding a space. A police officer loomed above me where I lay.

"Madam?" he inquired.

Madam. I wanted to laugh, but it didn't come out like that. My head was bleeding. Blood trickled from between my fingers, puddled on the rough stone. Scrapings from my jacket littered the surface of the bridge.

Another police officer held McLeod in an armlock. Tighter, I thought. Where's a bit of police brutality when you need it?

McLeod, sod him, looked as if he still had the energy for a sprint.

"Let me make the introductions," I said to the police officer, rising to that courteous *Madam* at last. "I'm Laura Principal, private investigator. And this is Kelsey McLeod, killer. The CID has been searching for him all day. I suggest, now that you've found him"—I turned and smiled at McLeod, as the lines of the song from *South Pacific* slipped into my head—"you never let him go."

Chapter 26

WE WAITED TWENTY minutes for our turn on the Ferris wheel, Sonny and I. We watched the operative who ran the ride, with one foot propped on a piece of machinery—how he maintained a contemptuous distance from the crowd. We saw shooters train their sights on coconuts at the rifle range. We eyed a woman in a cashmere coat who came away from the hoopla brandishing a spider made of lime-green acrylic. It looked like cotton candy. We registered a bloodcurdling scream from the Night Rider and decided it didn't call for action on our part—that we could relax. I put my hands inside the pockets of Sonny's greatcoat. We polished off a huge bag of popcorn and shared a hug.

In short, we concentrated on the moment, and steered clear of any further talk about the case. Until Sonny broke the ice.

"You never feel as elated as you expect, Laura, do you?"

He meant *we*. Or *I*. Or *one*.

"The finish of a case," he added. "It's an anticlimax."

Was it anticlimax, I wondered—this strange sensation I felt, this emptiness, this dislocation? I'd been on full rev for two weeks now, chasing questions: about Geraldine, about Daryll, about Edward King and Kelsey McLeod and Janet Flatt and the rest. And I'd done my level best to keep all options open. I hadn't been moved by an intuition of evil to chase one "murderer" against others. I hadn't allowed my sympathy for Daryll, my liking for Howard, my aversion to Mark Miller, to harden into a hunch. Like Prince Charming after the ball, I was open-minded—willing to try the glass slipper of guilt on the foot of every candidate, and to accept the evidence of the fit.

What unsettled me most was the brusqueness with which the investigation had ended. The day before yesterday, I could still spin a plausible story that would confirm Mark Miller, or Edward King, or Patrick Caudwell—or, in a reluctant pinch, Daryll Flatt—as the killer of Geraldine King. Forty-eight hours later I had to settle on Kelsey McLeod and let the others go.

It happened so suddenly—boom, finish—that my emotions hadn't had time to catch up with reality. My current mood was set not by elation at Daryll's innocence, but by the negative aspects of the case: by the sorrow that had burdened Daryll's childhood; by Geraldine's vulnerability, and McLeod's callous betrayal; by Mark Miller's brutality and his mother's bleak life; by the damage that had been done to Patrick Caudwell, as a child, and the damage that he'd done in turn.

I was haunted, too, by a fear that Daryll's "release"—like Patrick Caudwell's—might have come too late.

"There's not always this sense of anticlimax, Sonny," I said at last. "After all, when you completed your surveillance of the Bennetts, you didn't seem down in the mouth."

"Whatever rude remarks I might make about Frank and Bryan Bennett," Sonny replied, "pitting myself against them involved—or at least it did until the bastards went for you—a touch of gamesmanship. It wasn't the sort of case to give me nightmares."

We were directly in front of the Ferris wheel, at last, and

it was beginning to unload. Almost our turn. I couldn't resist a tease.

"Come now, Sonny. Gamesmanship wasn't the only thing that kept you cheerful when you were staking out the Bennetts, was it?"

He looked genuinely puzzled.

"Let's not forget the bookkeeper," I reminded him. "The one who provided information over drinks—'all in the line of duty,' you claimed. The one who made your eyes shine."

"Oh, that bookkeeper," Sonny declared, smiling broadly.

There it was again. That shine. "So tell me—what did she have that I don't?"

"You were here," Sonny shot back, quick enough to tell me that he meant it, "and she was there. Just kidding," he retracted immediately, pushing me gently in the direction of the loading platform. He gave me a reassuring squeeze. But that was the second time recently he'd said something along those lines. I filed it away to ponder when the time was right.

We settled into the swing seat and snapped the bar in place. The wheel lunged upward, lifting us by fits and starts above the crowds. Then the wrinkles of movement smoothed away, and we descended in a rush. I laughed as the ground swept toward me. My tummy remained in the air—but vertigo kept its distance, as it sometimes does, and I could enjoy the swoop down toward the common. The volume of noise from the fairground grew louder as we fell. Then it faded as we surged up again, into the sky, into the night wind. And silence.

Sonny dragged me away from the bookkeeper, back to Daryll Flatt. "Whereas your investigation—" he began.

"Was no game. There was a streak of cruelty throughout."

A nastiness that smudged the surface of the issues, I thought. Made it hard to wipe them clean.

"Like Miller's bullying of his little brother?" Sonny interrupted.

"Or the coldness between Edward King and his mother. Or, for that matter, the disparaging remarks that peppered William Holtby's descriptions of his wife."

"Above all," Sonny concluded, "there was the initial premise: the very possibility that a child could be a cold-blooded killer. Even with Daryll about to be cleared, it's hard to feel like celebrating. Somehow the good news is tainted by the fact that his own social worker set him up. If you take McLeod, and Miller—and Patrick Caudwell with his bloody bananas," Sonny added, shaking his head, "it's enough to make you despair of men."

By *you*, he meant *I* and *one*.

He shifted in the seat. Our swing teetered forward. I didn't like it.

"Hold on, Sonny." We leveled out again. "It's not like you to despair. Think again. Howard has to be high on anyone's list of decent people. Murray Eagleton is honorable and kindly. And Daryll . . . ? Well, Daryll is only a child, after all. Not a child killer. Just a child."

Sonny's openness about his own unease at the way the case ended had nudged me into a more positive position. I kissed him, gently and gratefully.

"And then, Sonny Mendlowitz—there's always you."

We skimmed the ground and ascended, flying backward. The wind rushed up behind us and tangled my hair. Then, with an ominous grinding, the wheel slowed. It crawled sedately for a few seconds, and bumped and churned the rest of the way to the top. Then our swinging seat lurched over the restraining pin and halted, at the very peak.

"And how do you feel now?" Sonny asked. He held my hand, just to be sure.

We jerked back and forth—once, twice, three times— before we finally settled. From our vantage point, the fairground below appeared to be bathed in a golden glow. Gusts of wind tossed the chestnut trees along Victoria Avenue, and the street lamps beyond them flashed into view. In the distance, making their way toward Jesus Green, I could discern three small familiar bodies—a man, a woman, a boy—walking close together, their bodies touching.

"Top of the world," I said.

Acknowledgments

MANY PEOPLE PROVIDED expert information in the making of this book. I should particularly like to thank Trevor Wakefield, Principal of Stamford House; Inspector Chris Bainbridge of Essex Police; Astrid Haslam, Jan Spurling, Alida McDowell and Veronica Purser of Cambridge Social Services; Dr. David Dean of Carleton University; Joshua Stanworth Held; Dr. Annie Bartlett; Dr. David Jayne; and Dr. Janet Reibstein. For my friend Su Kappeler, belated thanks.

I am grateful to Joe Blades, Julie Held, Rosa Held, Jane McCarren, Rosalind Miles, Gill Motley, Nicholas Ray, Ann Smith, Pat Spring and Gray Walker for ideas and assistance, and to Felicity Bryan, Jane Chelius, Yvette Goulden, and, above all, David Held for their help with the development of the story.

I found the following books useful in thinking about children and violence: Charles Patrick Ewing, *Children Who Kill,* Mondo (London, 1993); Gitta Sereny, *The Case of Mary Bell,* Pimlico (London, 1995); Rosalind Miles, *The Children We Deserve,* HarperCollins (London, 1995); Mark Thomas, *Every Mother's Nightmare,* Pan Books (London, 1993).

The partial lyric that appears before Chapter 1 is taken from "Liverpool Lullaby" by Stan Kelly, copyright 1958, Logo Songs / Heathside Music.

A CONVERSATION WITH
MICHELLE SPRING

Q. *Michelle, a lot of your fans know they can practically sing along with the titles of your novels.* Every Breath You Take, Running for Shelter, Standing in the Shadows. *And now* Nights in White Satin. *When and why did you devise the idea of adopting these song titles and lyrics for your Laura Principal mysteries?*

A. If I'd been born in an earlier era, I might have wanted to work in Tin Pan Alley. I've always been fascinated by the lyrics of popular songs. So it's not surprising that song lyrics sprang to mind as I wrote the books in the Laura Principal series. As I worked on the stories, the titles seemed to choose themselves!

Every Breath You Take, for example—from that wonderfully chilling song by the Police about obsessive love—was the obvious title for a novel focused on a woman who'd suffered the attentions of a stalker. The song always reminded me of the delicate line between adoring someone and seeking to control them.

My second book was about a girl who leaves a domineering employer and, in doing so, comes to even worse harm. She's a domestic worker. So the title, *Running for Shelter*, was particularly apt. It's from a Rolling Stones song that also mentions "mother's little helper."

And *Standing in the Shadows*—another fragment from a Stones lyric—made the perfect title for my third book, exploring as it did the inner world of a child who confessed to the murder of his foster mother.

My fourth book begins at an extravagant party at Cambridge University. A young woman arrives, full of excitement, stunningly turned out in a dress of pure white satin. Two hours later, she disappears. The Moody Blues might have written "Nights in White Satin" especially for her!

Q. *Who or what was your inspiration for Laura Principal?*
A. It's easier to say what the inspiration wasn't! I wasn't

inspired by images from the past of private investigators who are cynical loners, distrustful of other people, or driven by angst.

On the contrary, Laura Principal is a woman—like most of the women I know—who is deeply embedded in relationships. One tension that runs through the series stems from Laura's struggle to arrive at a workable balance between commitments—between the competing demands made by a long-term lover (Sonny), close women friends (Helen, Stevi, Claire), children (not her own), and her career. This particular struggle is something that Laura Principal has in common with me and, I suspect, with many other women in the modern world.

Laura Principal wasn't based on any individual. I've been asked, on occasion, whether Laura Principal was based on me. I should be so lucky! Unlike Michelle Spring, Laura Principal seldom worries about what to wear. She's good at lots of things I'm not—she's athletic, plays the saxophone, handles a car like she was born in the driving seat, and, when it's called for, can launch a vigorous physical defense of herself or others. So, no, she's not me; but she is a person I'd like to know. One of the things I most like about her is her reluctance to leap to conclusions about other people. Laura is rarely judgmental. She can often see the good, or simply the vulnerable, in people who are, on the surface, despicable. And if that causes her difficulties as a P.I., it also makes makes her human.

Q. *Your novels unfold in actual locales, principally Cambridge and London. Why did you make this choice? And what advantages and disadvantages have you discovered with this approach?*
A. When I began writing crime fiction, I set my books in England, in the locations that I knew best: Cambridge (where I live), London (less than an hour away), and the beautiful north Norfolk coast. But using two or more settings has a distinct disadvantage, I soon discovered—far too much traveling to do as Laura Principal moved back and forth between locations.

So I've focused more and more on Cambridge. Settled down there, so to speak. And I'm very happy with that decision.

The first advantage stems from the fact that Cambridge has everything a crime writer could want: from high-tech industry— the flat fen areas around Cambridge are known, with good reason, as Silicon Fen—and prosperous agricultural estates to a massive seasonal influx of visitors, which creates new tensions. And, of course, there's Cambridge University; the ancient colleges provide almost gothic settings for murder.

One of my hopes in writing this series is to contribute to a fresh image of Cambridge—not the romanticized picture that is presented on postcards, but something more true to life.

I've lived in the city of Cambridge for all but two years since I left Canada, and I find writing about the city as a novelist tremendously liberating. When I worked as an academic, I spent a great deal of my time living in my head. Being a novelist gives me license to look around. To look closely. I can leap up from my desk and rush down to the river to see the swans; spend an evening examining the police cells at Parkside Station; stroll along the Backs; have lunch at Browns Restaurant—and refer to it all as research! In some ways, using Cambridge as a setting has made me feel that I properly inhabit Cambridge for the very first time.

Disadvantages? Only one. If I vacationed in Tuscany or Tenerife, I couldn't claim any tax relief on the journey.

Q. *We know that you have dual citizenship—English and Canadian—by virtue of being born and raised in Victoria, Vancouver Island, British Columbia. Were you a reader of crime fiction at an early age?*
A. I started at the age of six. I was quarantined in hospital for several weeks, in a room on my own, and allowed no visitors. But my father—always a rebel—flaunted the rules. Each and every evening he crept up the fire escape to visit me with a rescue package: a container of eggnog, a meat pie, and a Nancy Drew novel. I learned what a good companion mysteries could be.

Two years later, while poring over *The Secret of the Sword Doll,* I fainted from excitement. My mother banned crime fiction—too stimulating, she said. Of course, for a child, that greatly increased its attractions.

In adolescence, when I came across some of the greats of crime fiction—Sir Arthur Conan Doyle, Daphne du Maurier, Dashiell Hammett, Dorothy Sayers, Mary Roberts Rinehart, Patricia Highsmith—my devotion deepened.

But I think it's fair to say that it's not just the quality of the writing that draws me to crime. I'm fascinated also with the way that crime weaves in and out of ordinary lives. I've had, in most respects, a very ordinary life. And yet there were killings in my neighborhood when I was a child that left an indelible mark. As an adult, I've been caught up in an armed raid on a bank, stalked by a former student, and rescued from a fate worse than death by a multiple murderer. I feel sometimes as if crime has always hovered at the edge of my vision. And—can you understand this?—it makes reading, and writing, crime fiction something of a relief.

Q. *Let us back up to that "rescued by a multiple murderer" statement. Can you elaborate?*

A. Well, that all happened in Venice Beach, California, many years ago, when I was young enough to wear a bikini and the area was still rough and tough. I was strolling home across the sand after a morning in the sun when I was approached by a group of men. They were tall, well spoken, and young; they looked as if they might be a college basketball team en route to a match. But they formed a horseshoe around me and began pushing and prodding, rerouting me toward Venice Pier. Let's play under the pier, they said, and I knew I was in trouble. Even with the L.A. sun blazing down, the area under the pier was as dark as sin.

I won't go into how I felt, except to say that that walk across the sand seemed like the longest journey of my life. It lasted until, a dozen yards short of the pier, we were intercepted by a short swaggering man. He was brown-skinned and muscular, and dressed like Huckleberry Finn in cutoffs and straw hat.

What's your name? he asked me.

I told him the truth. What did I have to lose?

He locked eyes with the six giants who surrounded me. Hey, brothers, he said. This here's my friend, Michelle.

There was a long, long pause. Then, one by one, my tormentors nodded, said goodbye, and trotted off toward the promenade, leaving me alone with Huckleberry. I took his arm. We headed off to buy ice cream. When the basketball team was out of earshot, I asked the obvious question: Who are you?

He took out his wallet and displayed, with pride, wanted notices from several states—for drug dealing, for armed robbery, many for murder. His name, I saw, was Rodrigo.

Honey, he said, I'm da King a da Beach.

And he was. Rodrigo called the shots. He put the word out that I was under his protection, and nobody on Venice Beach bothered me again.

In the end, Rodrigo was murdered himself—but that's another story.

Q. *Now to return to fiction. You've discussed your childhood reading passions. But what—after two and a half decades in an academic career (including a teaching stint at Cambridge University) and four academic books—inspired you to become a novelist? And what specific motivation was there to be a crime novelist?*
A. I write because I have to. I learned relatively late in life that writing keeps me sane and centered. That the rest of the day is easier if I start it out by putting words on paper.

And I also write because I have stories to tell. Until recently, writing had to be fitted around lectures, seminars, supervisions, marking essays. The writing got done, but there was no time to think ahead. When I gave up university teaching, I reached inside the filing cabinet and took stock of all the ideas for novels that had been tossed there, waiting for their moment. I'm glad to say there are enough new ones to keep me writing well into the new millennium.

And why, when I write, do I write crime fiction? In 1990, on sabbatical (California, again), I tried my hand for the first time at fiction. What I had in mind was a rather "serious" novel with little resemblance to crime fiction. I sat at a desk overlooking the bougainvillea for three months and didn't produce a word. I was just about to throw in the towel when the first chapter of *Every Breath You Take* flowed—unplanned, like automatic writing—from my pen. And there it was—to my amazement, a detective novel.

And now I'm well and truly hooked on crime fiction. I find the action, the pursuit, the danger exhilarating. I'm intrigued by the intellectual challenge—to construct a plot that will make readers scratch their heads along the way but where the awkward elements fall into place at the end. I delight in shaping my characters, in their individuality and their interaction, in watching them come alive. And I'm drawn to the opportunity to reflect, through the medium of crime, on the world in which we live.

I suppose you could say that this emphasis on crime is not a strategic decision. It is simply the case that stories involving crimes and their consequences and the complex motivations behind them are the stories I'm longing to tell.

Q. *In the mystery/suspense field, who are your favorite writers?*
A. From my early years of reading crime, there are two authors, whose writing styles are in some respects at opposite poles, who exerted a strong pull on my imagination. Sir Arthur Conan Doyle created Sherlock Holmes, the man of pure intellect, the hyper-rational detective—an early forensic scientist, really, with his systematic studies of tobacco ash and mud. And yet it isn't the plots that drew me to Conan Doyle. What captured me was the atmosphere.The swirling fogs of Victorian London, the stuffy claustrophobia of the rooms at 221B Baker Street, the poignant strains of violin music as Holmes descended into depression—all these created a highly charged context for Holmes' investigations.

And at the other end of the spectrum was Shirley Jackson. I first encountered *The Haunting of Hill House* in a *Reader's Digest* Condensed Book; even in that unpromising format, I adored it. On the surface, *Hill House* is a supernatural thriller with gothic overtones. Underneath, it is a piercing study of psychology and human relationships, with an immensely satisfying conclusion.

As for contemporary writers, I admire authors of many different kinds of books, for many different reasons. For brooding intensity, there is Frances Fyfield or Barbara Vine; for dialogue, Elmore Leonard or Val McDermid, who—though no one thinks of her as a comic author—often writes verbal exchanges that make me laugh aloud; for vivid characters, Liza Cody or Laurie R. King or Valerie Wilson Wesley; for economical plotting, L. R. Wright or Joan Didion; and, for atmosphere, Helen Dunmore, who is known as a "literary author" but whose *Talking to the Dead* is a masterpiece of psychological suspense.

And so on. More of my favorites are, I'm afraid, left out here than included.

Q. *For you as a practitioner of crime fiction, what are the appeals of the genre?*
A. Crime fiction lends itself beautifully to subjects that are important and difficult. Because of the focus on death, it necessitates the unfolding of lives, and of the context in which those lives are lived, in a way that often throws contemporary conditions into sharp relief. All my books deal, directly or indirectly, with difficult subjects. *Every Breath You Take* touched—more than touched—on homophobia and sexual harassment; *Running for Shelter* used the treatment of migrant domestic workers as a backdrop against which to explore the mystery of a missing girl; *Standing in the Shadows* explored the delicate and painful subject of murder committed by children; *Nights in White Satin* picks its way through the contemporary world of prostitution.

But crime fiction is—and should be—entertaining too. I don't hold with the puritanical line of thought which suggests that fun has to be sharply segregated from serious reflection. I always hope that readers will find something to think about in my books, perhaps even something that makes them "think again." But equally, I hope they are entertained.

It's when I create a corner of chaos—when a reader says to me ... "I couldn't put your book down" ... "I didn't get a wink of sleep" ... "I forgot to cook dinner " ... "The report went unwritten"—that's the moment that I'm happiest with this work.

Q. *When you wrote* Every Breath You Take, *did you know it would be the launch for a series?*
A. I had no idea. I wrote initially for my own satisfaction—to get a few things off my chest. And as I mentioned earlier, I was as surprised as anyone when the book I wrote turned out to be crime fiction. *Every Breath You Take* introduced Laura Principal; I assumed that that would be not only her first appearance but also her last.

But then two things happened. A publisher bought the manuscript and asked—no, pressed—for a series. And equally important, Laura Principal stubbornly refused to die. I was in London, a couple of months after completing that first novel, and browsing through Camden Market, not far from where I'd positioned the head office of Aardvark Investigations in *Every Breath You Take*. A voice said to me, clear as a bell: Why don't you drop in on Laura?

That's when I knew that she lived, at least in my head. That she'd have to come back again, for the second book, in what therefore became a series.

Q. *What is your daily (assuming you write daily) or weekly work schedule?*
A. Simple: Monday to Friday, after the children leave for school, I sit straight down at my desk—sometimes fully dressed, sometimes not—and write a thousand words. That can take two hours, or six. After it's done, I polish the writing from earlier days. On Saturday and Sunday, if family activities allow, I write more.

My aim is to do a thousand words a day. But some days the stuff starts to flow and I end up with three thousand words and a headache—and a major editing job the following morning. Other days, the sun shines too enticingly, and I never quite settle at my desk.

And then, of course, there are those exhilarating occasions when I get carried away by research—when I spend my morning poking my nose into police cells, or touring the pathology labs, or talking to strippers, and fail to write at all.

Q. *In 1998,* The London Times *named you one of the "100 masters of crime fiction"—quite an honor, considering so many other occupants of that list are not only legendary but long dead. What was your reaction to being in that roll call?*
A. Astonishment, first.

Then delight.

And a continuing sense of unease, when I think of the many excellent writers who could have been named in my place.

To be quite truthful, I don't feel like a master—or even a mistress! Writing is a demanding craft—writing crime fiction doubly so. My first book was a stab in the dark. Through the experience of writing the second and the third, I gained confidence as a writer and learned a lot about both the discipline and the technique of writing.

Now, with the fourth book, I do at last begin to feel that I'm getting the hang of it. At this rate, I'll be eighty years old before I feel I've really earned the title of "master."